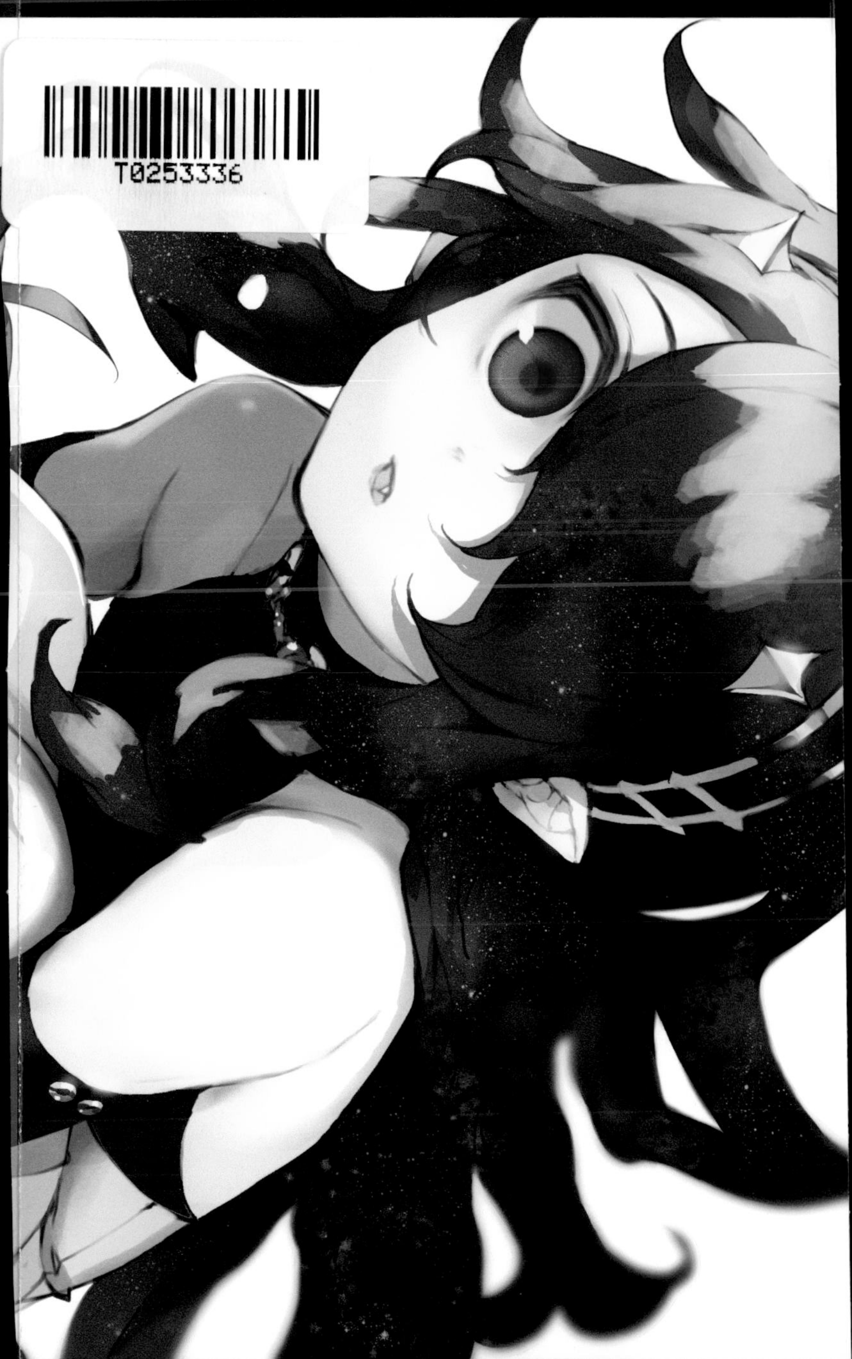

Seraph of the End

─VAMPIRE REIGN─

4

STORY BY **Takaya Kagami**
ART BY **Yamato Yamamoto**
STORYBOARDS BY **Daisuke Furuya**

YUICHIRO HYAKUYA

A boy who escaped from the vampire capital, he has both great kindness and a great desire for revenge. Lone wolf.

GUREN ICHINOSE

Lieutenant Colonel of the Moon Demon Company, a Vampire Extermination Unit. He recruited Yuichiro into the Japanese Imperial Demon Army.

YOICHI SAOTOME

Yuichiro's friend.
His sister was killed by a vampire.

SHIHO KIMIZUKI

Yuichiro's friend.
Smart but abrasive.

SHINOA HIRAGI

Guren's subordinate and Yuichiro's surveillance officer. Member of the illustrious Hiragi family.

MITSUBA SANGU

An elite soldier who has been part of the Moon Demon Company since age 13. Bossy.

STORY

A mysterious virus decimates the human population, and vampires claim dominion over the world. Yuichiro and his adopted family of orphans are kept as vampire fodder in an underground city until the day Mikaela, Yuichiro's best friend, plots an ill-fated escape for the orphans. Only Yuichiro survives and reaches the surface.

Four years later, Yuichiro enters into the Moon Demon Company, a Vampire Extermination Unit in the Japanese Imperial Demon Army, to enact his revenge. It is there he gains Asuramaru, a demon-possessed weapon capable of killing vampires.

Along with his squad mates Shinoa, Yoichi, Kimizuki and Mitsuba, Yuichiro deploys to Shinjuku with orders to thwart a vampire attack. However, in the battle he spots someone who looks a lot like Mika...

Seraph of the End
VAMPIRE REIGN

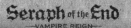

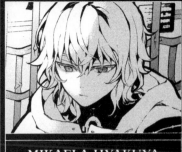

MIKAELA HYAKUYA

Yuichiro's best friend. He was supposedly killed but has come back to life as a vampire.

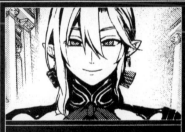

FERID BATHORY

A Seventh Progenitor vampire, he killed Mikaela.

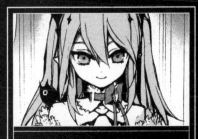

KRUL TEPES

Queen of the Vampires and a Third Progenitor.

Seraph of the End
—VAMPIRE REIGN—

4

CONTENTS

CHAPTER 12
A Very Safe Supplement 005

CHAPTER 13
Reunion of Childhood Friends 051

CHAPTER 14
Everyone's a Sinner 099

CHAPTER 15
Complicated Connections 147

Four Years Ago

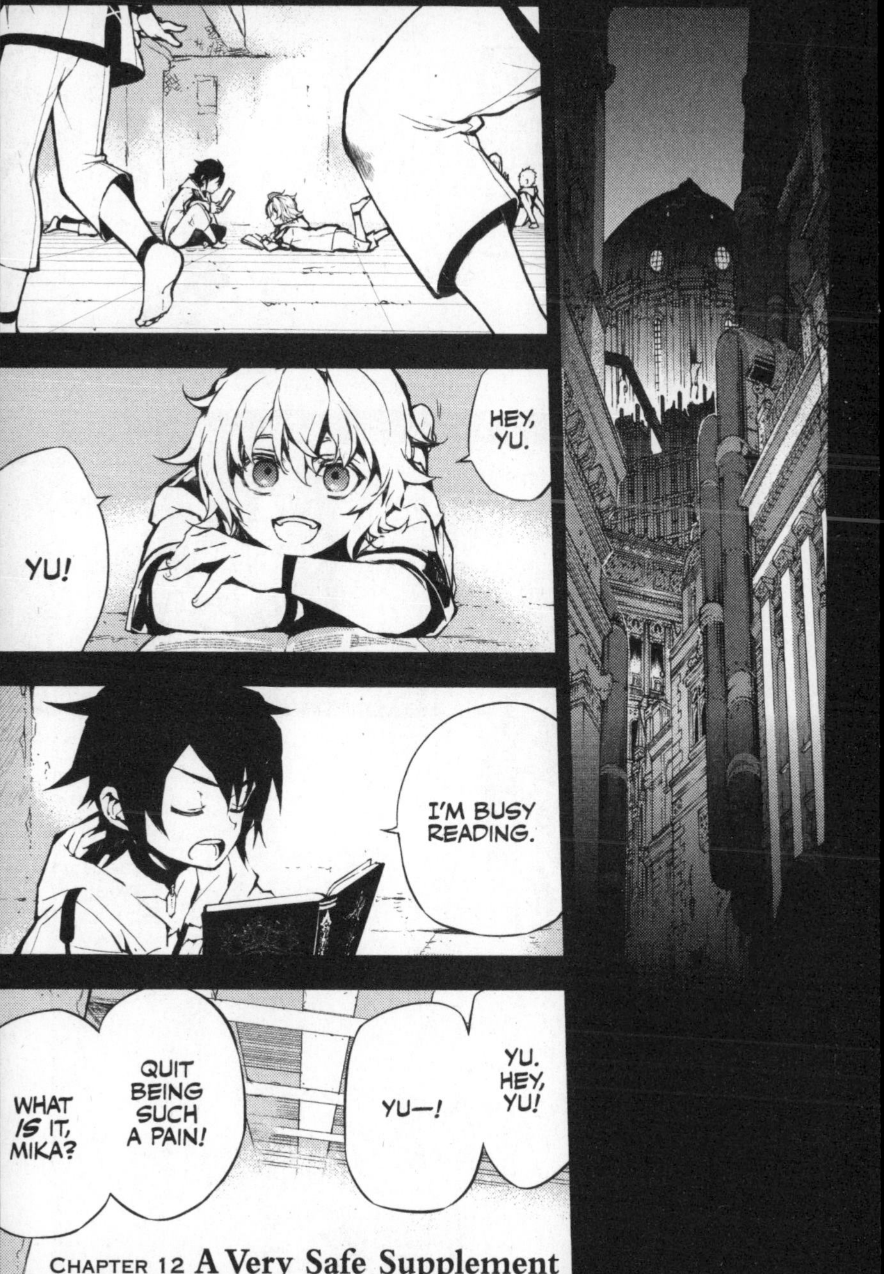
HEY, YU.
YU!
I'M BUSY READING.
YU. HEY, YU!
YU—!
QUIT BEING SUCH A PAIN!
WHAT *IS* IT, MIKA?

CHAPTER 12 A Very Safe Supplement

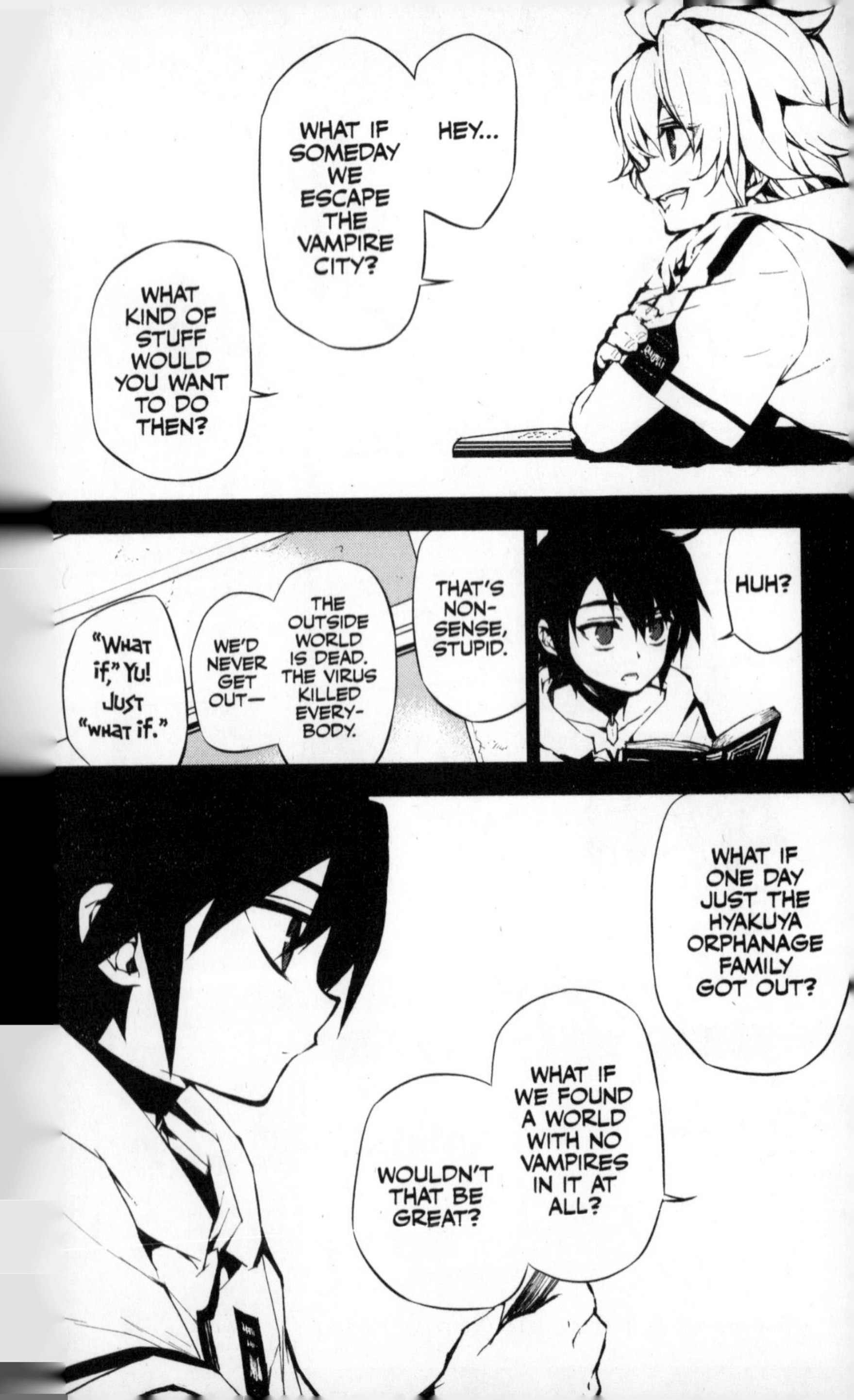
HEY...
WHAT IF SOMEDAY WE ESCAPE THE VAMPIRE CITY?
WHAT KIND OF STUFF WOULD YOU WANT TO DO THEN?
HUH?
THAT'S NON-SENSE, STUPID.
THE OUTSIDE WORLD IS DEAD. THE VIRUS KILLED EVERY-BODY.
WE'D NEVER GET OUT—
"WHAT IF," YU! JUST "WHAT IF."
WHAT IF ONE DAY JUST THE HYAKUYA ORPHANAGE FAMILY GOT OUT?
WHAT IF WE FOUND A WORLD WITH NO VAMPIRES IN IT AT ALL?
WOULDN'T THAT BE GREAT?

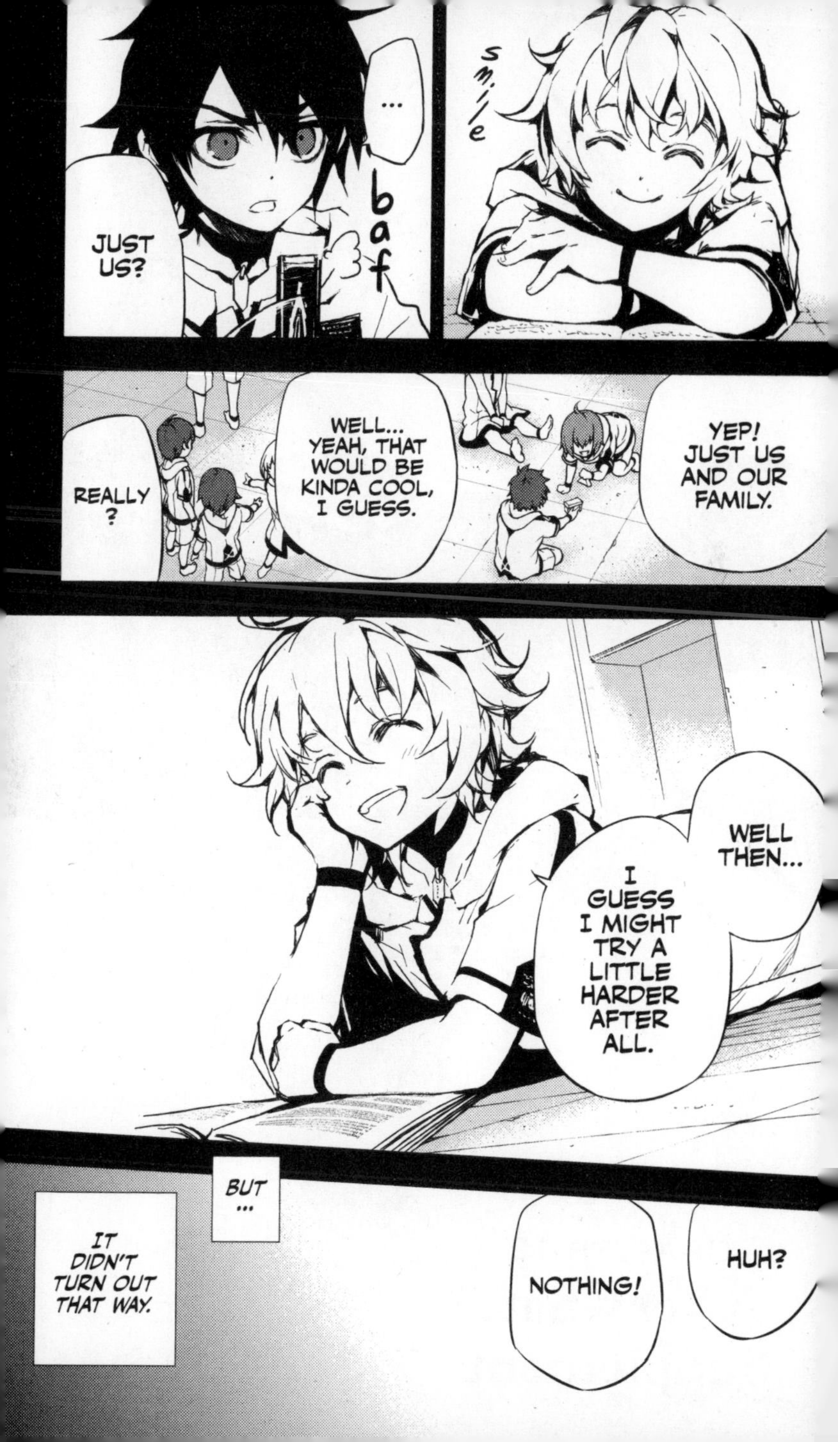
smile
...
baf
JUST US?
YEP! JUST US AND OUR FAMILY.
WELL... YEAH, THAT WOULD BE KINDA COOL, I GUESS.
REALLY ?
WELL THEN...
I GUESS I MIGHT TRY A LITTLE HARDER AFTER ALL.
HUH?
NOTHING!
BUT...
IT DIDN'T TURN OUT THAT WAY.

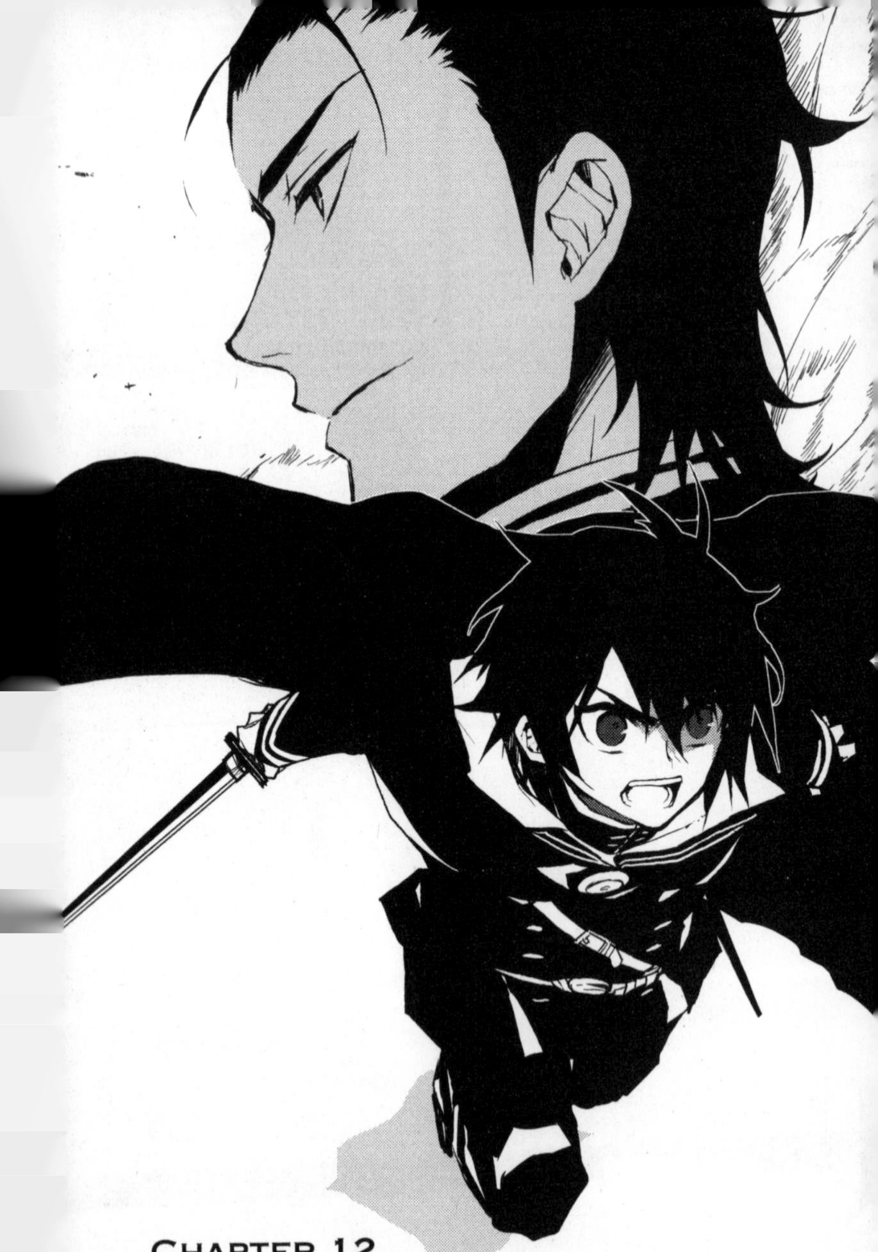

CHAPTER 12

A Very Safe Supplement

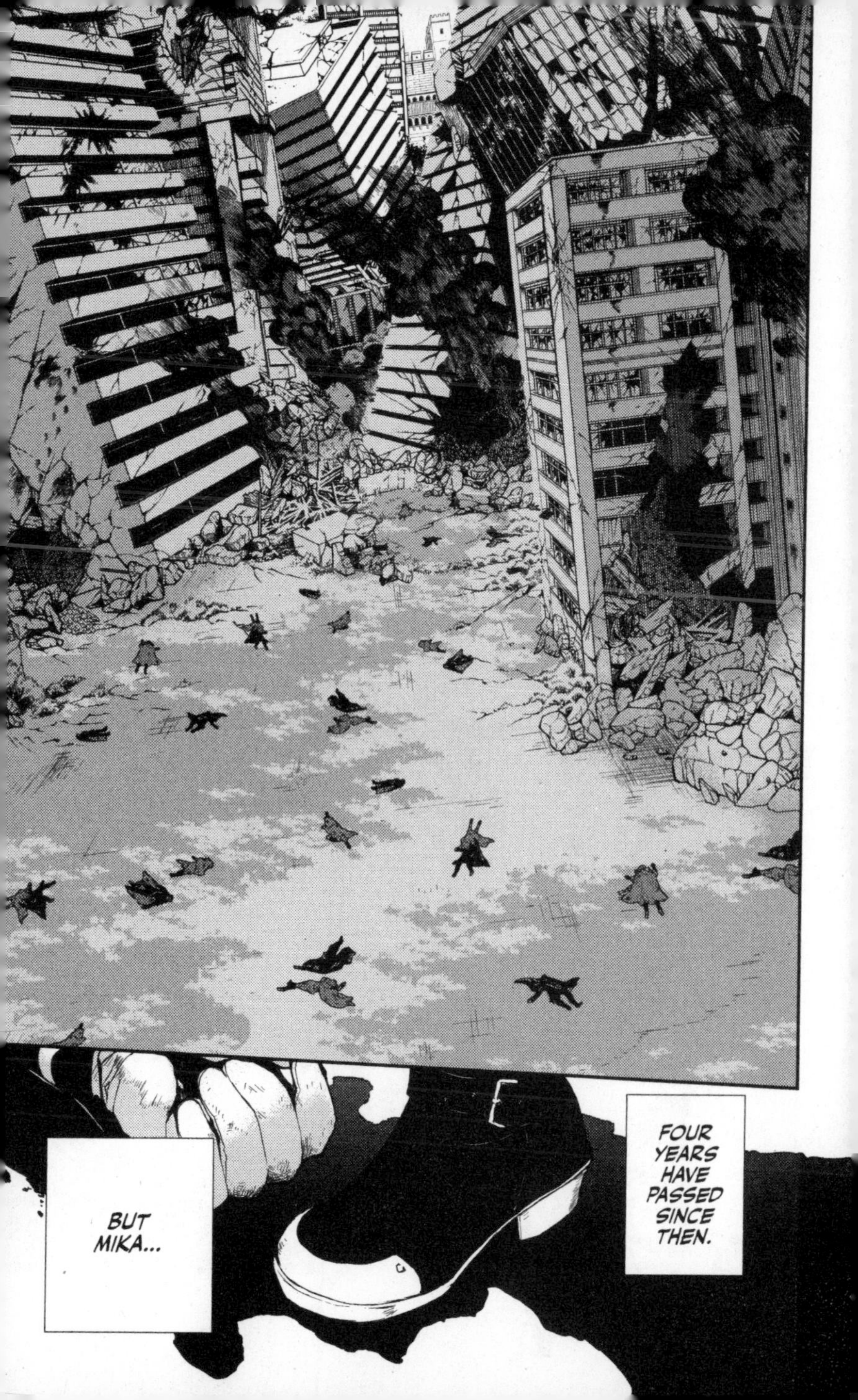
FOUR YEARS HAVE PASSED SINCE THEN.
BUT MIKA...

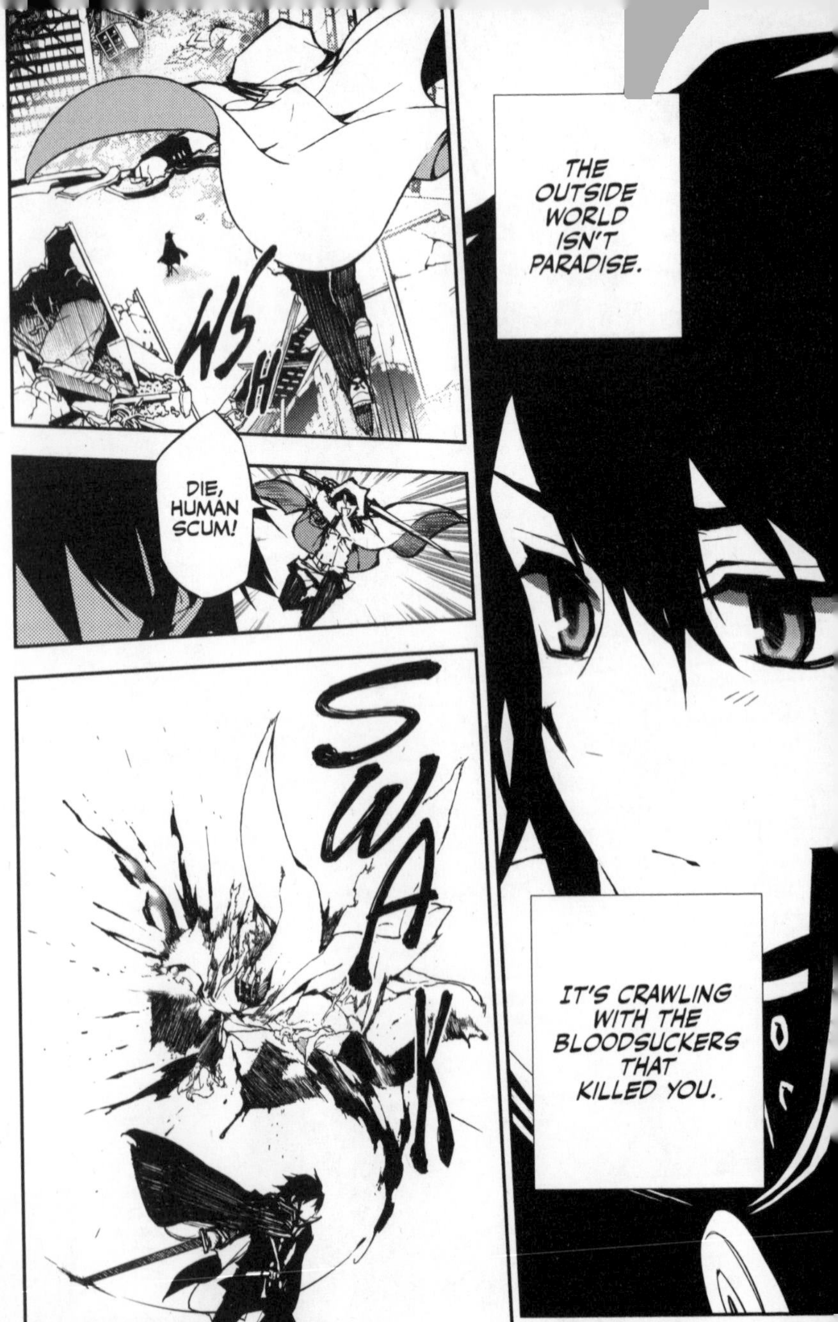
THE OUTSIDE WORLD ISN'T PARADISE.
IT'S CRAWLING WITH THE BLOODSUCKERS THAT KILLED YOU.
WSH
DIE, HUMAN SCUM!
SWAK

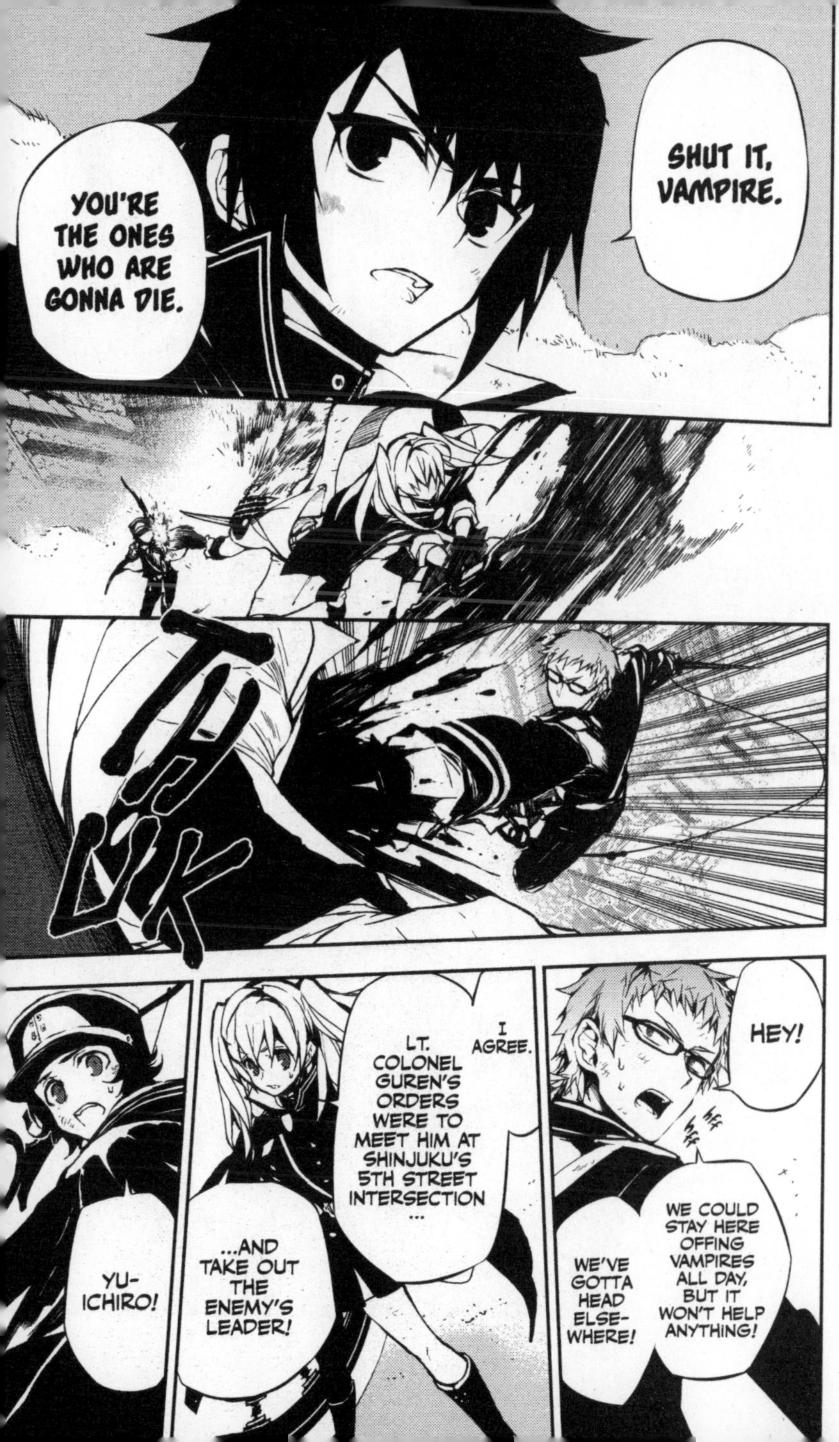
SHUT IT, VAMPIRE.
YOU'RE THE ONES WHO ARE GONNA DIE.
THUK
HEY!
hff hff
WE COULD STAY HERE OFFING VAMPIRES ALL DAY, BUT IT WON'T HELP ANYTHING!
WE'VE GOTTA HEAD ELSE-WHERE!
I AGREE.
LT. COLONEL GUREN'S ORDERS WERE TO MEET HIM AT SHINJUKU'S 5TH STREET INTERSECTION...
...AND TAKE OUT THE ENEMY'S LEADER!
YU-ICHIRO!

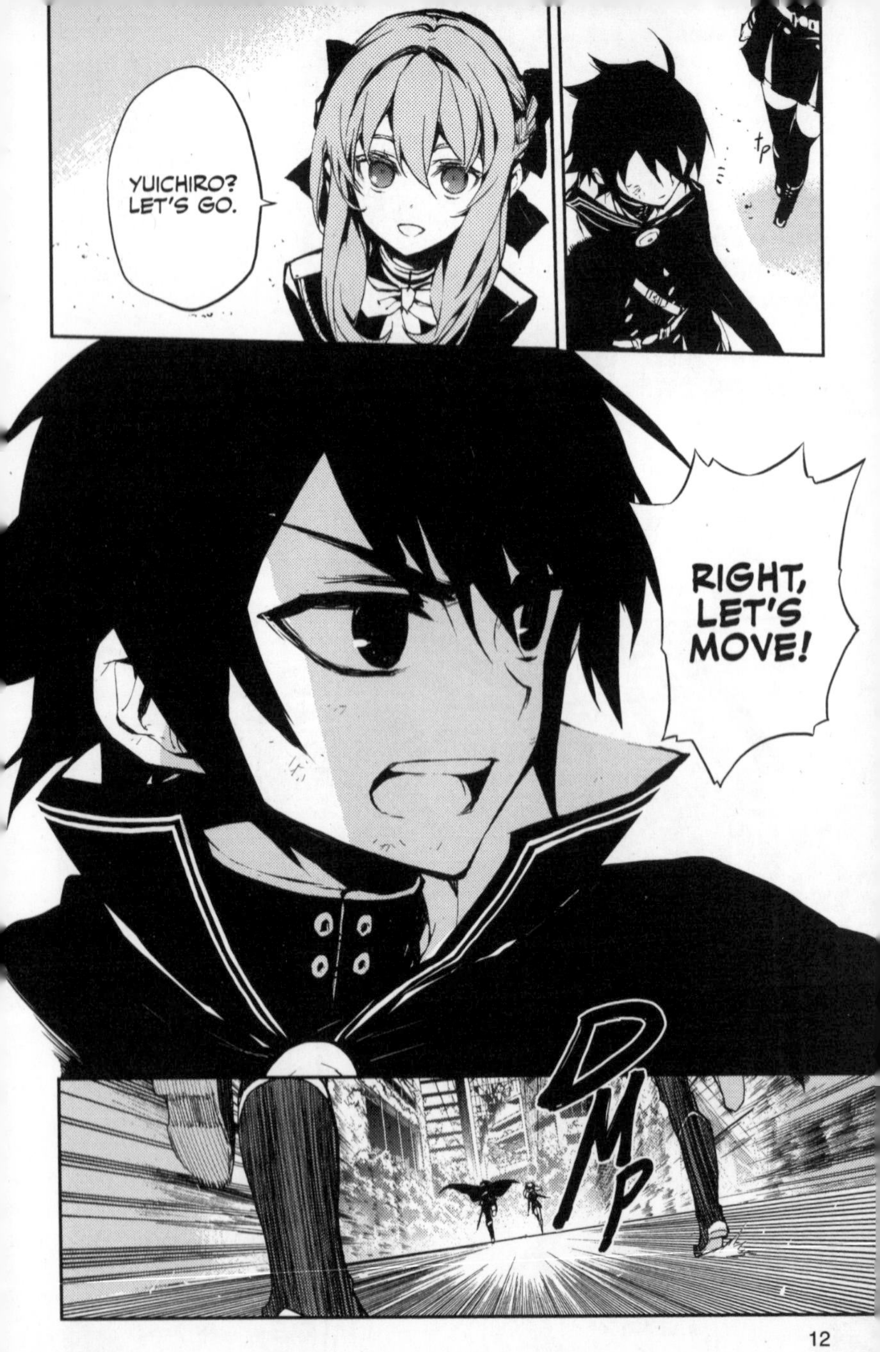
tp
YUICHIRO? LET'S GO.
RIGHT, LET'S MOVE!
DMP

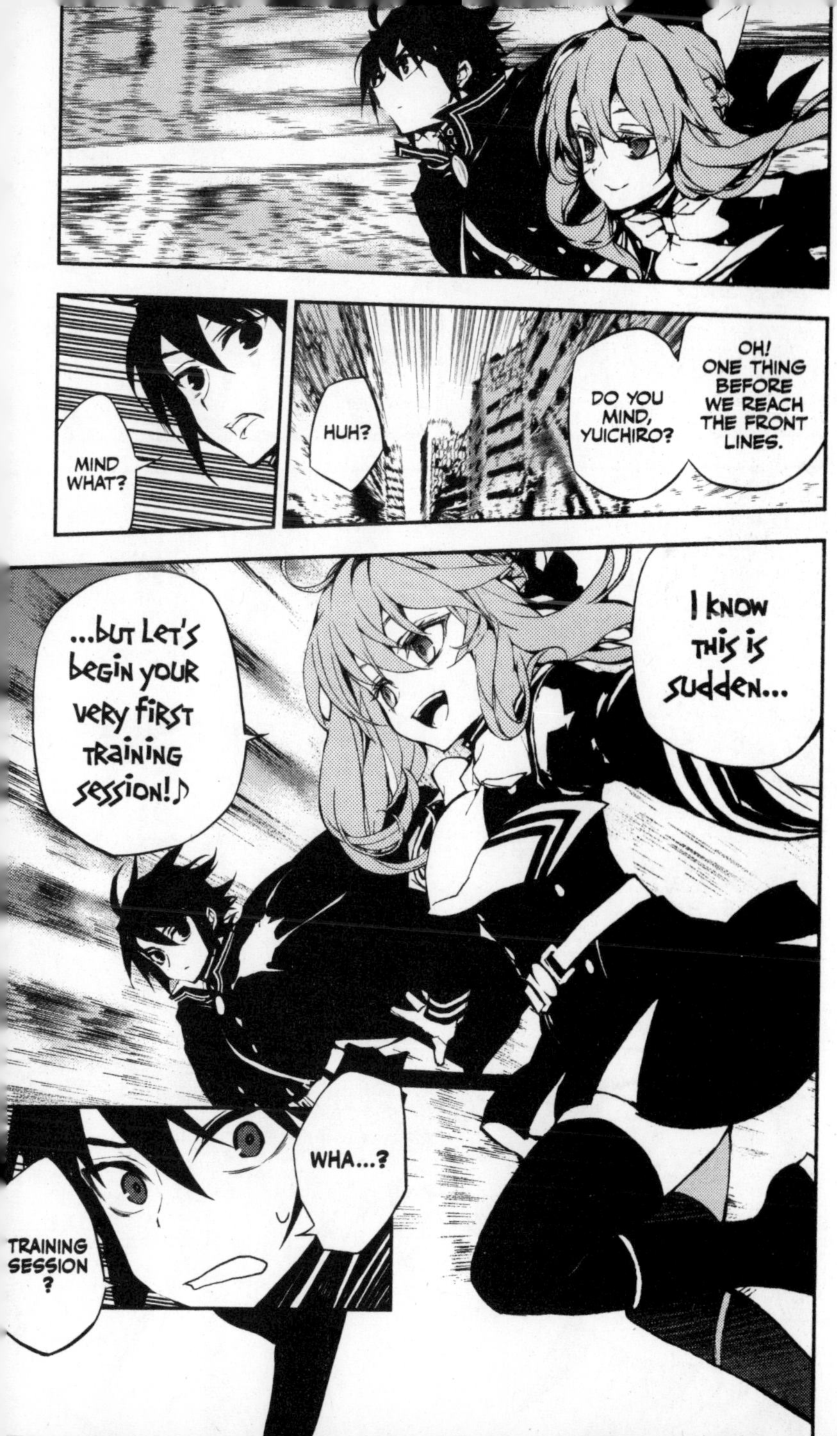
OH! ONE THING BEFORE WE REACH THE FRONT LINES.
DO YOU MIND, YUICHIRO?
HUH?
MIND WHAT?
I KNOW THIS IS SUDDEN...
...BUT LET'S BEGIN YOUR VERY FIRST TRAINING SESSION!♪
WHA...?
TRAINING SESSION?

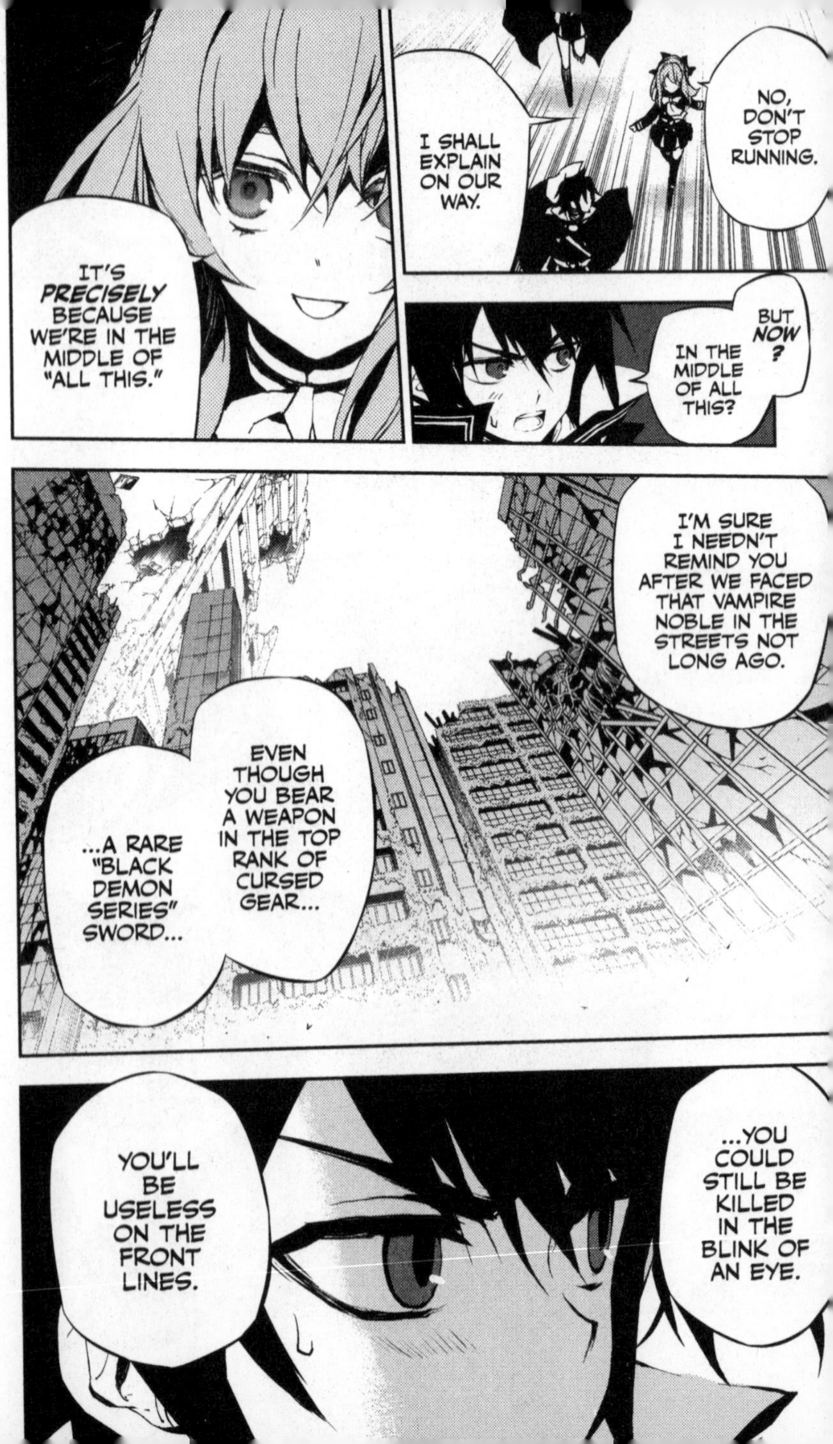
NO, DON'T STOP RUNNING.
I SHALL EXPLAIN ON OUR WAY.
BUT *NOW*? IN THE MIDDLE OF ALL THIS?
IT'S *PRECISELY* BECAUSE WE'RE IN THE MIDDLE OF "ALL THIS."
I'M SURE I NEEDN'T REMIND YOU AFTER WE FACED THAT VAMPIRE NOBLE IN THE STREETS NOT LONG AGO.
EVEN THOUGH YOU BEAR A WEAPON IN THE TOP RANK OF CURSED GEAR...
...A RARE "BLACK DEMON SERIES" SWORD...
...YOU COULD STILL BE KILLED IN THE BLINK OF AN EYE.
YOU'LL BE USELESS ON THE FRONT LINES.

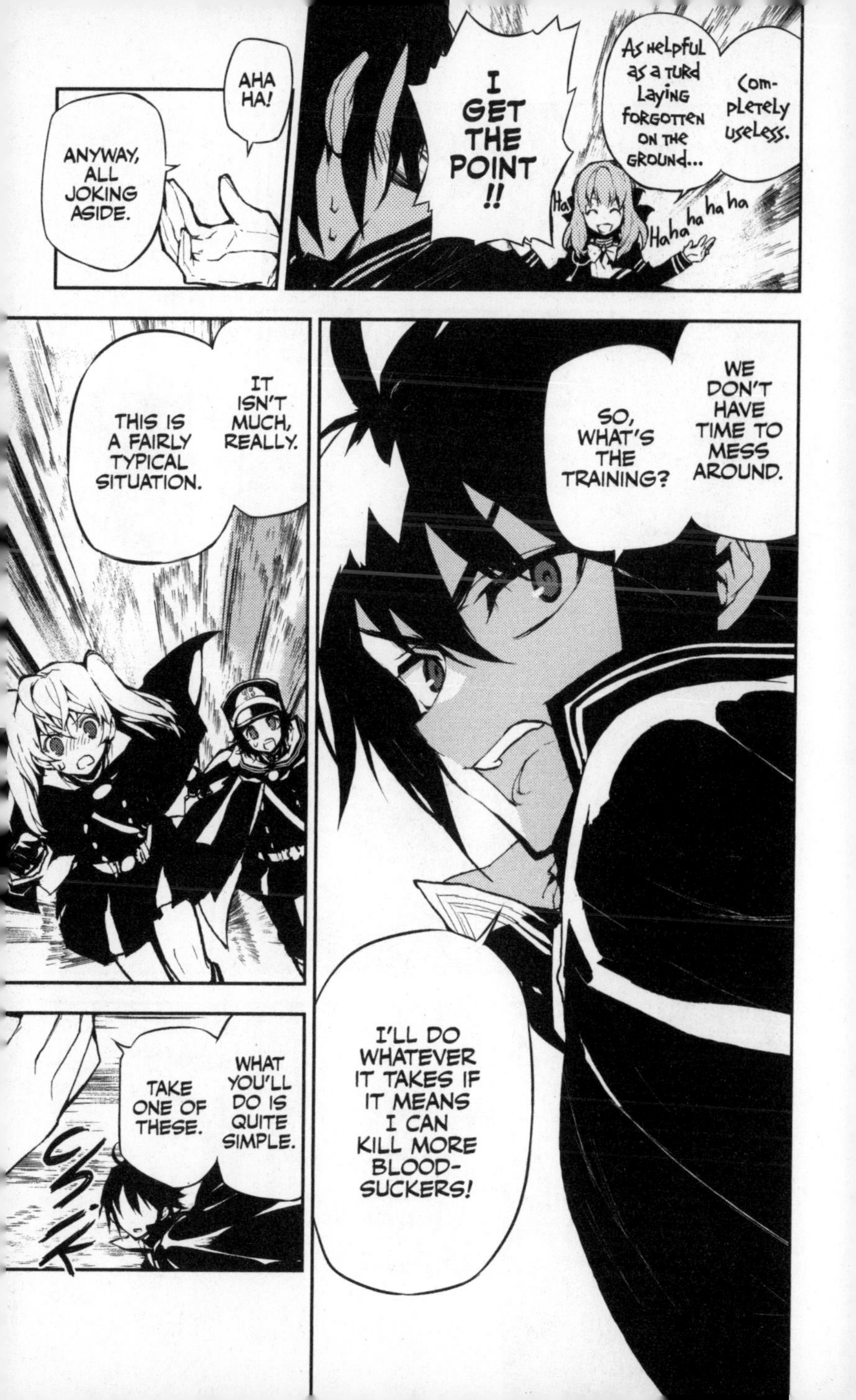
Com-pletely useless.
As helpful as a turd laying forgotten on the ground...
Ha Haha ha ha ha
I GET THE POINT!!
AHA HA!
ANYWAY, ALL JOKING ASIDE.
WE DON'T HAVE TIME TO MESS AROUND.
SO, WHAT'S THE TRAINING?
I'LL DO WHATEVER IT TAKES IF IT MEANS I CAN KILL MORE BLOOD-SUCKERS!
IT ISN'T MUCH, REALLY.
THIS IS A FAIRLY TYPICAL SITUATION.
WHAT YOU'LL DO IS QUITE SIMPLE.
TAKE ONE OF THESE.
SHIK

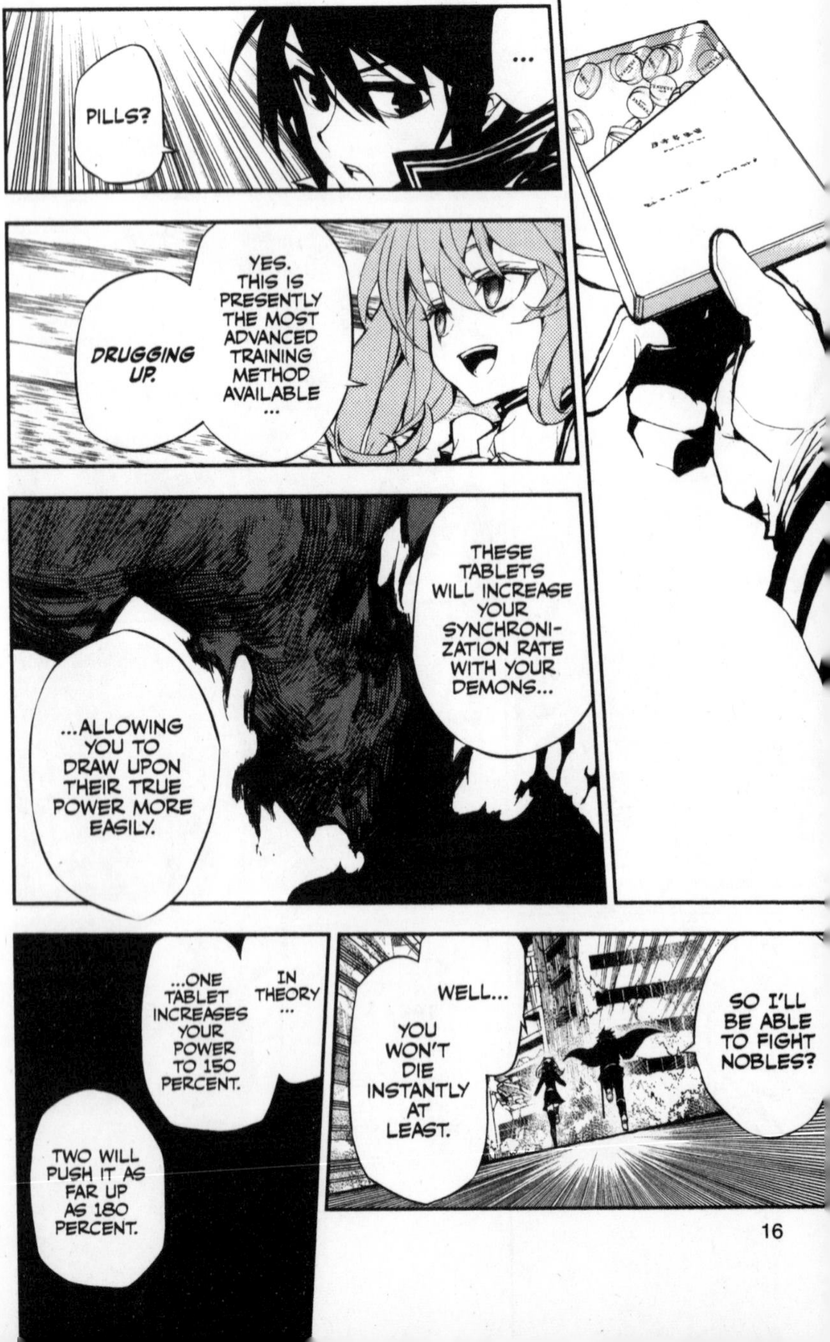
...
PILLS?
YES. THIS IS PRESENTLY THE MOST ADVANCED TRAINING METHOD AVAILABLE ...
DRUGGING UP.
THESE TABLETS WILL INCREASE YOUR SYNCHRONIZATION RATE WITH YOUR DEMONS...
...ALLOWING YOU TO DRAW UPON THEIR TRUE POWER MORE EASILY.
SO I'LL BE ABLE TO FIGHT NOBLES?
WELL...
YOU WON'T DIE INSTANTLY AT LEAST.
IN THEORY ...
...ONE TABLET INCREASES YOUR POWER TO 150 PERCENT.
TWO WILL PUSH IT AS FAR UP AS 180 PERCENT.

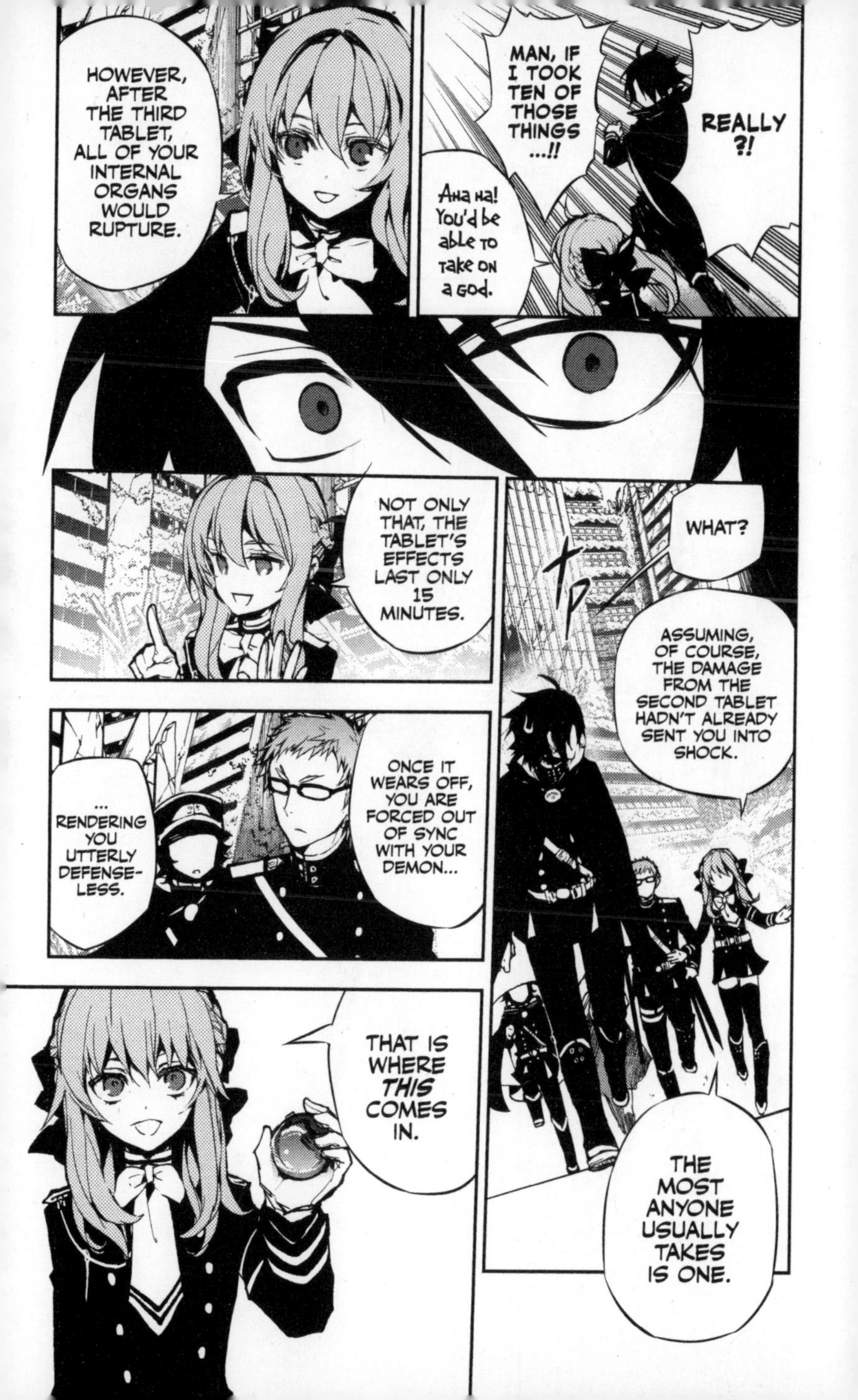
MAN, IF I TOOK TEN OF THOSE THINGS ...!!
Aha ha! You'd be able to take on a god.
REALLY ?!
HOWEVER, AFTER THE THIRD TABLET, ALL OF YOUR INTERNAL ORGANS WOULD RUPTURE.
WHAT?
ASSUMING, OF COURSE, THE DAMAGE FROM THE SECOND TABLET HADN'T ALREADY SENT YOU INTO SHOCK.
THE MOST ANYONE USUALLY TAKES IS ONE.
NOT ONLY THAT, THE TABLET'S EFFECTS LAST ONLY 15 MINUTES.
ONCE IT WEARS OFF, YOU ARE FORCED OUT OF SYNC WITH YOUR DEMON...
... RENDERING YOU UTTERLY DEFENSE-LESS.
THAT IS WHERE *THIS* COMES IN.

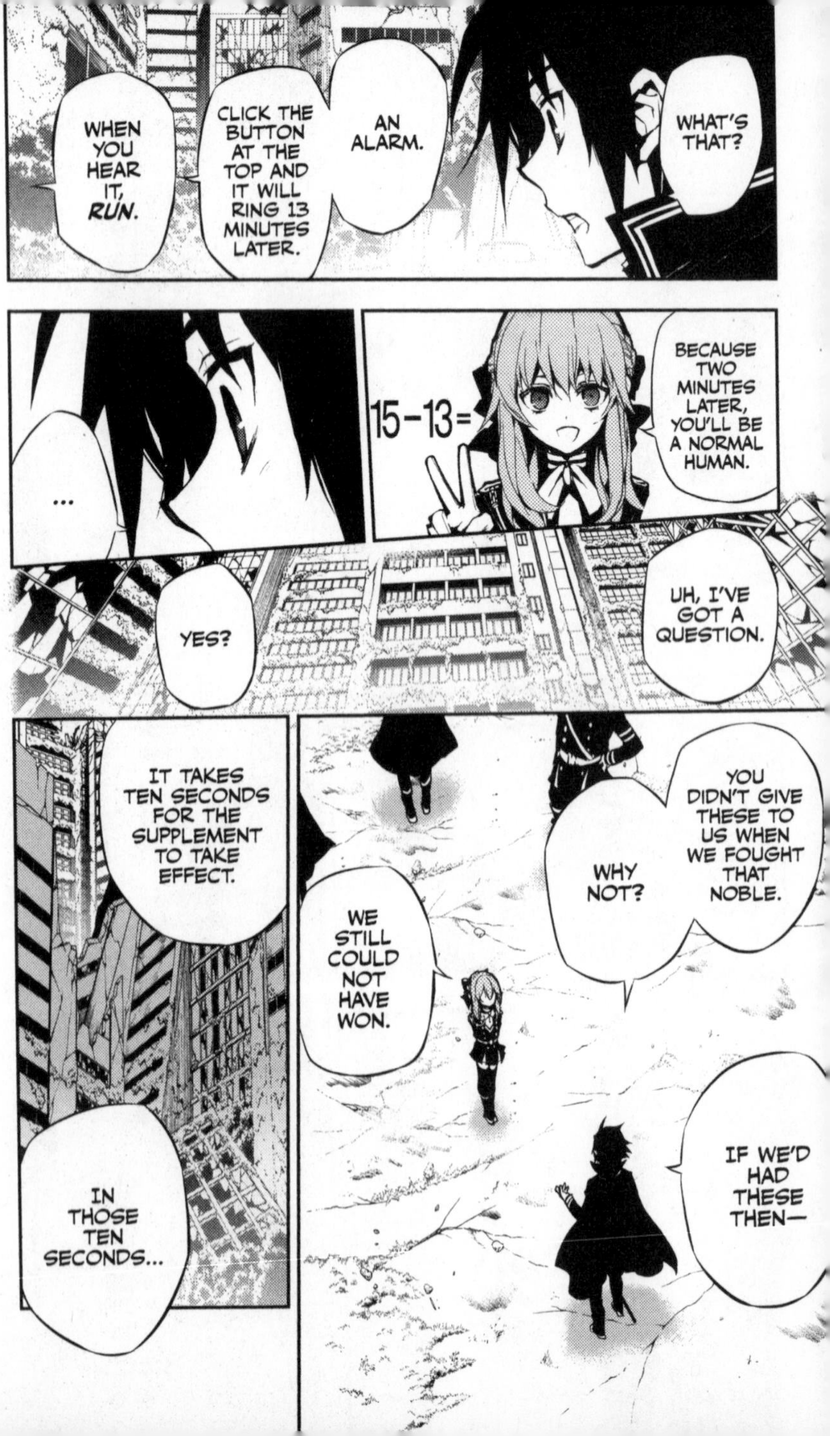
WHAT'S THAT?
AN ALARM.
CLICK THE BUTTON AT THE TOP AND IT WILL RING 13 MINUTES LATER.
WHEN YOU HEAR IT, *RUN*.
BECAUSE TWO MINUTES LATER, YOU'LL BE A NORMAL HUMAN.
15-13=
...
UH, I'VE GOT A QUESTION.
YES?
YOU DIDN'T GIVE THESE TO US WHEN WE FOUGHT THAT NOBLE.
WHY NOT?
IF WE'D HAD THESE THEN—
WE STILL COULD NOT HAVE WON.
IT TAKES TEN SECONDS FOR THE SUPPLEMENT TO TAKE EFFECT.
IN THOSE TEN SECONDS...

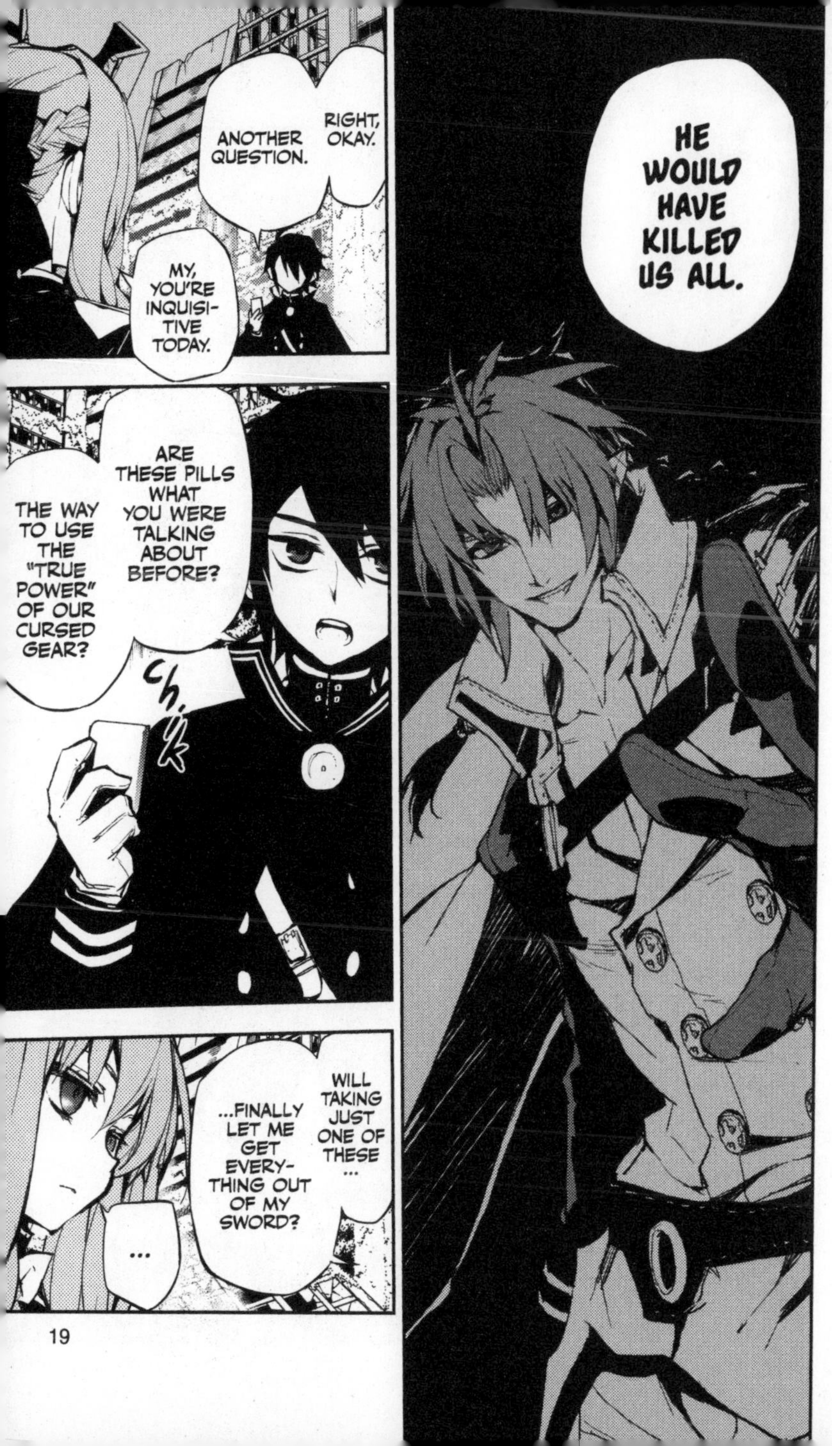
HE WOULD HAVE KILLED US ALL.
RIGHT, OKAY.
ANOTHER QUESTION.
MY, YOU'RE INQUISI-TIVE TODAY.
ARE THESE PILLS WHAT YOU WERE TALKING ABOUT BEFORE?
THE WAY TO USE THE "TRUE POWER" OF OUR CURSED GEAR?
chik
WILL TAKING JUST ONE OF THESE...
...FINALLY LET ME GET EVERY-THING OUT OF MY SWORD?
...

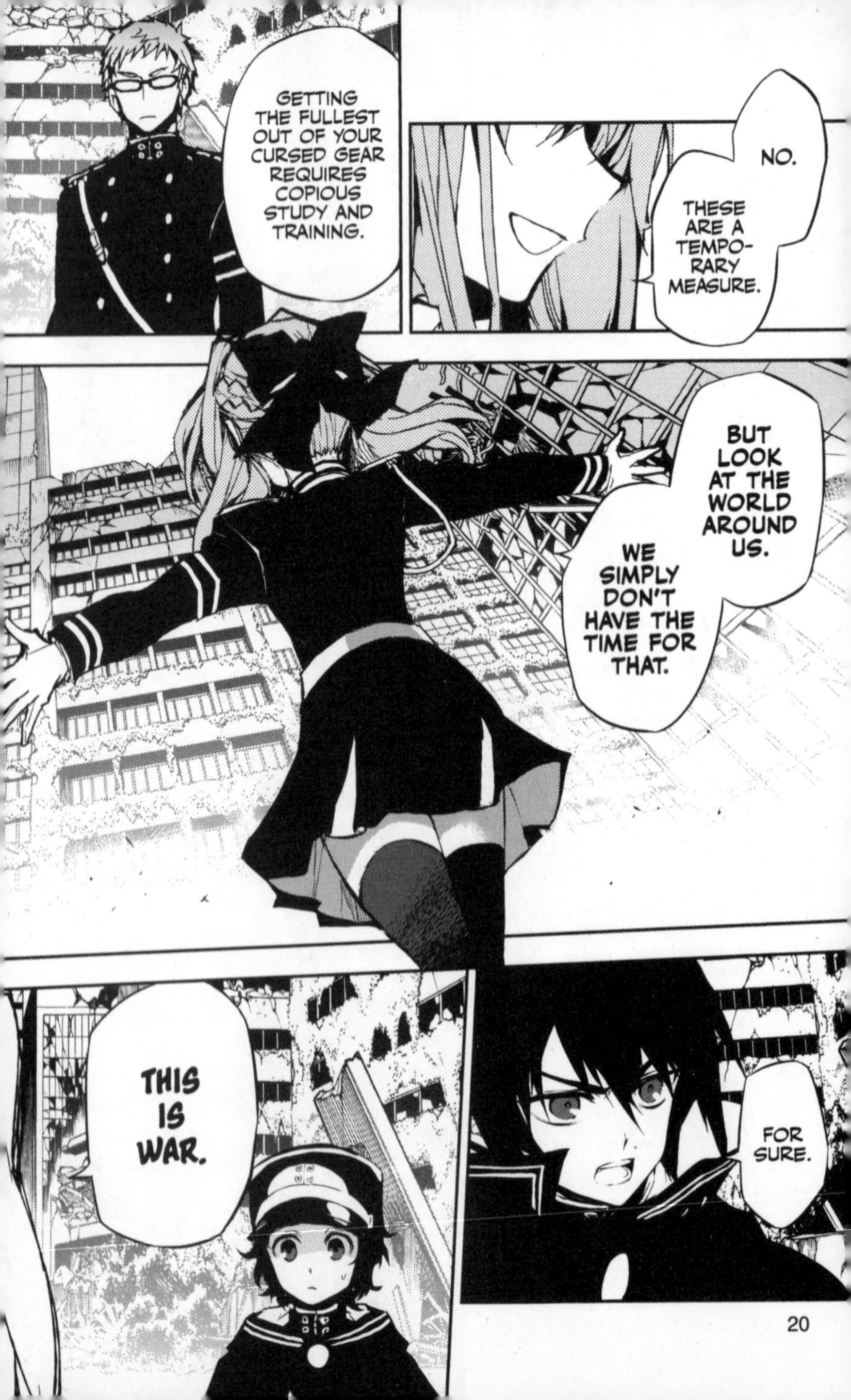
NO.
THESE ARE A TEMPORARY MEASURE.
GETTING THE FULLEST OUT OF YOUR CURSED GEAR REQUIRES COPIOUS STUDY AND TRAINING.
BUT LOOK AT THE WORLD AROUND US.
WE SIMPLY DON'T HAVE THE TIME FOR THAT.
FOR SURE.
THIS IS WAR.

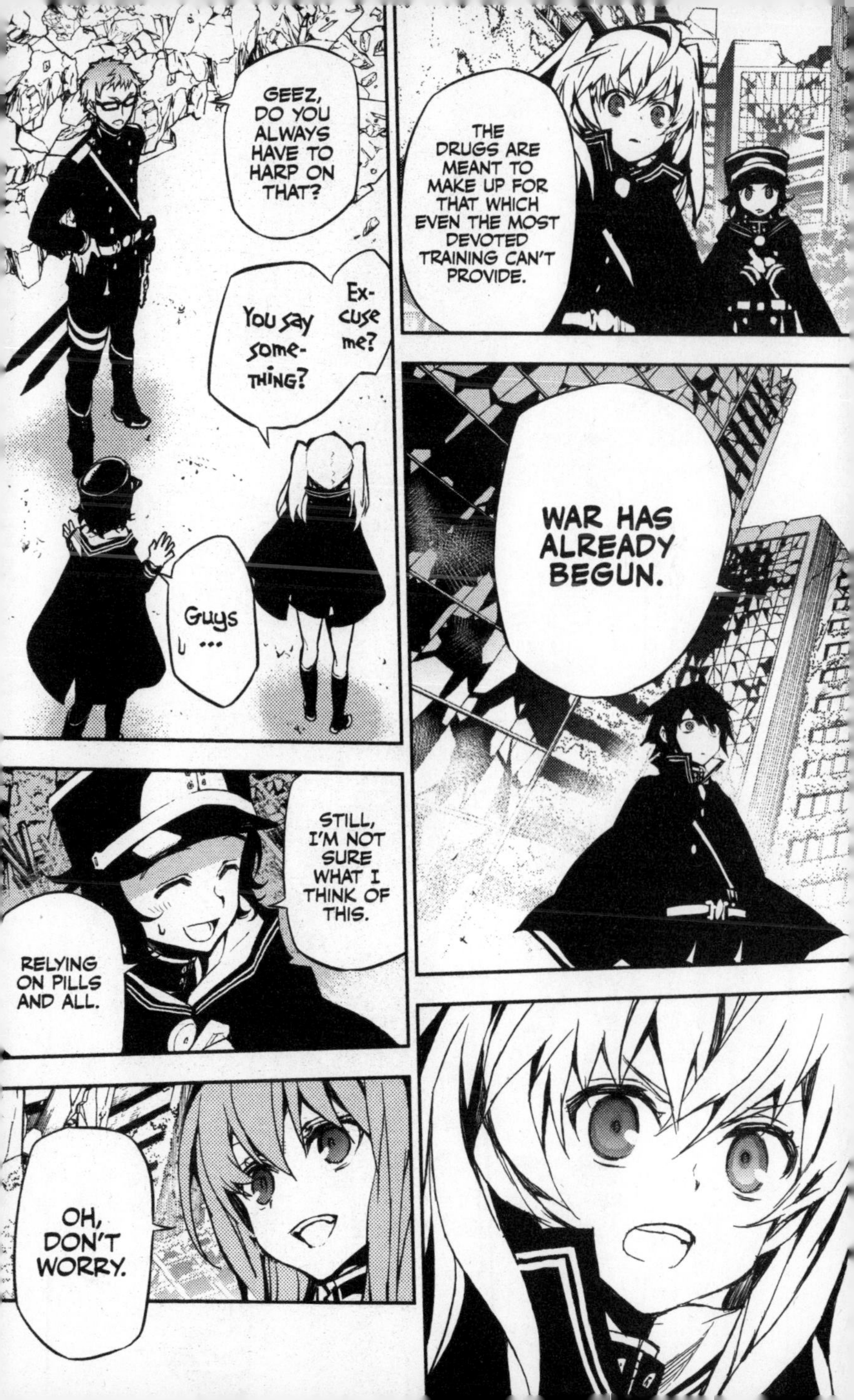
THE DRUGS ARE MEANT TO MAKE UP FOR THAT WHICH EVEN THE MOST DEVOTED TRAINING CAN'T PROVIDE.
GEEZ, DO YOU ALWAYS HAVE TO HARP ON THAT?
Ex-cuse me?
You say some-thing?
Guys ...
WAR HAS ALREADY BEGUN.
STILL, I'M NOT SURE WHAT I THINK OF THIS.
RELYING ON PILLS AND ALL.
OH, DON'T WORRY.

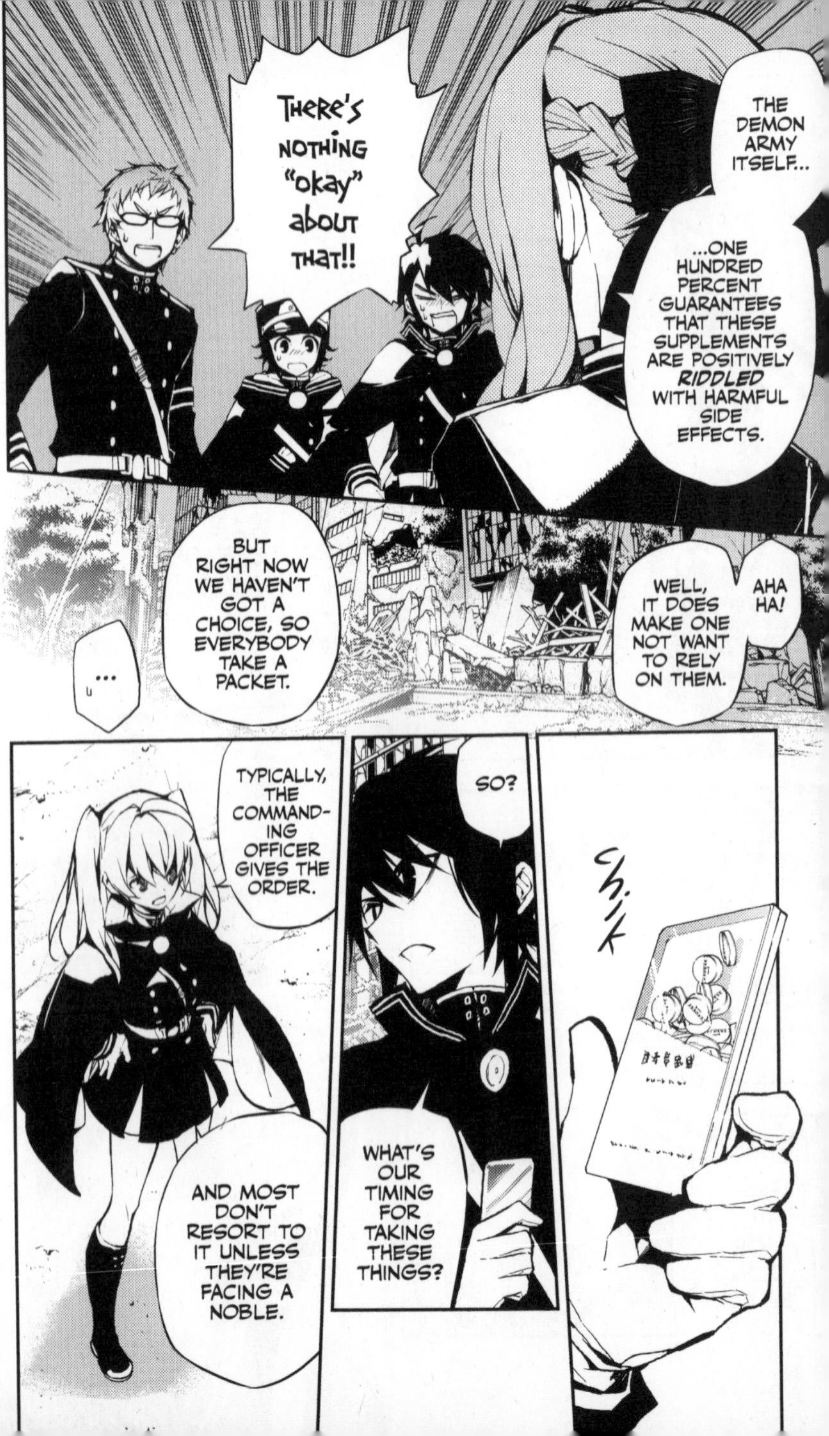
THE DEMON ARMY ITSELF...
...ONE HUNDRED PERCENT GUARANTEES THAT THESE SUPPLEMENTS ARE POSITIVELY *RIDDLED* WITH HARMFUL SIDE EFFECTS.
There's nothing "okay" about that!!
AHA HA!
WELL, IT DOES MAKE ONE NOT WANT TO RELY ON THEM.
BUT RIGHT NOW WE HAVEN'T GOT A CHOICE, SO EVERYBODY TAKE A PACKET.
...
Chik
SO?
WHAT'S OUR TIMING FOR TAKING THESE THINGS?
TYPICALLY, THE COMMAND-ING OFFICER GIVES THE ORDER.
AND MOST DON'T RESORT TO IT UNLESS THEY'RE FACING A NOBLE.

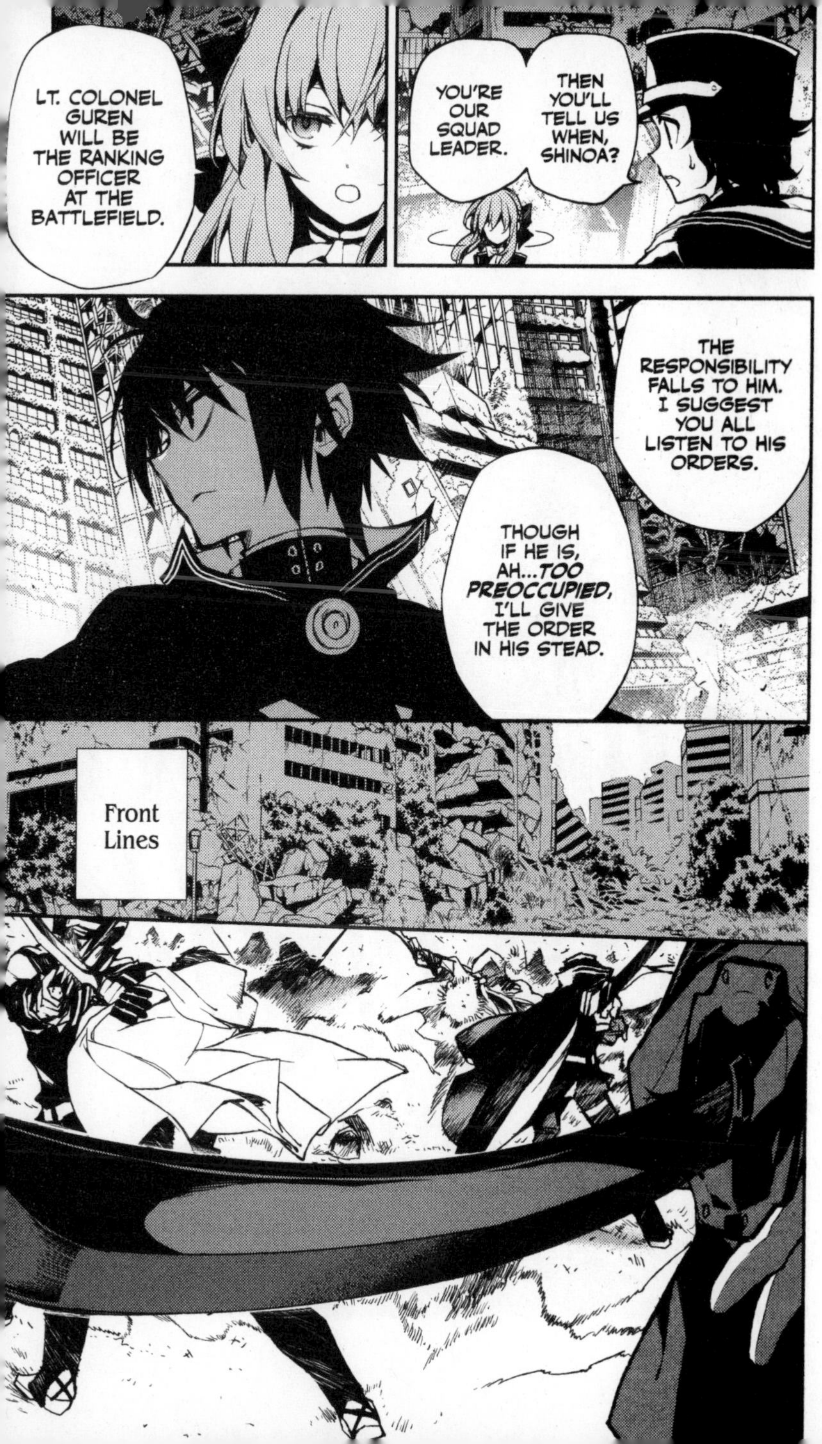
THEN YOU'LL TELL US WHEN, SHINOA?
YOU'RE OUR SQUAD LEADER.
LT. COLONEL GUREN WILL BE THE RANKING OFFICER AT THE BATTLEFIELD.
THE RESPONSIBILITY FALLS TO HIM. I SUGGEST YOU ALL LISTEN TO HIS ORDERS.
THOUGH IF HE IS, AH...*TOO PREOCCUPIED*, I'LL GIVE THE ORDER IN HIS STEAD.
Front Lines

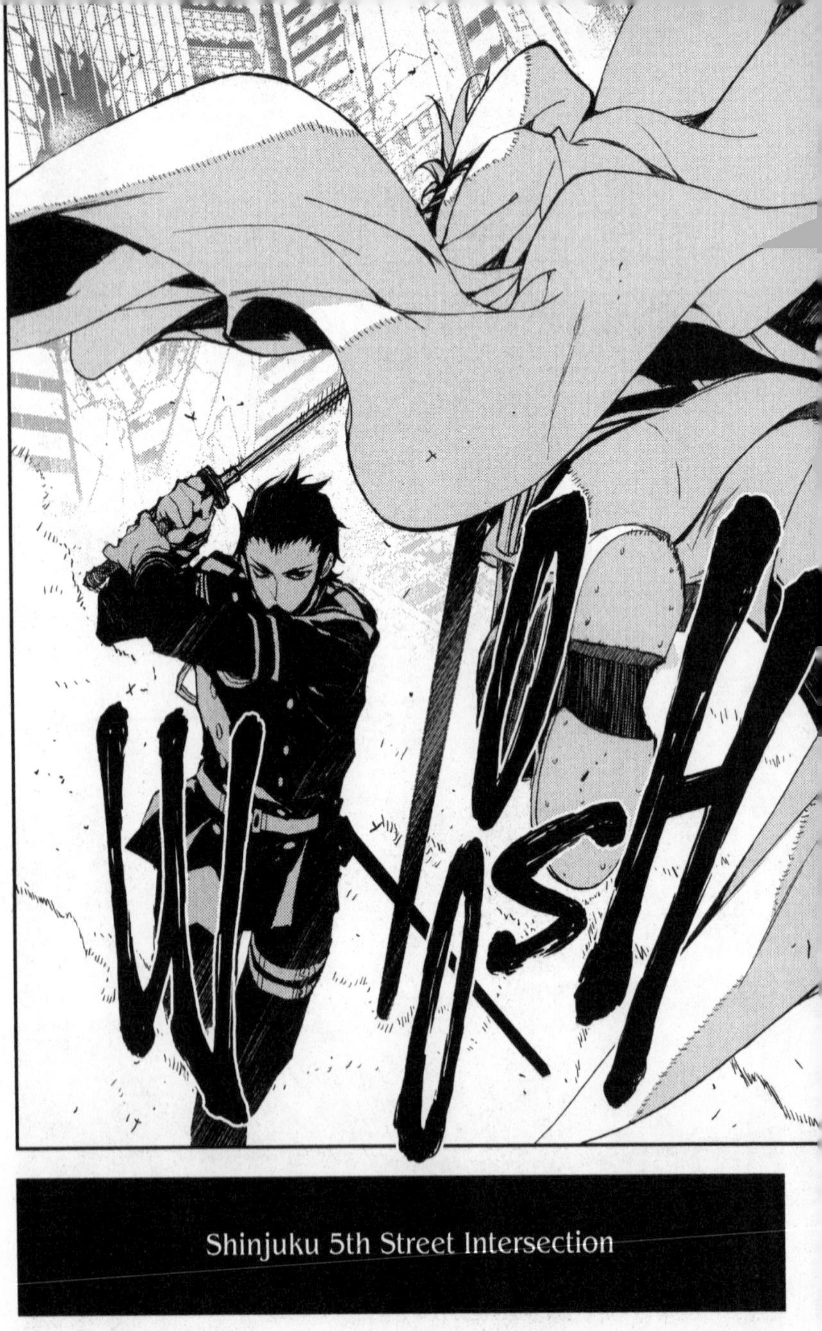
WHOOSH

Shinjuku 5th Street Intersection

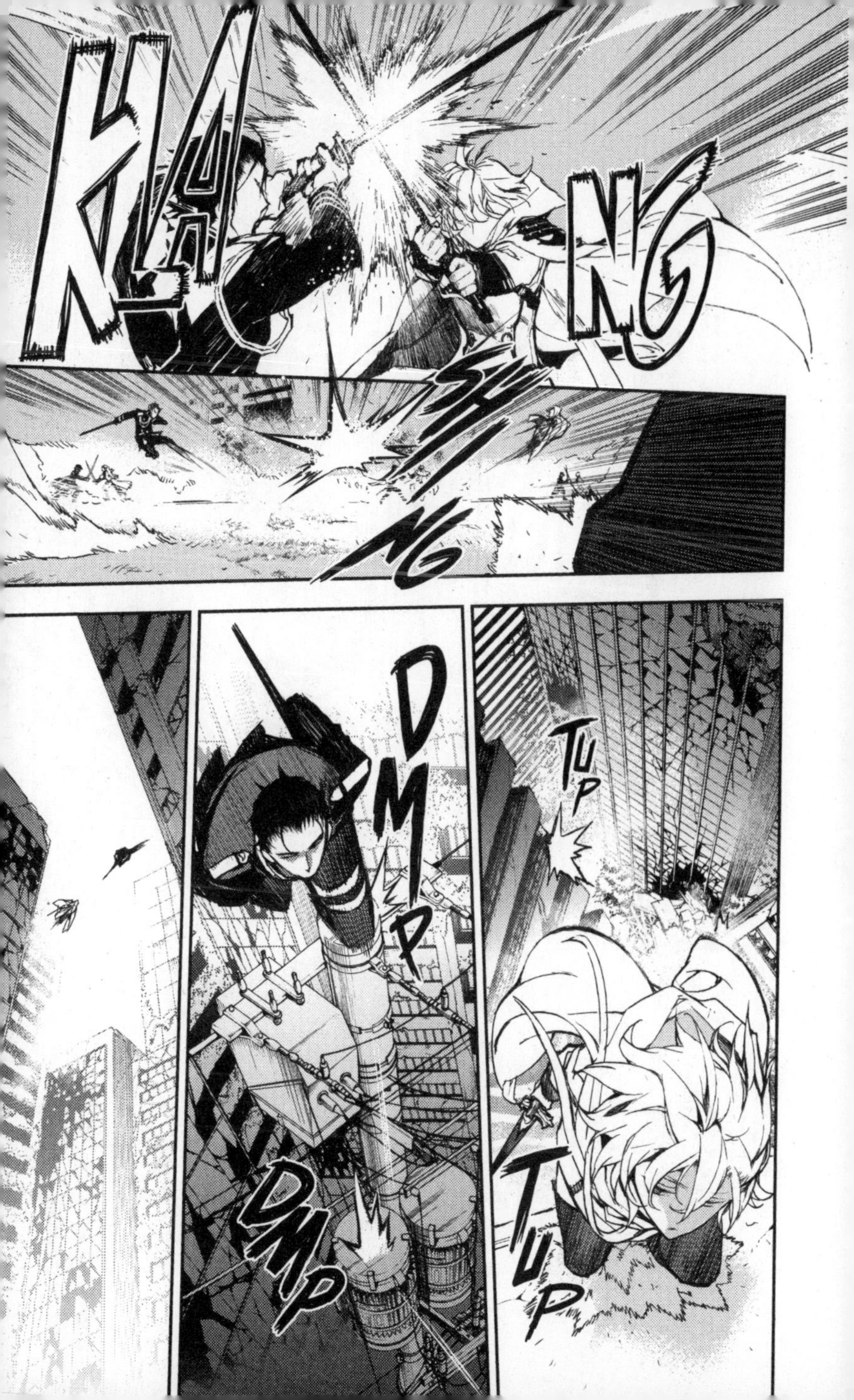
KLANG
SHING
TUP
TUP
DMP
DUMP

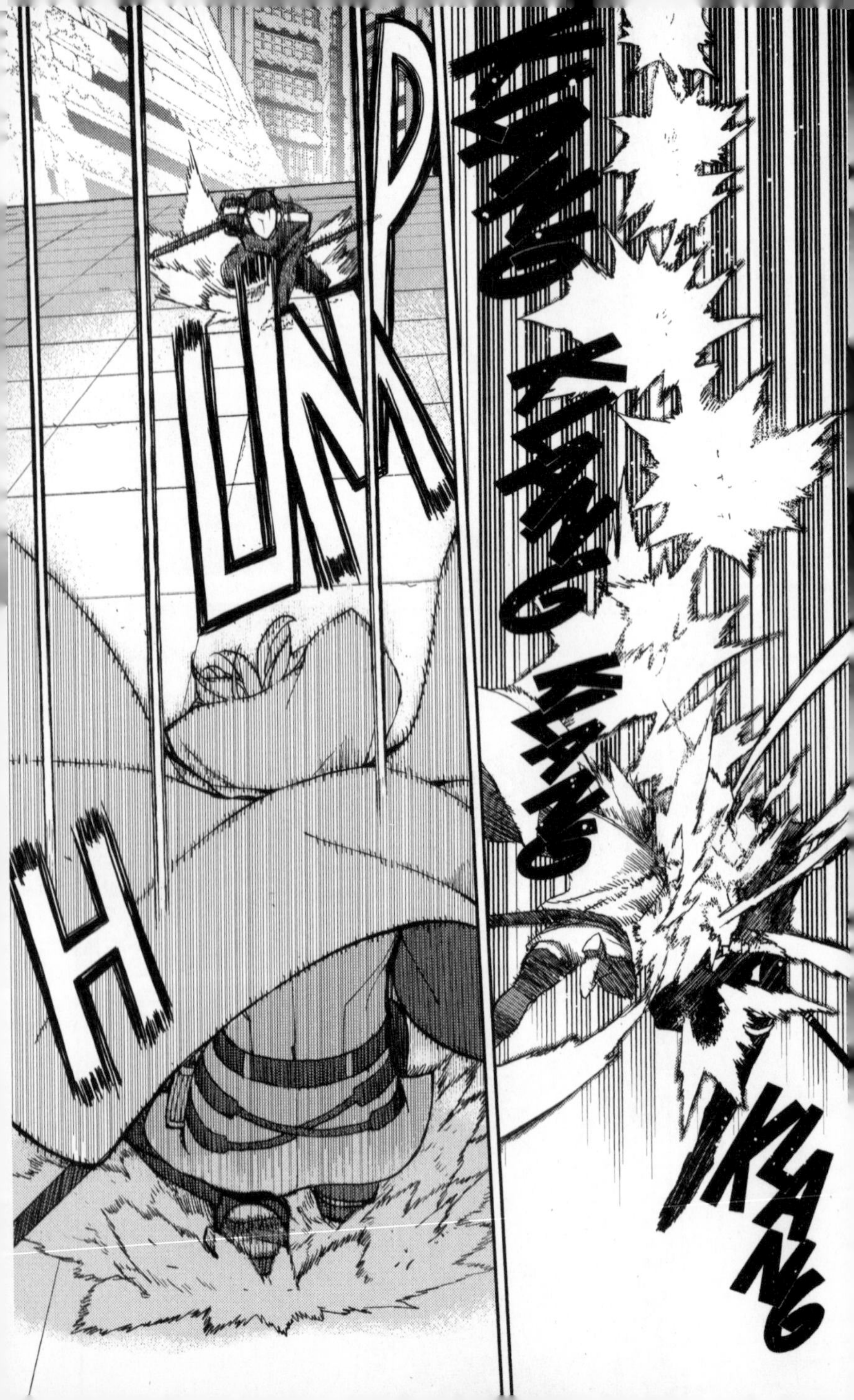
KLANG KLANG KLANG
KLANG

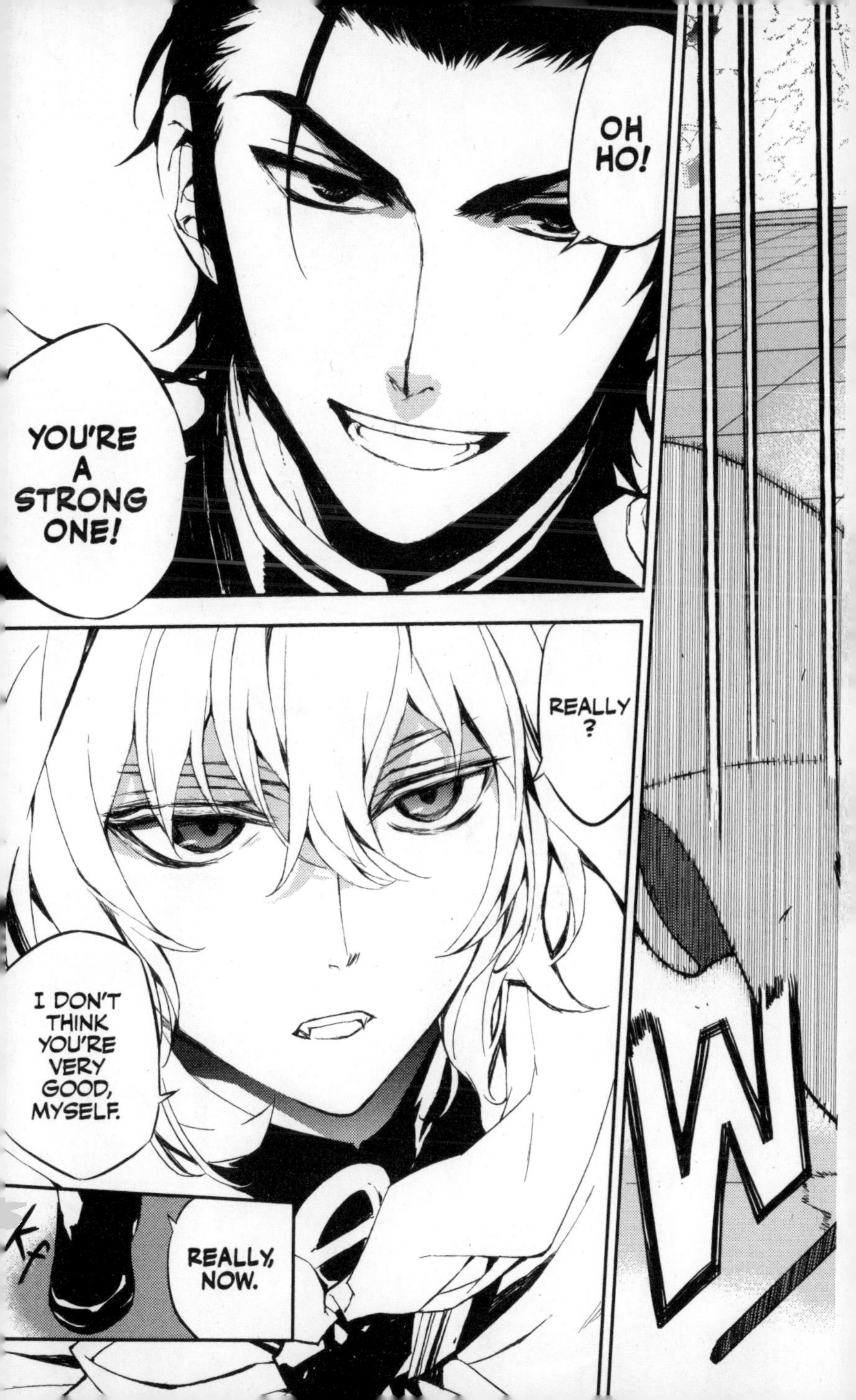
OH HO!
YOU'RE A STRONG ONE!
REALLY?
I DON'T THINK YOU'RE VERY GOOD, MYSELF.
REALLY, NOW.
Kf

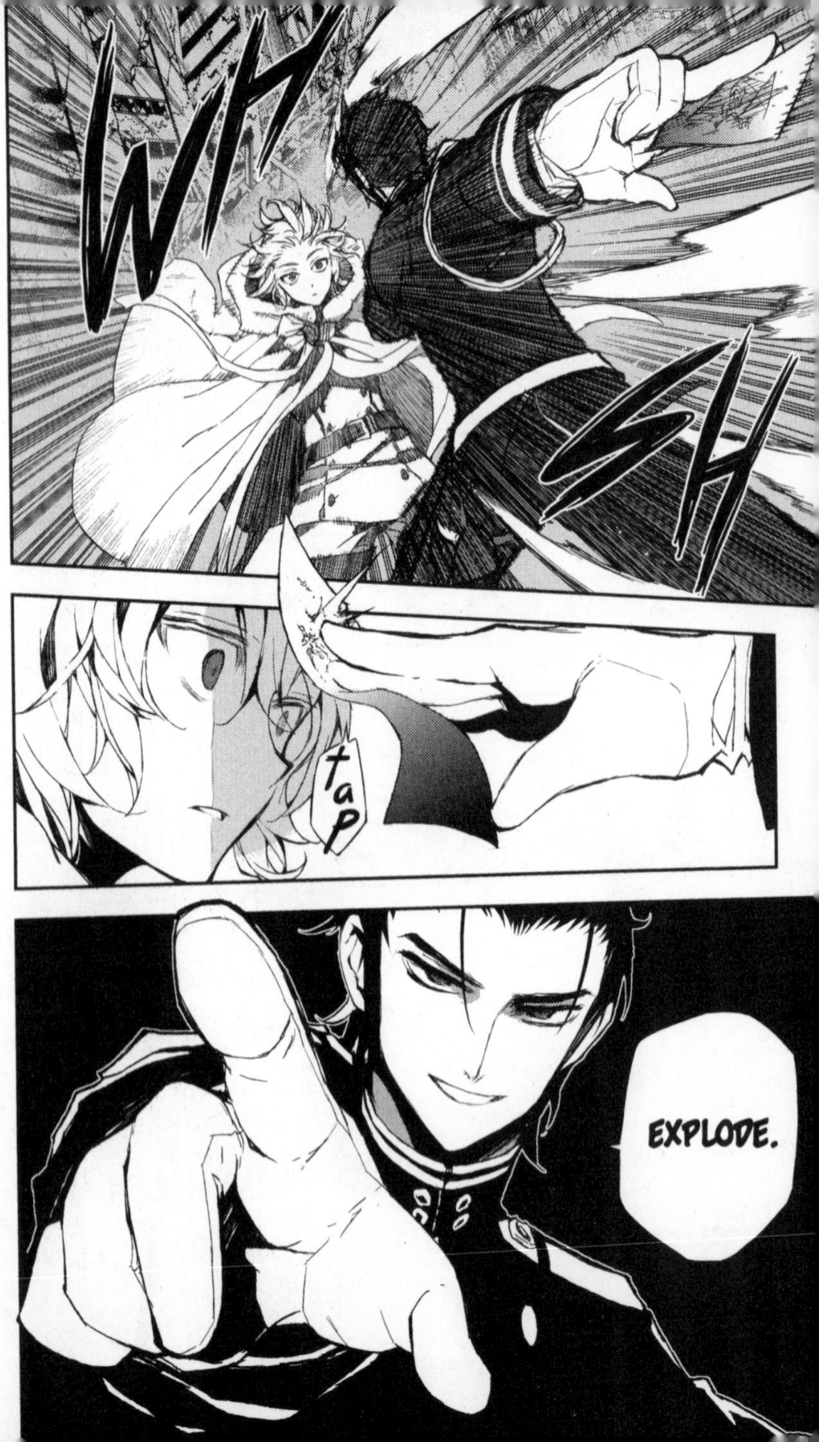

WHSH
tap
EXPLODE.

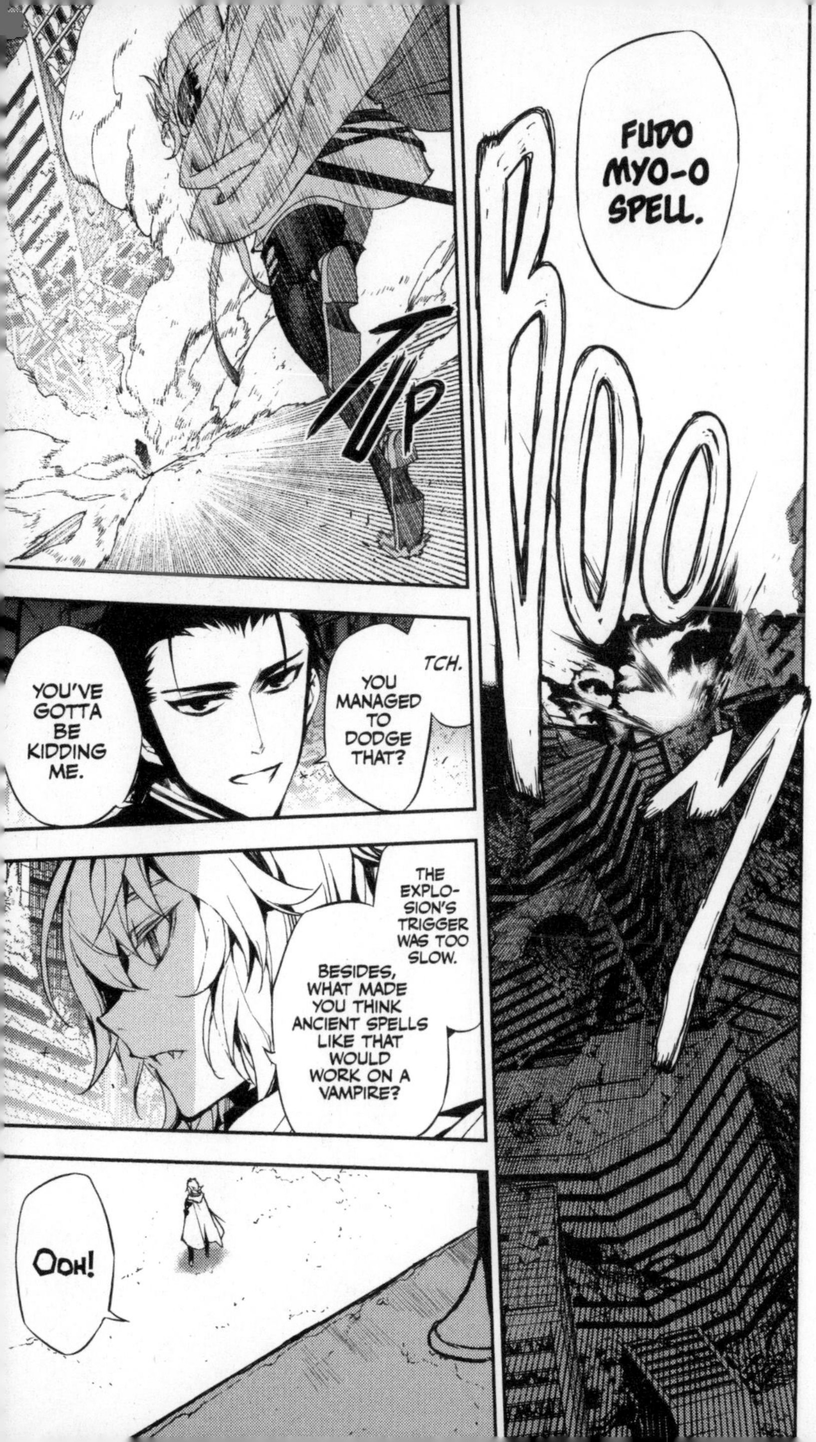
FUDO MYO-O SPELL.
BOOOOM
ZIP
TCH.
YOU MANAGED TO DODGE THAT?
YOU'VE GOTTA BE KIDDING ME.
THE EXPLOSION'S TRIGGER WAS TOO SLOW.
BESIDES, WHAT MADE YOU THINK ANCIENT SPELLS LIKE THAT WOULD WORK ON A VAMPIRE?
OOH!

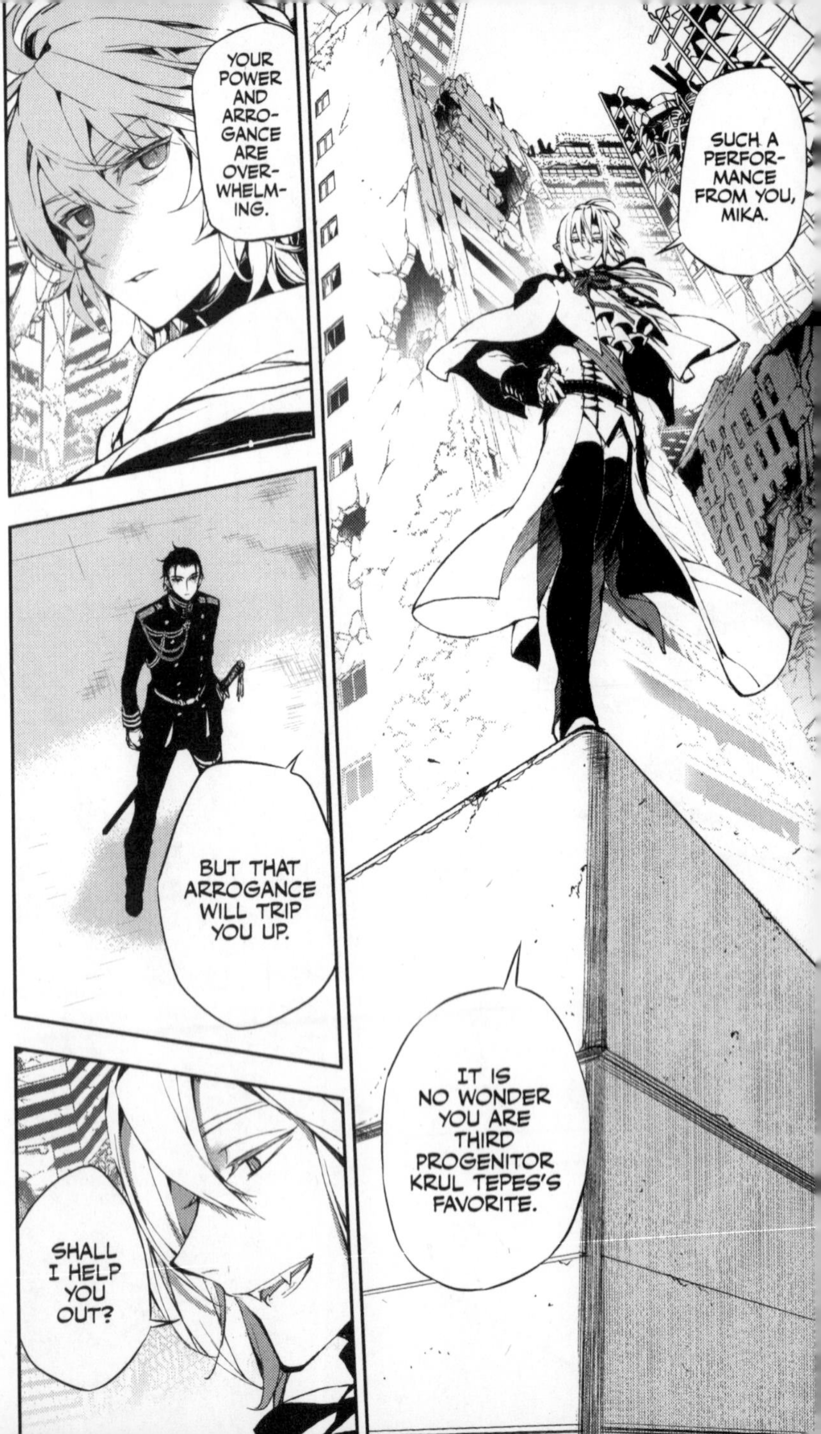
SUCH A PERFORMANCE FROM YOU, MIKA.
IT IS NO WONDER YOU ARE THIRD PROGENITOR KRUL TEPES'S FAVORITE.
YOUR POWER AND ARROGANCE ARE OVERWHELMING.
BUT THAT ARROGANCE WILL TRIP YOU UP.
SHALL I HELP YOU OUT?

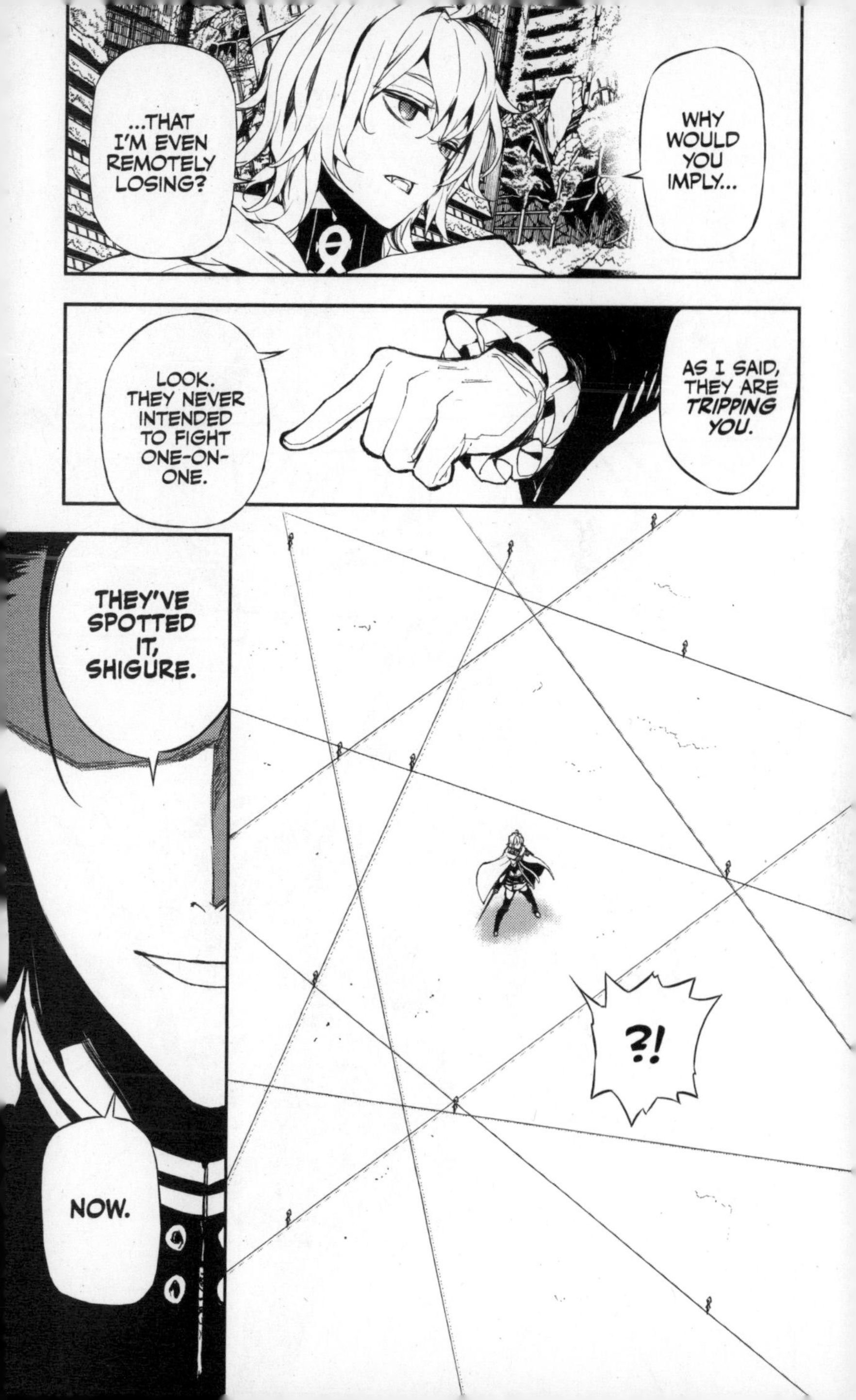
WHY WOULD YOU IMPLY...
...THAT I'M EVEN REMOTELY LOSING?
AS I SAID, THEY ARE TRIPPING YOU.
LOOK. THEY NEVER INTENDED TO FIGHT ONE-ON-ONE.
?!
THEY'VE SPOTTED IT, SHIGURE.
NOW.

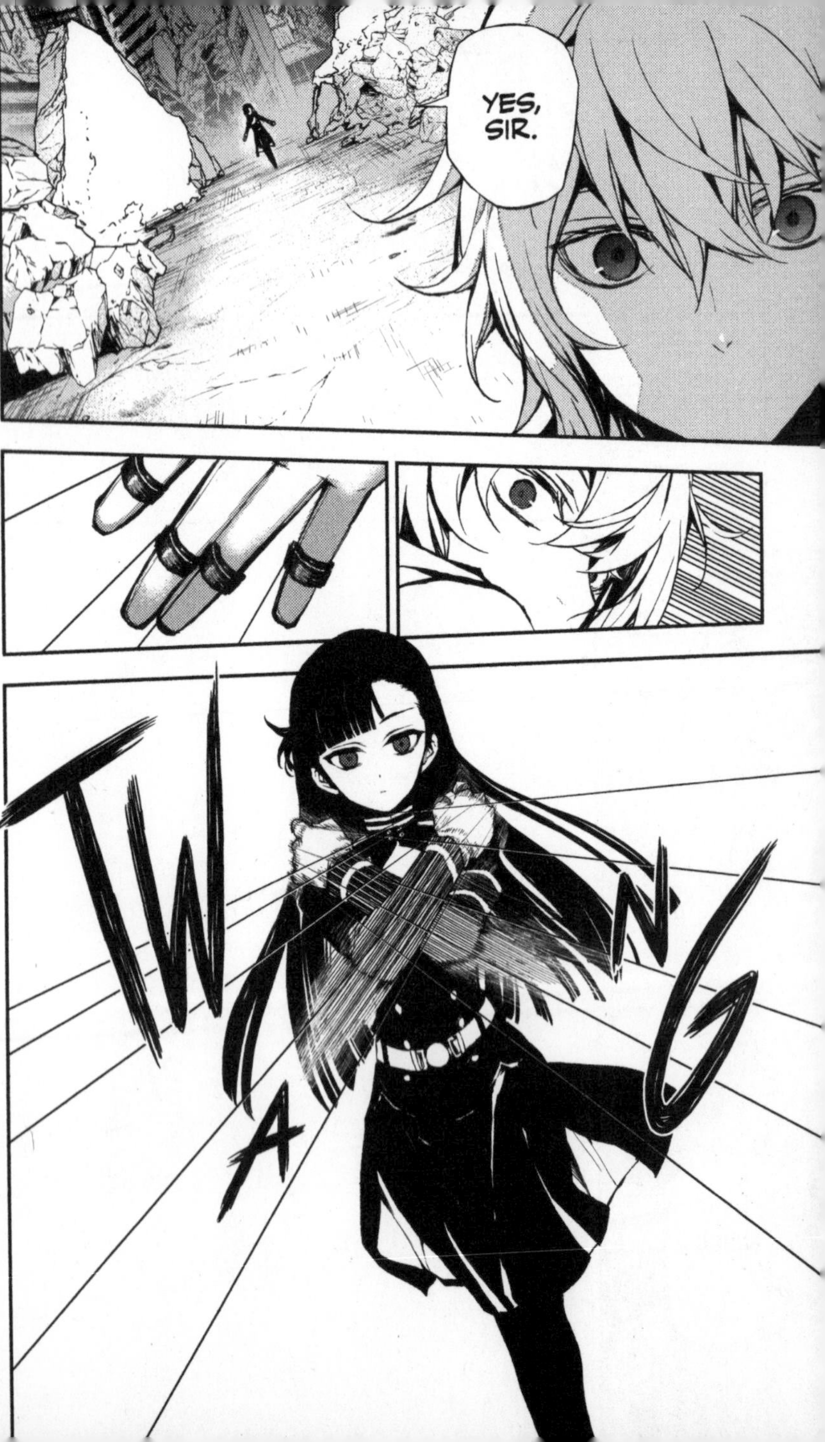
YES, SIR.
TWANG

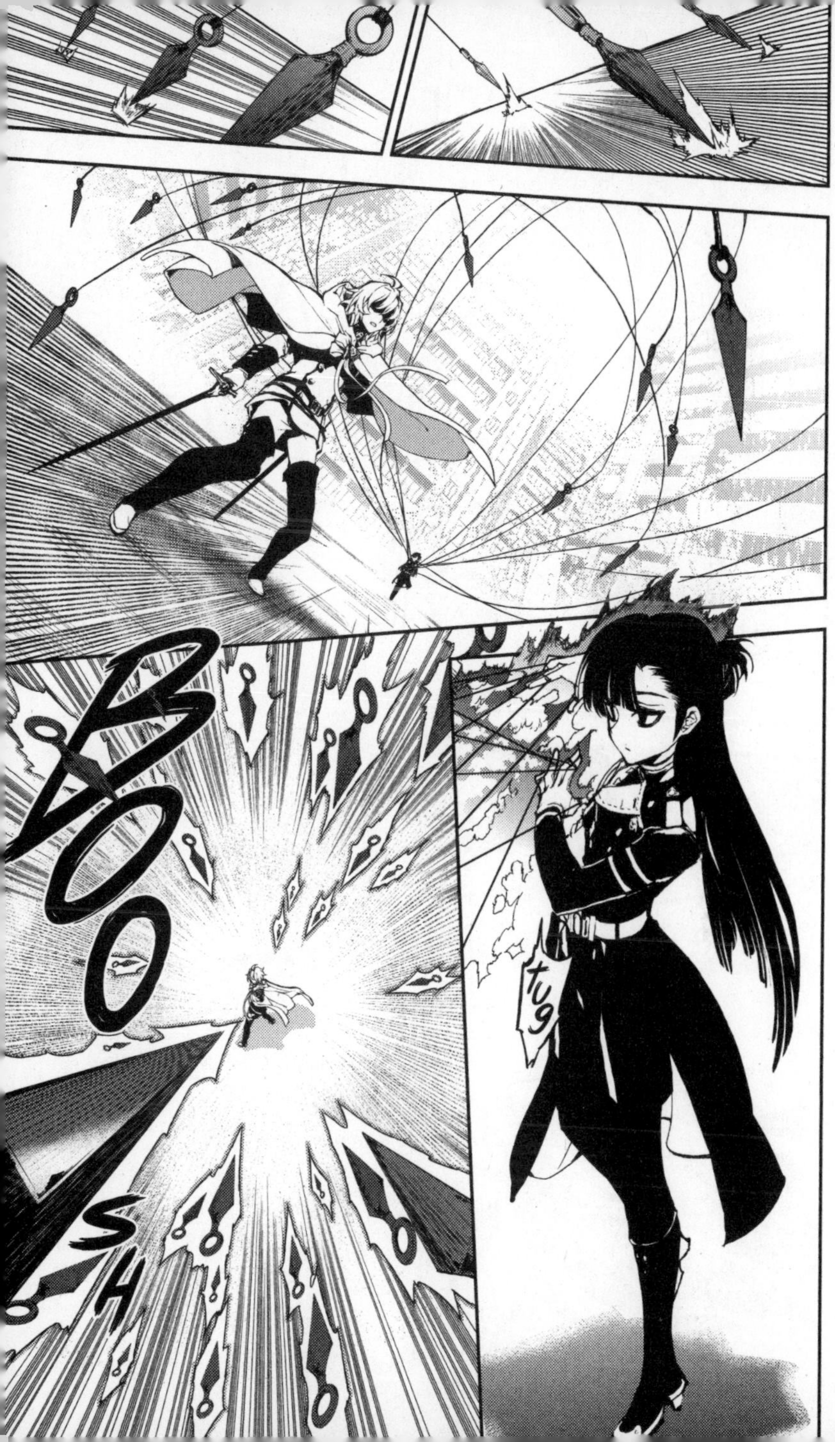
tug
BOOOSH

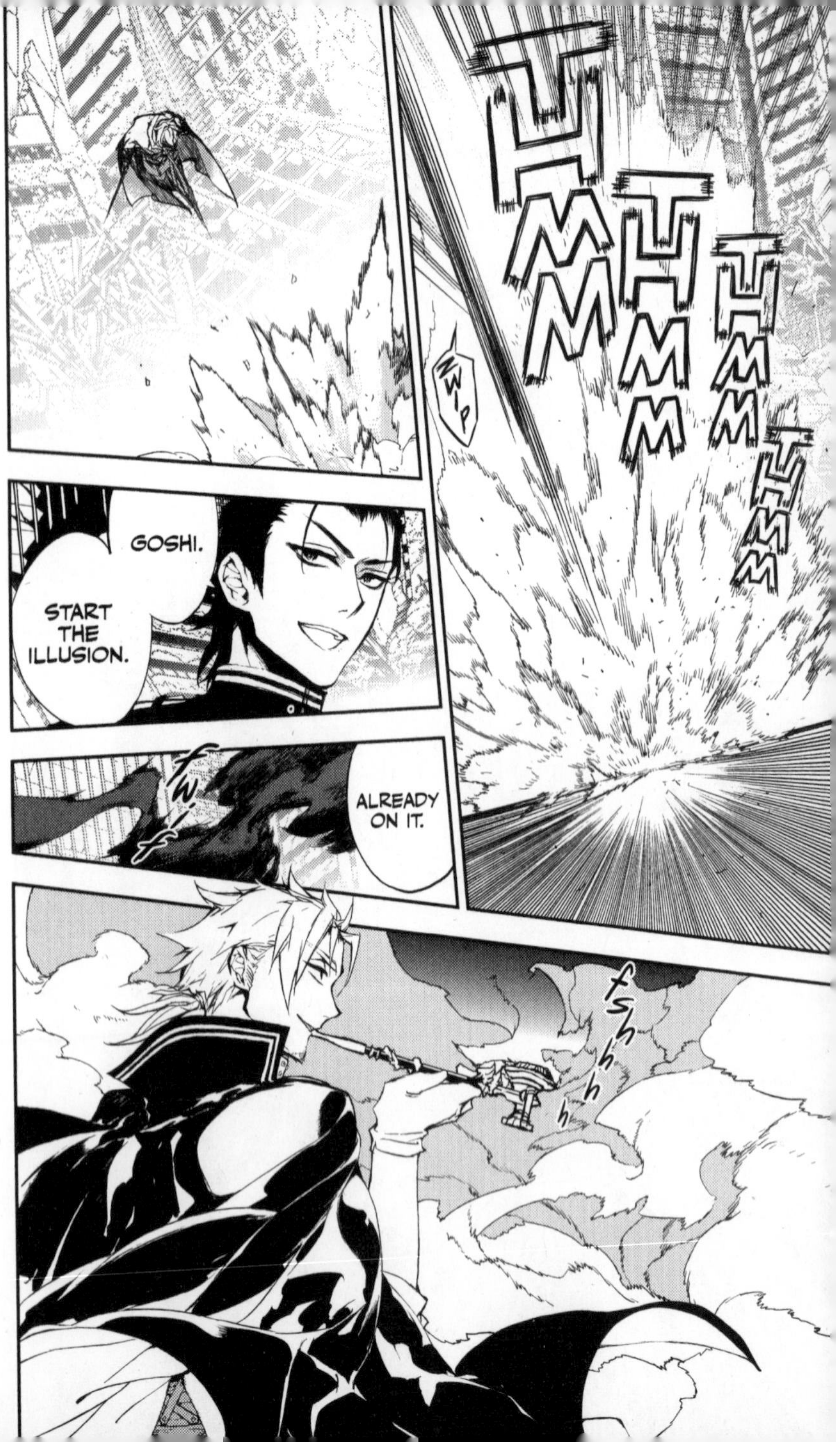
THHMM
THHMM
THHMM
THHMM
WHIP
GOSHI.
START THE ILLUSION.
fwiff
ALREADY ON IT.
fshhhh

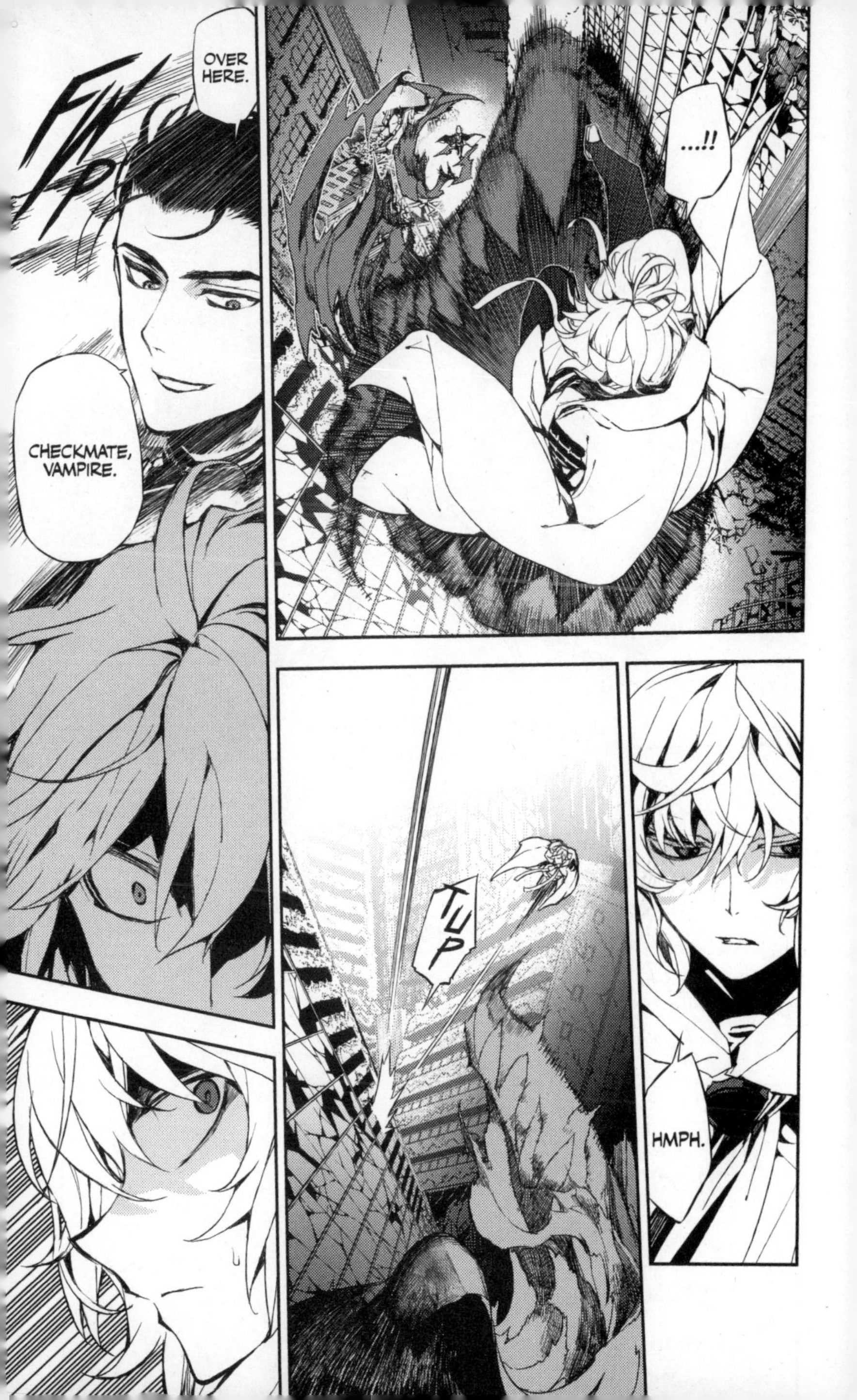
...!!
OVER HERE.
FWP
CHECKMATE, VAMPIRE.
HMPH.
TUP

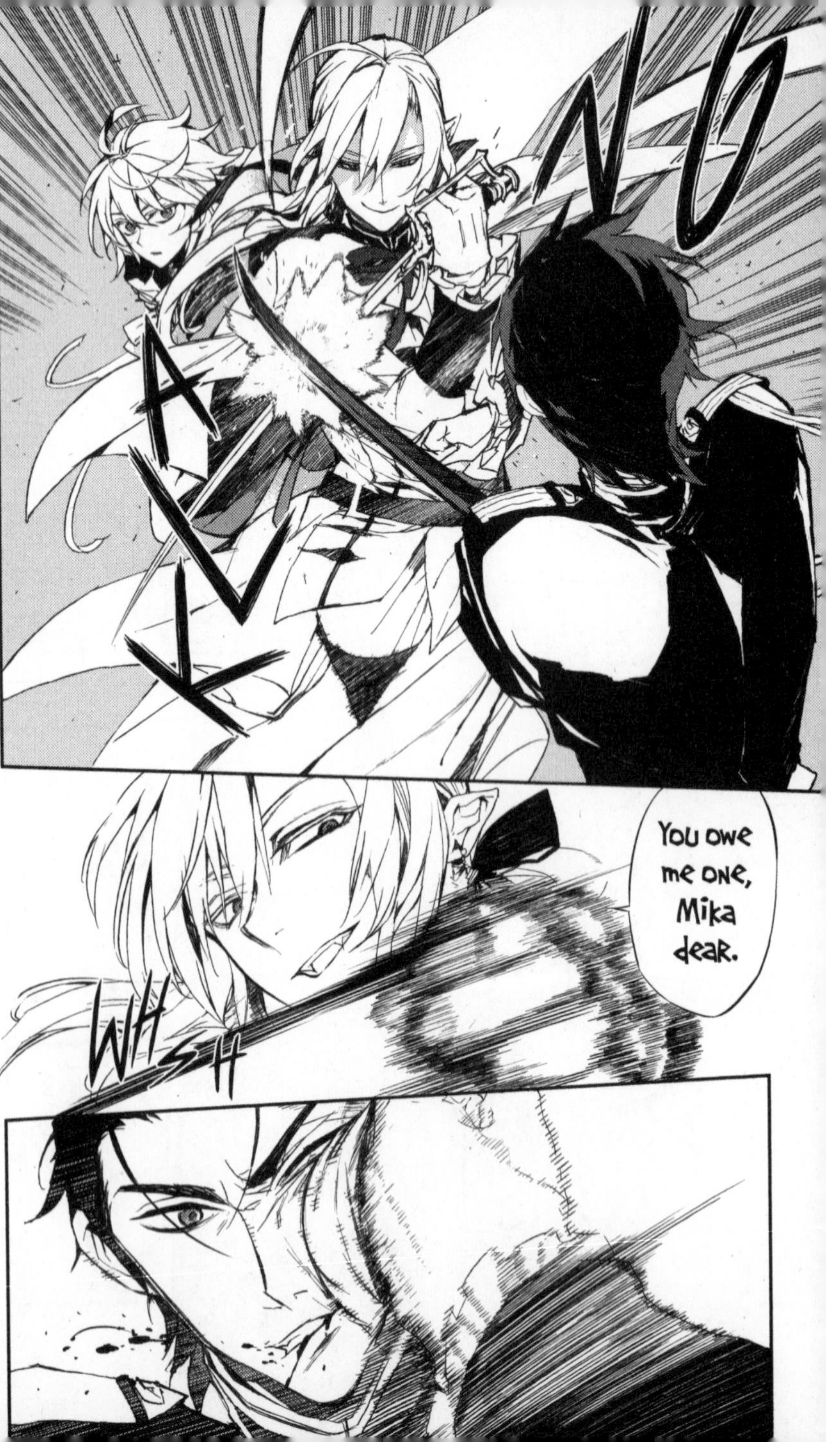
You owe me one, Mika dear.
WHSH

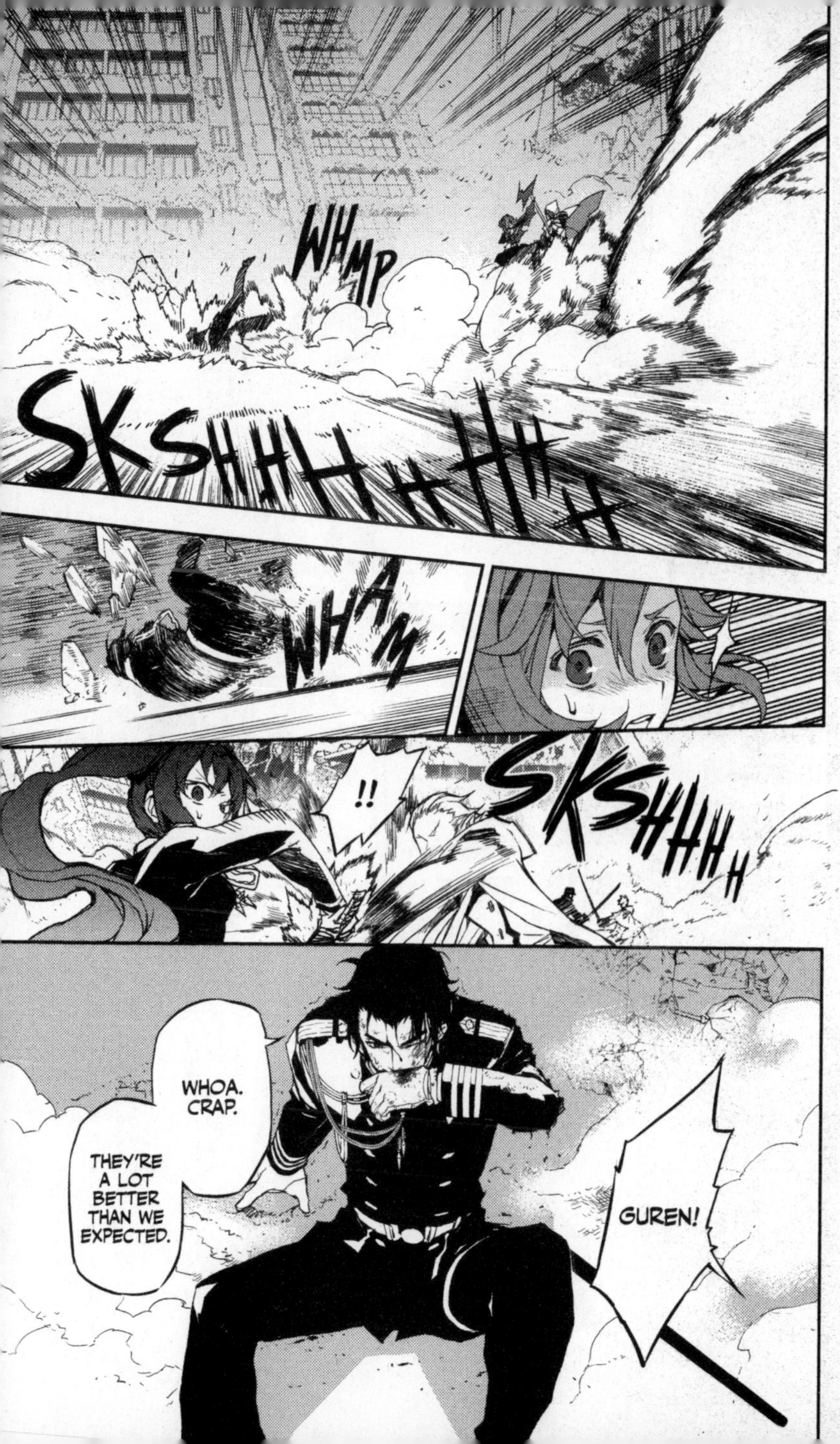

WHMP
SKSHHHHHHH
WHAM
SKSHHHHHH
!!
GUREN!
WHOA. CRAP.
THEY'RE A LOT BETTER THAN WE EXPECTED.

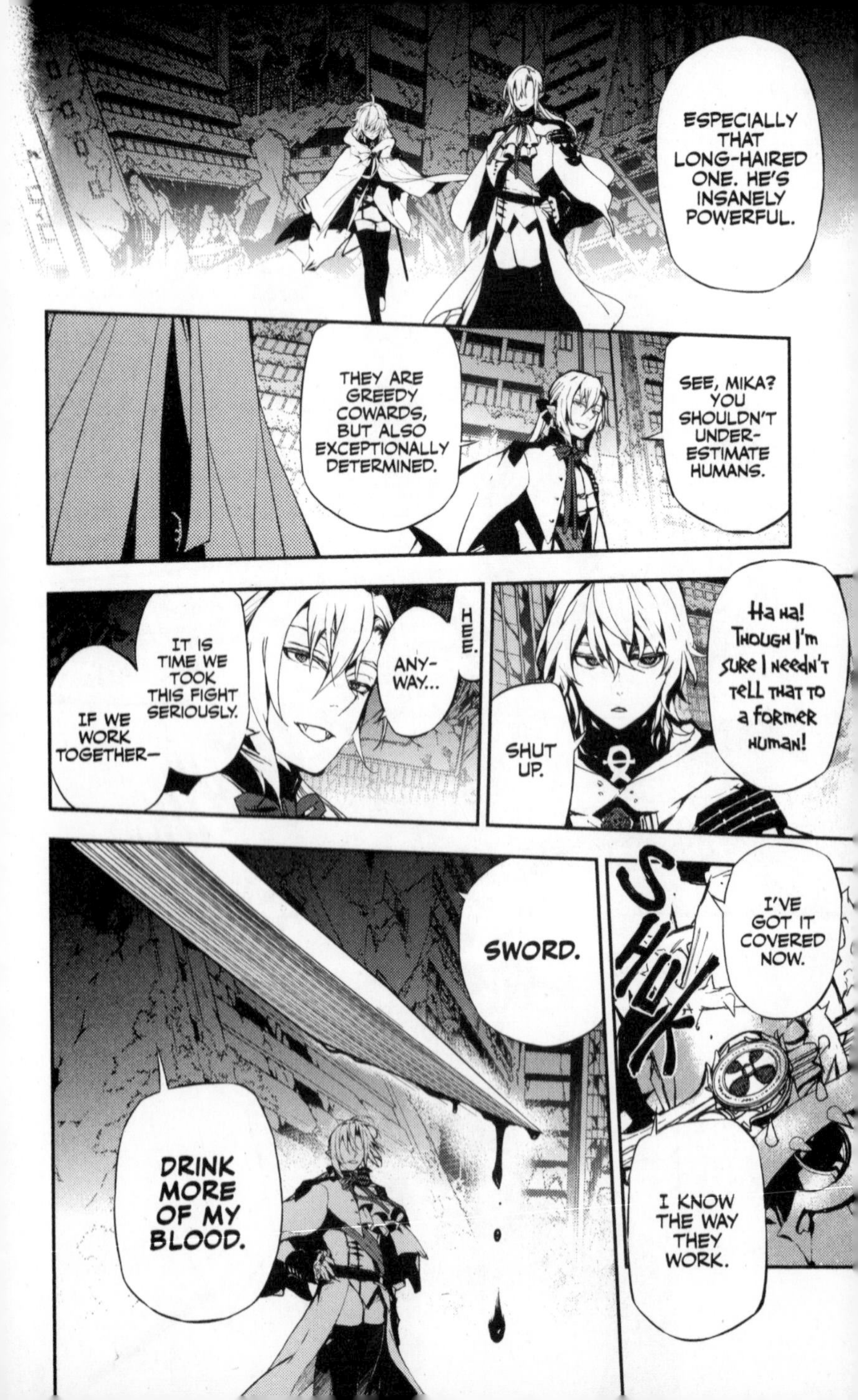
ESPECIALLY THAT LONG-HAIRED ONE. HE'S INSANELY POWERFUL.
SEE, MIKA? YOU SHOULDN'T UNDER-ESTIMATE HUMANS.
THEY ARE GREEDY COWARDS, BUT ALSO EXCEPTIONALLY DETERMINED.
Ha ha! Though I'm sure I needn't tell that to a former human!
SHUT UP.
HEE.
ANY-WAY...
IT IS TIME WE TOOK THIS FIGHT SERIOUSLY.
IF WE WORK TOGETHER—
I'VE GOT IT COVERED NOW.
SHOK
I KNOW THE WAY THEY WORK.
SWORD.
DRINK MORE OF MY BLOOD.

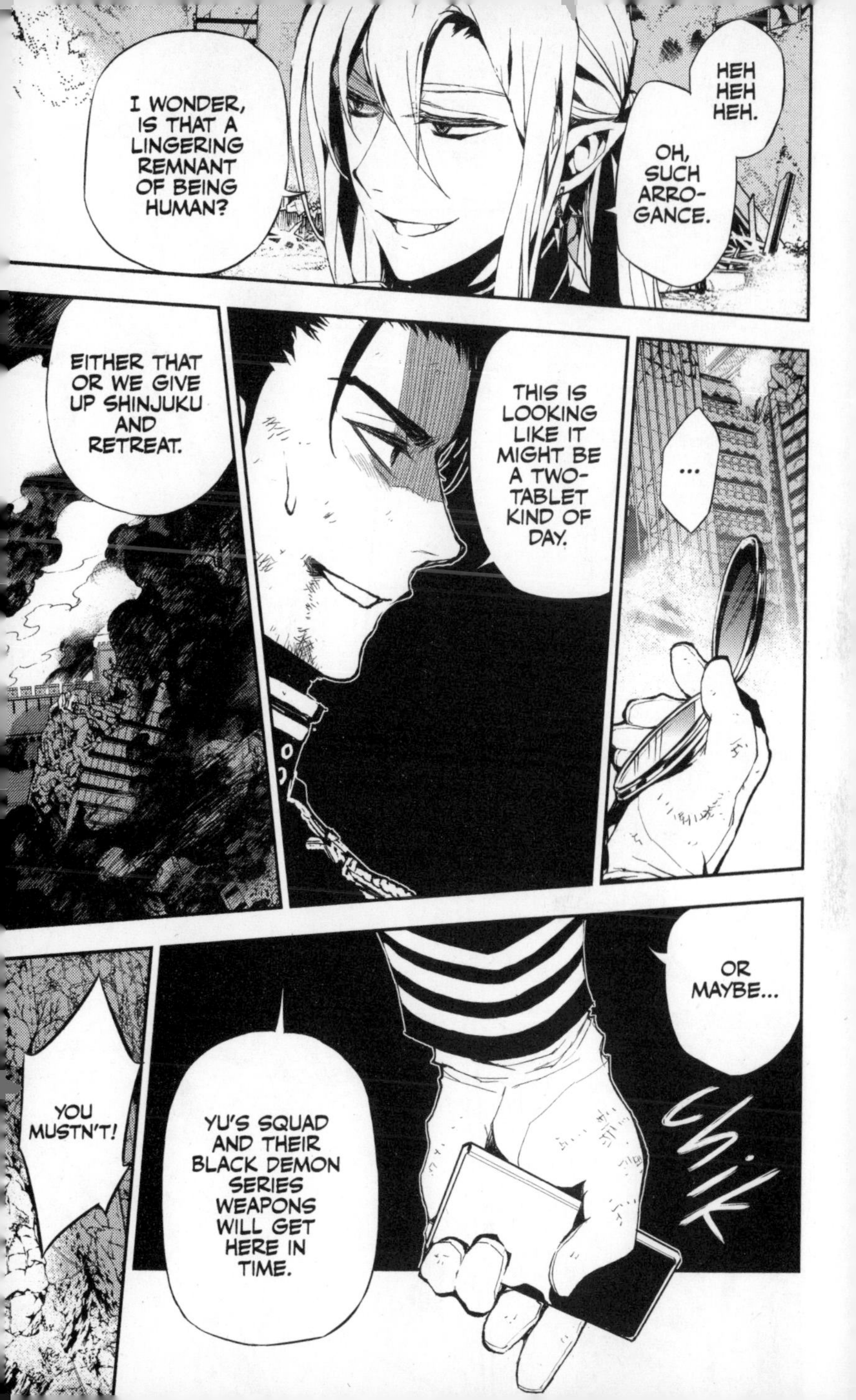
HEH HEH HEH.
OH, SUCH ARRO-GANCE.
I WONDER, IS THAT A LINGERING REMNANT OF BEING HUMAN?
...
THIS IS LOOKING LIKE IT MIGHT BE A TWO-TABLET KIND OF DAY.
EITHER THAT OR WE GIVE UP SHINJUKU AND RETREAT.
OR MAYBE...
SHIK
YU'S SQUAD AND THEIR BLACK DEMON SERIES WEAPONS WILL GET HERE IN TIME.
YOU MUSTN'T!

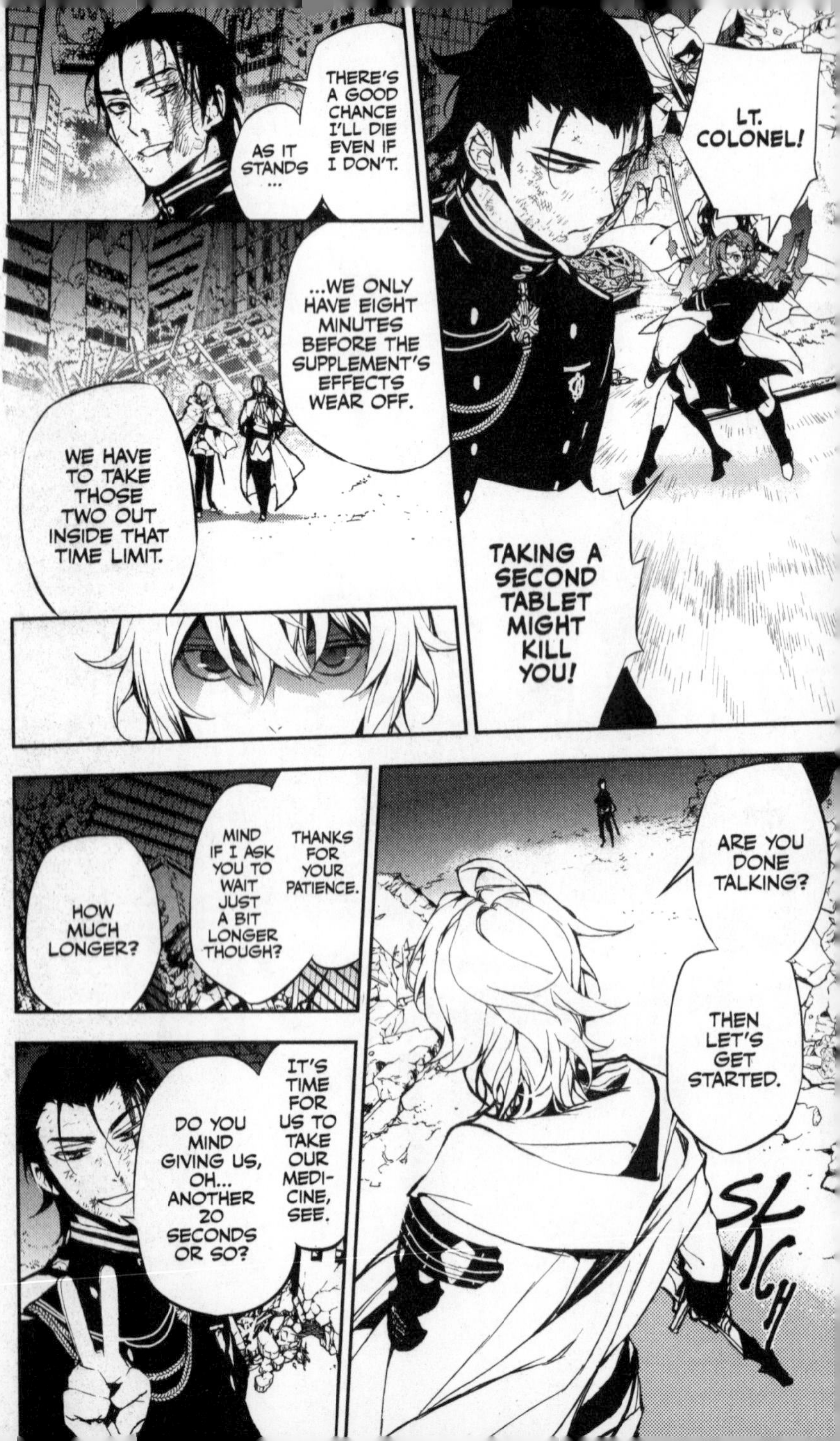
LT. COLONEL!
TAKING A SECOND TABLET MIGHT KILL YOU!
THERE'S A GOOD CHANCE I'LL DIE EVEN IF I DON'T.
AS IT STANDS...
...WE ONLY HAVE EIGHT MINUTES BEFORE THE SUPPLEMENT'S EFFECTS WEAR OFF.
WE HAVE TO TAKE THOSE TWO OUT INSIDE THAT TIME LIMIT.
ARE YOU DONE TALKING?
THEN LET'S GET STARTED.
SKCH
THANKS FOR YOUR PATIENCE.
MIND IF I ASK YOU TO WAIT JUST A BIT LONGER THOUGH?
HOW MUCH LONGER?
IT'S TIME FOR US TO TAKE OUR MEDICINE, SEE.
DO YOU MIND GIVING US, OH... ANOTHER 20 SECONDS OR SO?

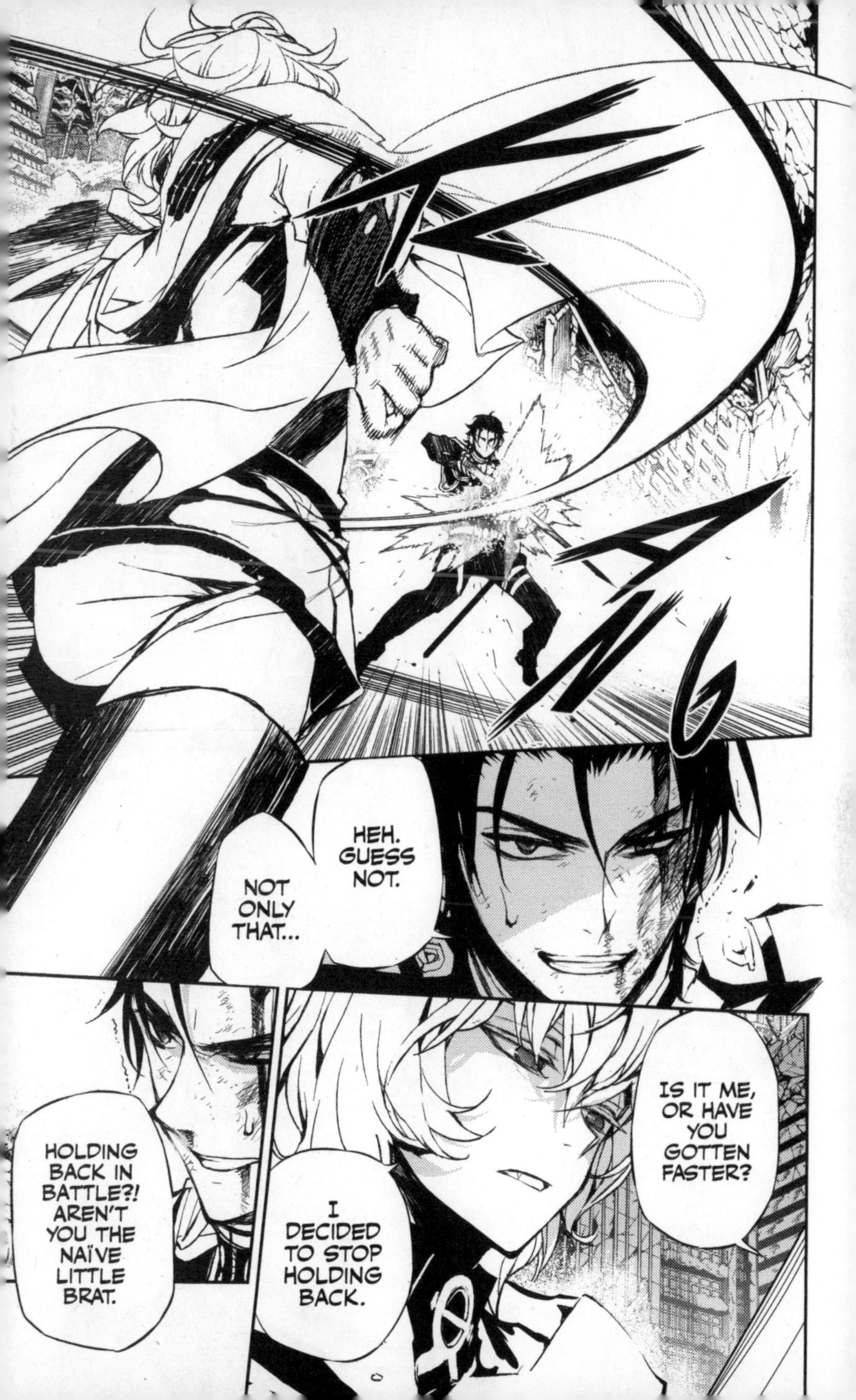
HEH. GUESS NOT.
NOT ONLY THAT...
IS IT ME, OR HAVE YOU GOTTEN FASTER?
I DECIDED TO STOP HOLDING BACK.
HOLDING BACK IN BATTLE?! AREN'T YOU THE NAÏVE LITTLE BRAT.

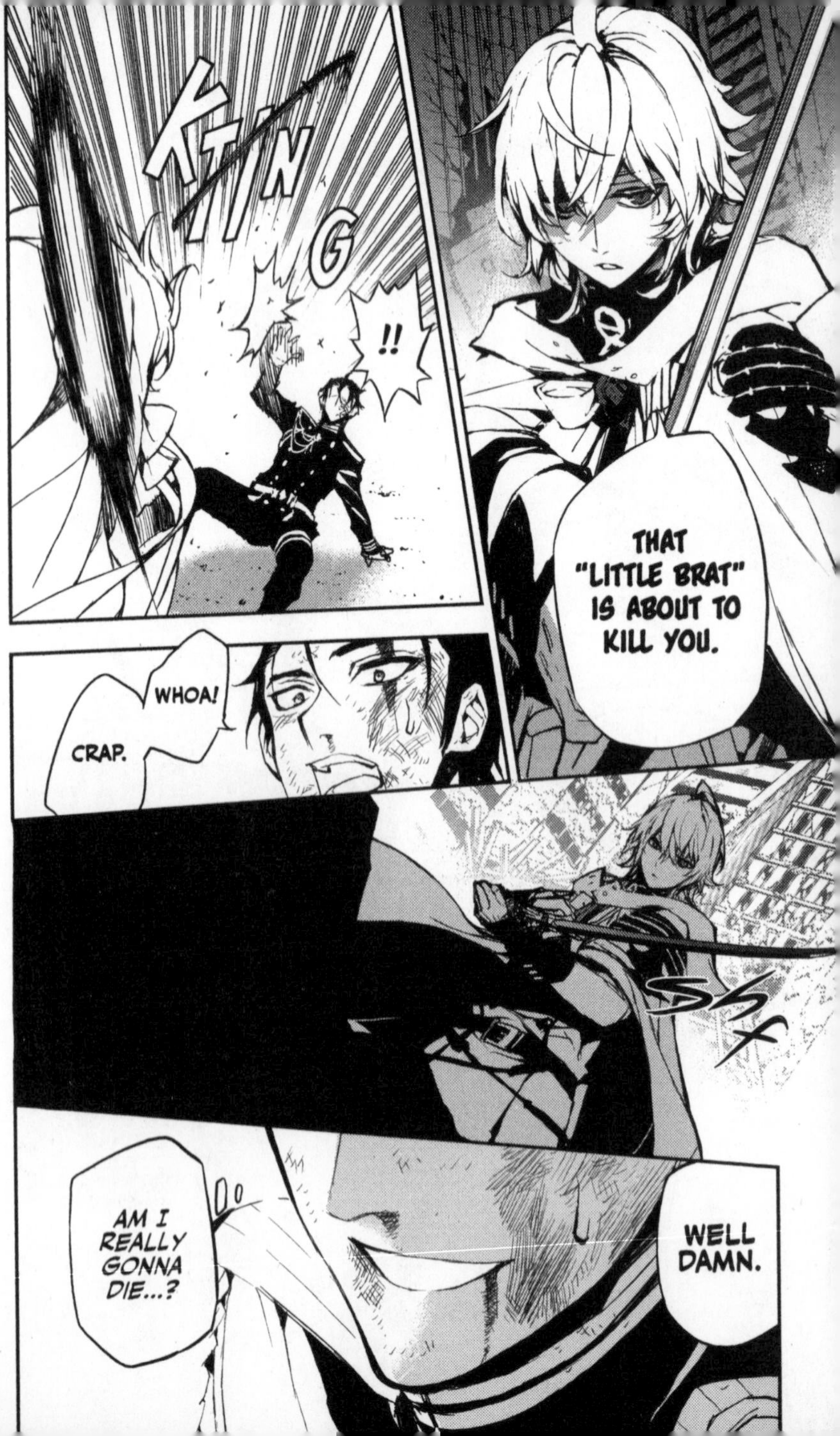
THAT "LITTLE BRAT" IS ABOUT TO KILL YOU.
KTING
!!
WHOA!
CRAP.
SHF
WELL DAMN.
AM I REALLY GONNA DIE...?

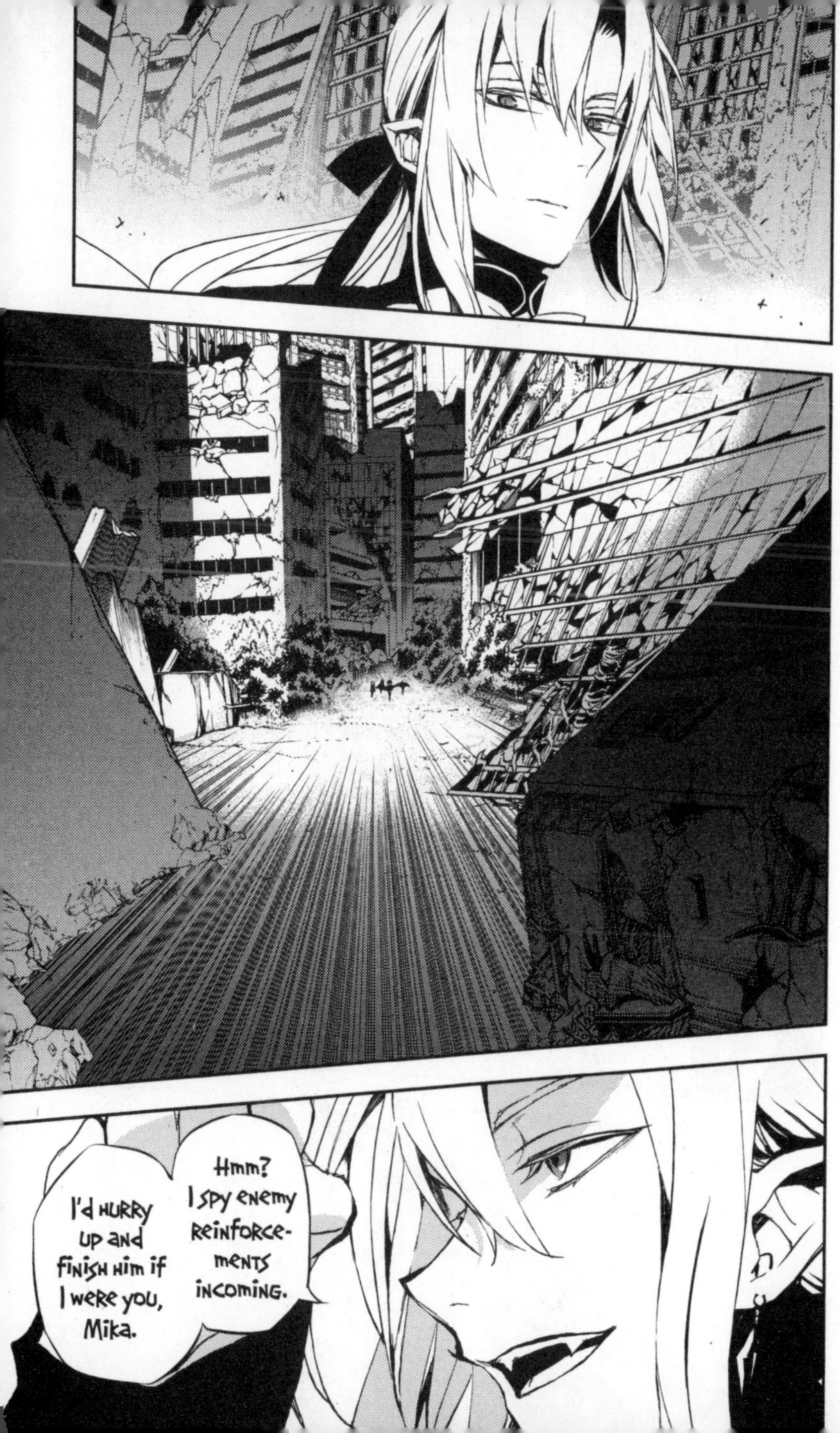
Hmm? I spy enemy reinforcements incoming.
I'd hurry up and finish him if I were you, Mika.

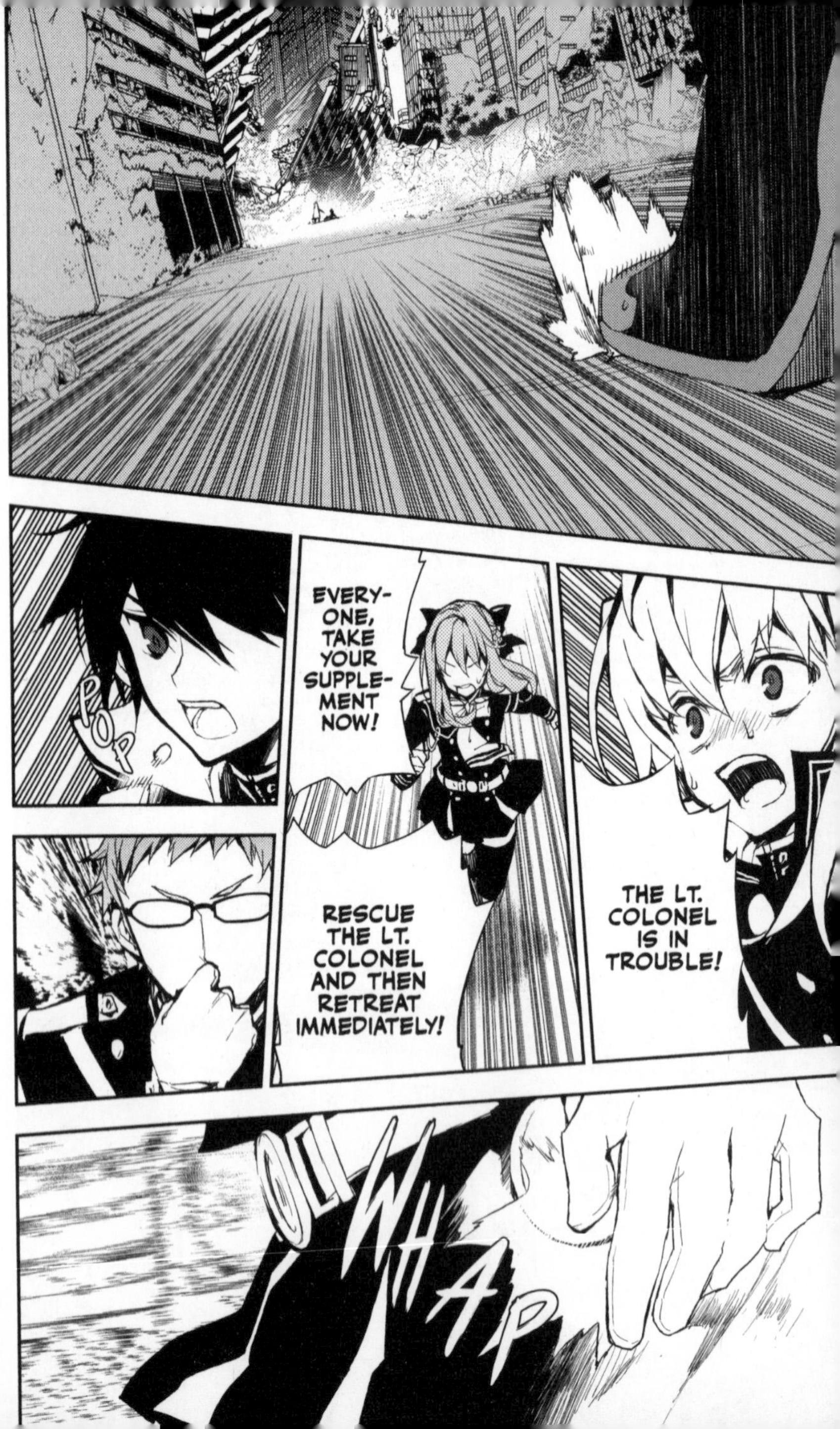
THE LT. COLONEL IS IN TROUBLE!
EVERY-ONE, TAKE YOUR SUPPLE-MENT NOW!
RESCUE THE LT. COLONEL AND THEN RETREAT IMMEDIATELY!
POP
WHAP

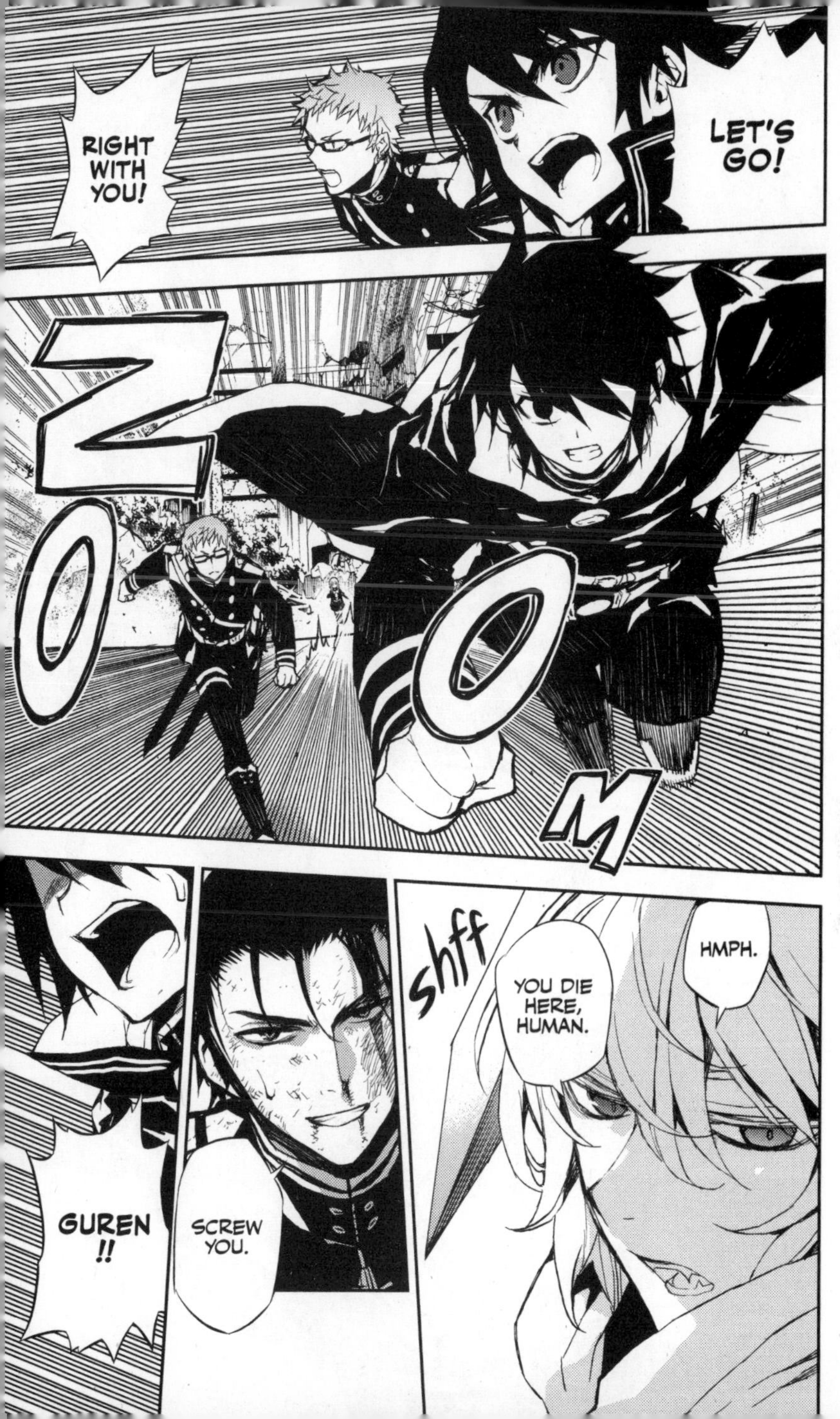
LET'S GO!
RIGHT WITH YOU!
ZOOOM
HMPH.
YOU DIE HERE, HUMAN.
shff
SCREW YOU.
GUREN!!

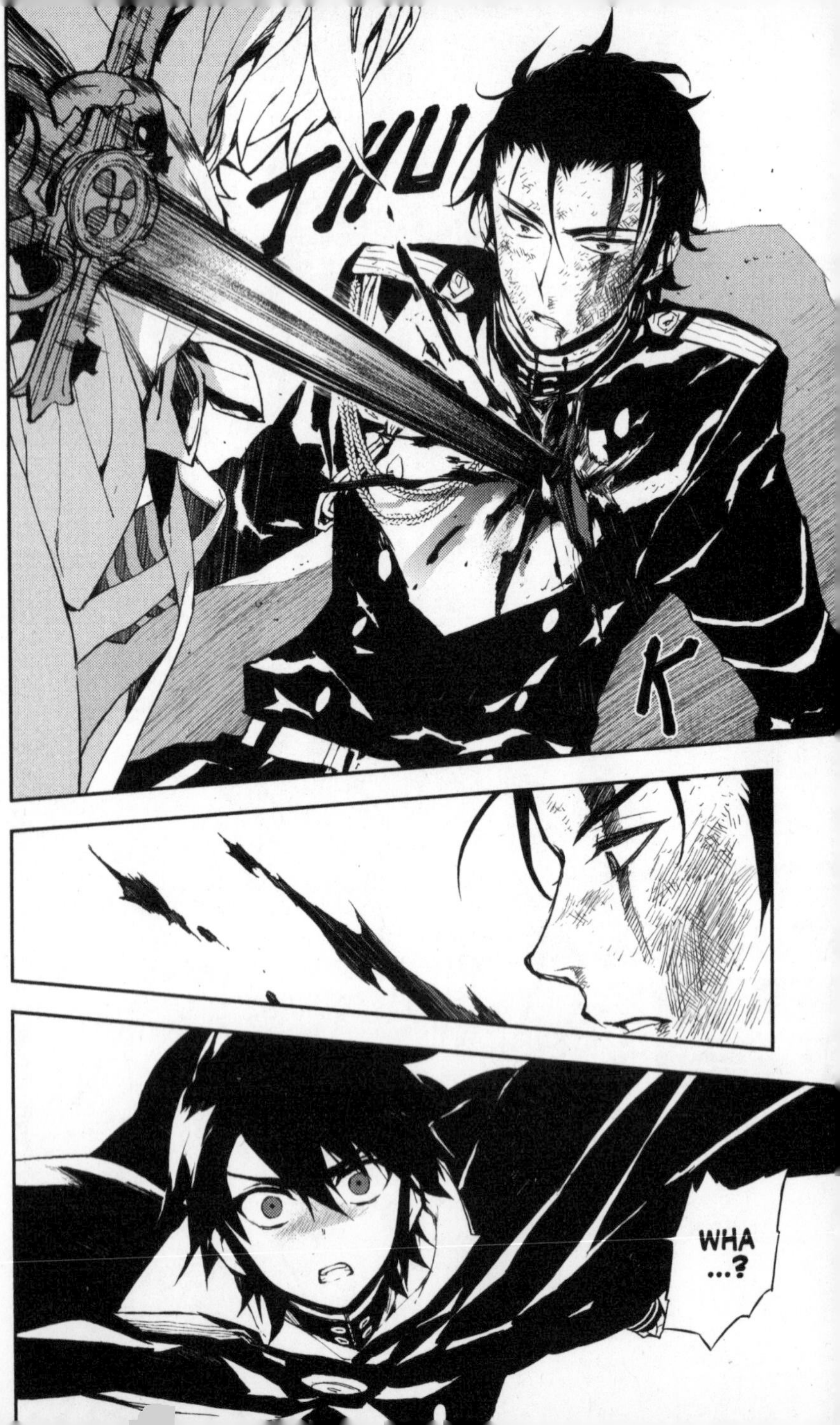
THUD
K
WHA ...?

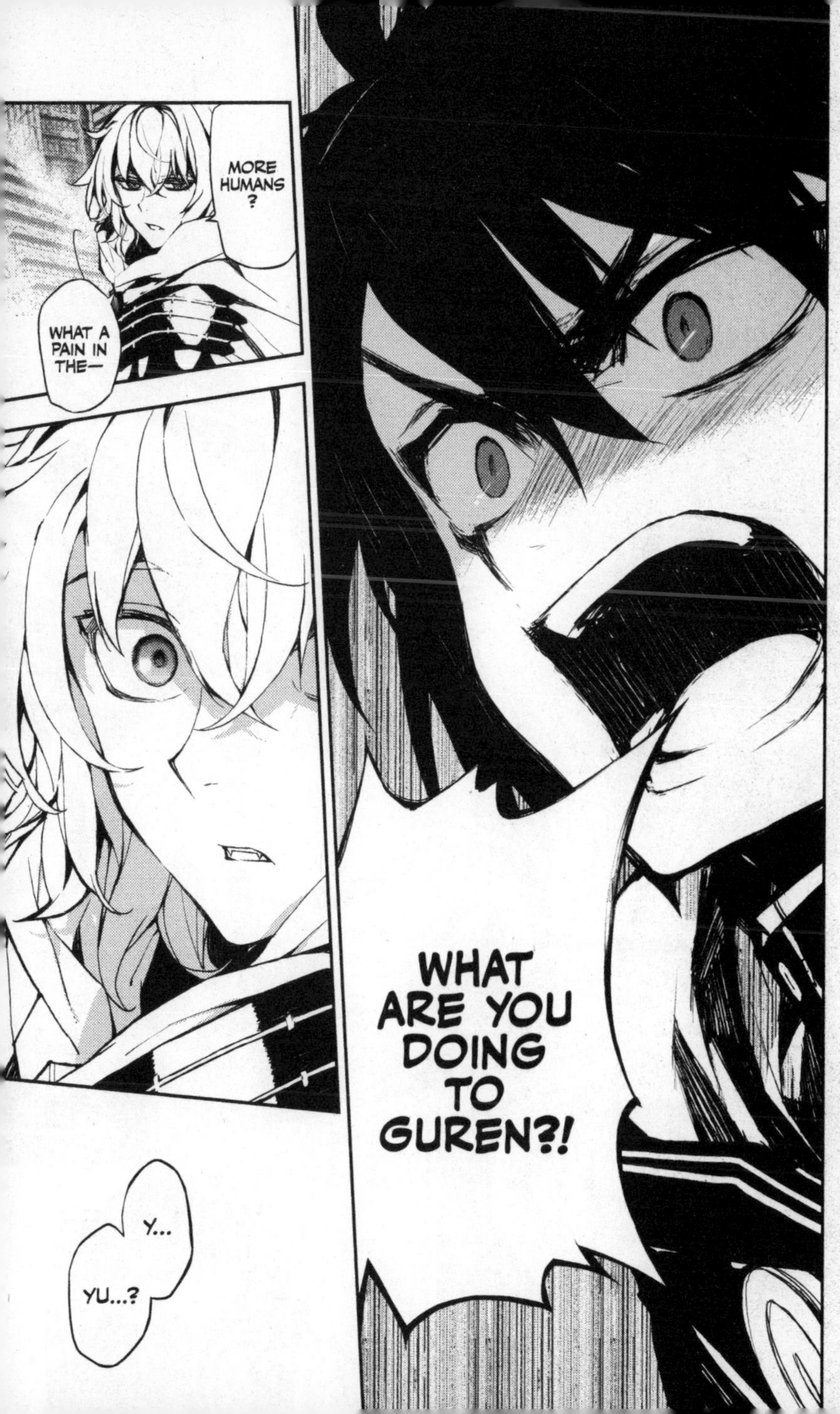
WHAT ARE YOU DOING TO GUREN?!
MORE HUMANS?
WHAT A PAIN IN THE—
Y...
YU...?

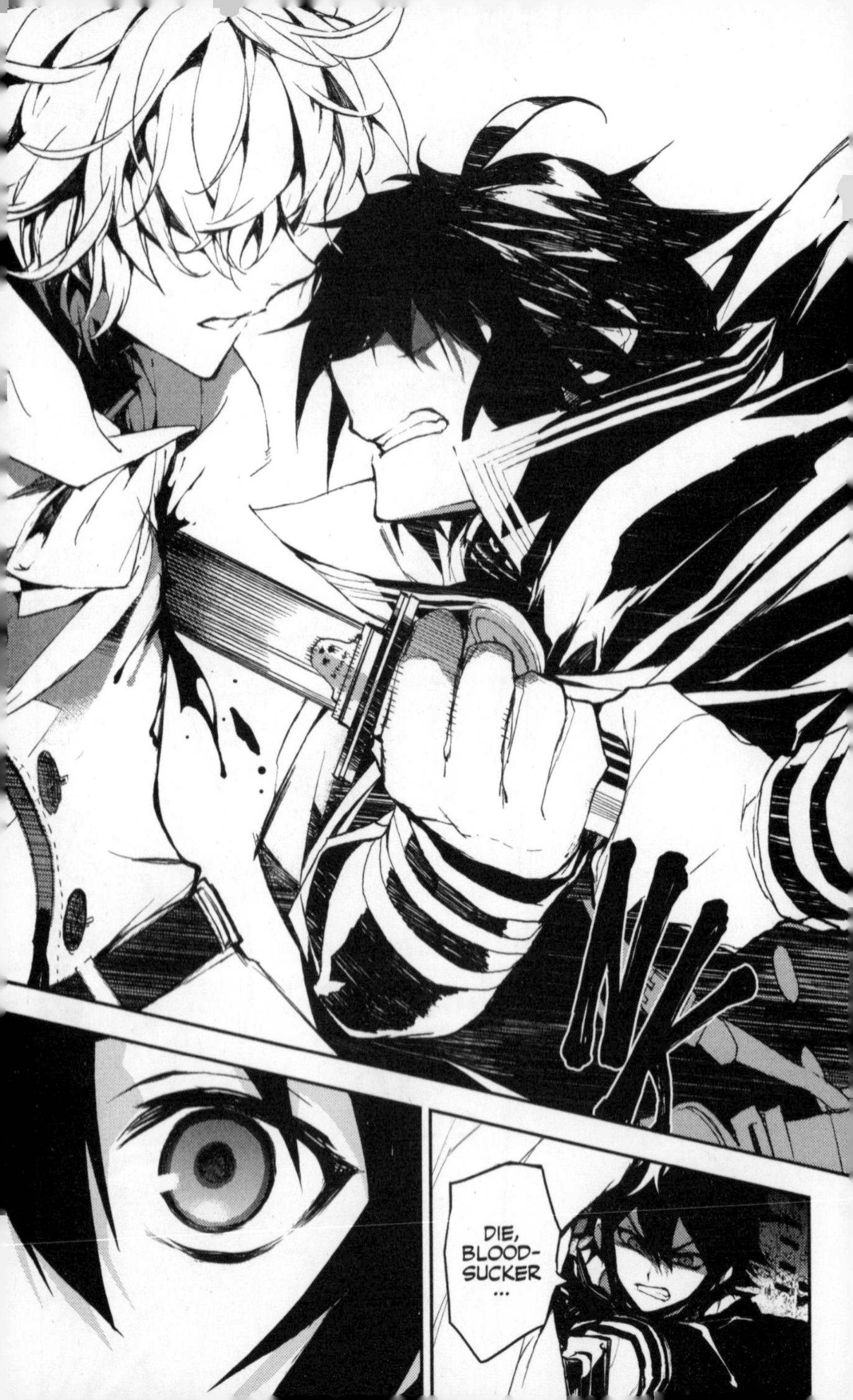
DIE, BLOOD-SUCKER ...

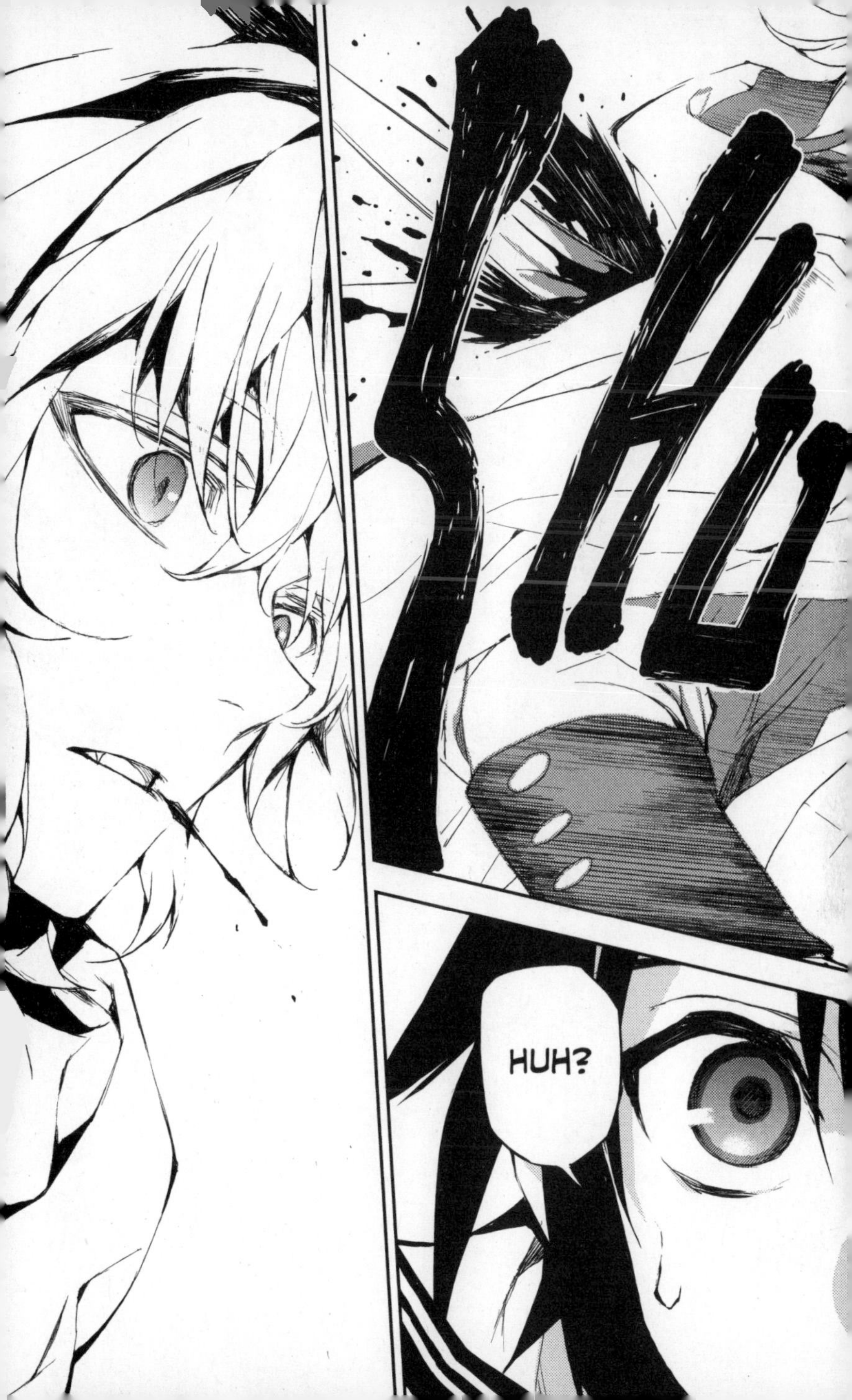
HUH?

Seraph of the End
—VAMPIRE REIGN—

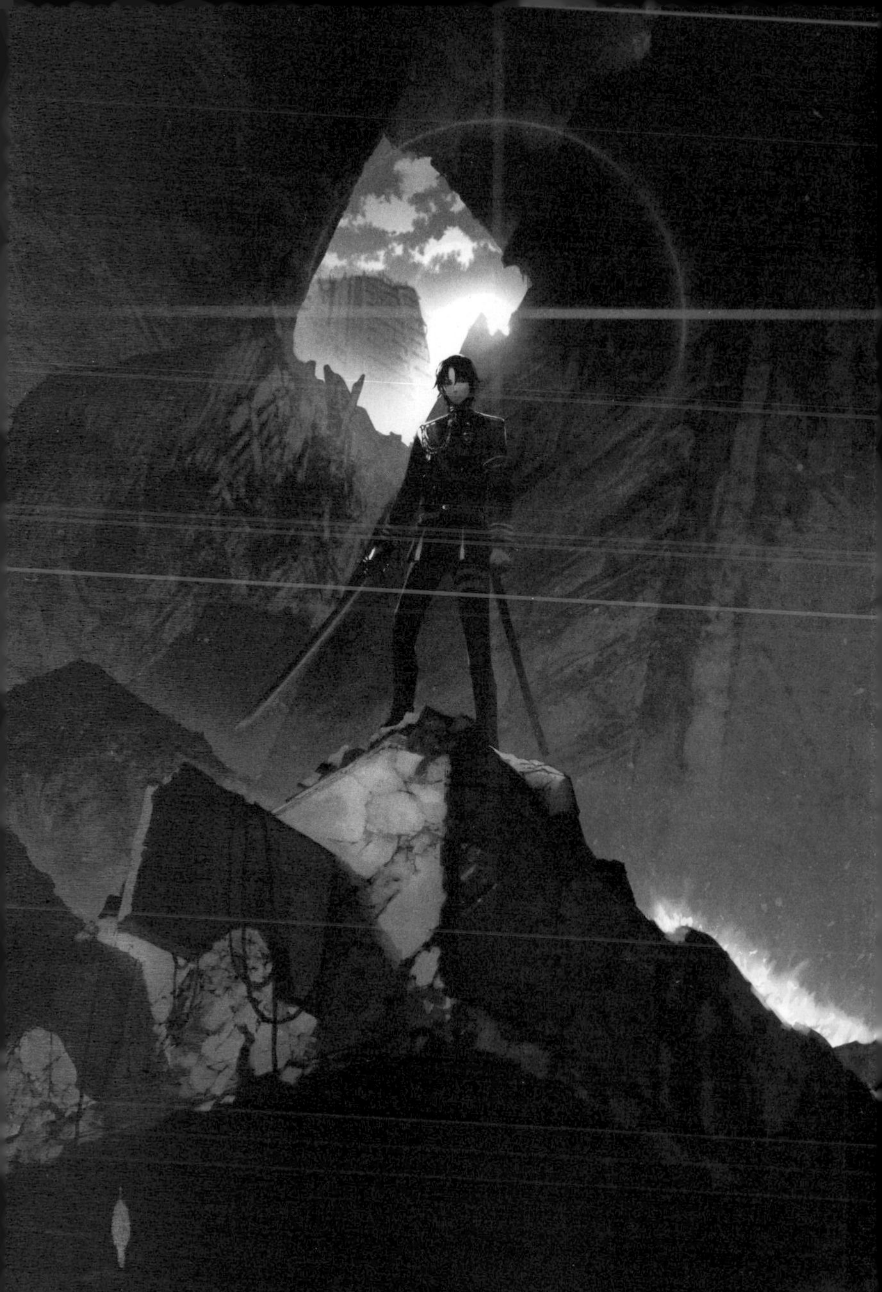

CHAPTER 13

Reunion of Childhood Friends

Seraph of the End
VAMPIRE REIGN

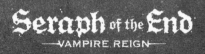

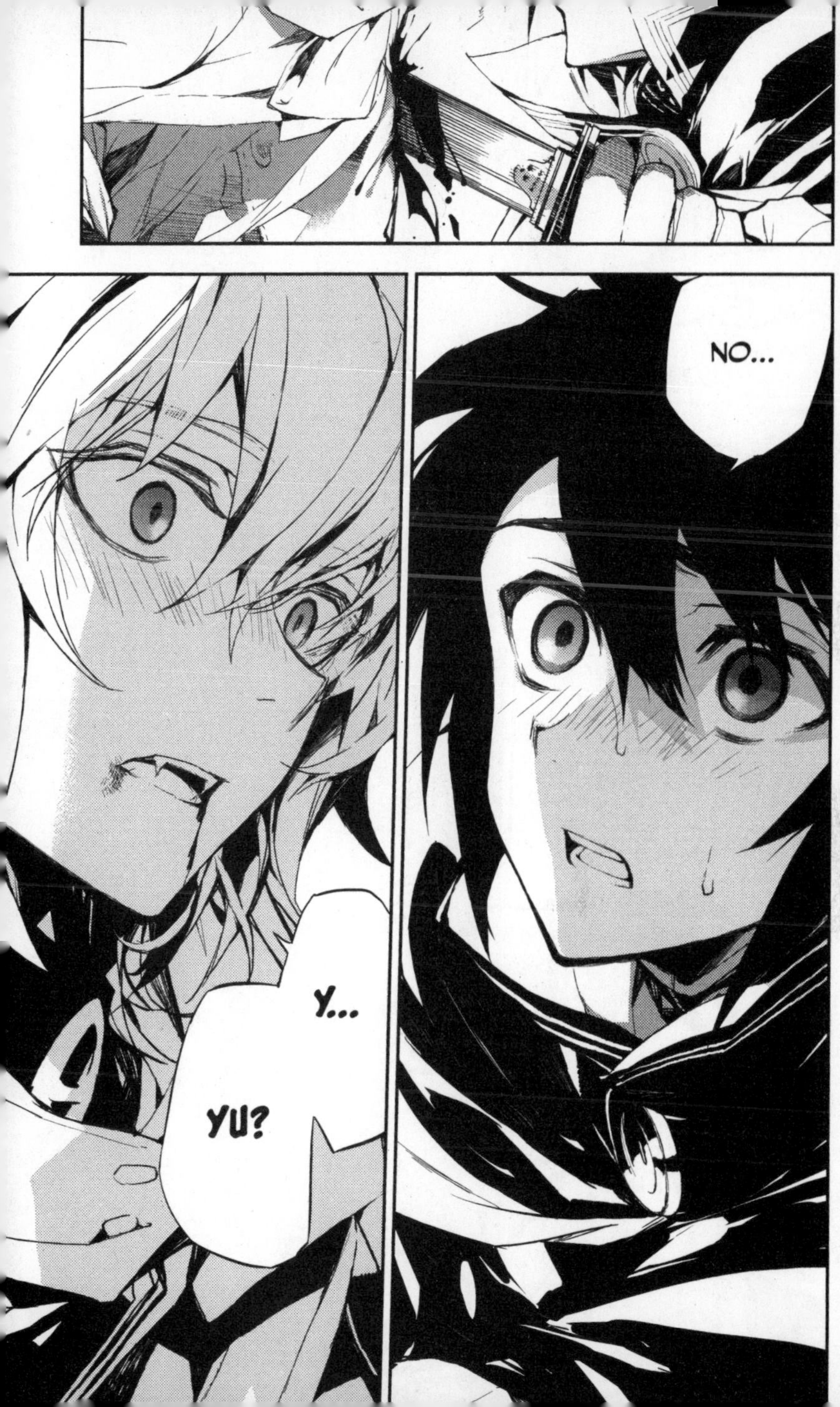
NO...
Y...
YU?

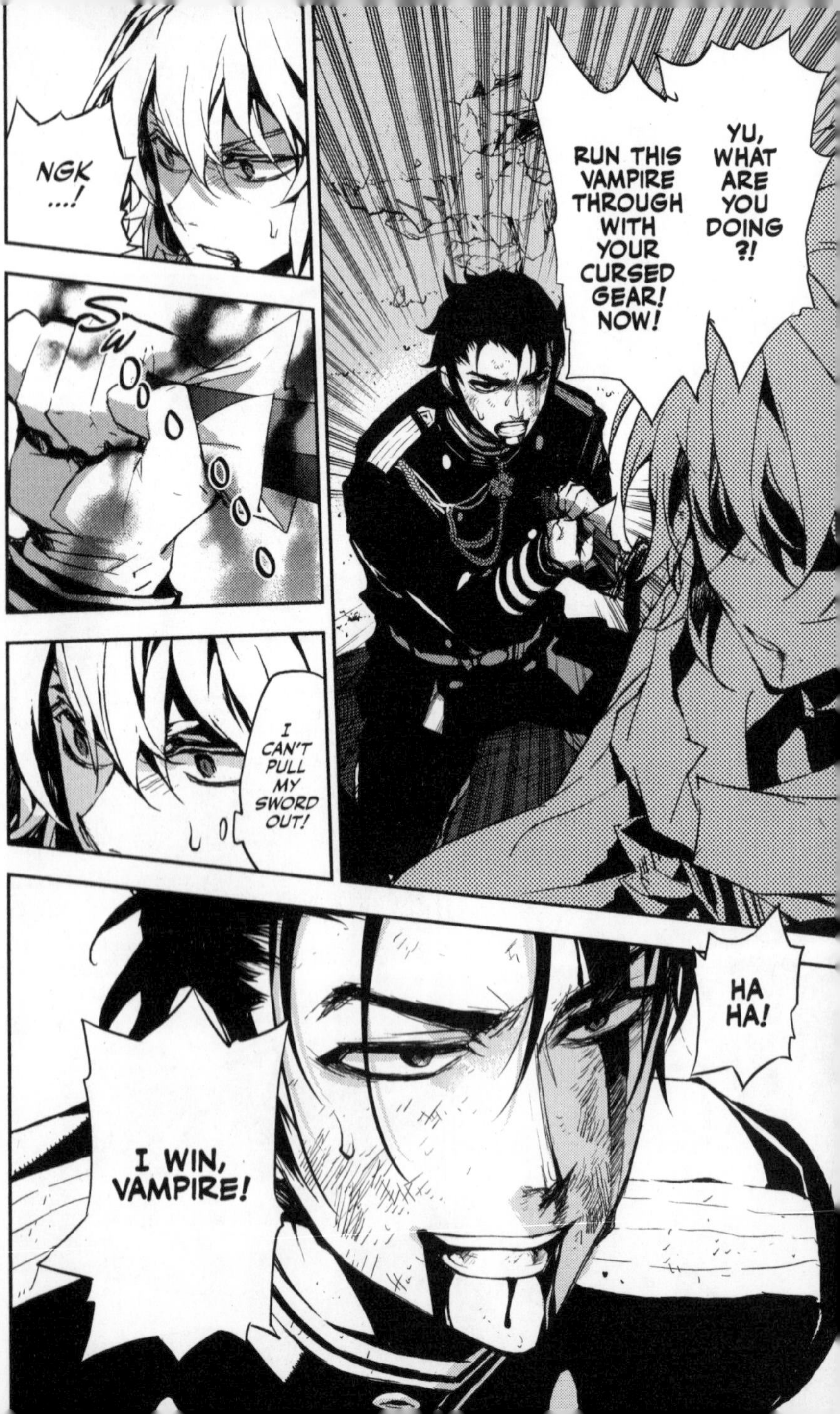
YU, WHAT ARE YOU DOING?!
RUN THIS VAMPIRE THROUGH WITH YOUR CURSED GEAR! NOW!
NGK ...!
SW
I CAN'T PULL MY SWORD OUT!
HA HA!
I WIN, VAMPIRE!

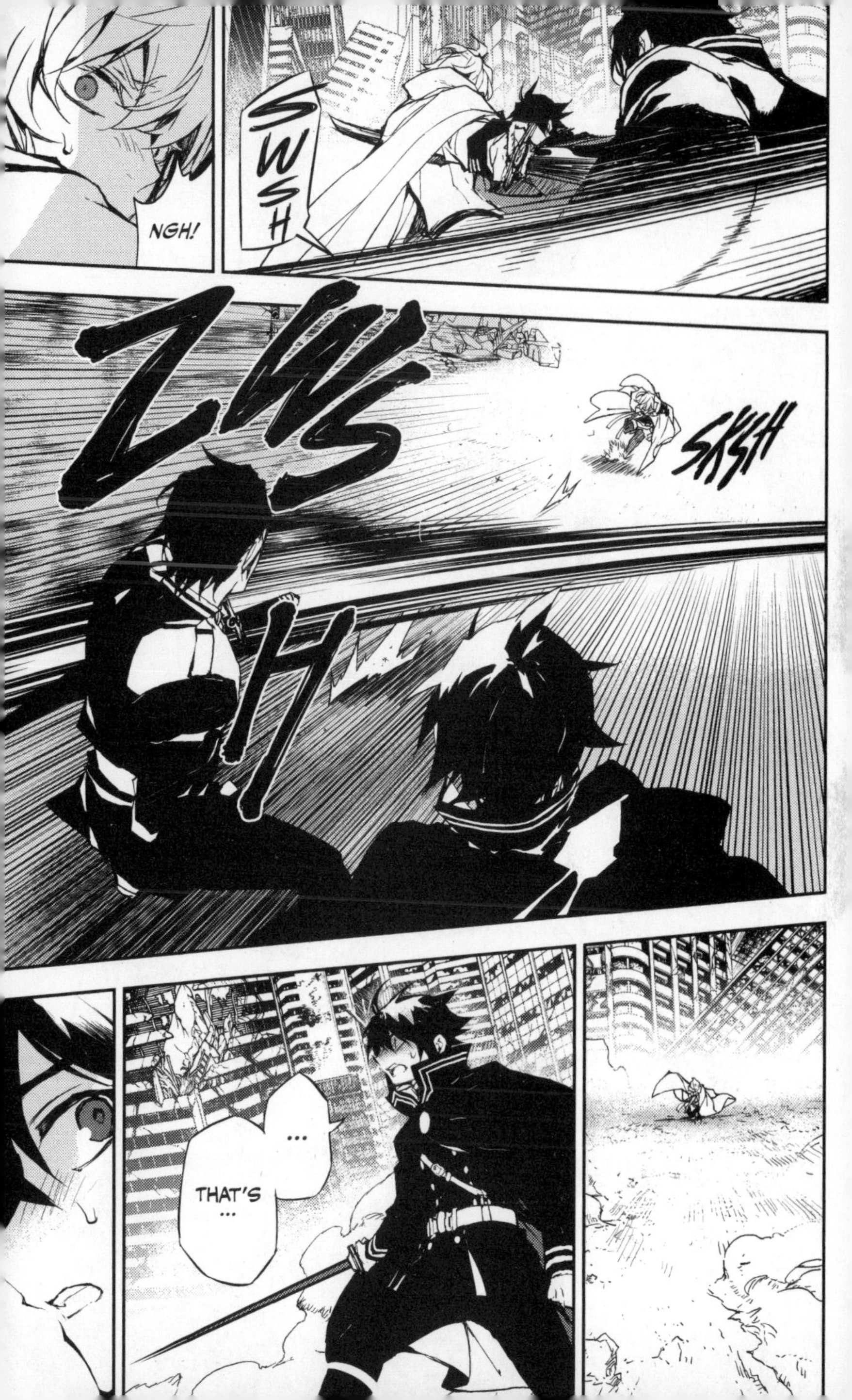
SWSH
NGH!
SKSH
ZWSH
...
THAT'S ...

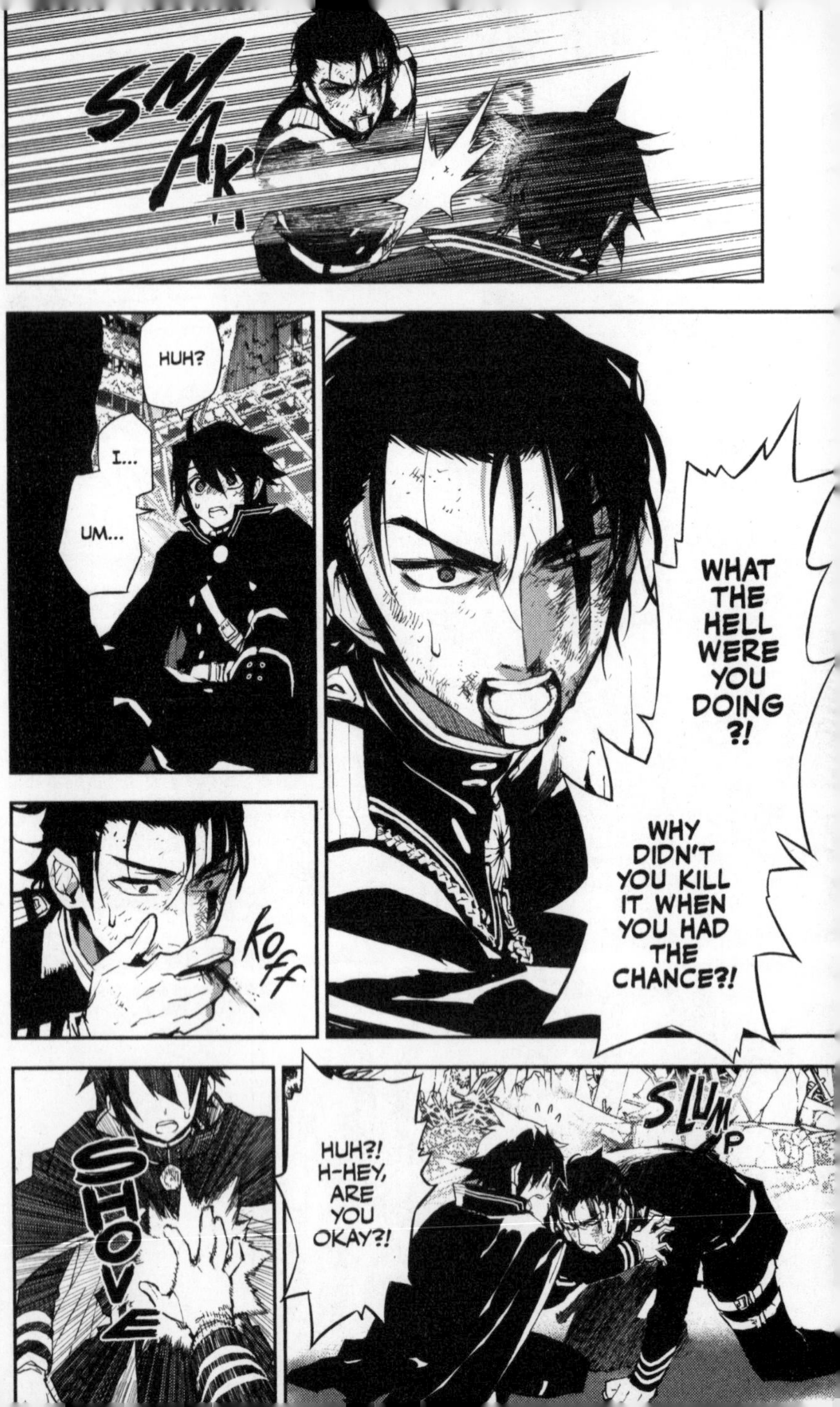
SMAK
WHAT THE HELL WERE YOU DOING?!
WHY DIDN'T YOU KILL IT WHEN YOU HAD THE CHANCE?!
HUH?
I...
UM...
KOFF
SLUMP
HUH?! H-HEY, ARE YOU OKAY?!
SHOVE

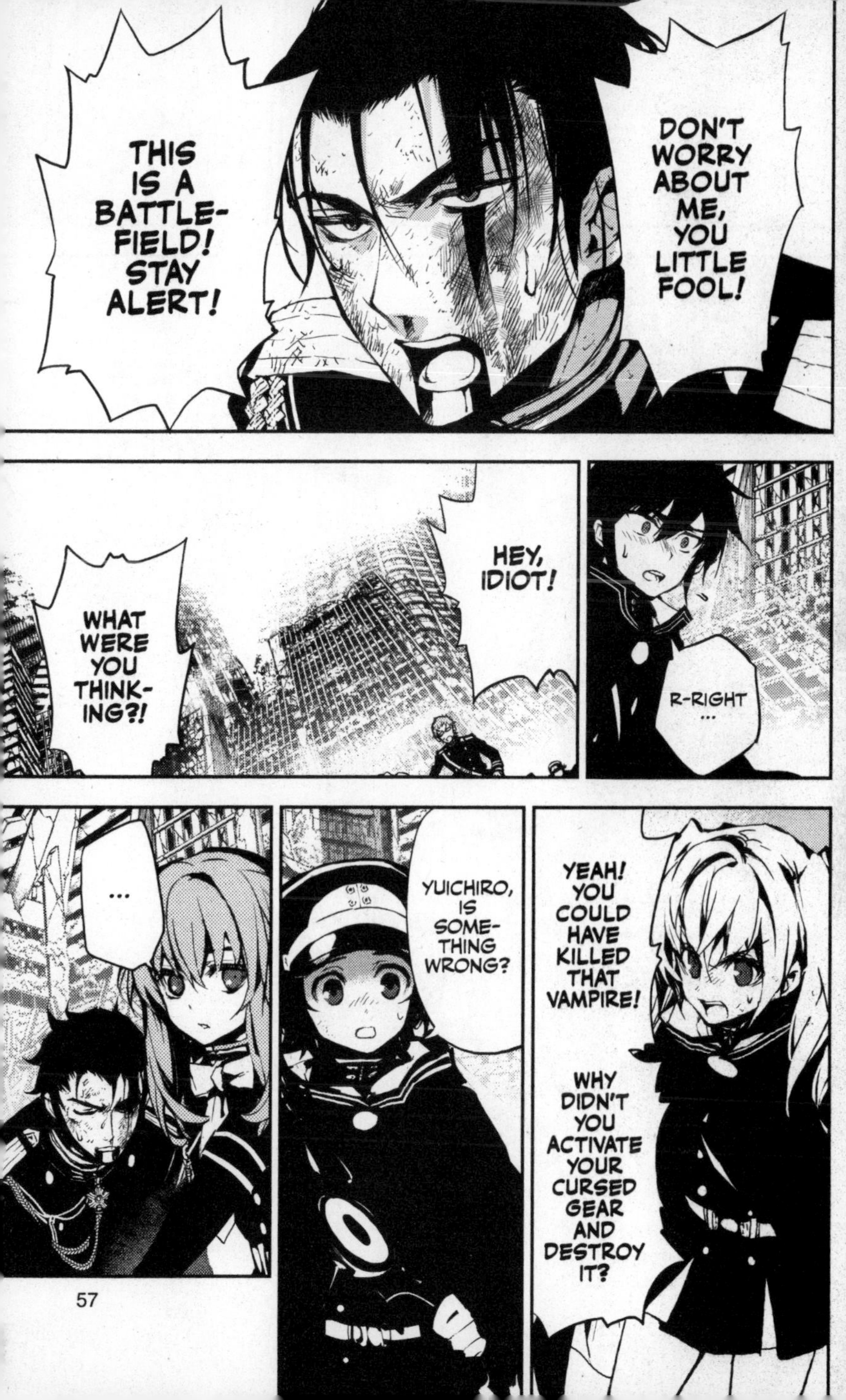
DON'T WORRY ABOUT ME, YOU LITTLE FOOL!
THIS IS A BATTLE-FIELD! STAY ALERT!
R-RIGHT ...
HEY, IDIOT!
WHAT WERE YOU THINK-ING?!
YEAH! YOU COULD HAVE KILLED THAT VAMPIRE!
WHY DIDN'T YOU ACTIVATE YOUR CURSED GEAR AND DESTROY IT?
YUICHIRO, IS SOME-THING WRONG?
...

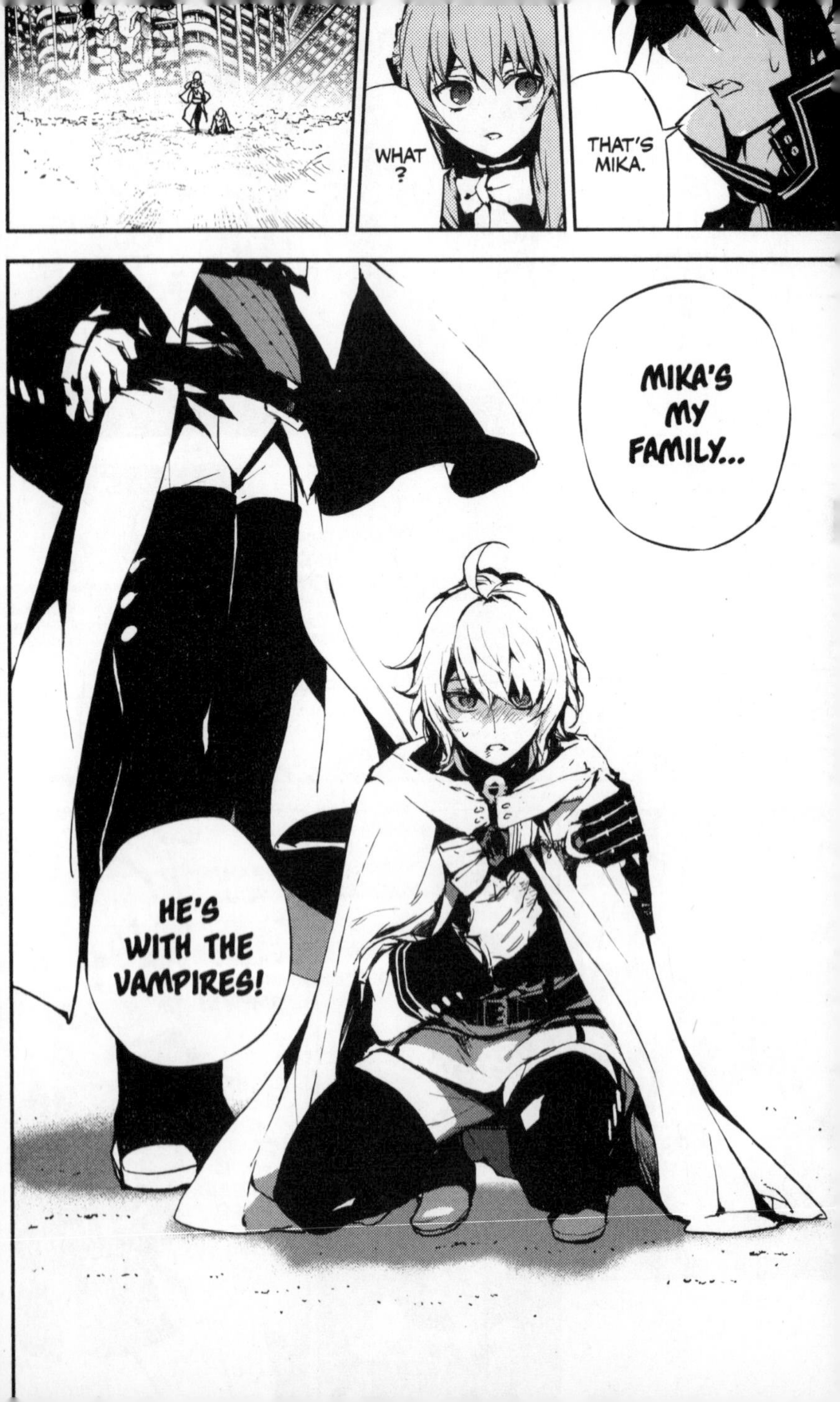
THAT'S MIKA.
WHAT ?
MIKA'S MY FAMILY...
HE'S WITH THE VAMPIRES!

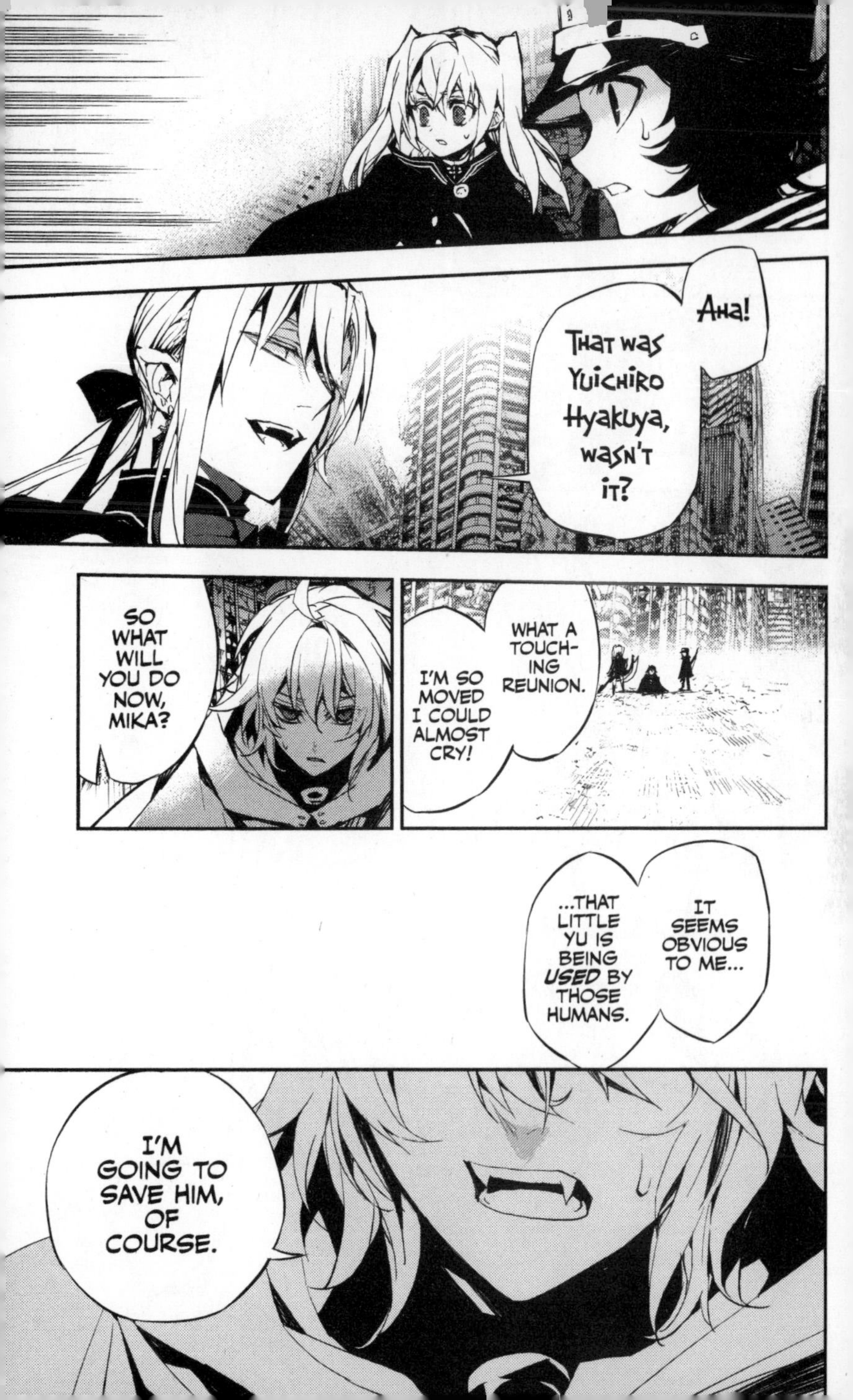
AHA!
THAT WAS YUICHIRO HYAKUYA, WASN'T IT?
WHAT A TOUCHING REUNION.
I'M SO MOVED I COULD ALMOST CRY!
SO WHAT WILL YOU DO NOW, MIKA?
IT SEEMS OBVIOUS TO ME...
...THAT LITTLE YU IS BEING *USED* BY THOSE HUMANS.
I'M GOING TO SAVE HIM, OF COURSE.

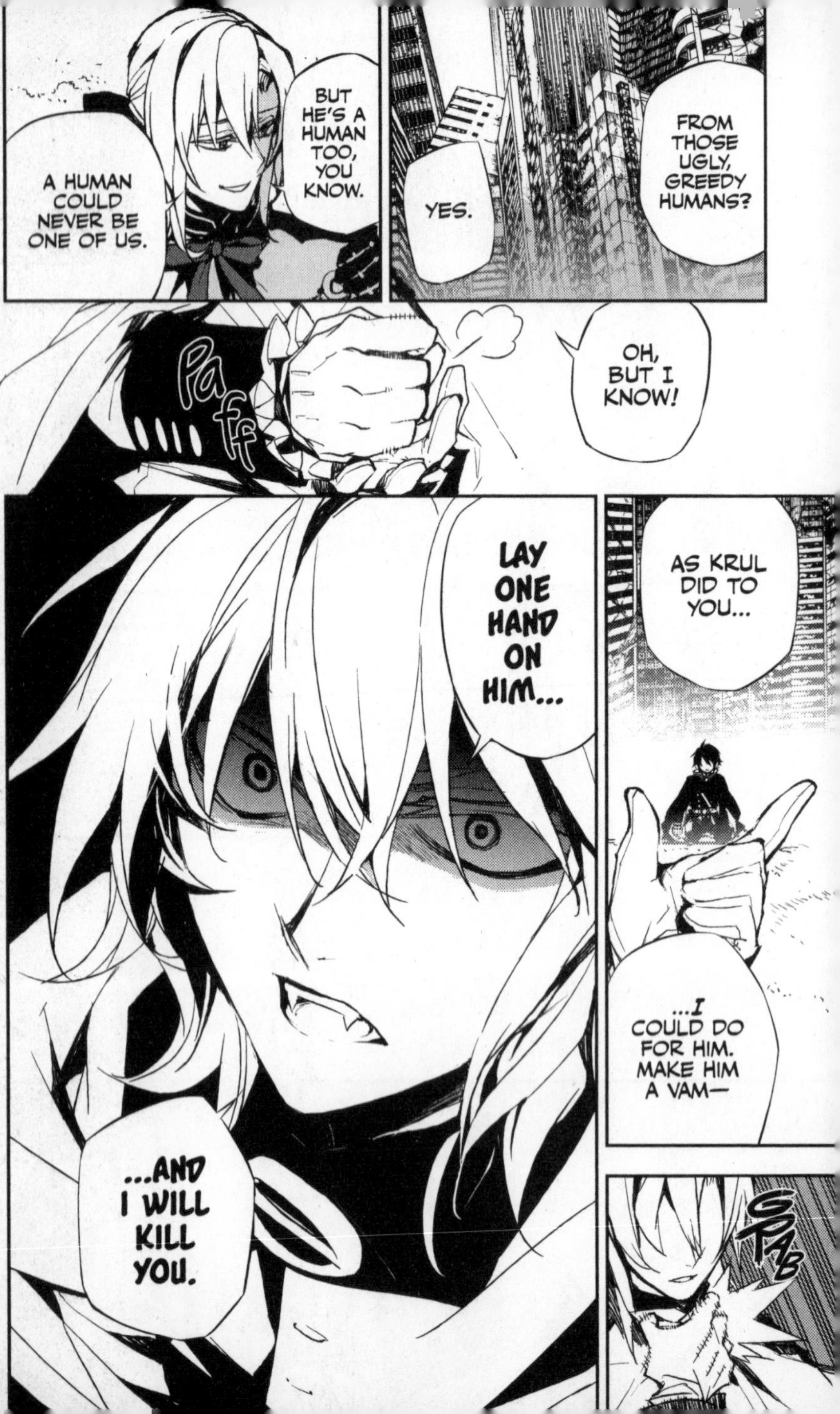
FROM THOSE UGLY, GREEDY HUMANS?
YES.
BUT HE'S A HUMAN TOO, YOU KNOW.
A HUMAN COULD NEVER BE ONE OF US.
OH, BUT I KNOW!
Paff
AS KRUL DID TO YOU...
...I COULD DO FOR HIM. MAKE HIM A VAM—
GRAB
LAY ONE HAND ON HIM...
...AND I WILL KILL YOU.

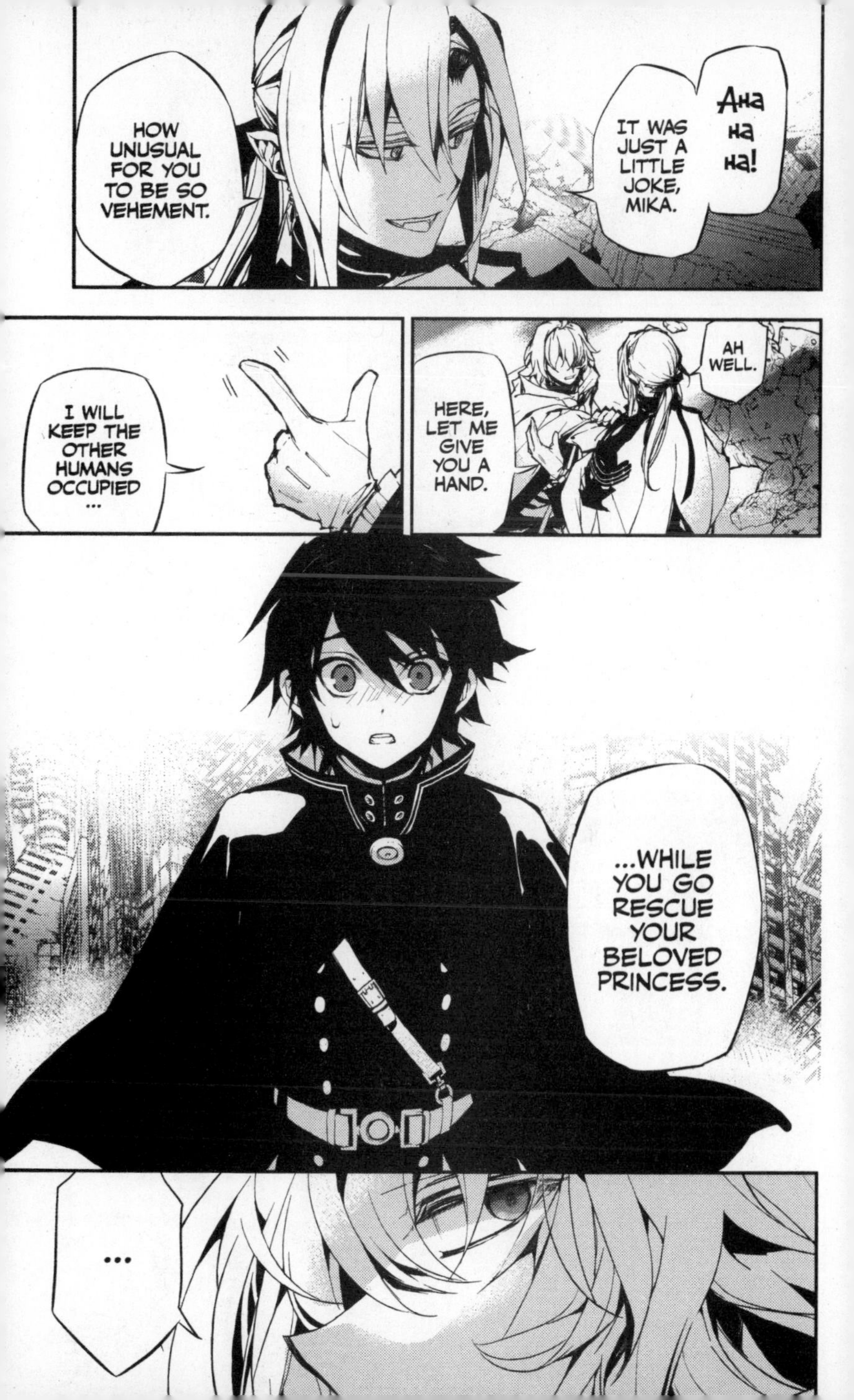
Aha ha ha!
IT WAS JUST A LITTLE JOKE, MIKA.
HOW UNUSUAL FOR YOU TO BE SO VEHEMENT.
AH WELL.
HERE, LET ME GIVE YOU A HAND.
I WILL KEEP THE OTHER HUMANS OCCUPIED ...
...WHILE YOU GO RESCUE YOUR BELOVED PRINCESS.
...

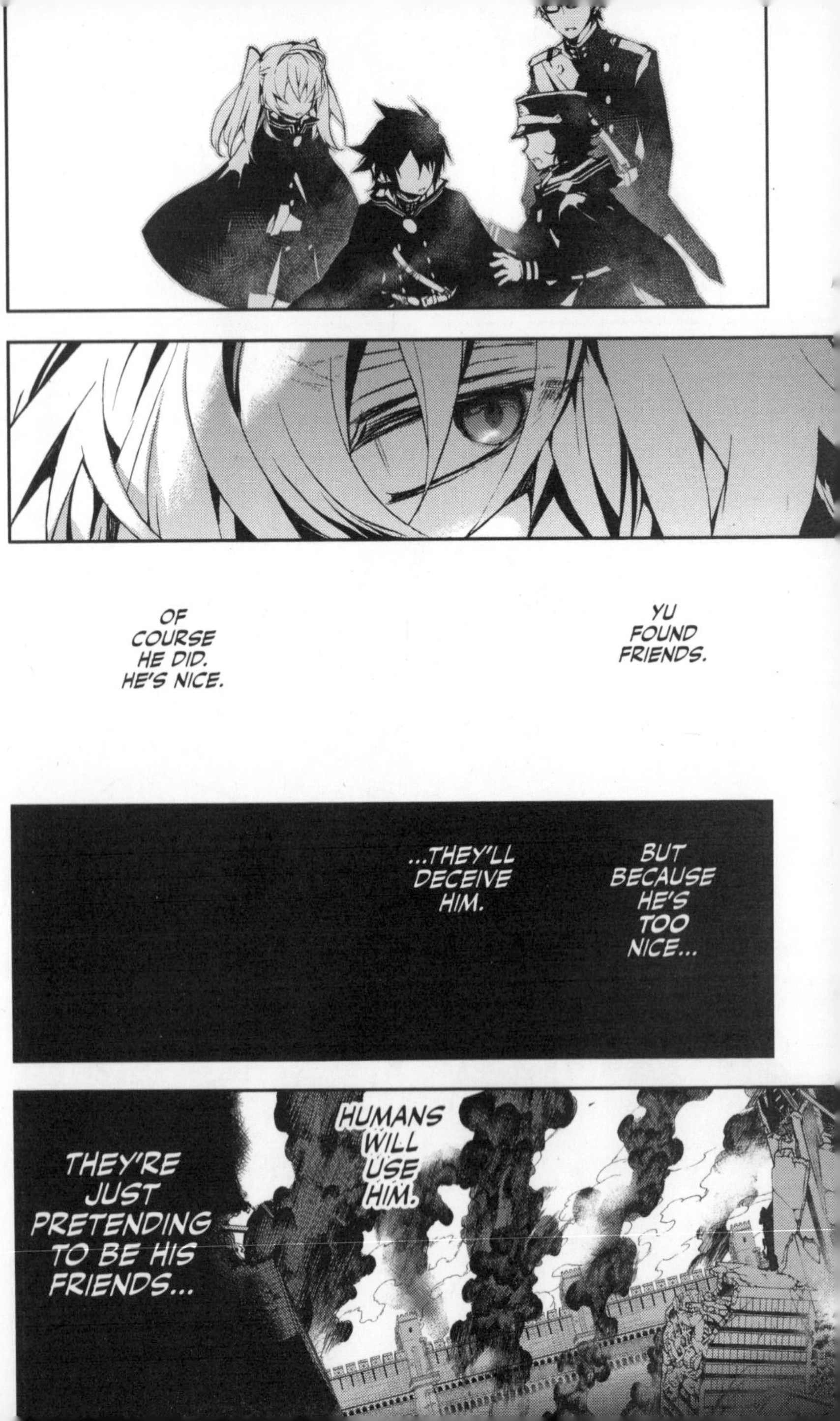
YU FOUND FRIENDS.
OF COURSE HE DID. HE'S NICE.
BUT BECAUSE HE'S TOO NICE...
...THEY'LL DECEIVE HIM.
HUMANS WILL USE HIM.
THEY'RE JUST PRETENDING TO BE HIS FRIENDS...

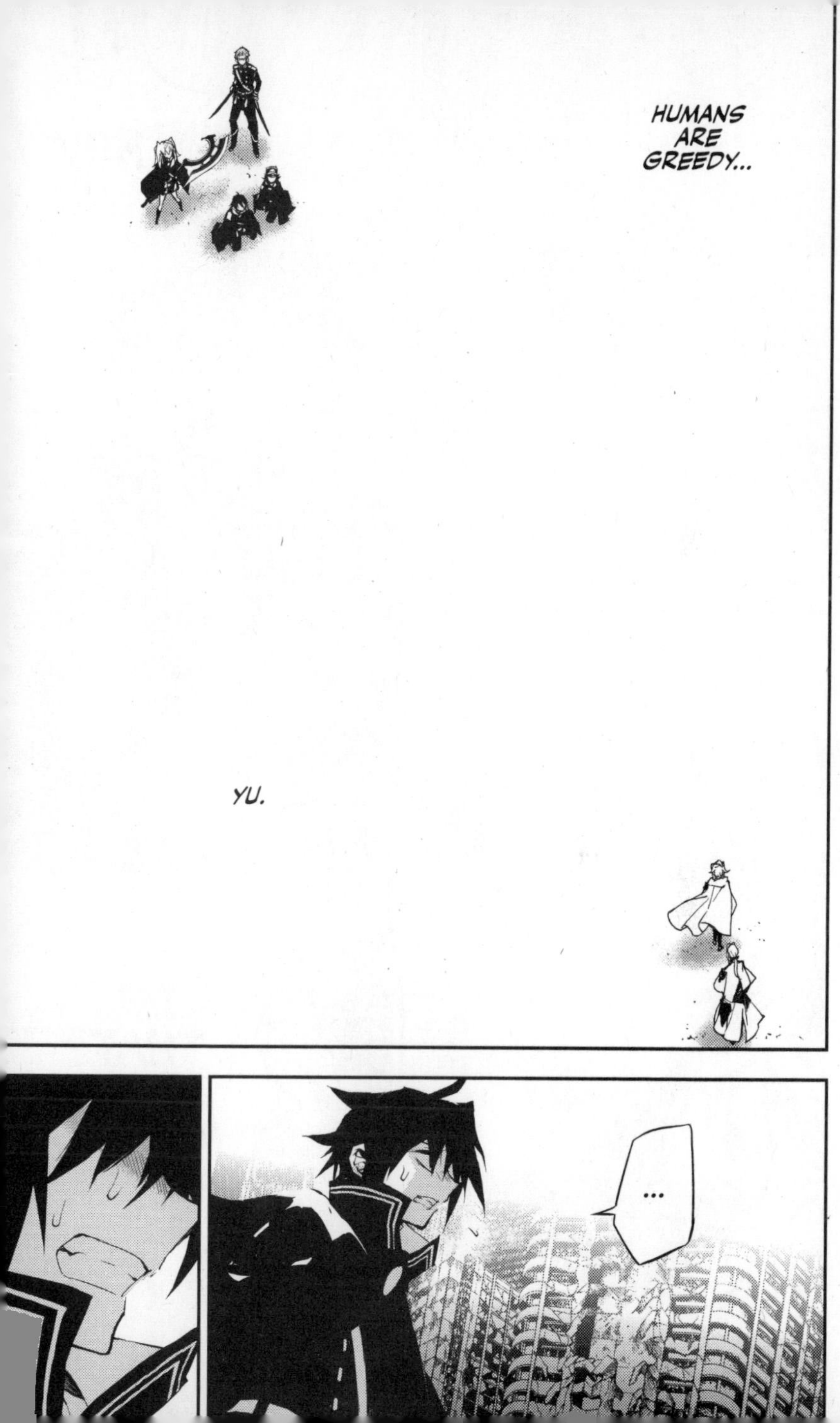
HUMANS ARE GREEDY...
YU.
...

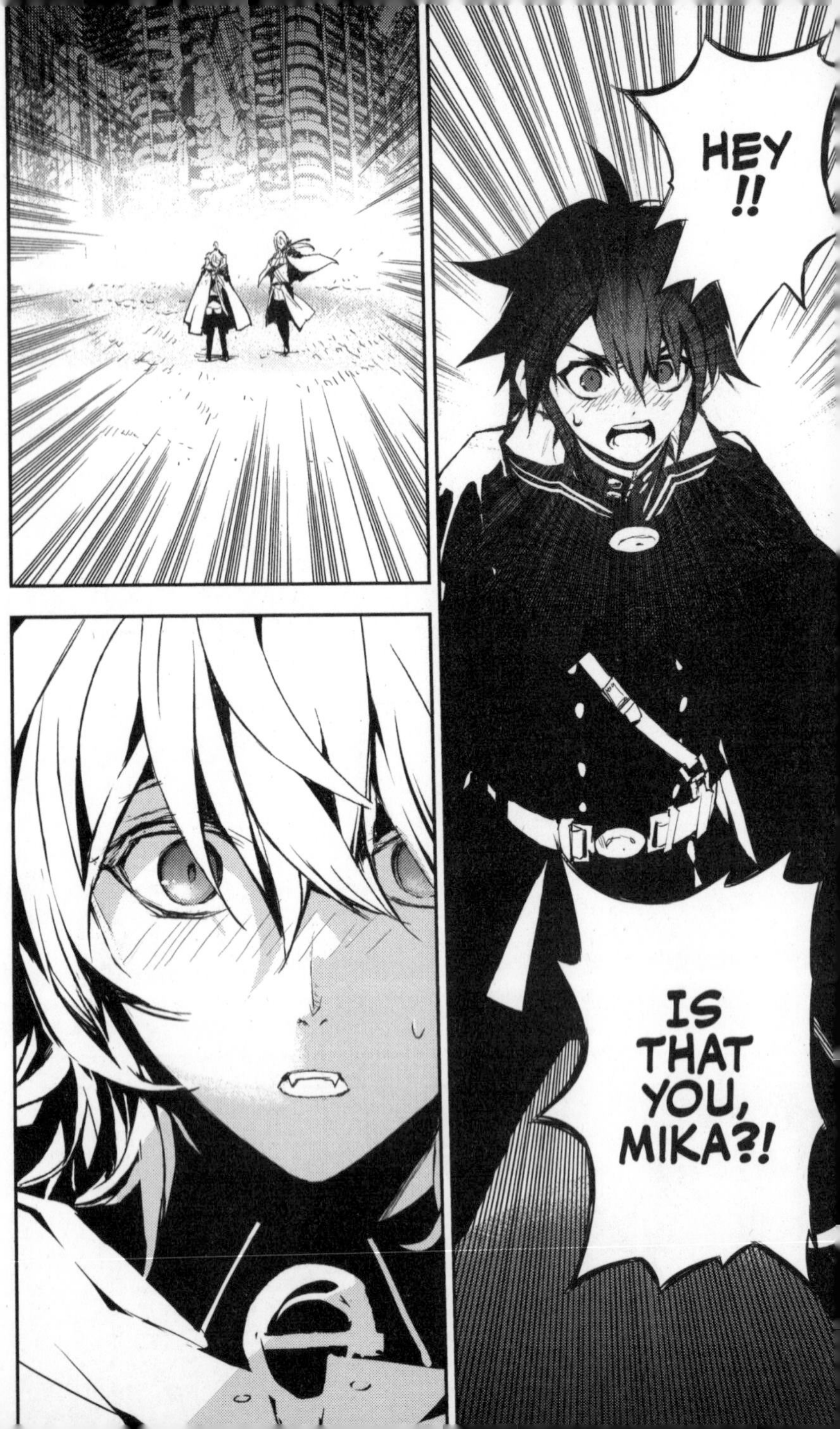
HEY !!
IS THAT YOU, MIKA?!

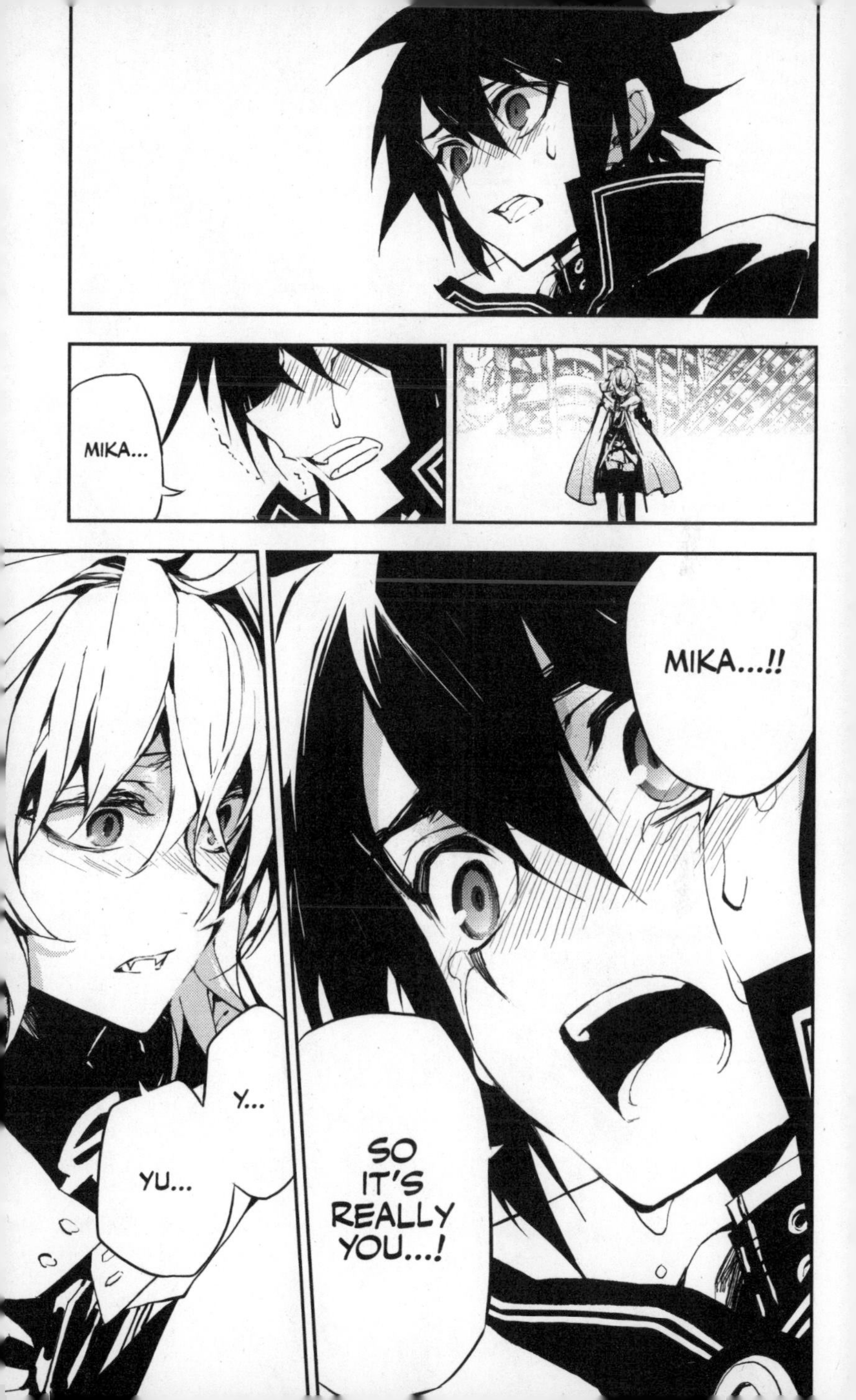
MIKA...
MIKA...!!
SO IT'S REALLY YOU...!
Y...
YU...

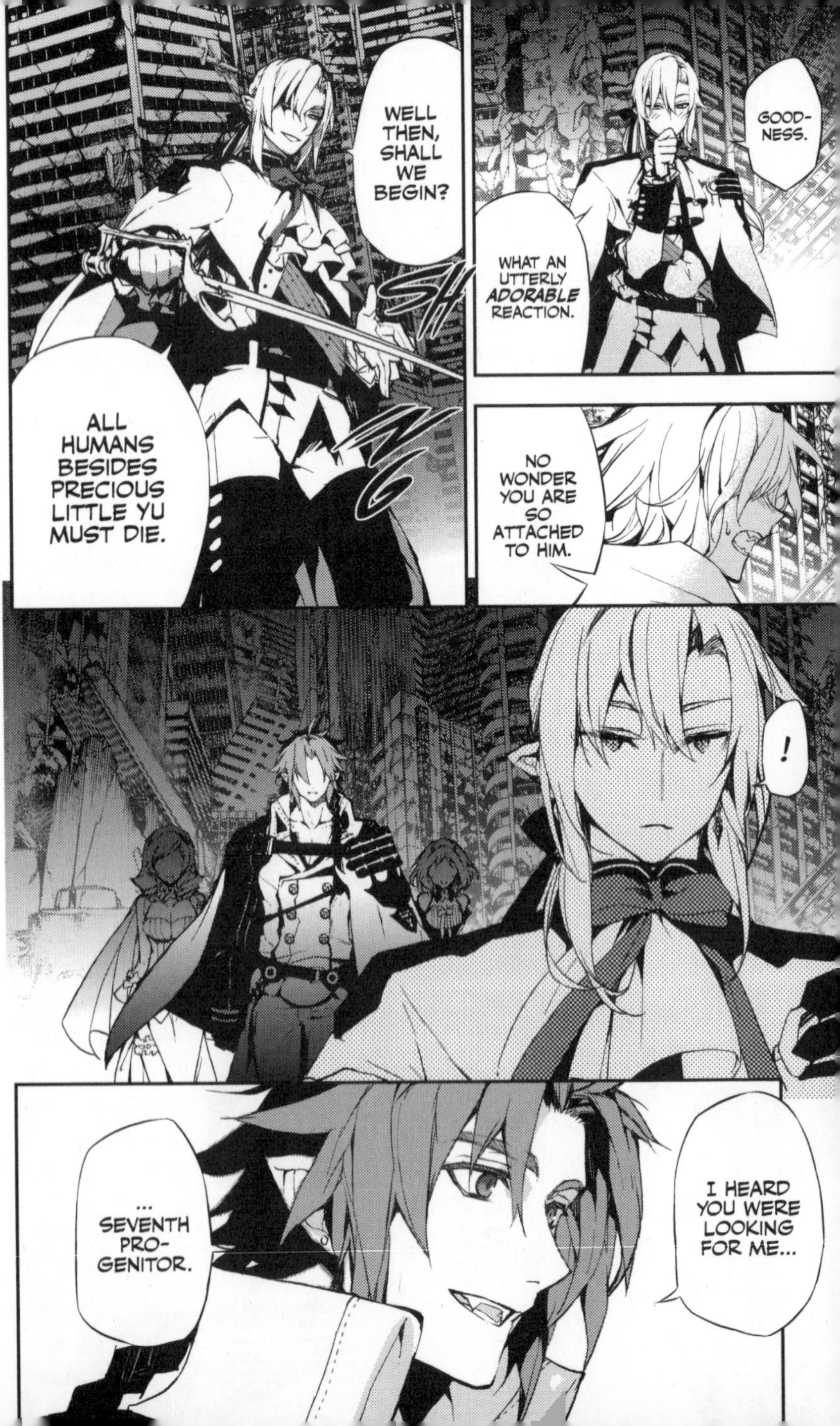

GOODNESS.
WHAT AN UTTERLY *ADORABLE* REACTION.
NO WONDER YOU ARE SO ATTACHED TO HIM.
WELL THEN, SHALL WE BEGIN?
SHING
ALL HUMANS BESIDES PRECIOUS LITTLE YU MUST DIE.
!
I HEARD YOU WERE LOOKING FOR ME...
...SEVENTH PROGENITOR.

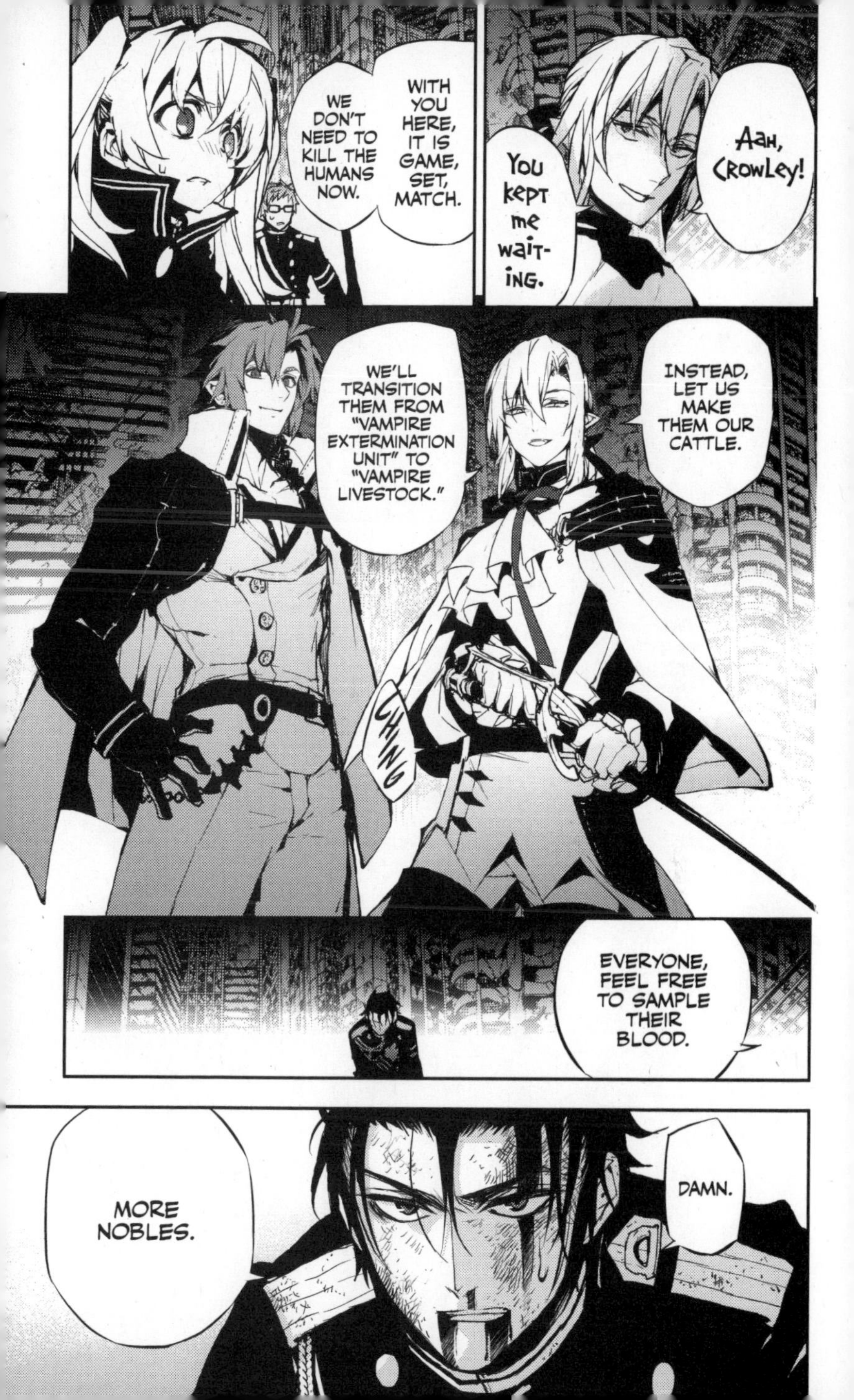
Aah, Crowley!
You kept me wait-ing.
WITH YOU HERE, IT IS GAME, SET, MATCH.
WE DON'T NEED TO KILL THE HUMANS NOW.
INSTEAD, LET US MAKE THEM OUR CATTLE.
WE'LL TRANSITION THEM FROM "VAMPIRE EXTERMINATION UNIT" TO "VAMPIRE LIVESTOCK."
CHING
EVERYONE, FEEL FREE TO SAMPLE THEIR BLOOD.
DAMN.
MORE NOBLES.

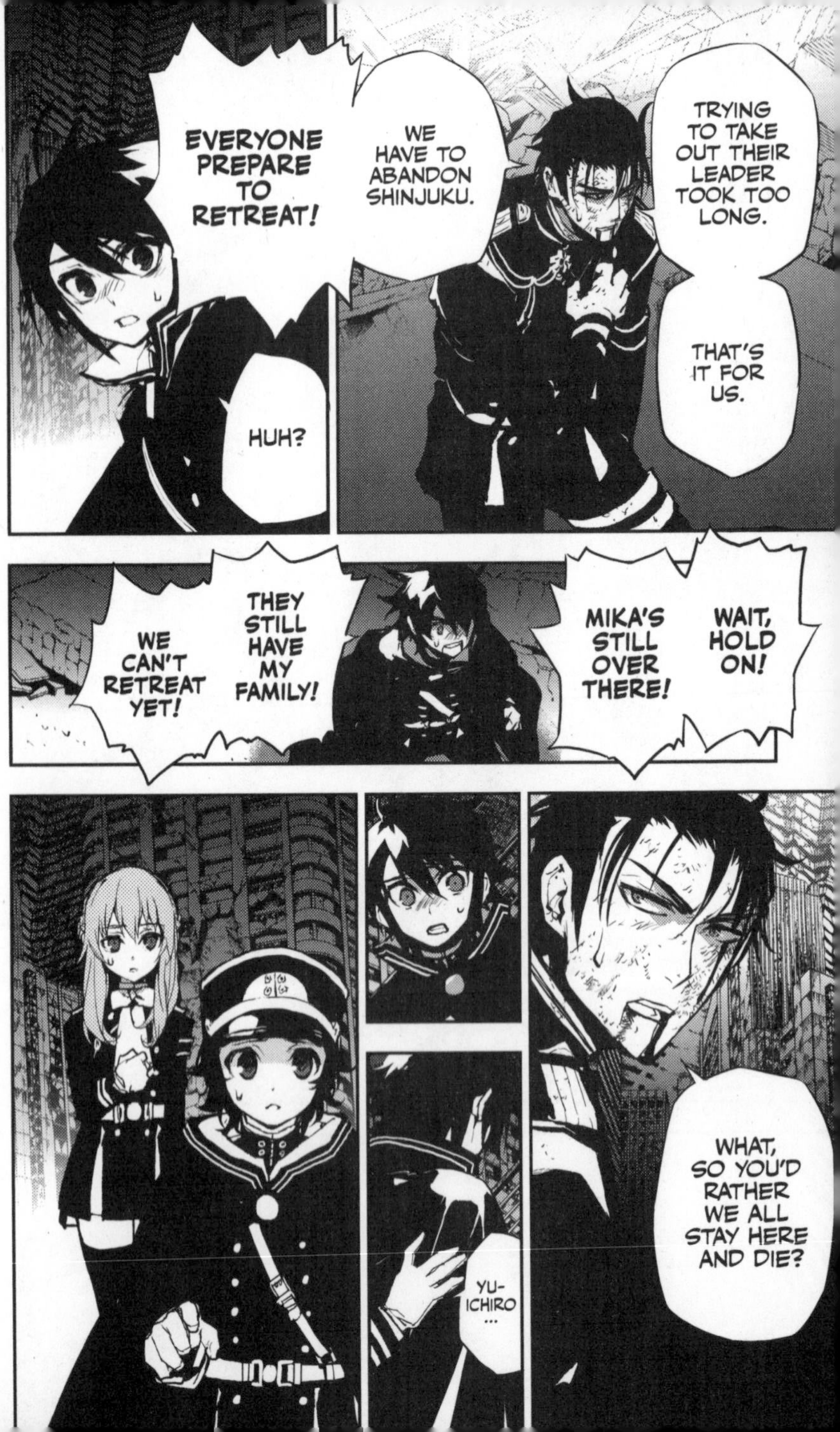
TRYING TO TAKE OUT THEIR LEADER TOOK TOO LONG.
THAT'S IT FOR US.
WE HAVE TO ABANDON SHINJUKU.
EVERYONE PREPARE TO RETREAT!
HUH?
WAIT, HOLD ON!
MIKA'S STILL OVER THERE!
THEY STILL HAVE MY FAMILY!
WE CAN'T RETREAT YET!
WHAT, SO YOU'D RATHER WE ALL STAY HERE AND DIE?
YU-ICHIRO...

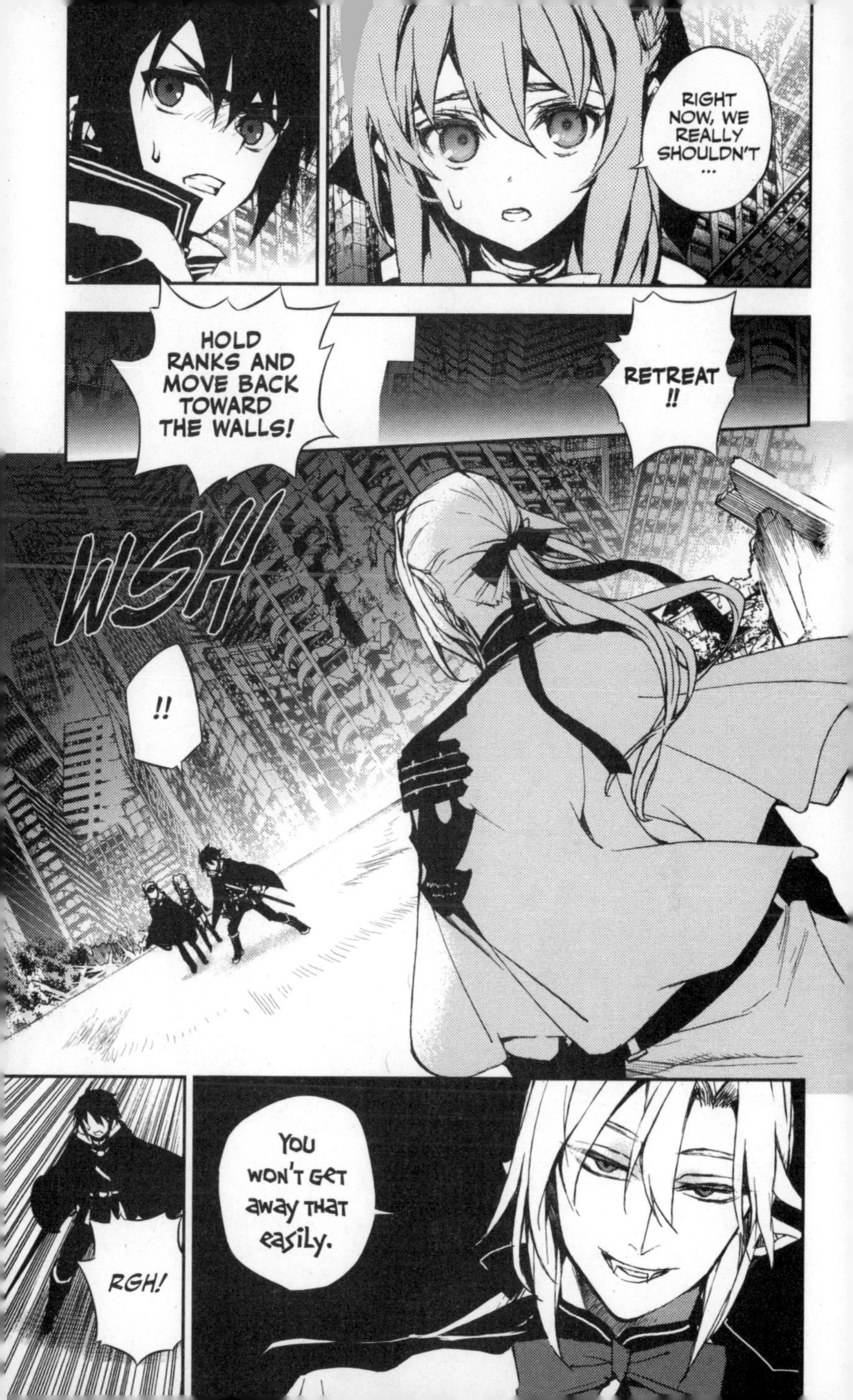
RIGHT NOW, WE REALLY SHOULDN'T ...
RETREAT !!
HOLD RANKS AND MOVE BACK TOWARD THE WALLS!
WSH
!!
YOU WON'T GET AWAY THAT EASILY.
RGH!

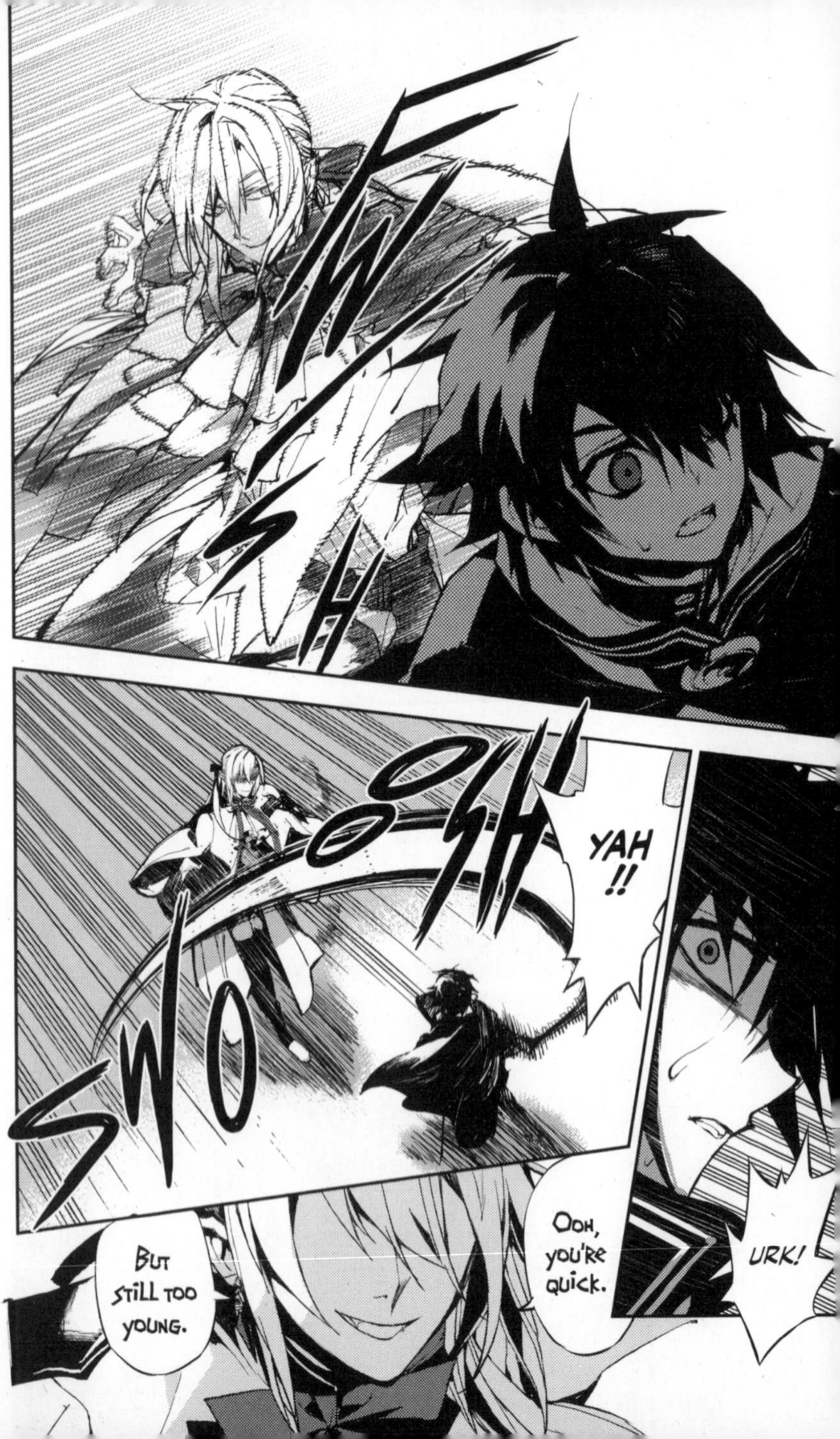
FWISH!
YAH!!
SWOOOSH
URK!
Ooh, you're quick.
But still too young.

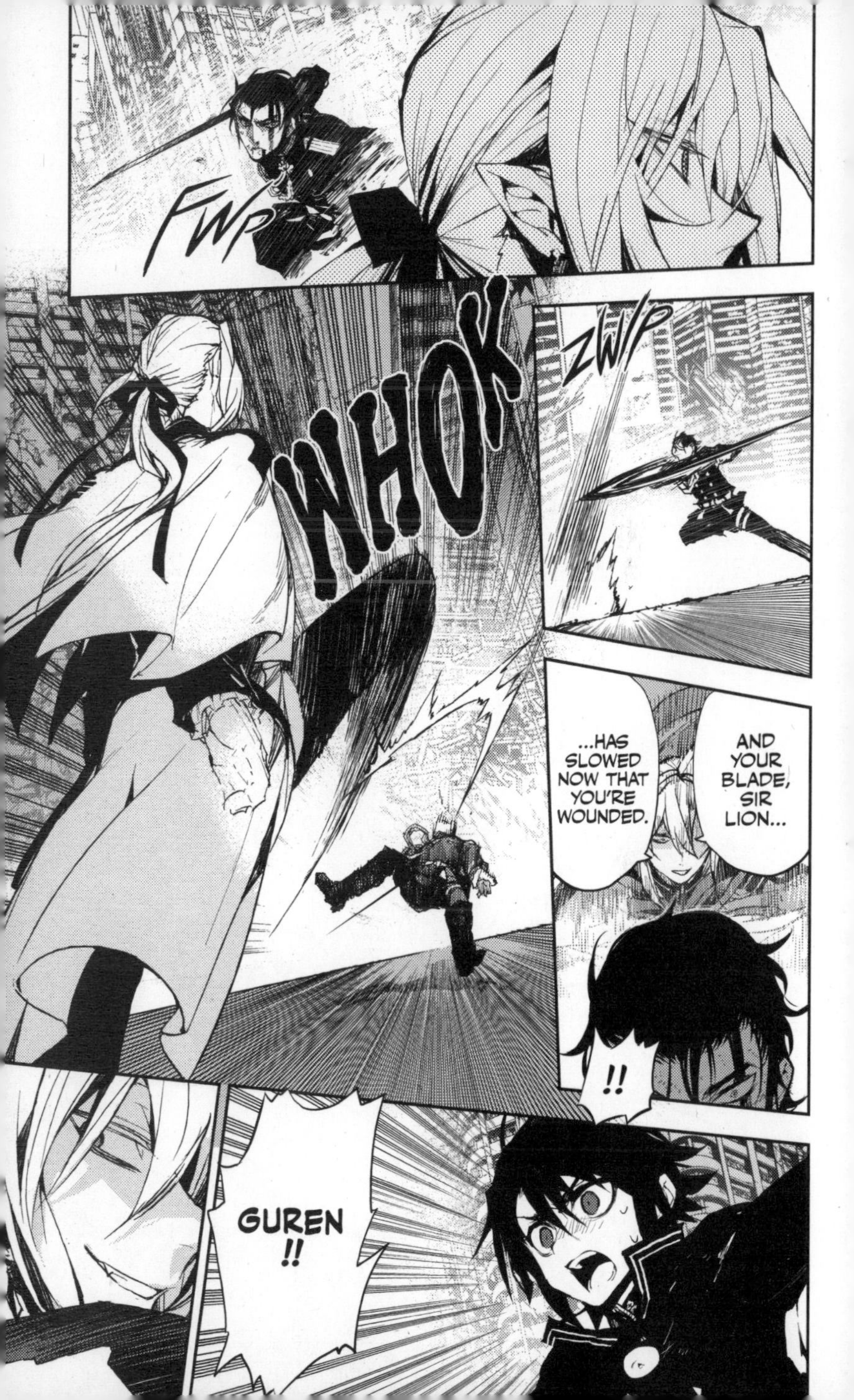
FWP
ZWIP
AND YOUR BLADE, SIR LION...
...HAS SLOWED NOW THAT YOU'RE WOUNDED.
!!
WHOK
GUREN !!

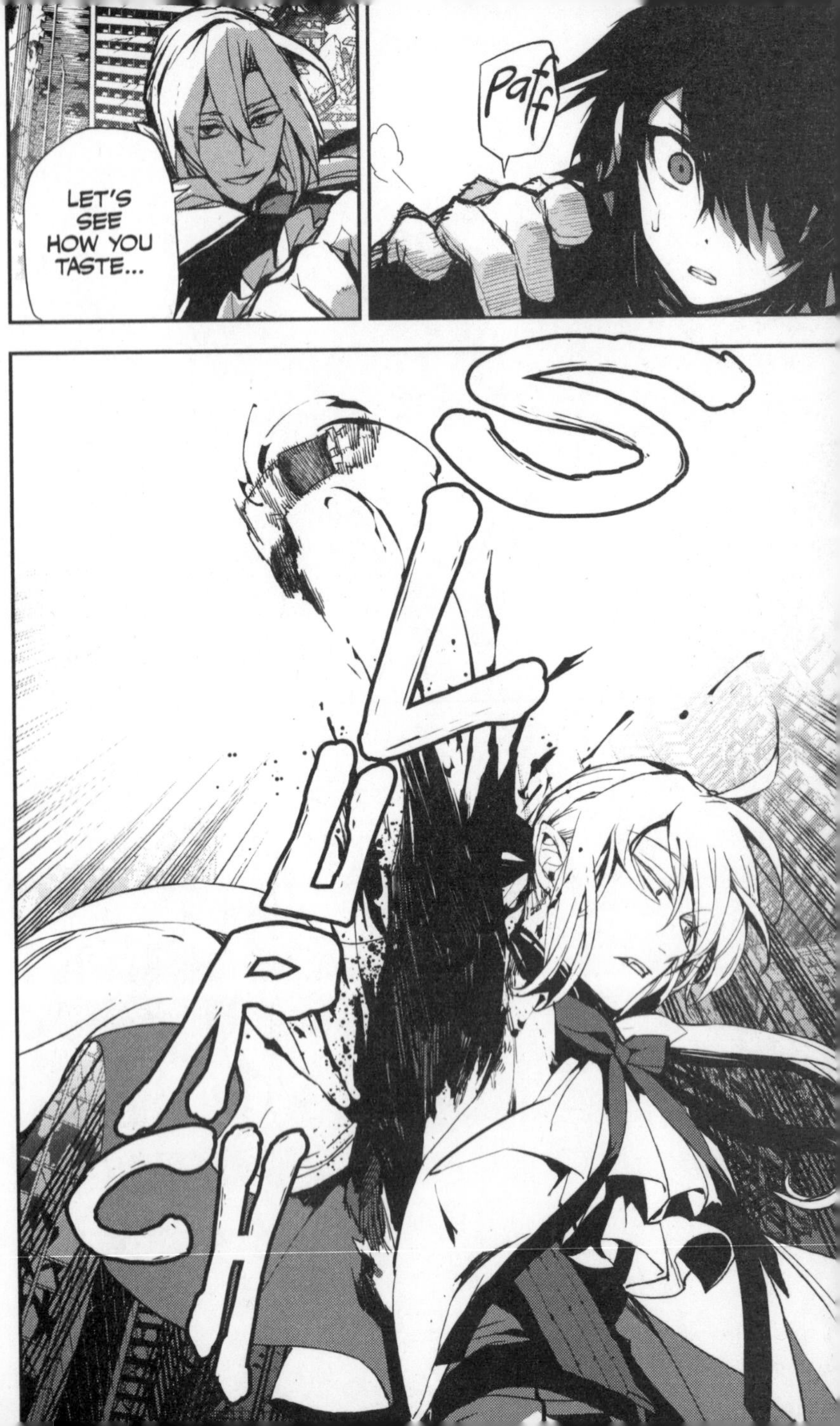
Paff
LET'S SEE HOW YOU TASTE...

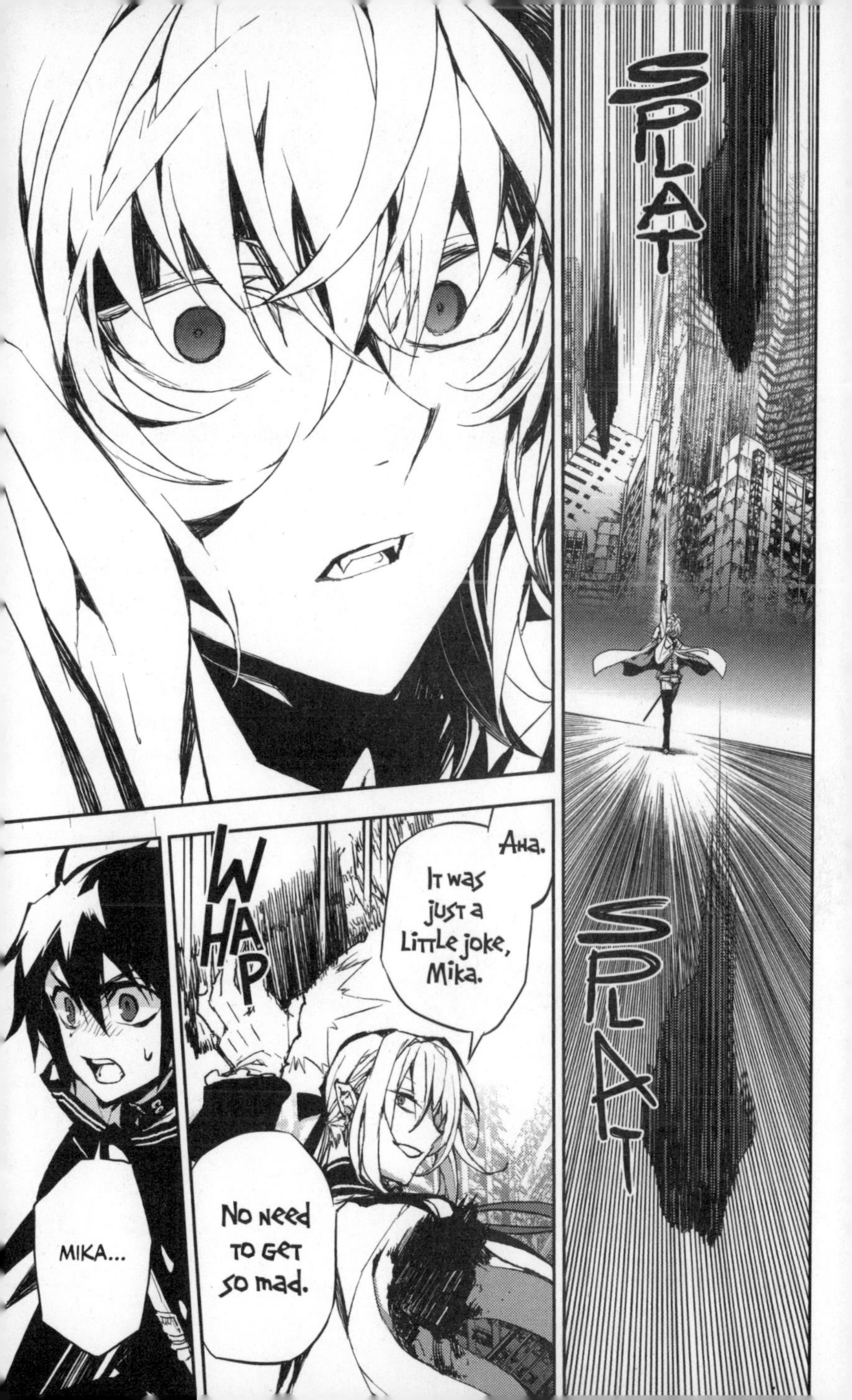
SPLAT
SPLAT
WHAP
Aha.
It was just a little joke, Mika.
No need to get so mad.
MIKA...

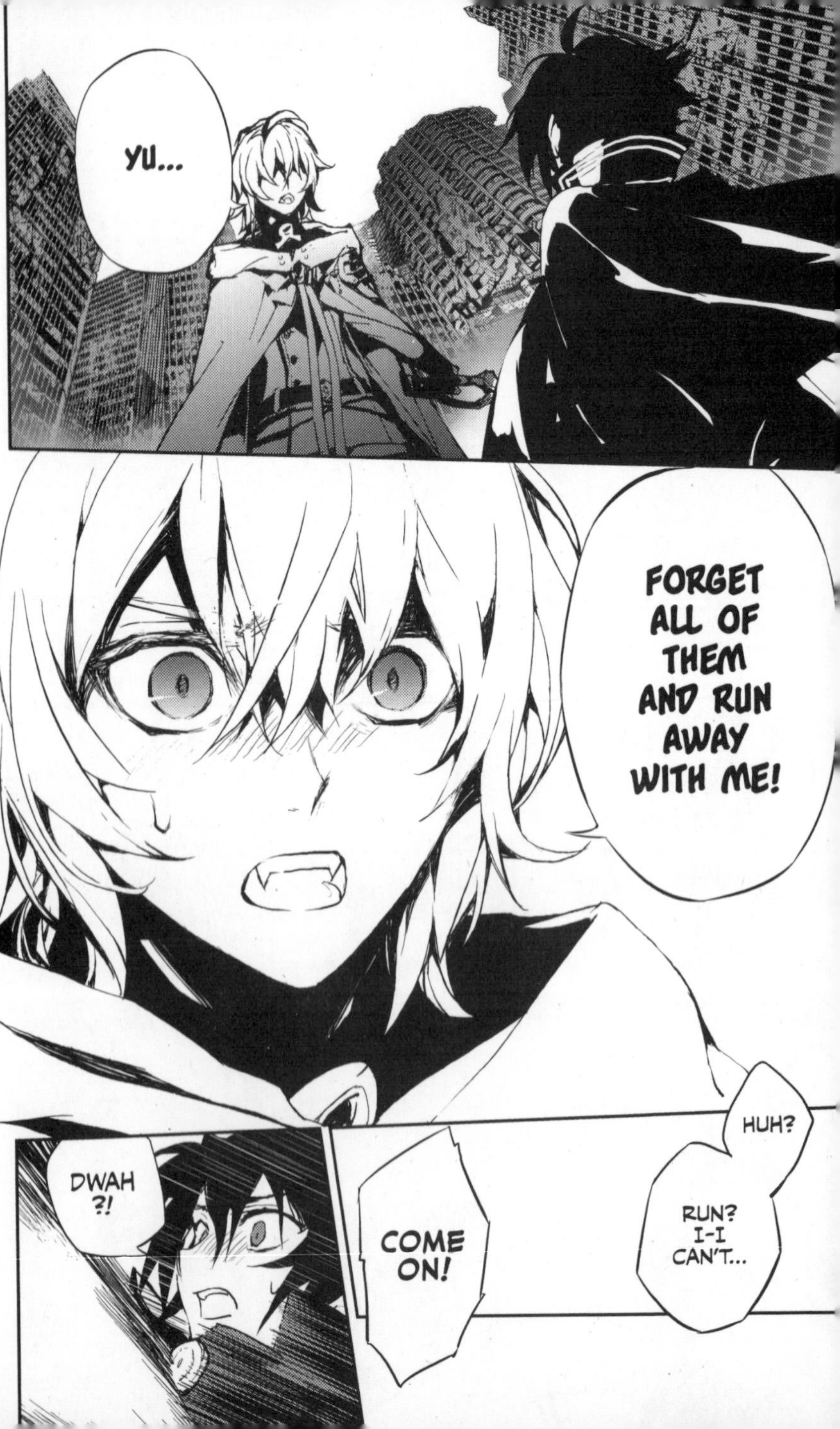
YU...
FORGET ALL OF THEM AND RUN AWAY WITH ME!
HUH?
RUN? I-I CAN'T...
COME ON!
DWAH ?!

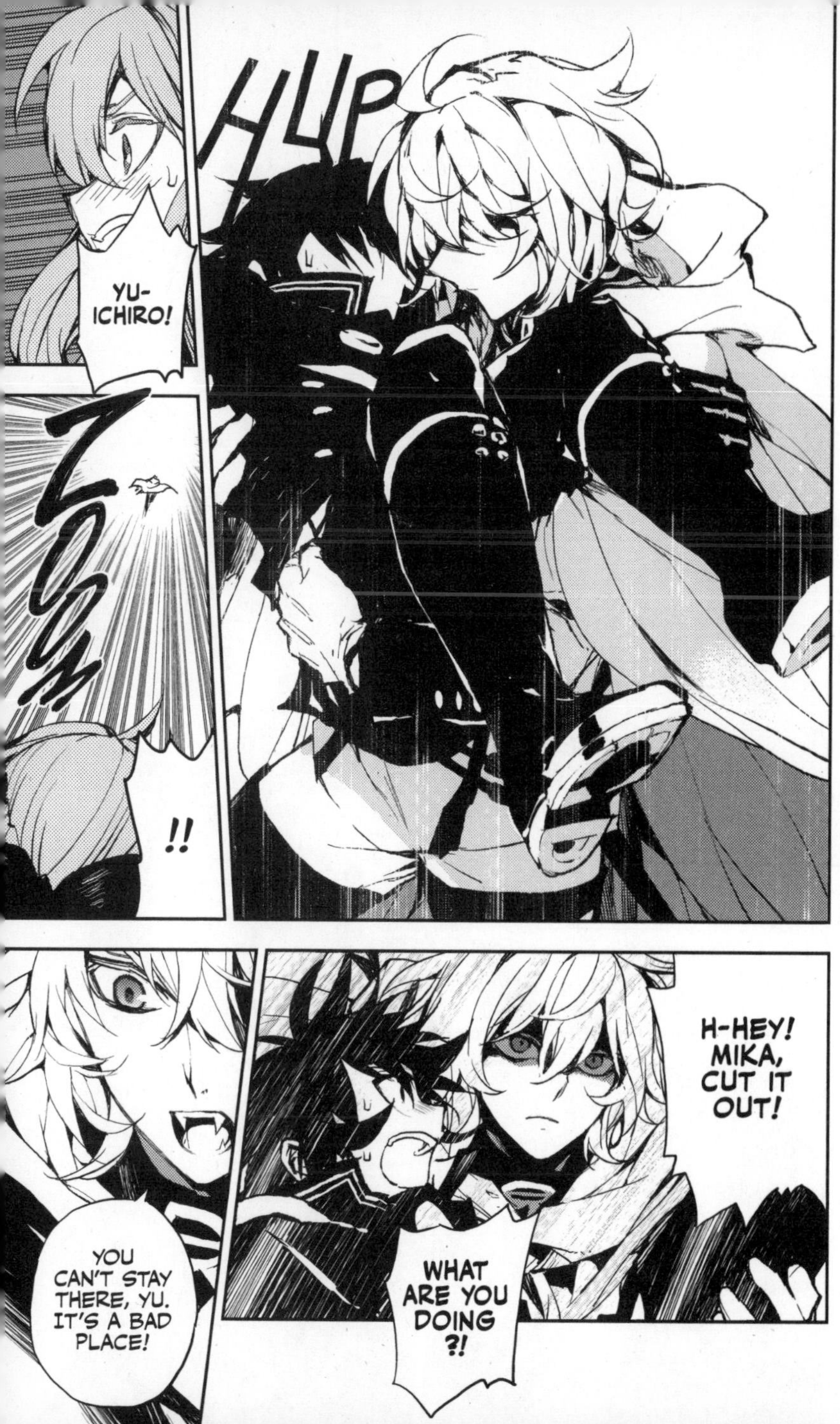
HUP
YU-ICHIRO!
ZOOM
!!
H-HEY! MIKA, CUT IT OUT!
WHAT ARE YOU DOING?!
YOU CAN'T STAY THERE, YU. IT'S A BAD PLACE!

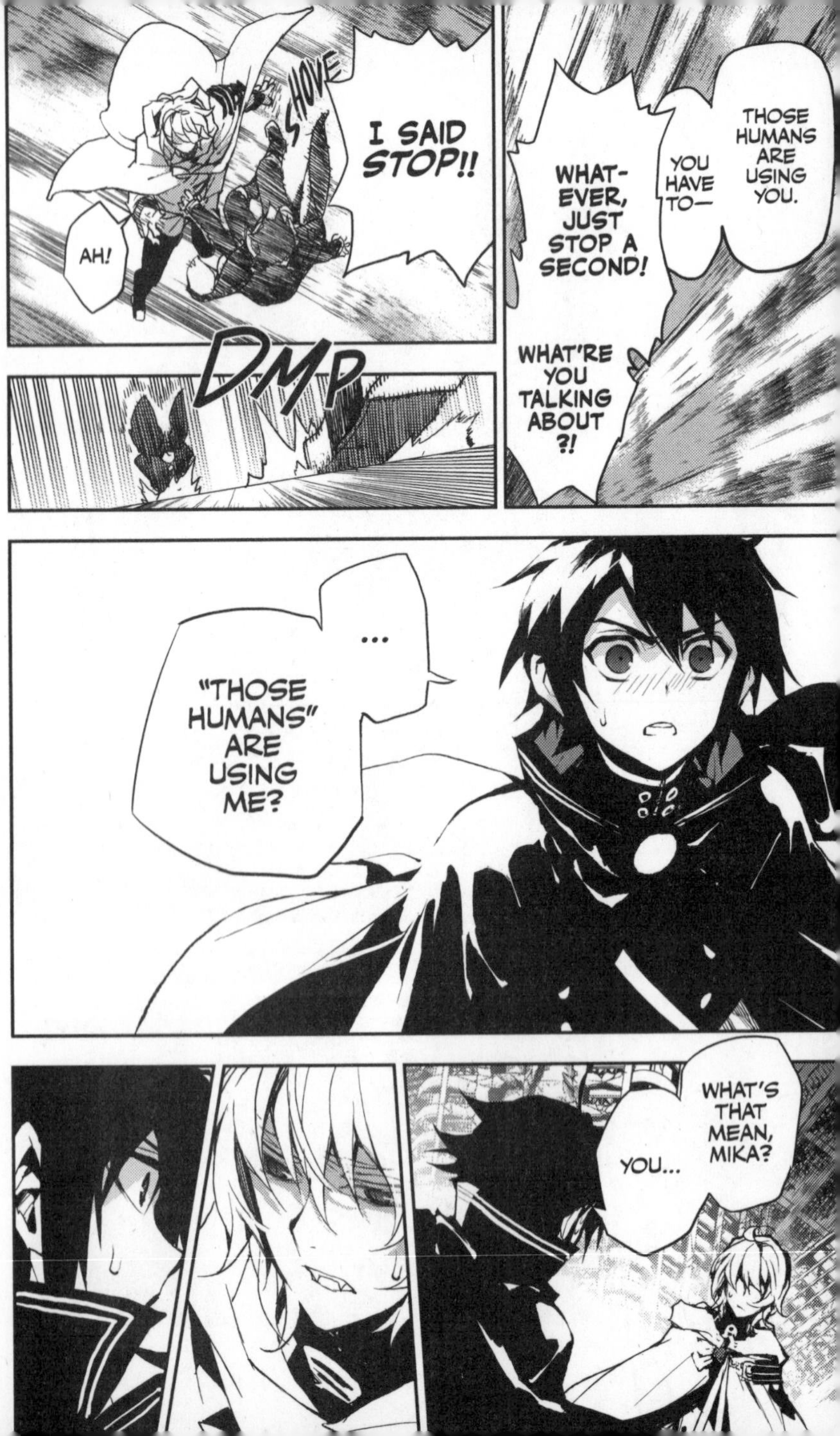
THOSE HUMANS ARE USING YOU.
YOU HAVE TO—
WHAT-EVER, JUST STOP A SECOND!
WHAT'RE YOU TALKING ABOUT?!
SHOVE
I SAID STOP!!
AH!
DMP
...
"THOSE HUMANS" ARE USING ME?
WHAT'S THAT MEAN, MIKA?
YOU...

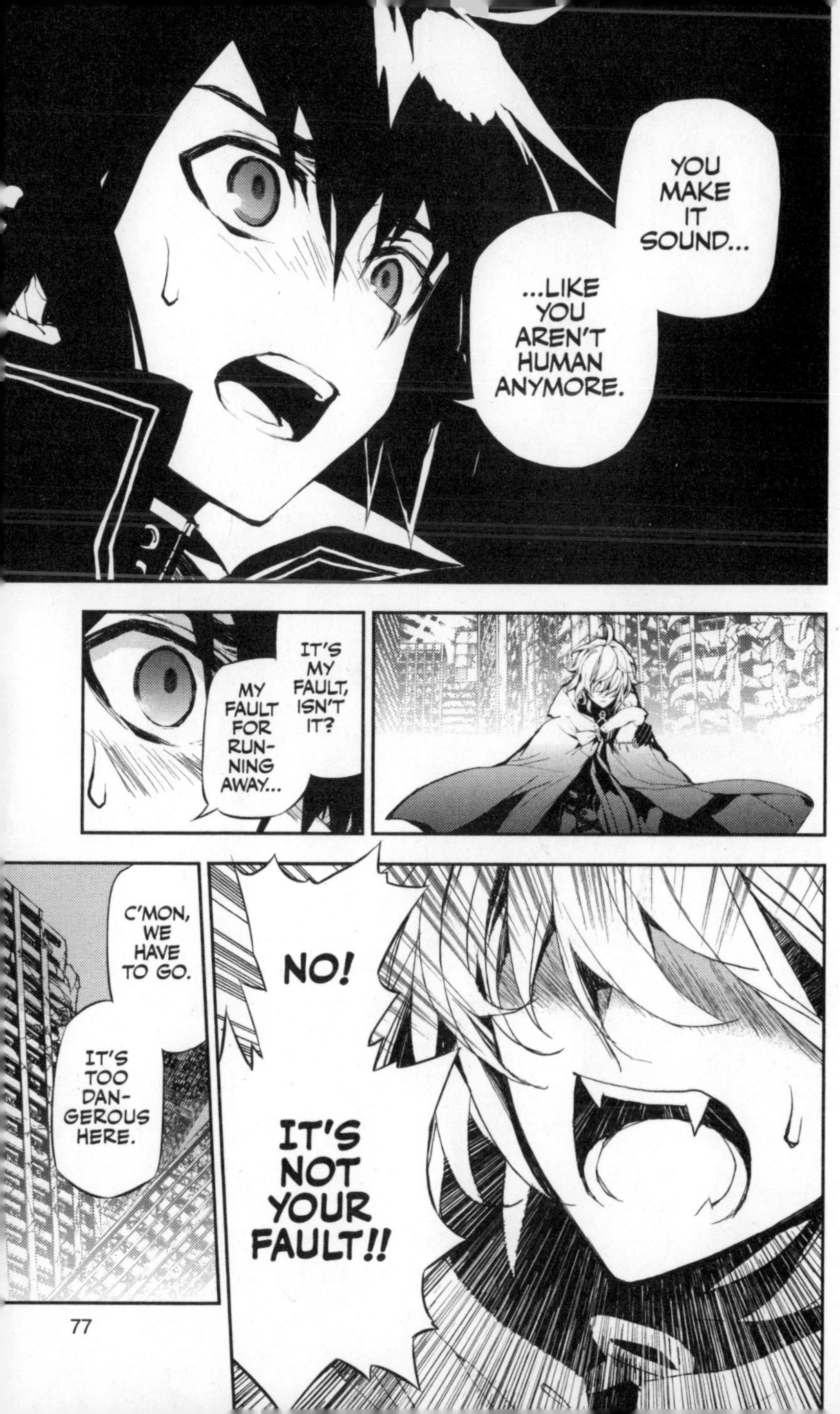
YOU MAKE IT SOUND...
...LIKE YOU AREN'T HUMAN ANYMORE.
IT'S MY FAULT, ISN'T IT?
MY FAULT FOR RUN-NING AWAY...
NO!
IT'S NOT YOUR FAULT!!
C'MON, WE HAVE TO GO.
IT'S TOO DAN-GEROUS HERE.

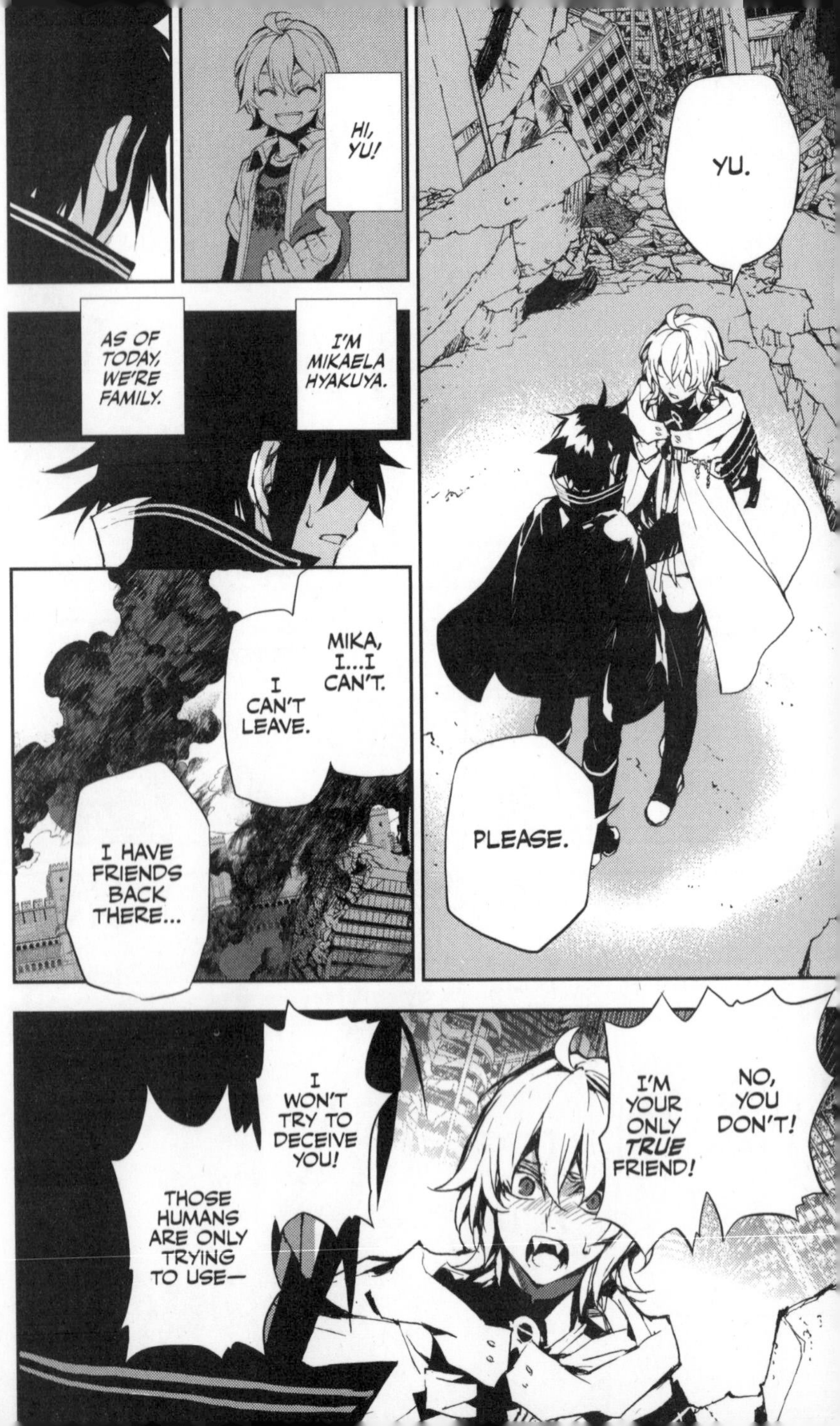
YU.
PLEASE.
HI, YU!
I'M MIKAELA HYAKUYA.
AS OF TODAY, WE'RE FAMILY.
MIKA, I...I CAN'T.
I CAN'T LEAVE.
I HAVE FRIENDS BACK THERE...
NO, YOU DON'T!
I'M YOUR ONLY *TRUE* FRIEND!
I WON'T TRY TO DECEIVE YOU!
THOSE HUMANS ARE ONLY TRYING TO USE—

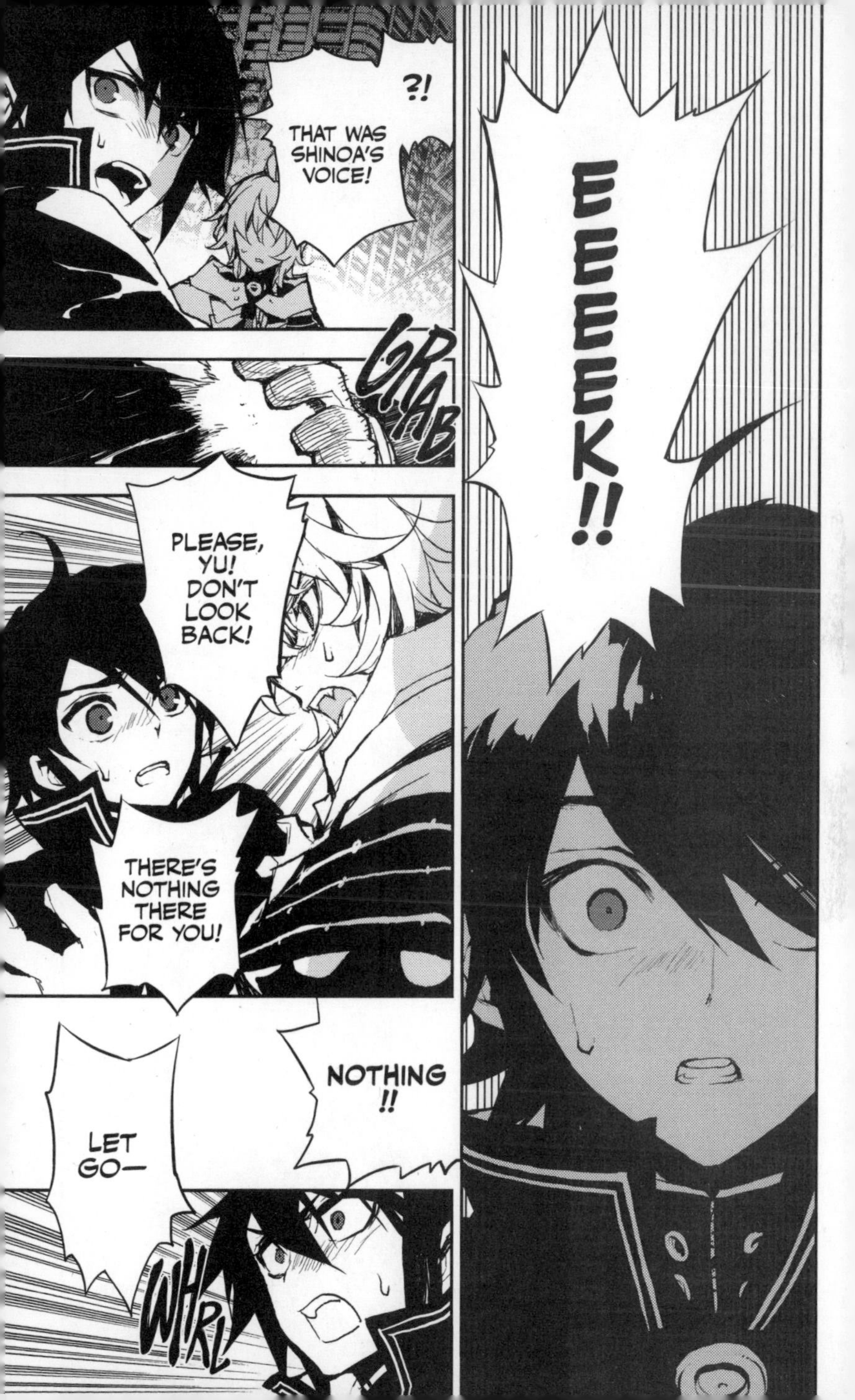
EEEEEK!!
?!
THAT WAS SHINOA'S VOICE!
GRAB
PLEASE, YU! DON'T LOOK BACK!
THERE'S NOTHING THERE FOR YOU!
NOTHING!!
LET GO—
WHIRL

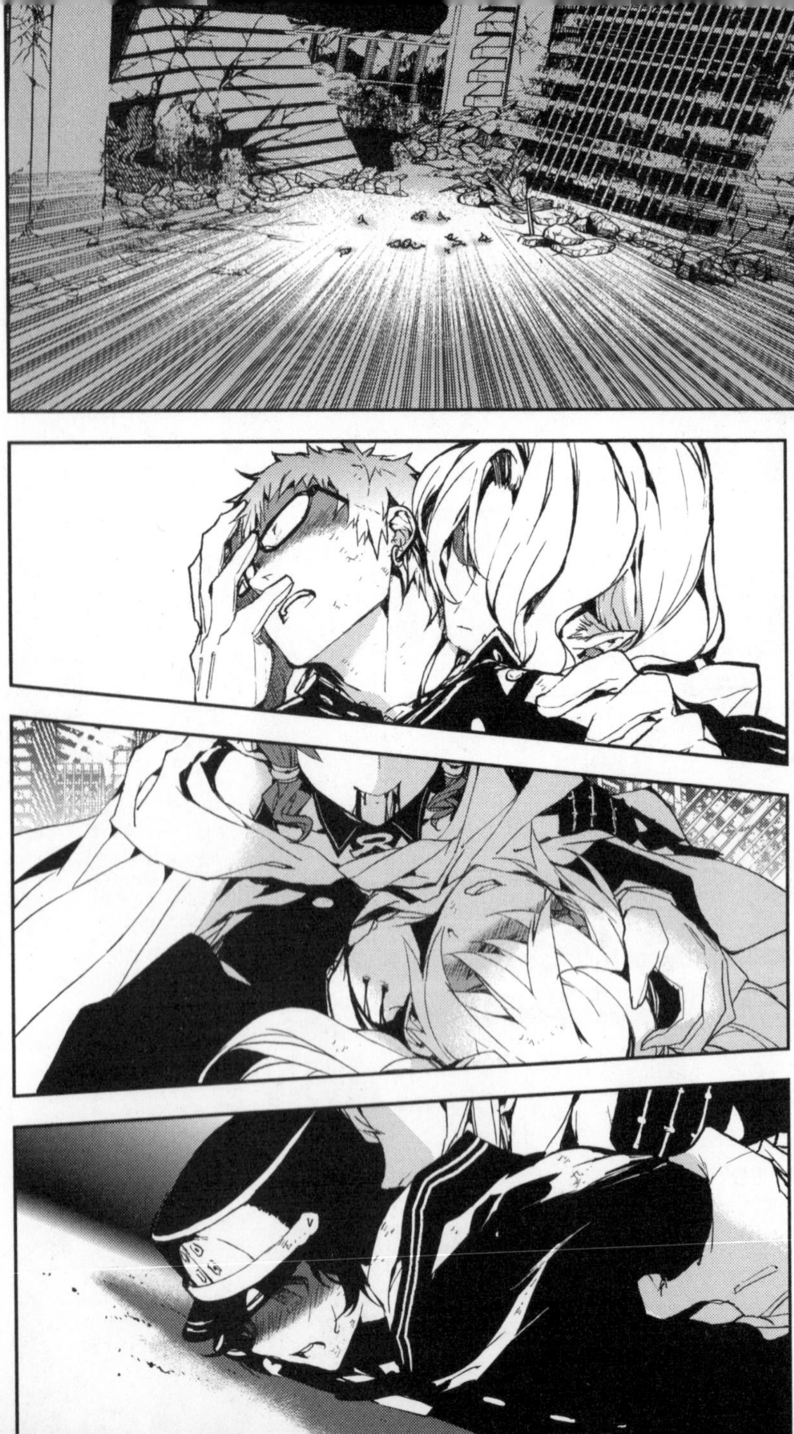

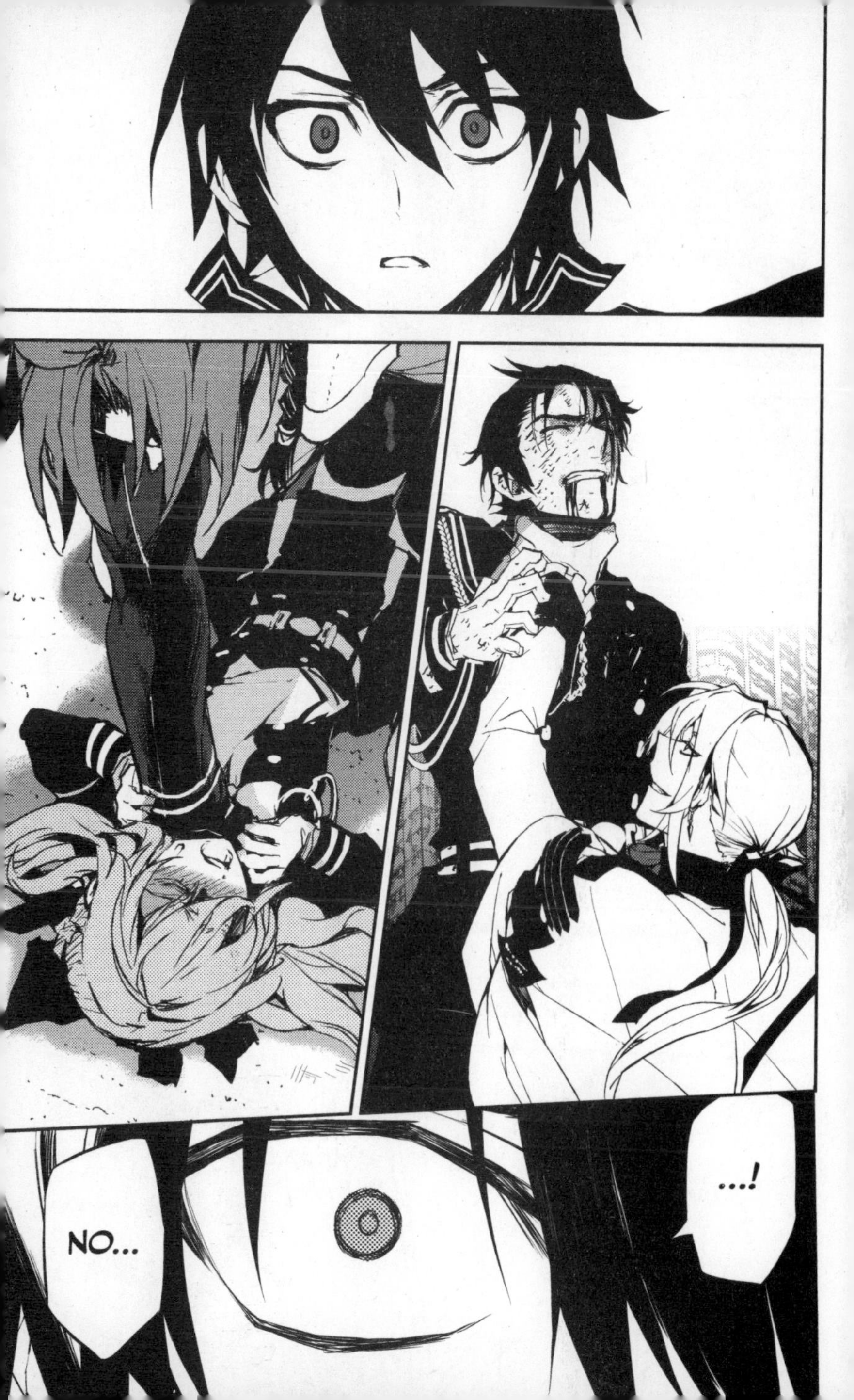
...!
NO...

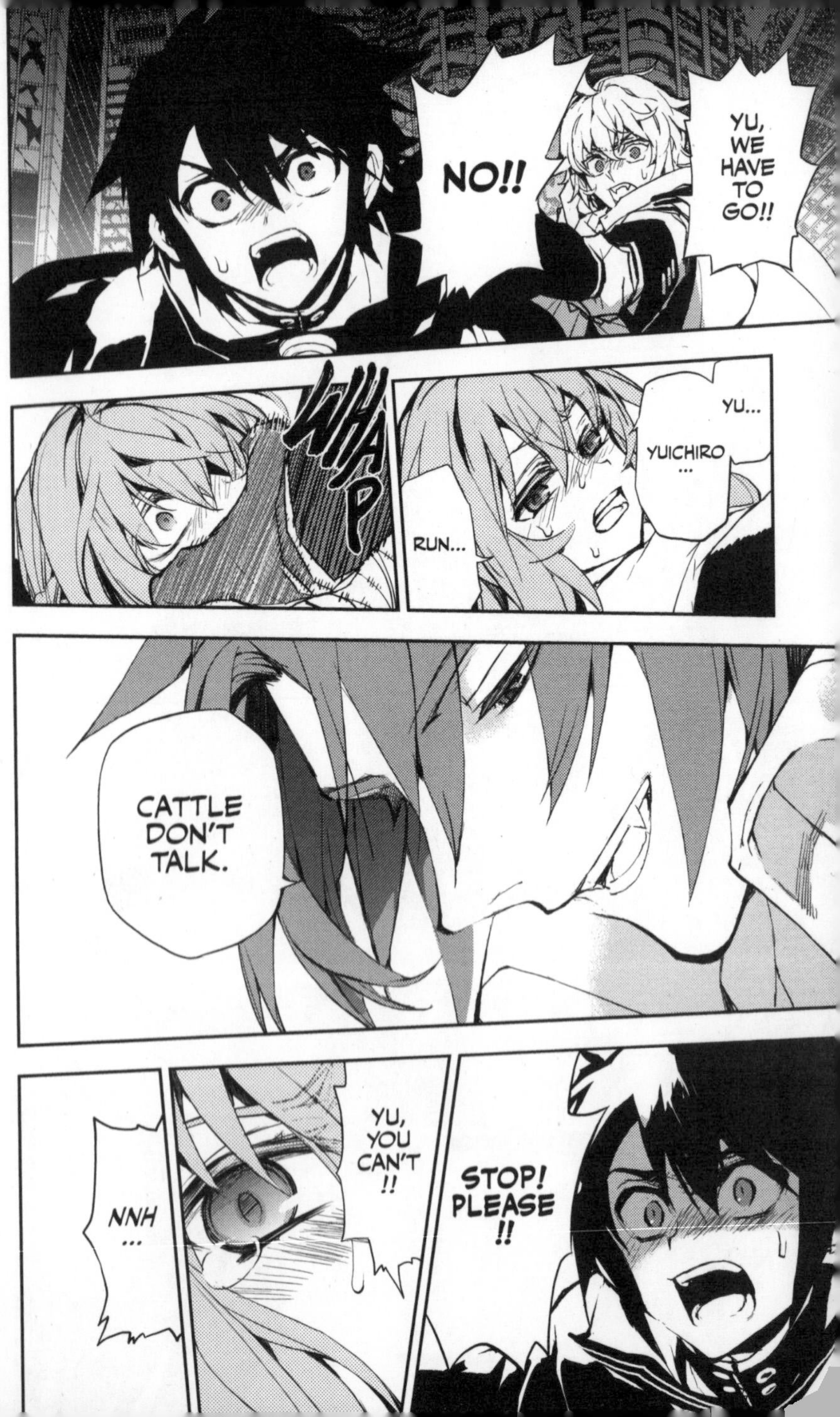
YU, WE HAVE TO GO!!
NO!!
YU...
YUICHIRO...
RUN...
WHAP
CATTLE DON'T TALK.
STOP! PLEASE!!
YU, YOU CAN'T!!
NNH...

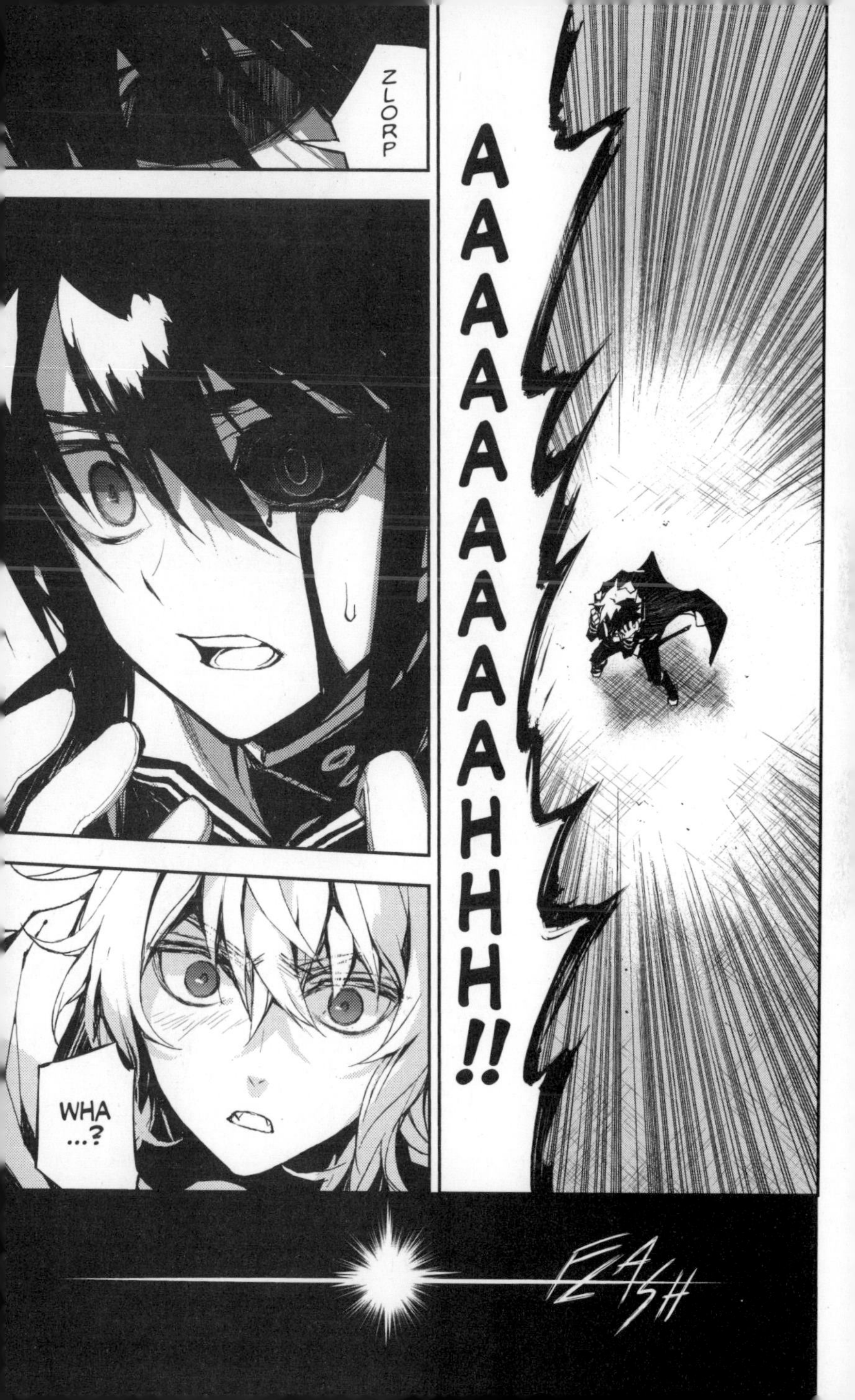
AAAAAAAAAAAHHH!!
ZLORP
WHA ...?
FLASH

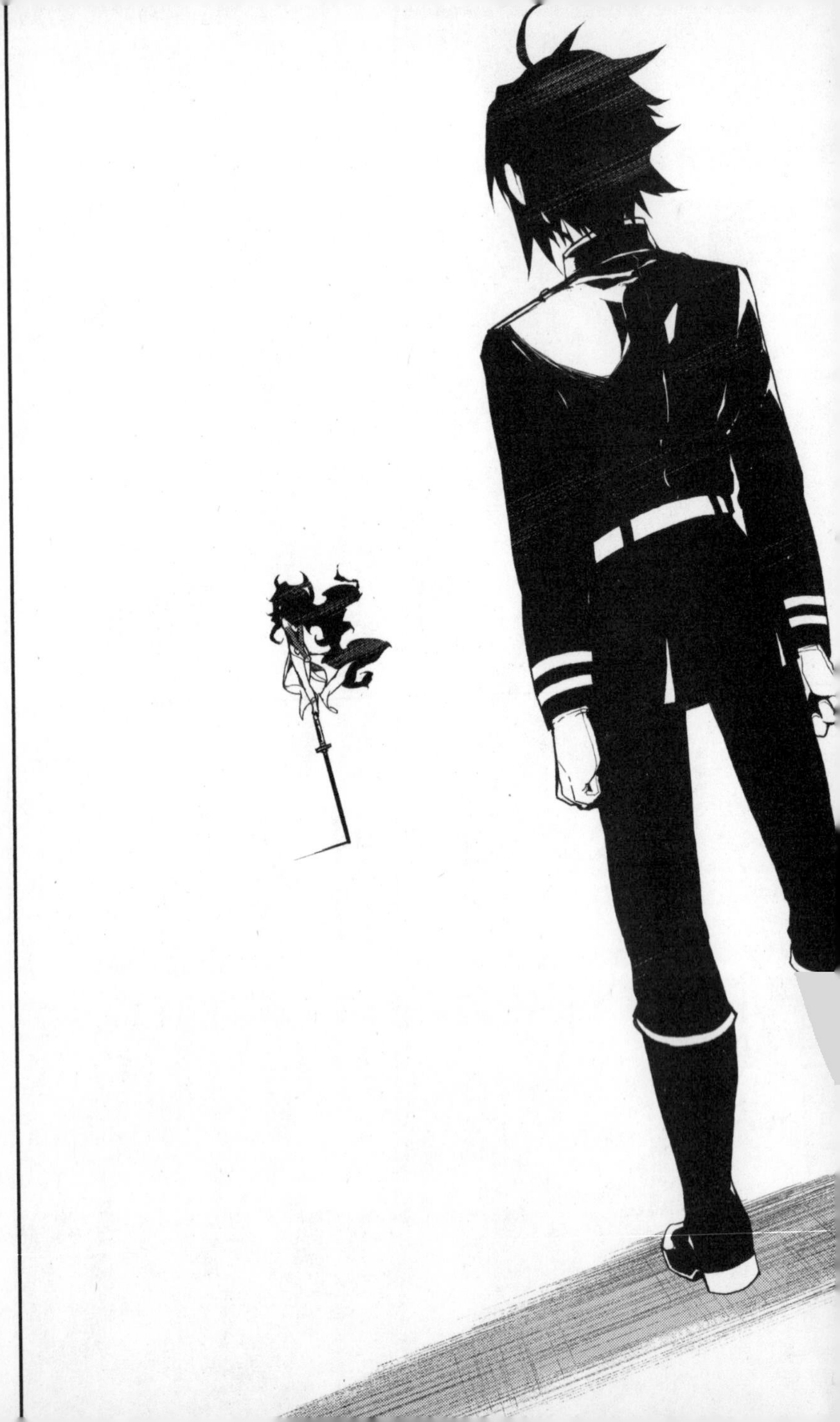

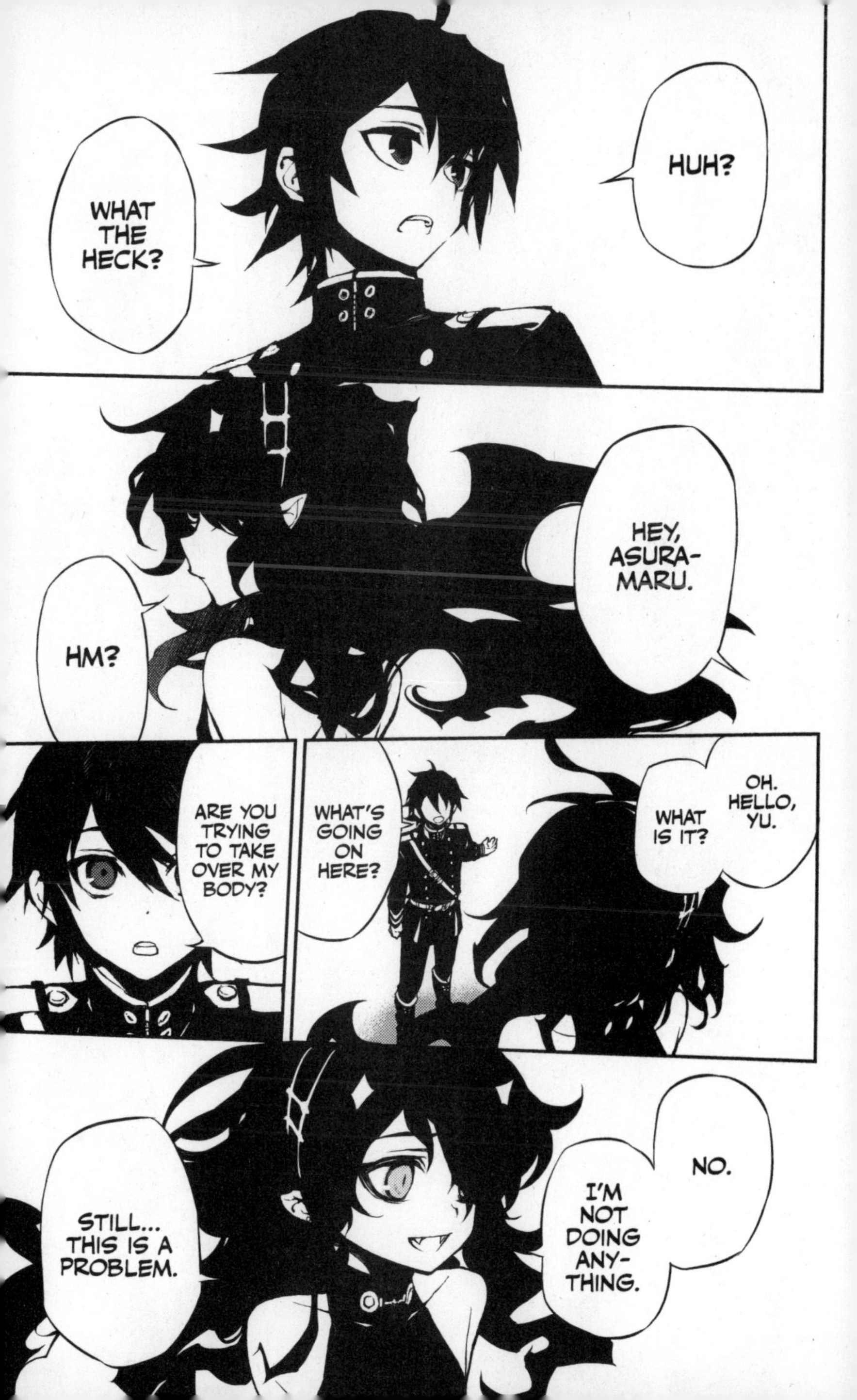
HUH?
WHAT THE HECK?
HEY, ASURA-MARU.
HM?
OH. HELLO, YU.
WHAT IS IT?
WHAT'S GOING ON HERE?
ARE YOU TRYING TO TAKE OVER MY BODY?
NO.
I'M NOT DOING ANY-THING.
STILL... THIS IS A PROBLEM.

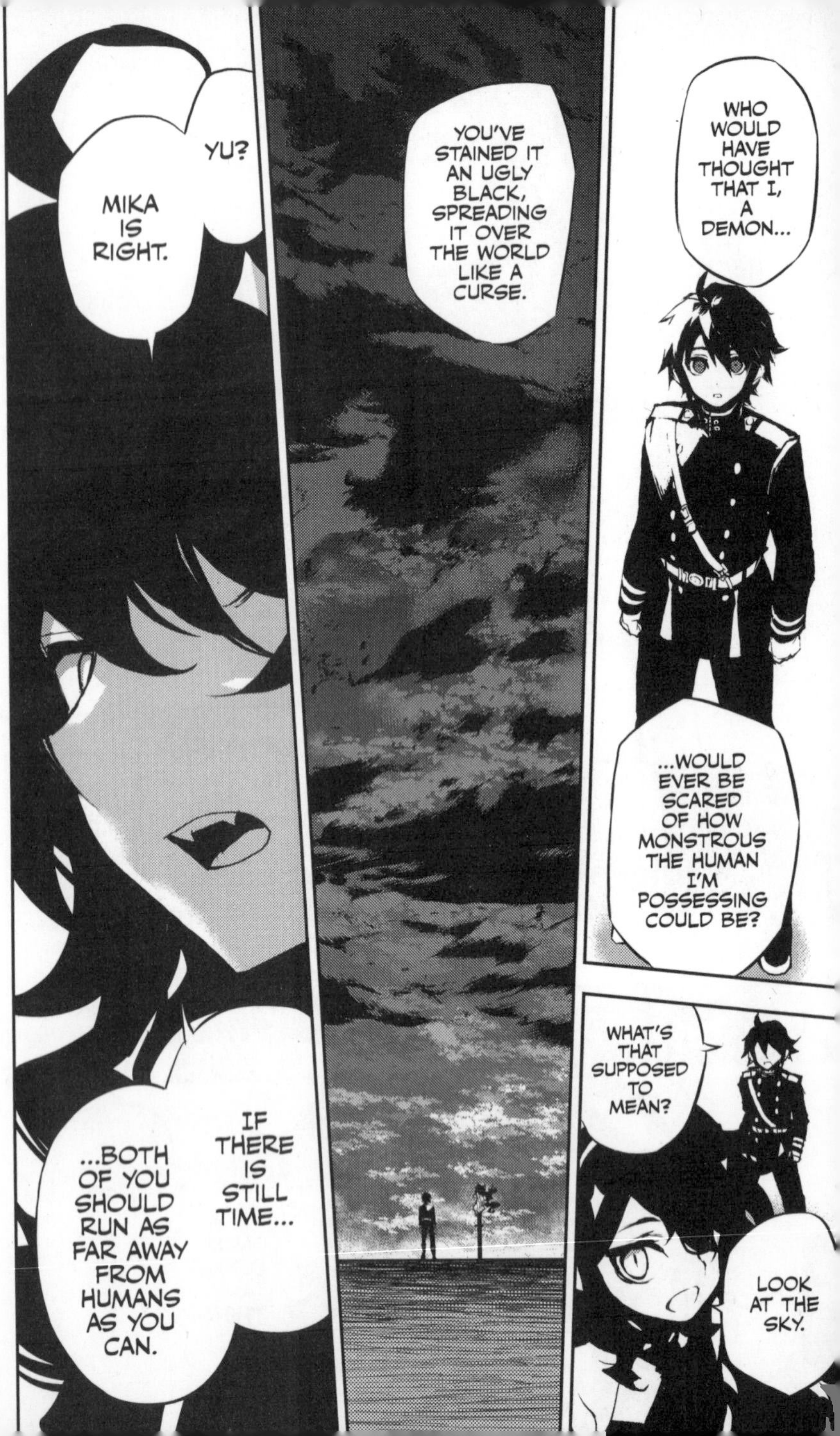
WHO WOULD HAVE THOUGHT THAT I, A DEMON...
...WOULD EVER BE SCARED OF HOW MONSTROUS THE HUMAN I'M POSSESSING COULD BE?
WHAT'S THAT SUPPOSED TO MEAN?
LOOK AT THE SKY.
YOU'VE STAINED IT AN UGLY BLACK, SPREADING IT OVER THE WORLD LIKE A CURSE.
YU?
MIKA IS RIGHT.
IF THERE IS STILL TIME...
...BOTH OF YOU SHOULD RUN AS FAR AWAY FROM HUMANS AS YOU CAN.

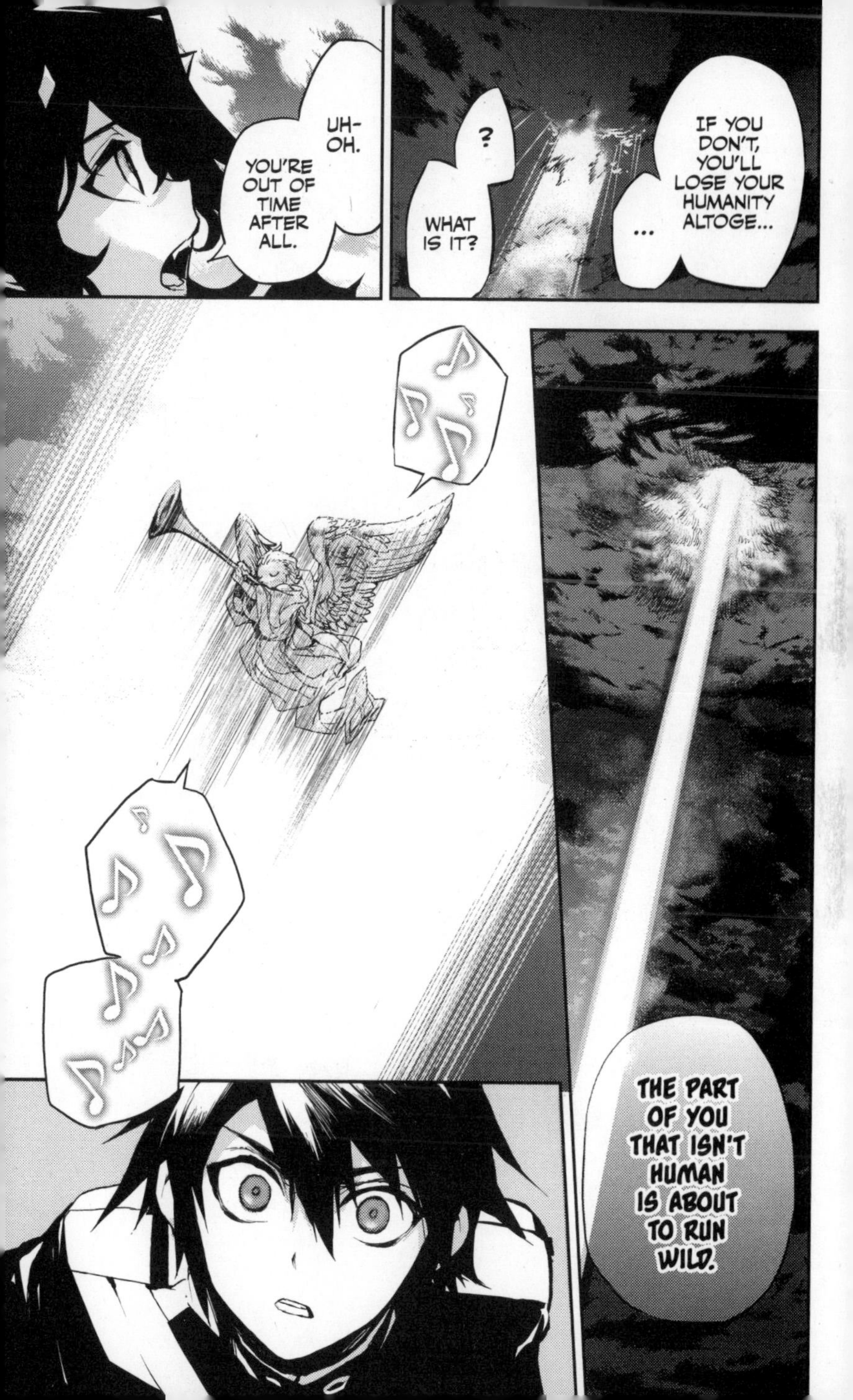
IF YOU DON'T, YOU'LL LOSE YOUR HUMANITY ALTOGE...
...
?
WHAT IS IT?
UH-OH.
YOU'RE OUT OF TIME AFTER ALL.
THE PART OF YOU THAT ISN'T HUMAN IS ABOUT TO RUN WILD.

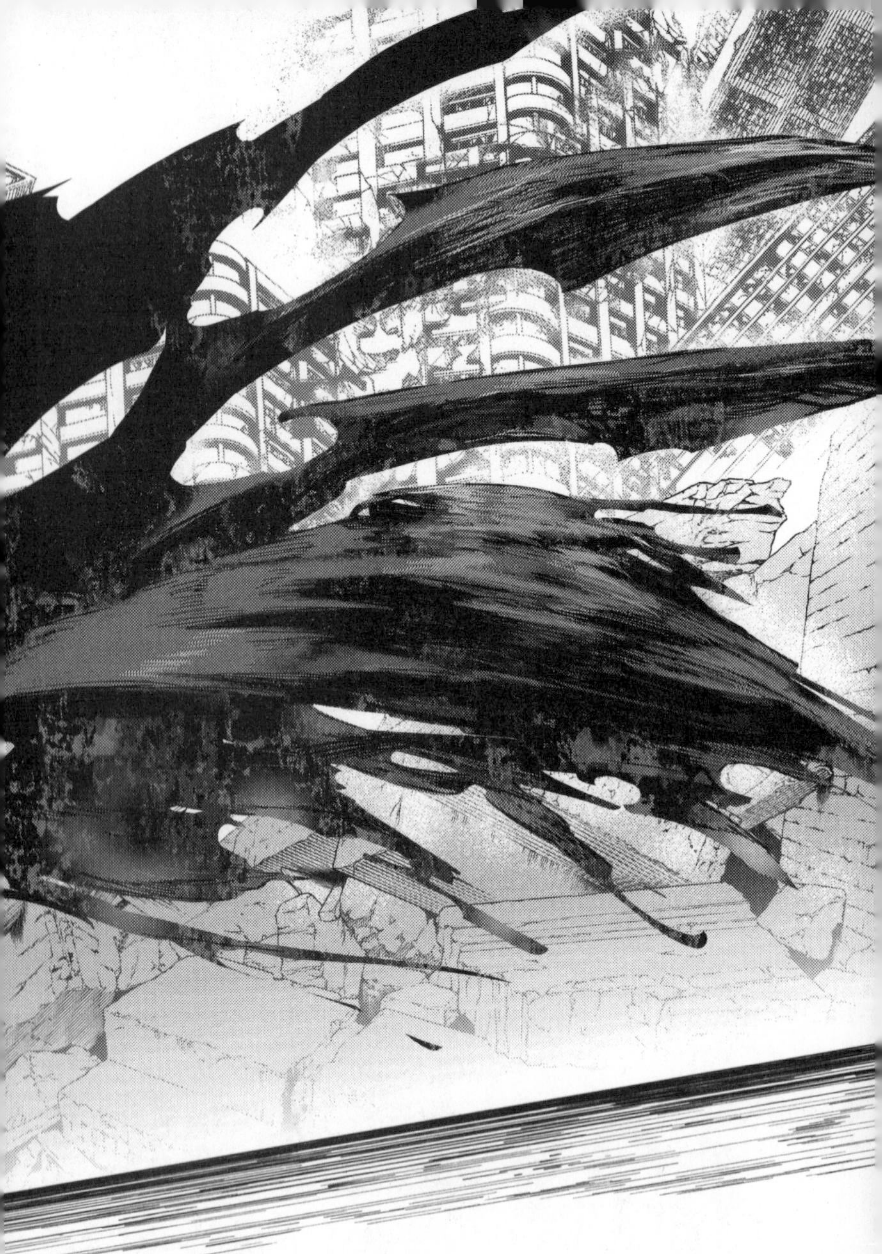

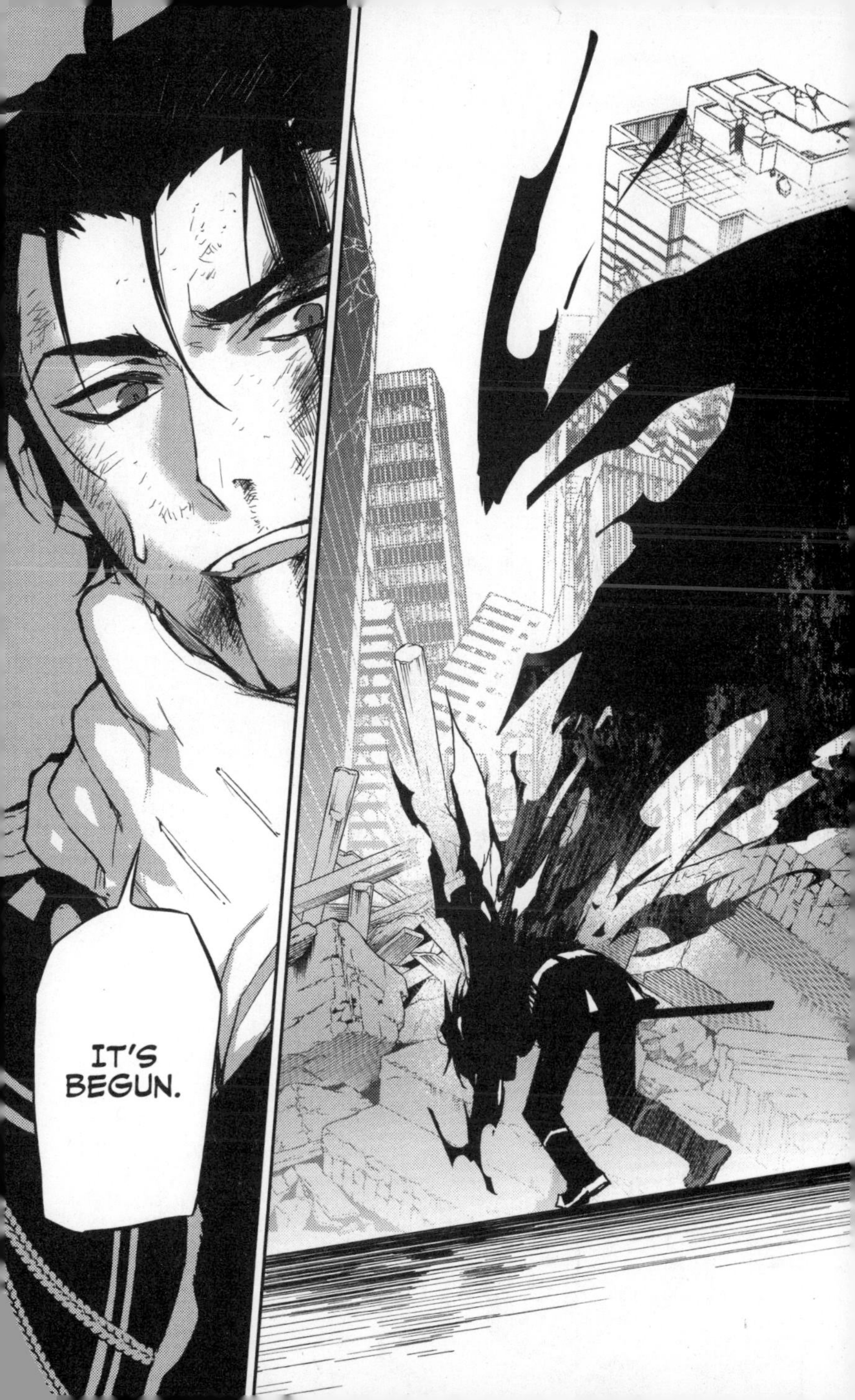
IT'S BEGUN.

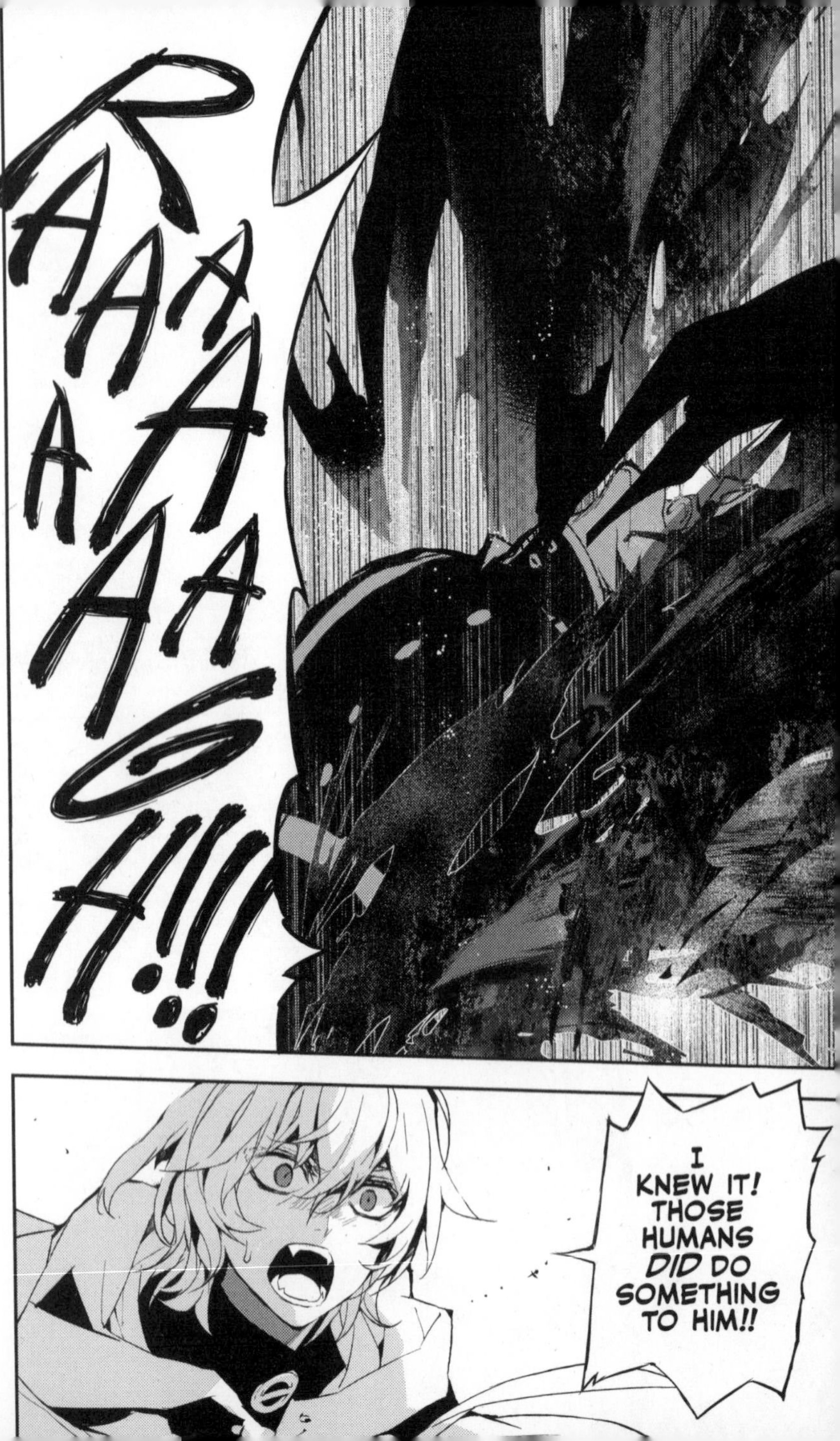
RAAAAAAAGH!!!
I KNEW IT! THOSE HUMANS *DID* DO SOMETHING TO HIM!!

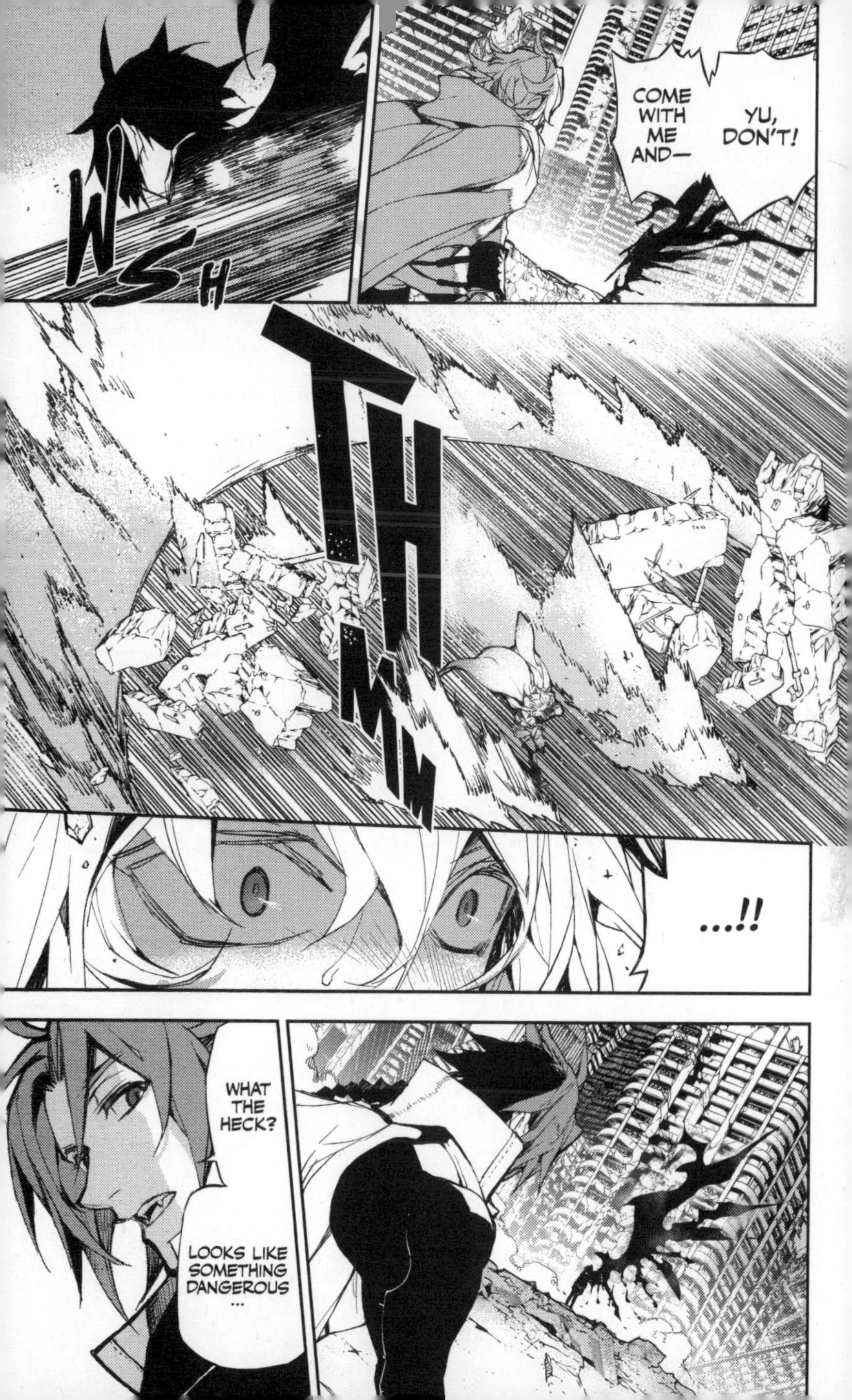
YU, DON'T!
COME WITH ME AND—
WSH
THMM
...!!
WHAT THE HECK?
LOOKS LIKE SOMETHING DANGEROUS ...

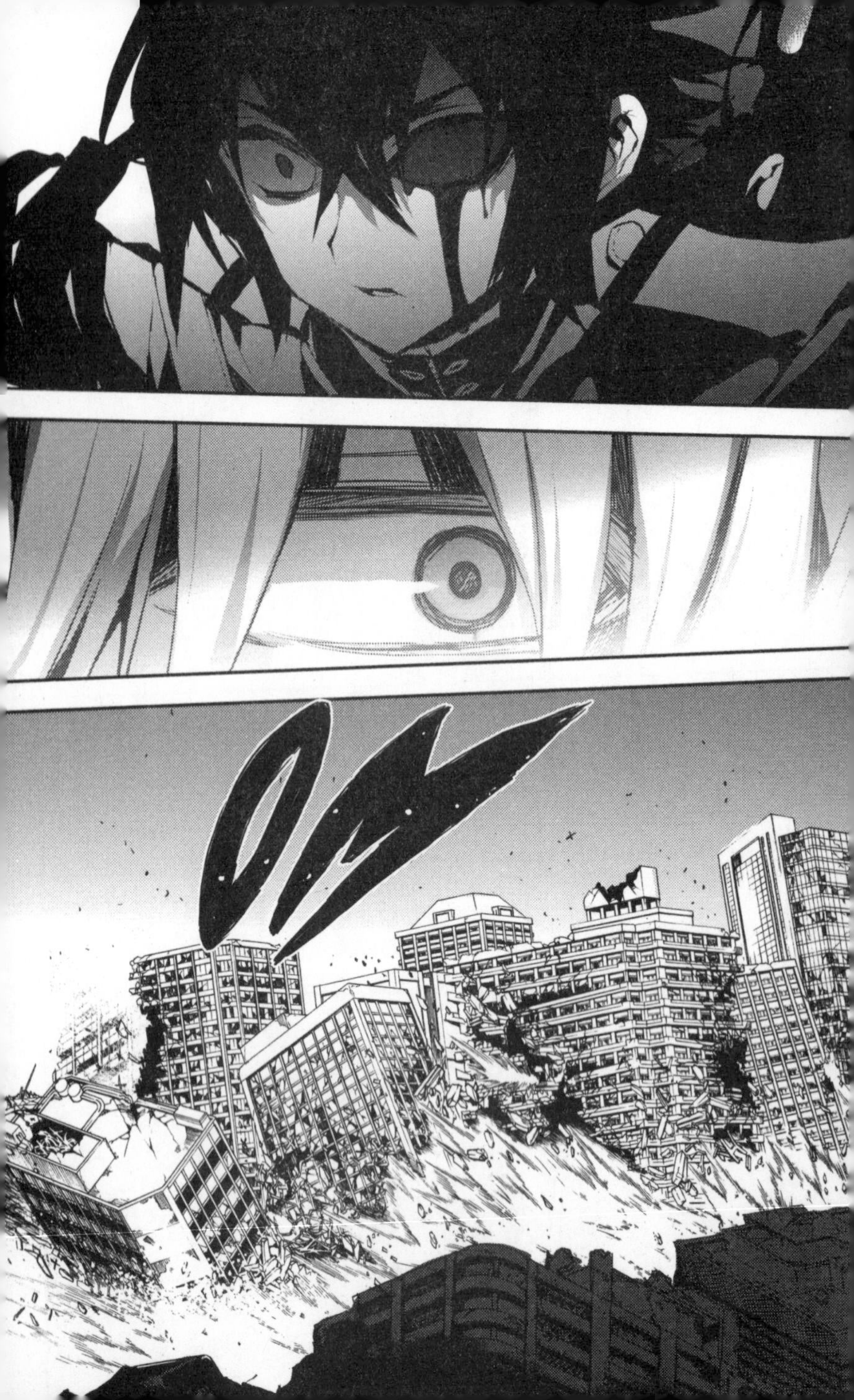

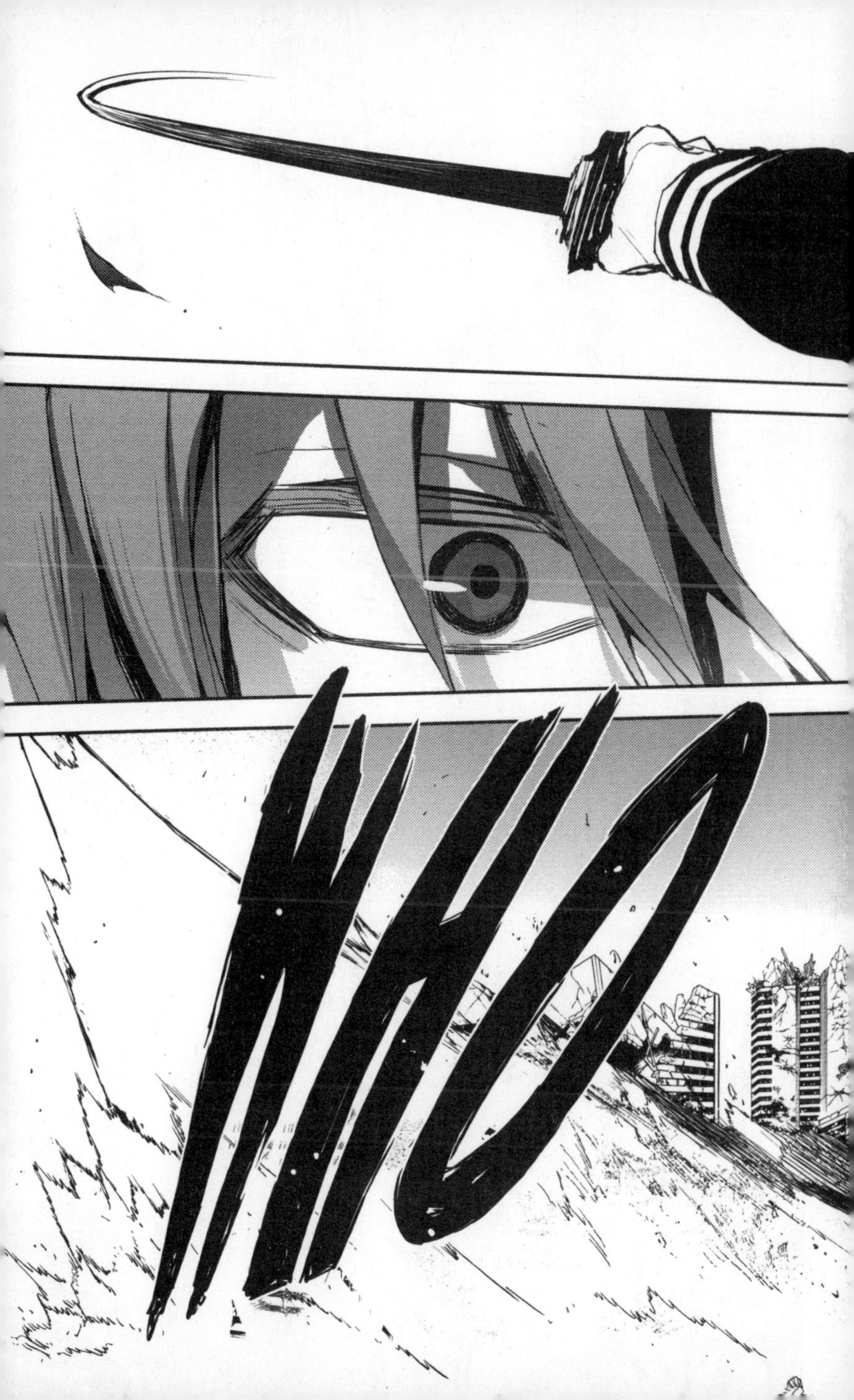
WHO

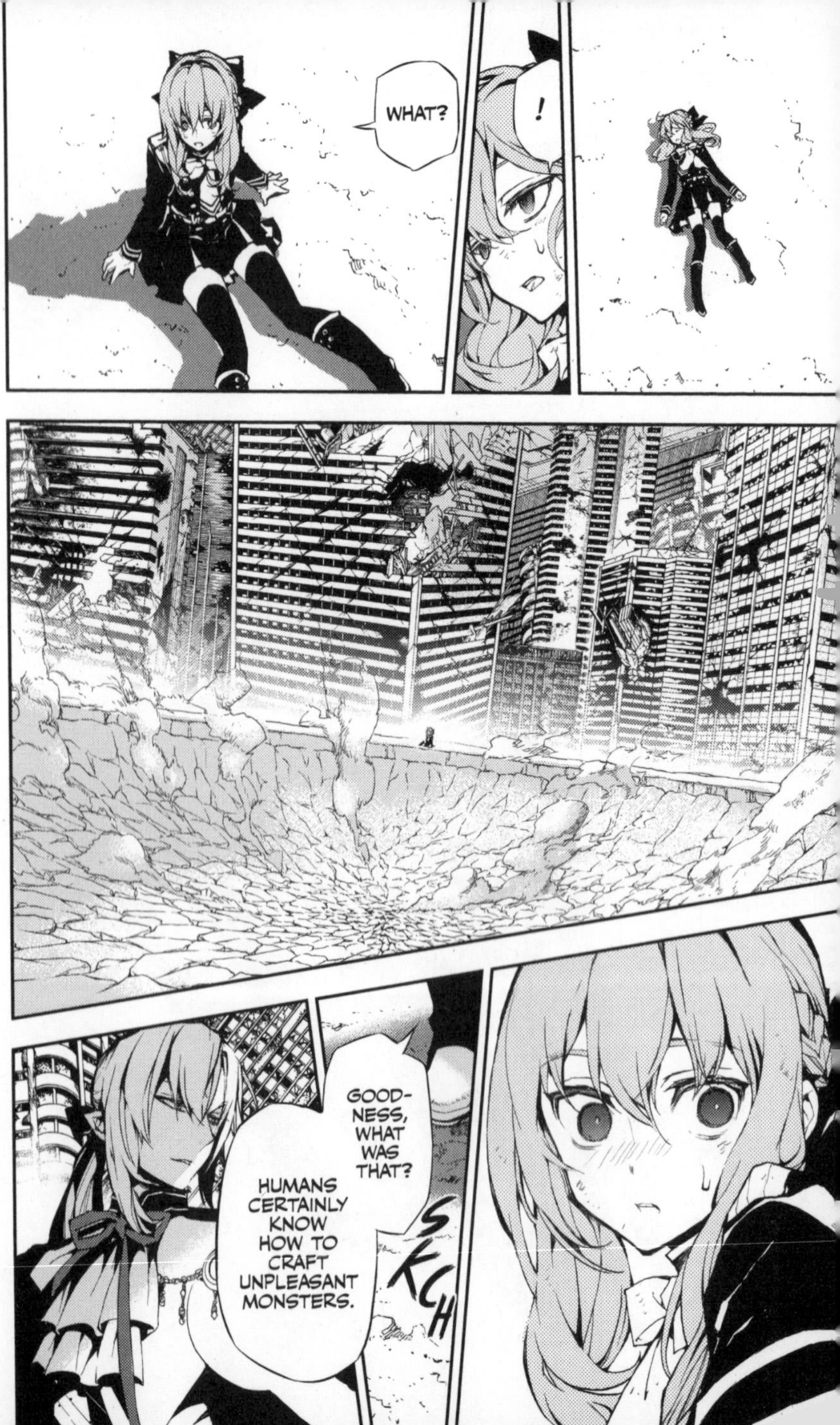
!
WHAT?
GOODNESS, WHAT WAS THAT?
HUMANS CERTAINLY KNOW HOW TO CRAFT UNPLEASANT MONSTERS.
SKCH

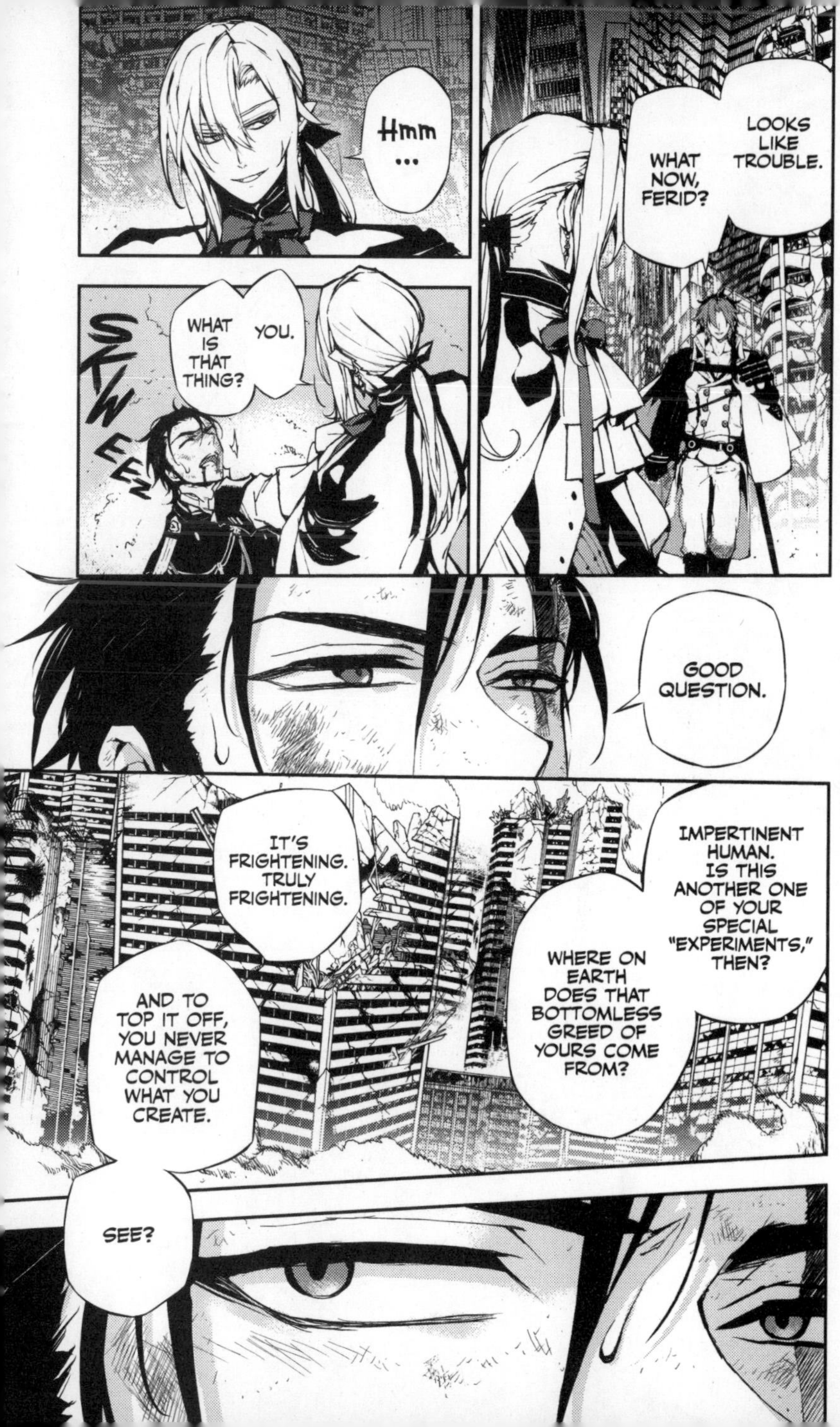
LOOKS LIKE TROUBLE.
WHAT NOW, FERID?
Hmm...
YOU.
WHAT IS THAT THING?
SKWEEZ
GOOD QUESTION.
IMPERTINENT HUMAN. IS THIS ANOTHER ONE OF YOUR SPECIAL "EXPERIMENTS," THEN?
WHERE ON EARTH DOES THAT BOTTOMLESS GREED OF YOURS COME FROM?
IT'S FRIGHTENING. TRULY FRIGHTENING.
AND TO TOP IT OFF, YOU NEVER MANAGE TO CONTROL WHAT YOU CREATE.
SEE?

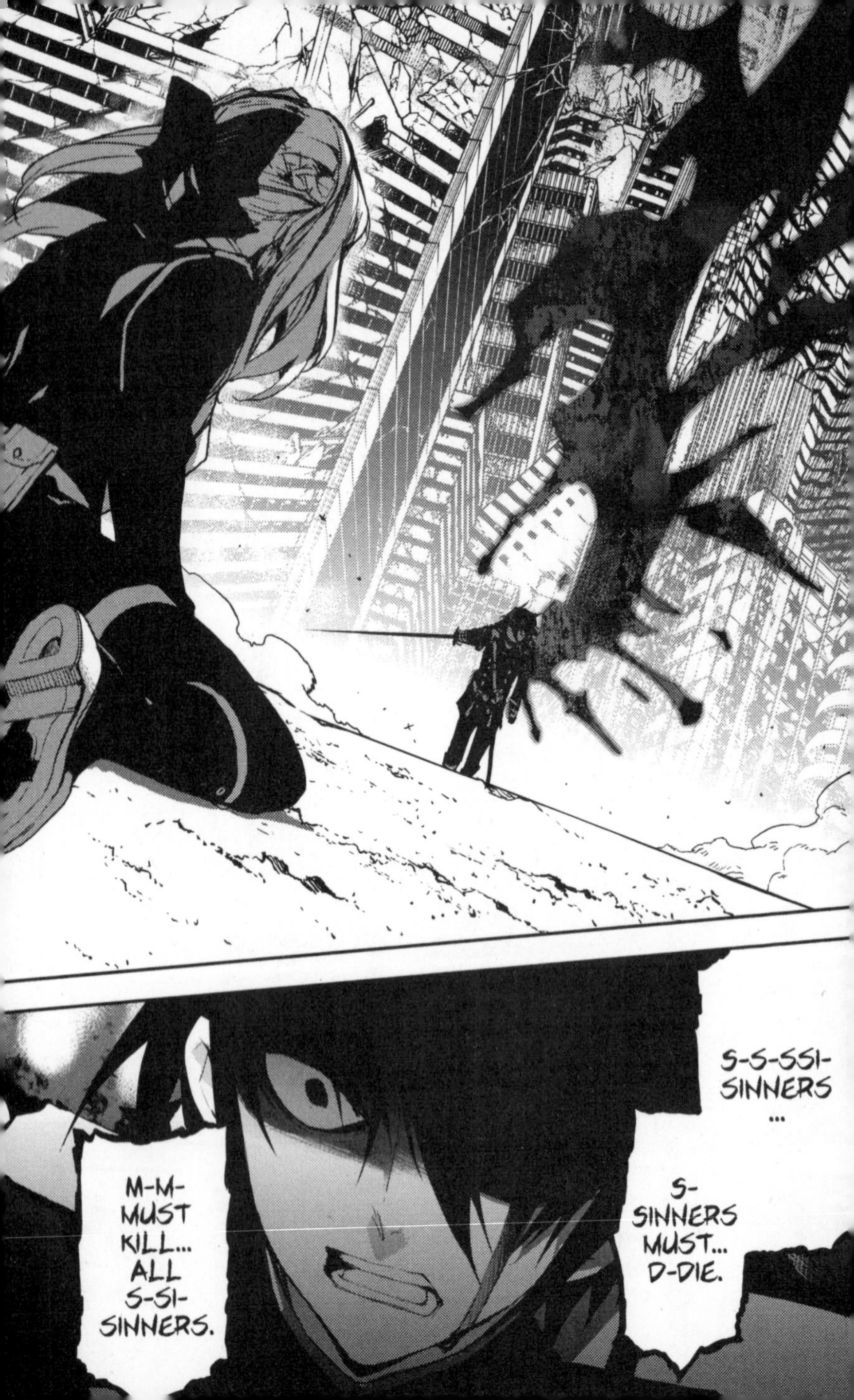
S-S-SSI-SINNERS ...
S-SINNERS MUST... D-DIE.
M-M-MUST KILL... ALL S-SI-SINNERS.

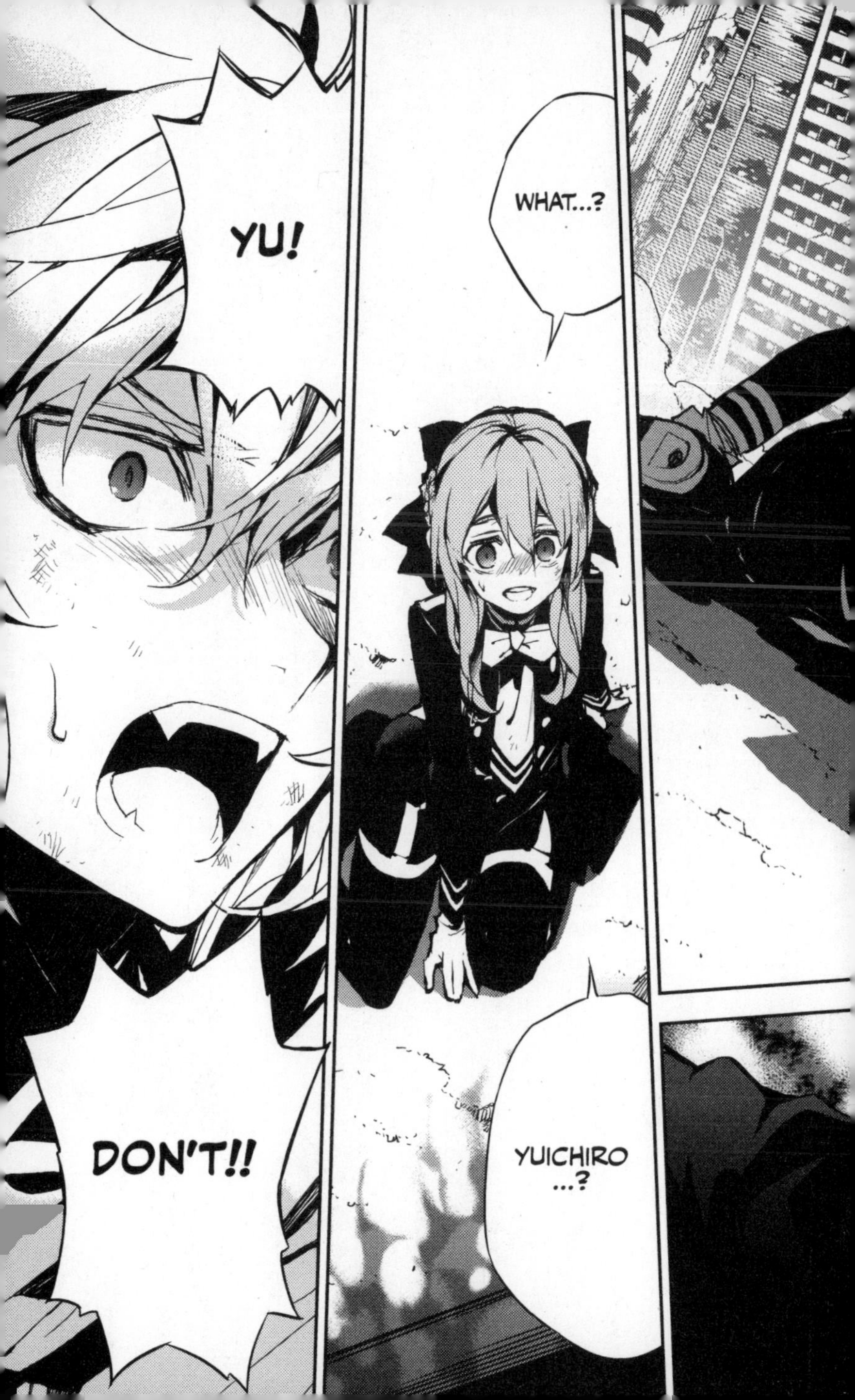
WHAT...?
YUICHIRO ...?
YU!
DON'T!!

Seraph of the End
VAMPIRE REIGN

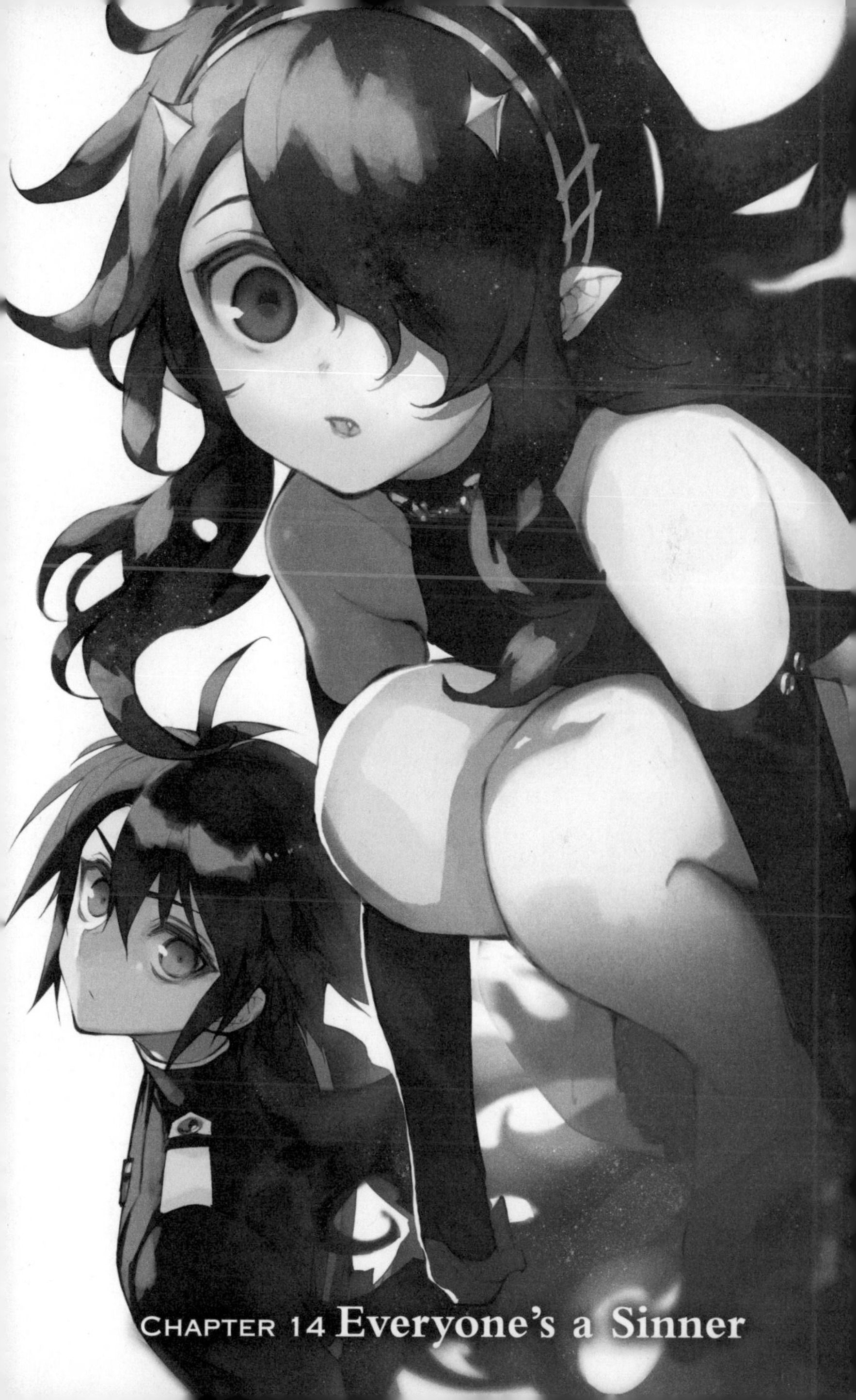

Chapter 14 Everyone's a Sinner

Seraph of the End
VAMPIRE REIGN

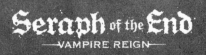

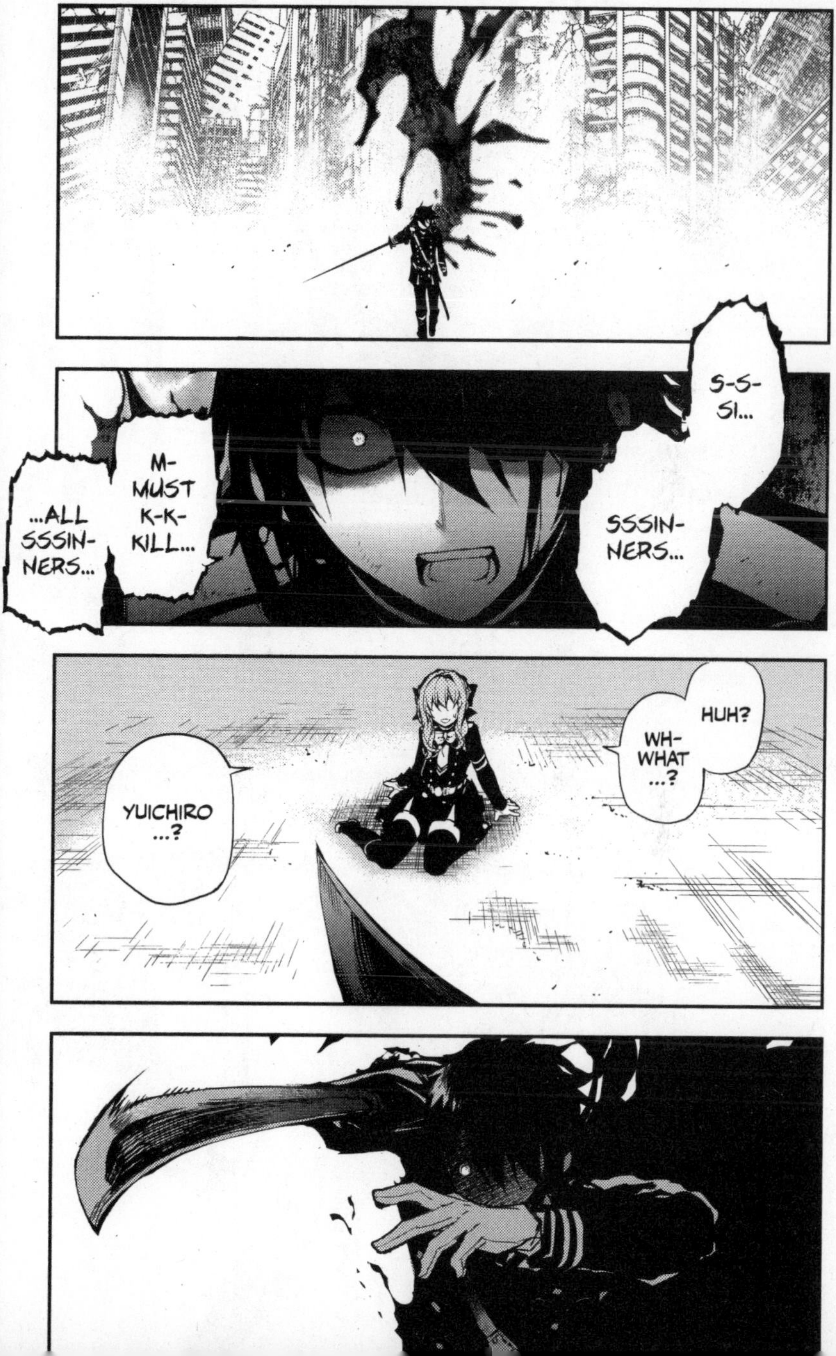
S-S-SI...
SSSIN-NERS...
M-MUST K-K-KILL...
...ALL SSSIN-NERS...
HUH? WH-WHAT...?
YUICHIRO...?

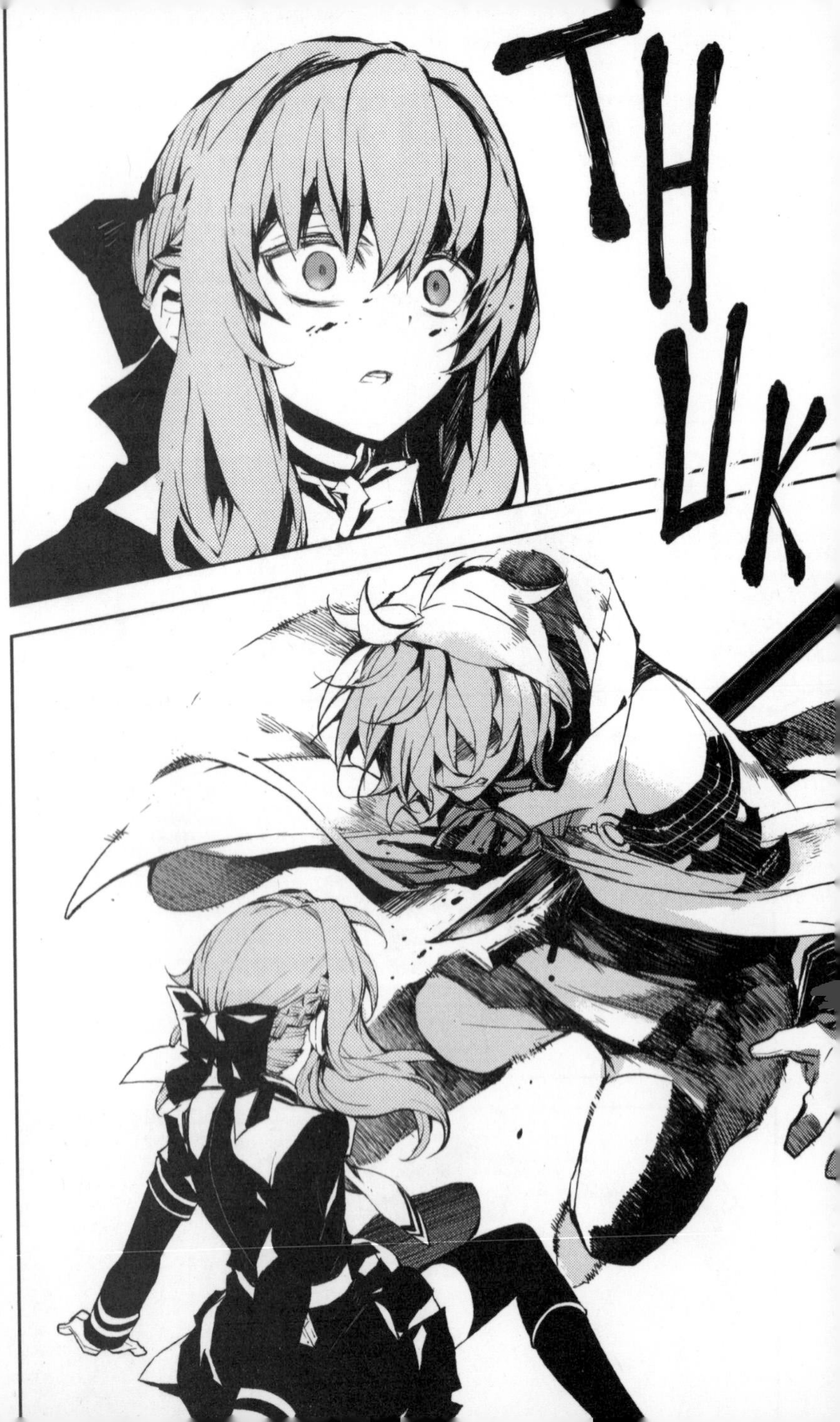
THUK

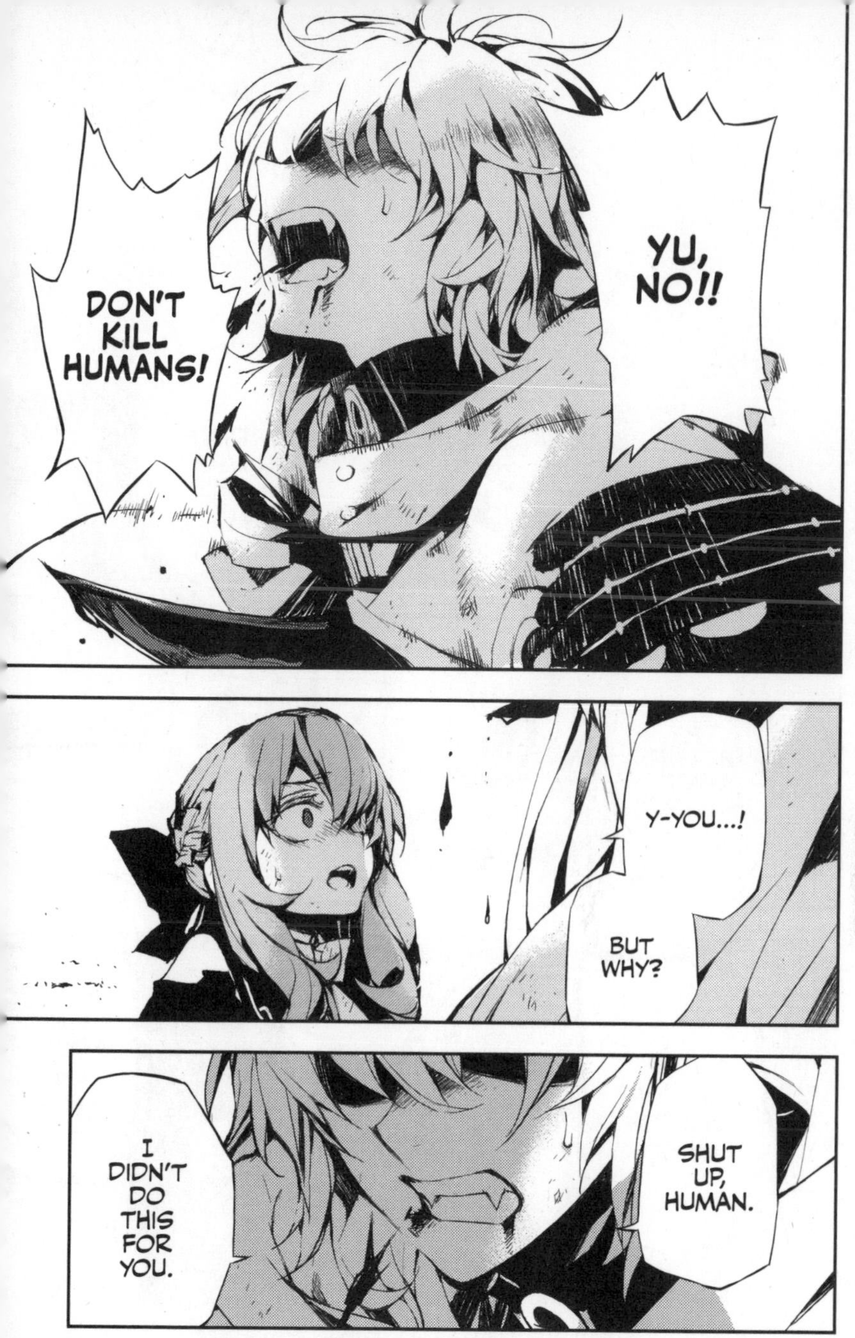
YU, NO!!
DON'T KILL HUMANS!
Y-YOU...!
BUT WHY?
SHUT UP, HUMAN.
I DIDN'T DO THIS FOR YOU.

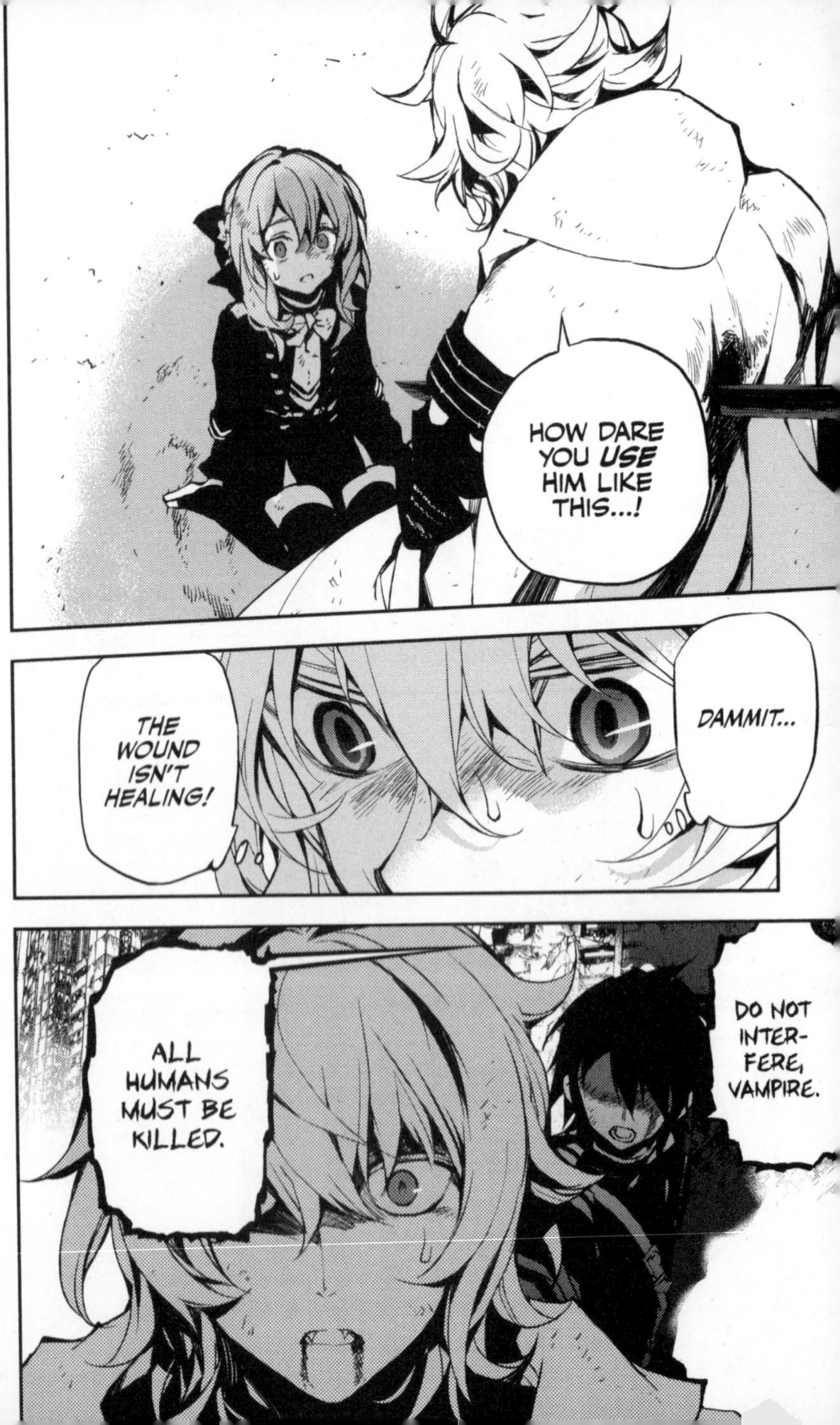
HOW DARE YOU USE HIM LIKE THIS...!
DAMMIT...
THE WOUND ISN'T HEALING!
DO NOT INTER-FERE, VAMPIRE.
ALL HUMANS MUST BE KILLED.

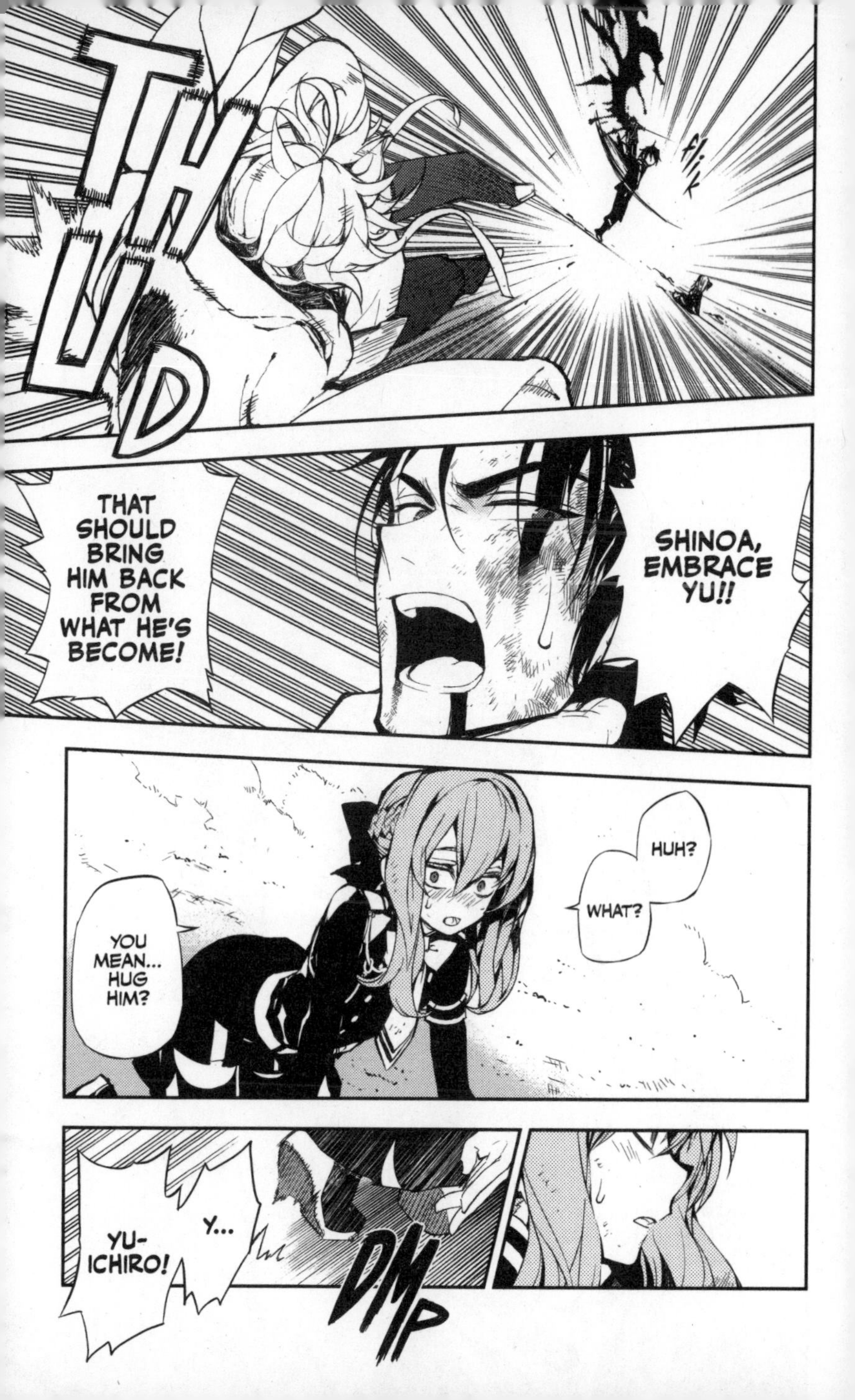
flik
THUD
SHINOA, EMBRACE YU!!
THAT SHOULD BRING HIM BACK FROM WHAT HE'S BECOME!
HUH?
WHAT?
YOU MEAN... HUG HIM?
Y...
YU-ICHIRO!
DMP

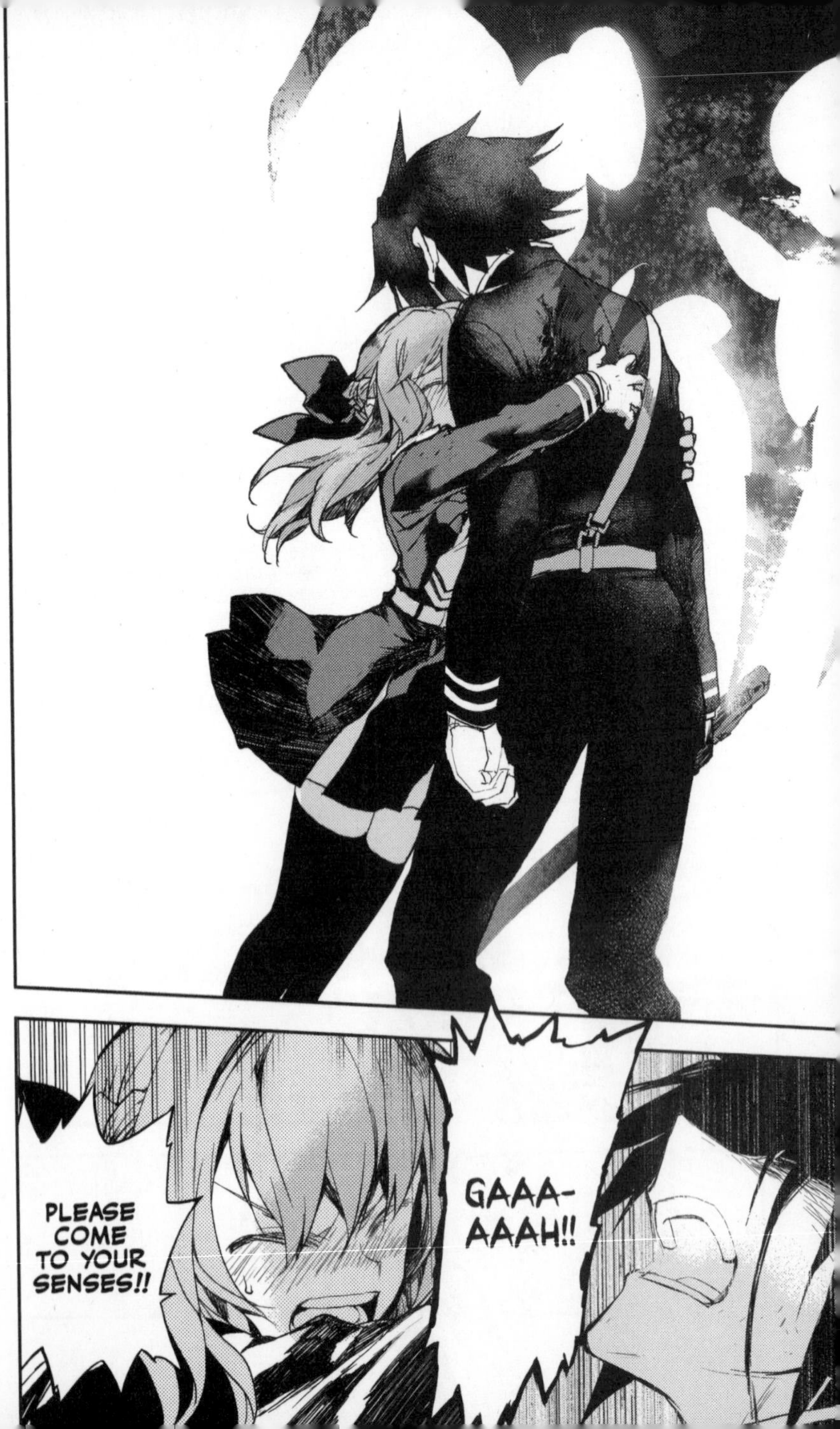
GAAA-AAAH!!
PLEASE COME TO YOUR SENSES!!

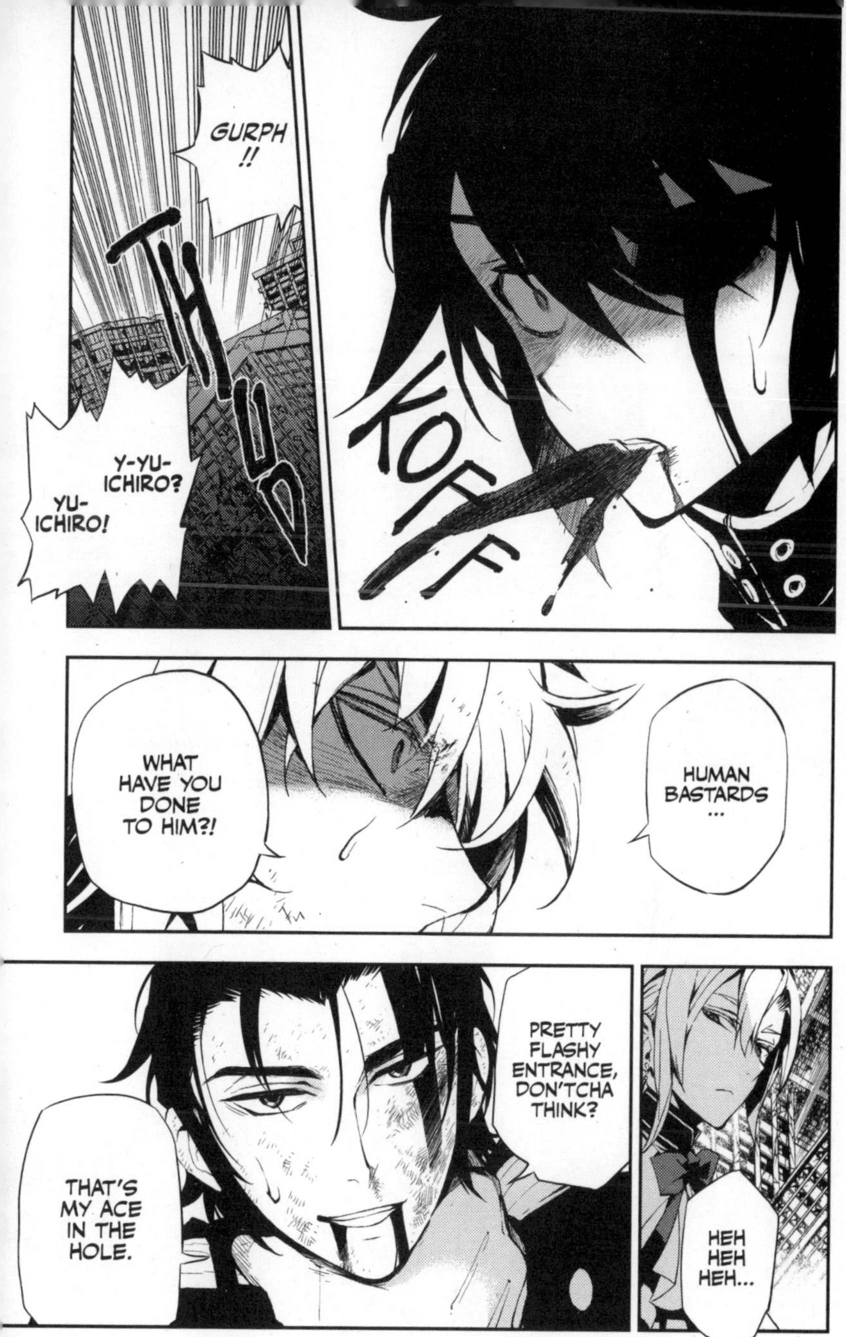
KOFF
GURPH !!
THUD
Y-YU-ICHIRO?
YU-ICHIRO!
HUMAN BASTARDS ...
WHAT HAVE YOU DONE TO HIM?!
HEH HEH HEH...
PRETTY FLASHY ENTRANCE, DON'TCHA THINK?
THAT'S MY ACE IN THE HOLE.

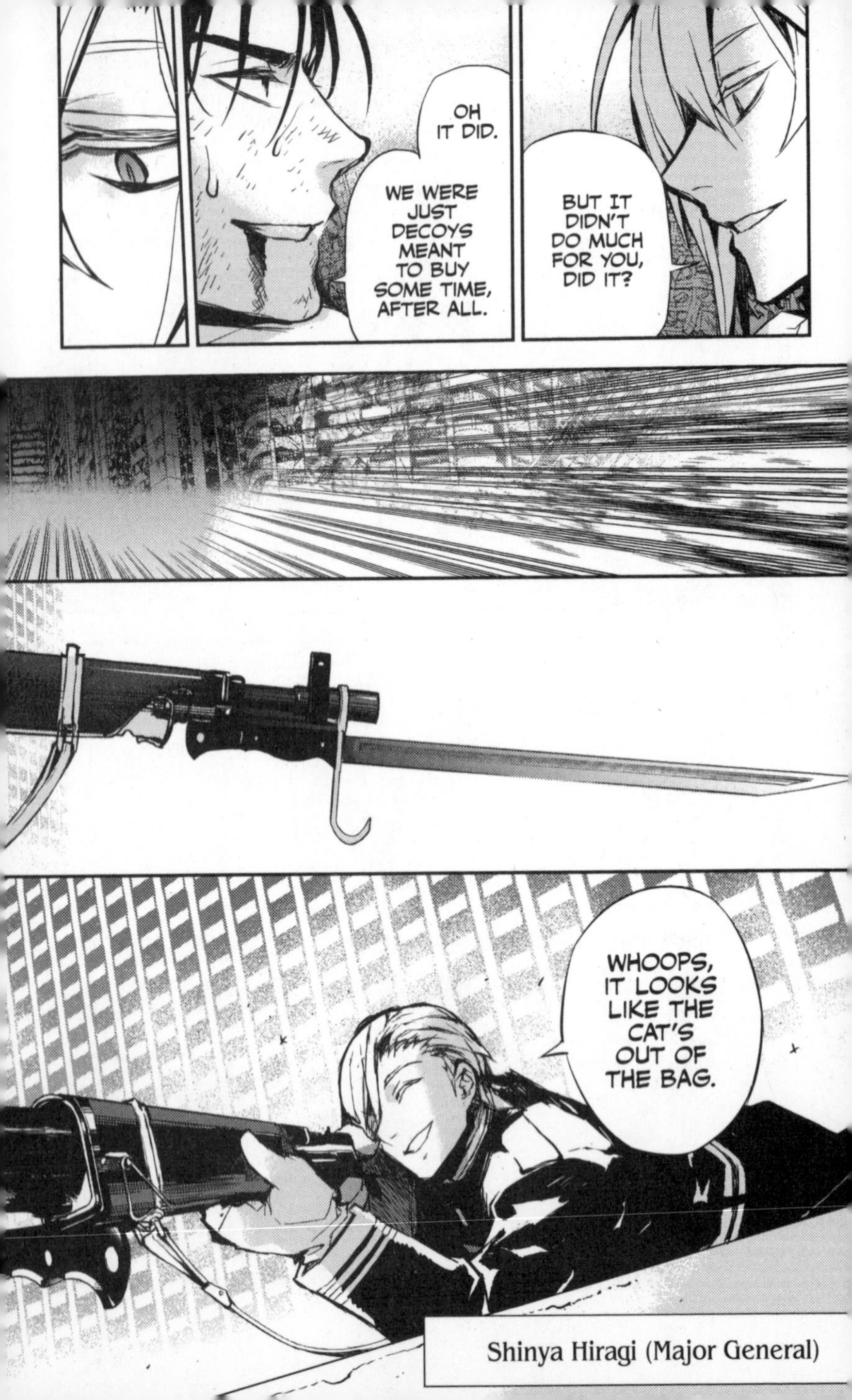
BUT IT DIDN'T DO MUCH FOR YOU, DID IT?
OH IT DID.
WE WERE JUST DECOYS MEANT TO BUY SOME TIME, AFTER ALL.
WHOOPS, IT LOOKS LIKE THE CAT'S OUT OF THE BAG.
Shinya Hiragi (Major General)

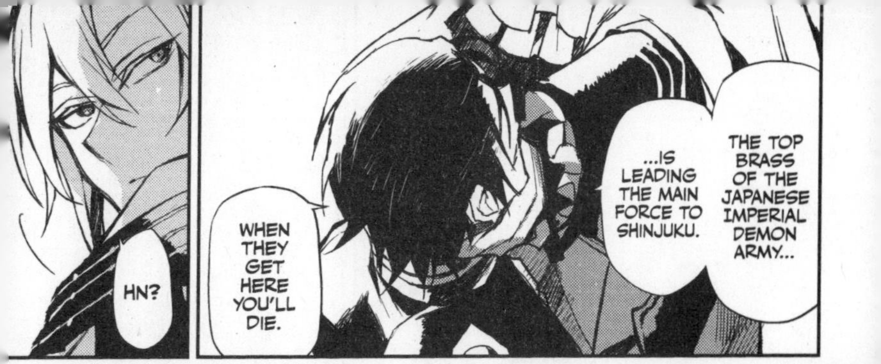
THE TOP BRASS OF THE JAPANESE IMPERIAL DEMON ARMY...
...IS LEADING THE MAIN FORCE TO SHINJUKU.
WHEN THEY GET HERE YOU'LL DIE.
HN?

*Ed: Byakkomaru = "White Tiger"

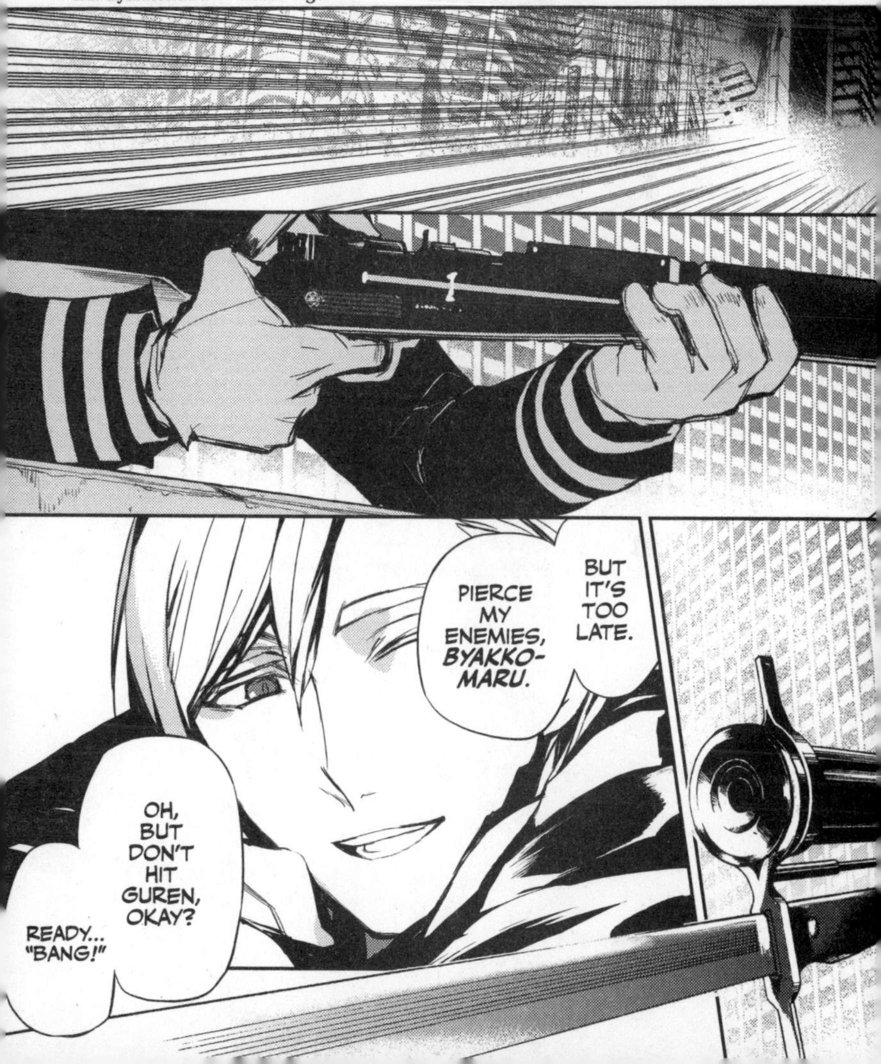
BUT IT'S TOO LATE.
PIERCE MY ENEMIES, *BYAKKO-MARU.*
OH, BUT DON'T HIT GUREN, OKAY?
READY... "BANG!"

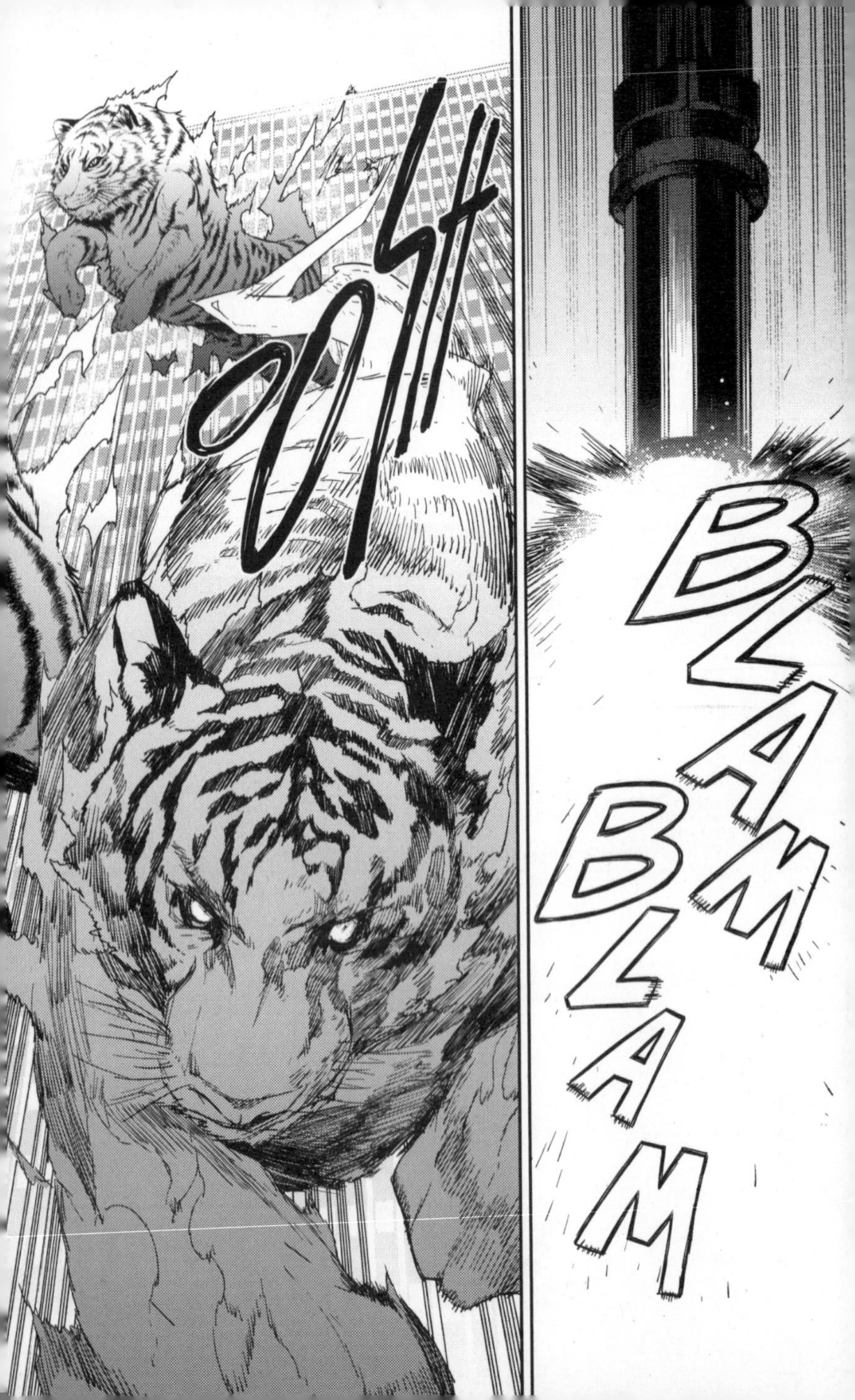
BLAM
BLAM

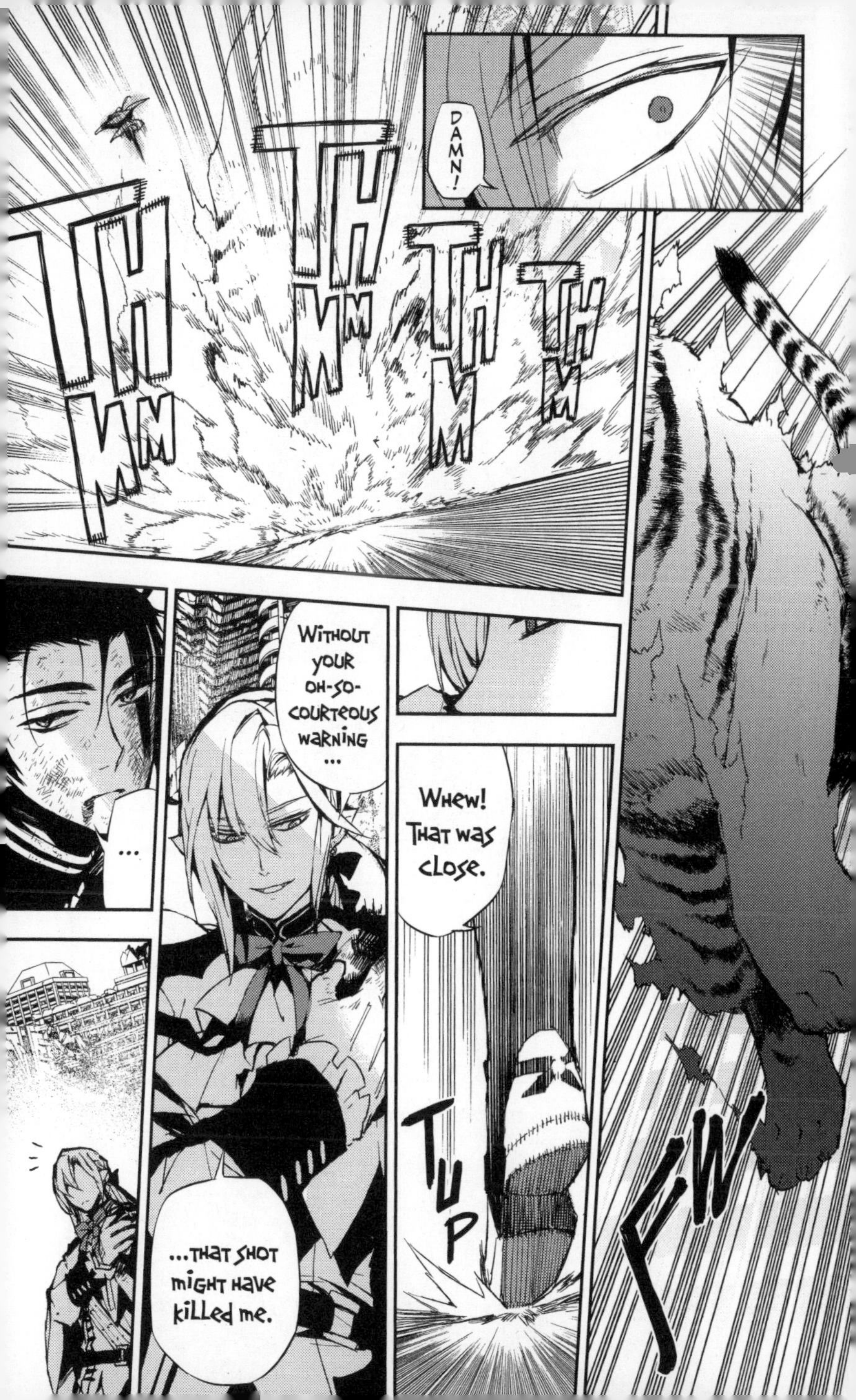

DAMN!
THMM
THMM
THMM
THMM
FW
WHEW! THAT WAS CLOSE.
TUP
WITHOUT YOUR OH-SO-COURTEOUS WARNING...
...THAT SHOT MIGHT HAVE KILLED ME.
...

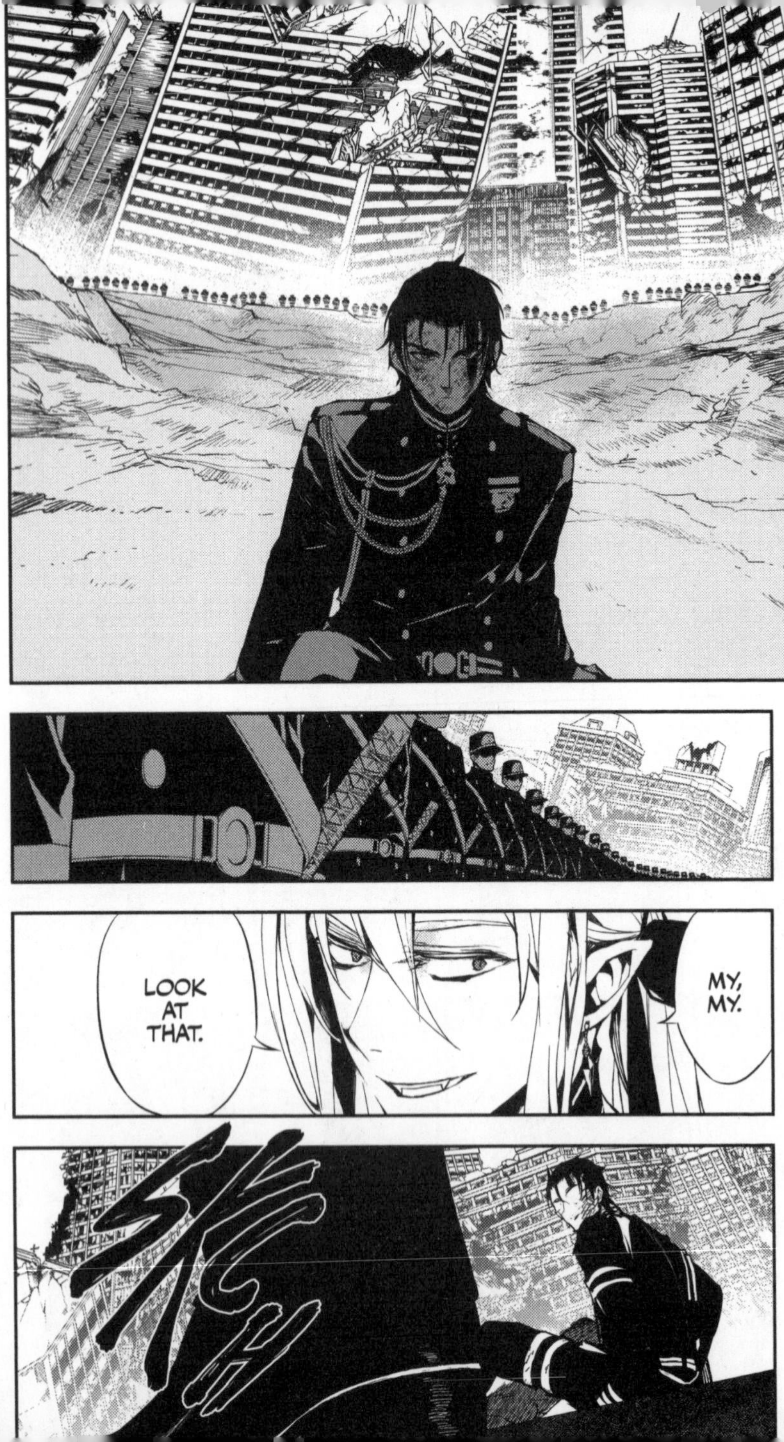
MY, MY.
LOOK AT THAT.

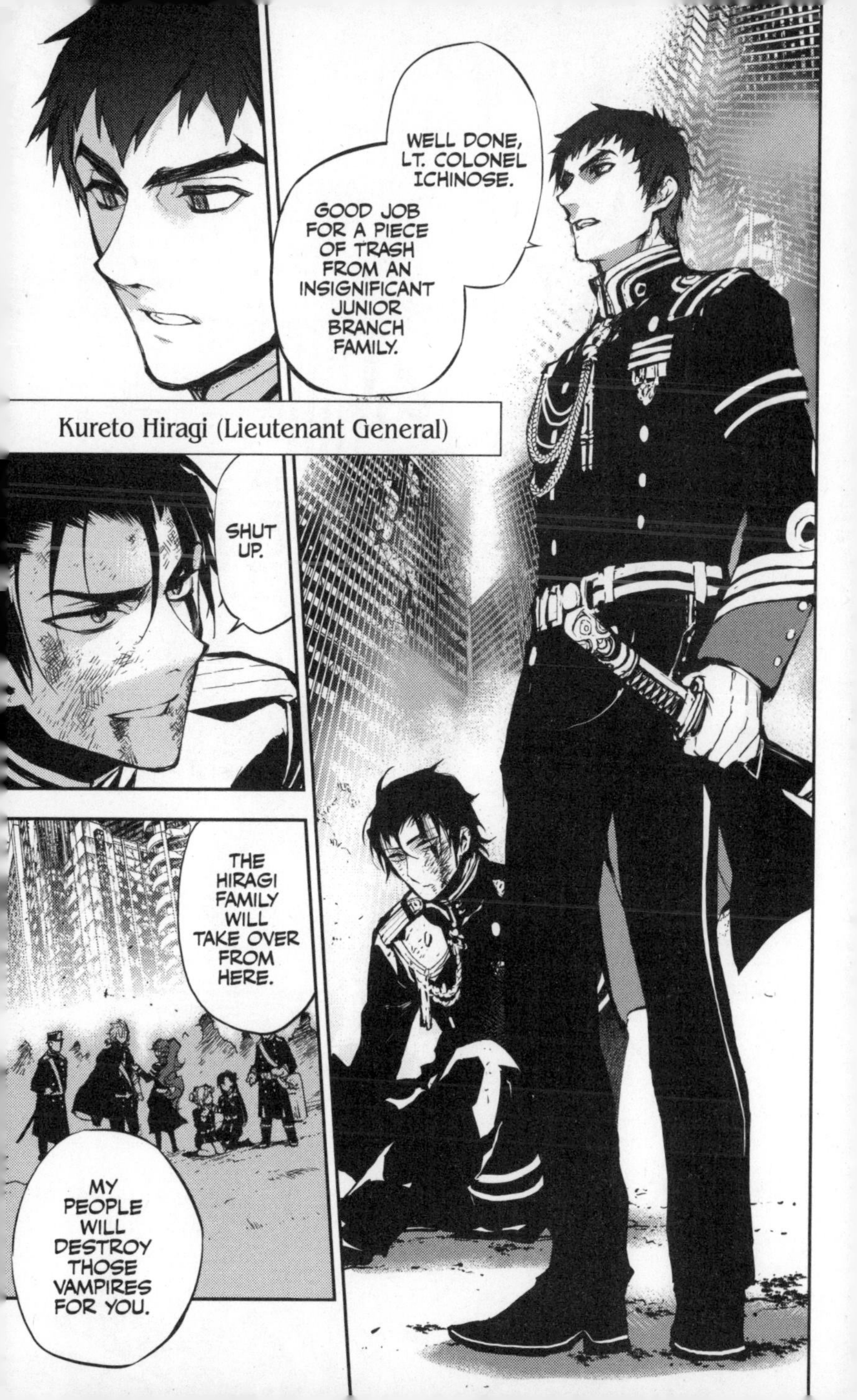
WELL DONE, LT. COLONEL ICHINOSE.
GOOD JOB FOR A PIECE OF TRASH FROM AN INSIGNIFICANT JUNIOR BRANCH FAMILY.
Kureto Hiragi (Lieutenant General)
SHUT UP.
THE HIRAGI FAMILY WILL TAKE OVER FROM HERE.
MY PEOPLE WILL DESTROY THOSE VAMPIRES FOR YOU.

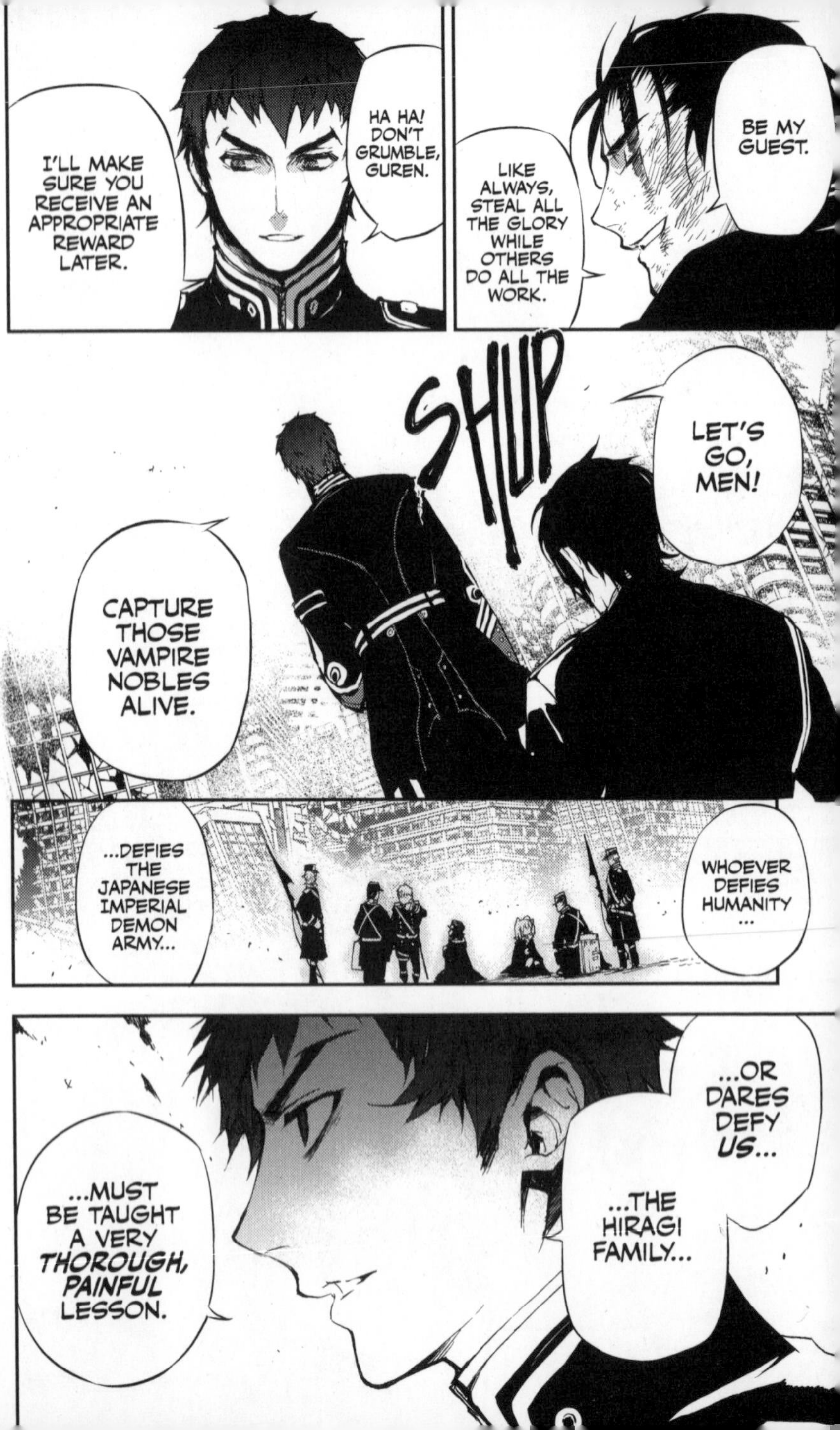
BE MY GUEST.
LIKE ALWAYS, STEAL ALL THE GLORY WHILE OTHERS DO ALL THE WORK.
HA HA! DON'T GRUMBLE, GUREN.
I'LL MAKE SURE YOU RECEIVE AN APPROPRIATE REWARD LATER.
SHUP
LET'S GO, MEN!
CAPTURE THOSE VAMPIRE NOBLES ALIVE.
WHOEVER DEFIES HUMANITY ...
...DEFIES THE JAPANESE IMPERIAL DEMON ARMY...
...OR DARES DEFY *US*...
...THE HIRAGI FAMILY...
...MUST BE TAUGHT A VERY *THOROUGH, PAINFUL* LESSON.

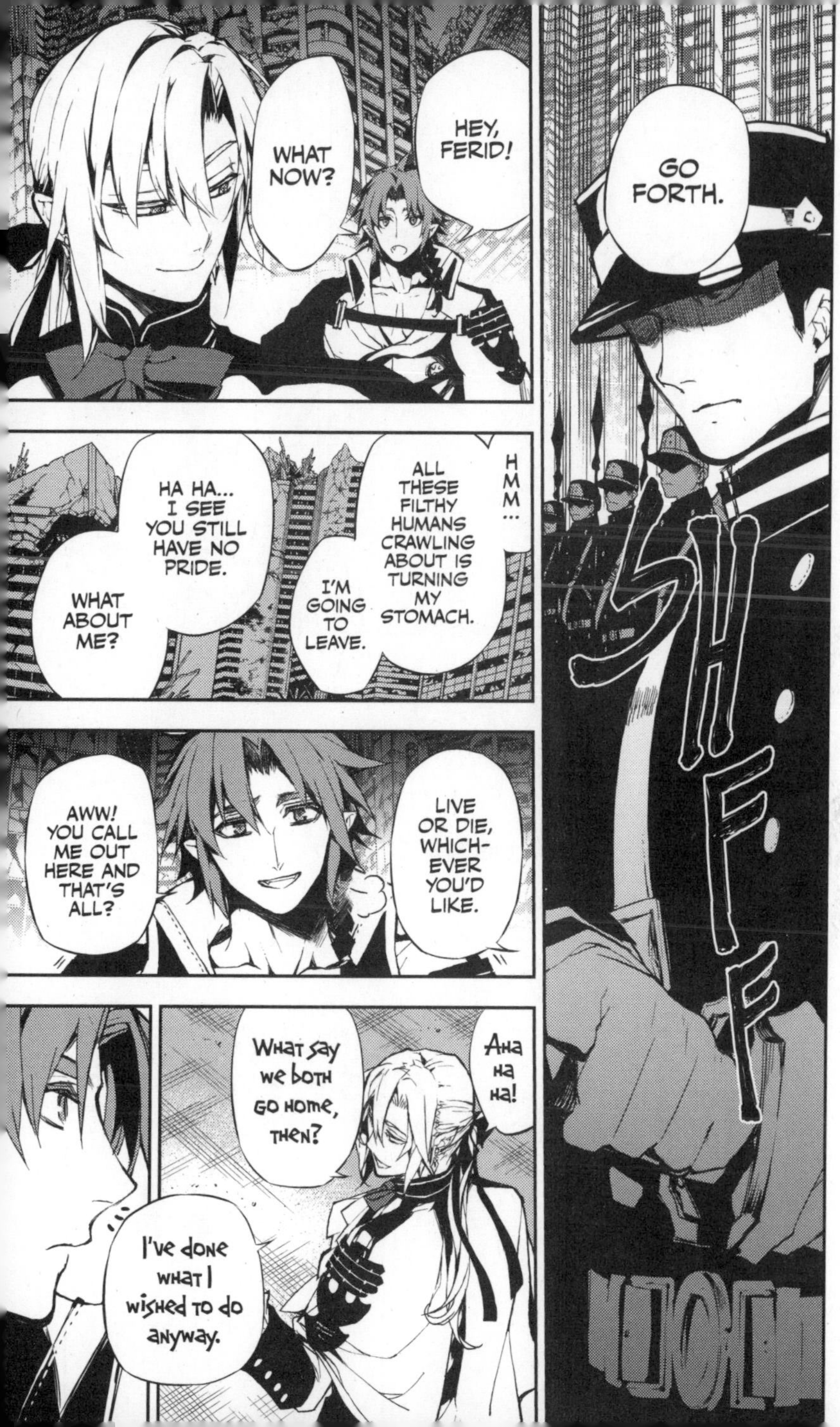
GO FORTH.
SHFF
HEY, FERID!
WHAT NOW?
HMM...
ALL THESE FILTHY HUMANS CRAWLING ABOUT IS TURNING MY STOMACH.
I'M GOING TO LEAVE.
HA HA... I SEE YOU STILL HAVE NO PRIDE.
WHAT ABOUT ME?
LIVE OR DIE, WHICH-EVER YOU'D LIKE.
AWW! YOU CALL ME OUT HERE AND THAT'S ALL?
Aha ha ha!
What say we both go home, then?
I've done what I wished to do anyway.

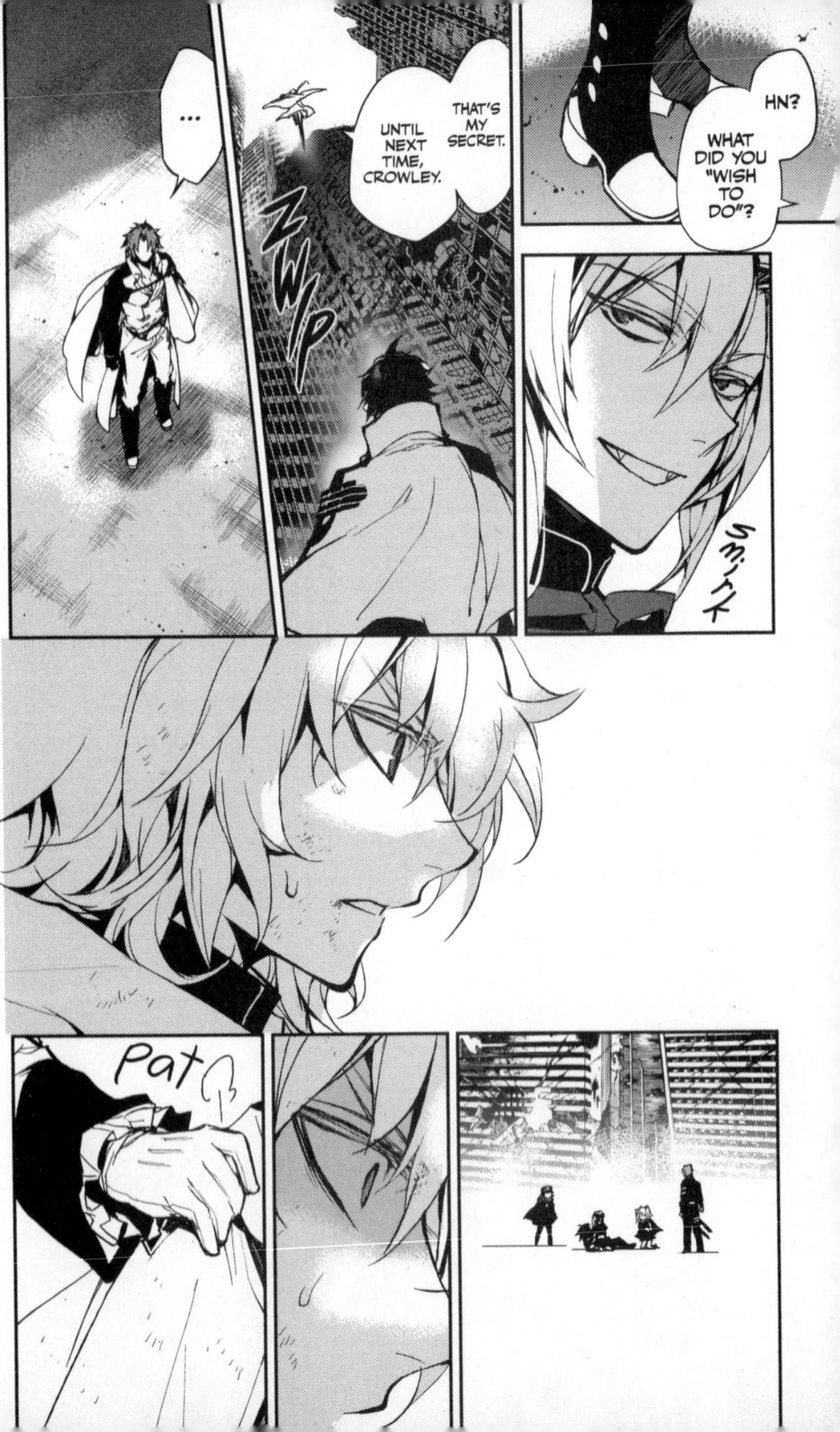
HN?
WHAT DID YOU "WISH TO DO"?
SMIRK
THAT'S MY SECRET.
UNTIL NEXT TIME, CROWLEY.
ZWIP
...
Pat

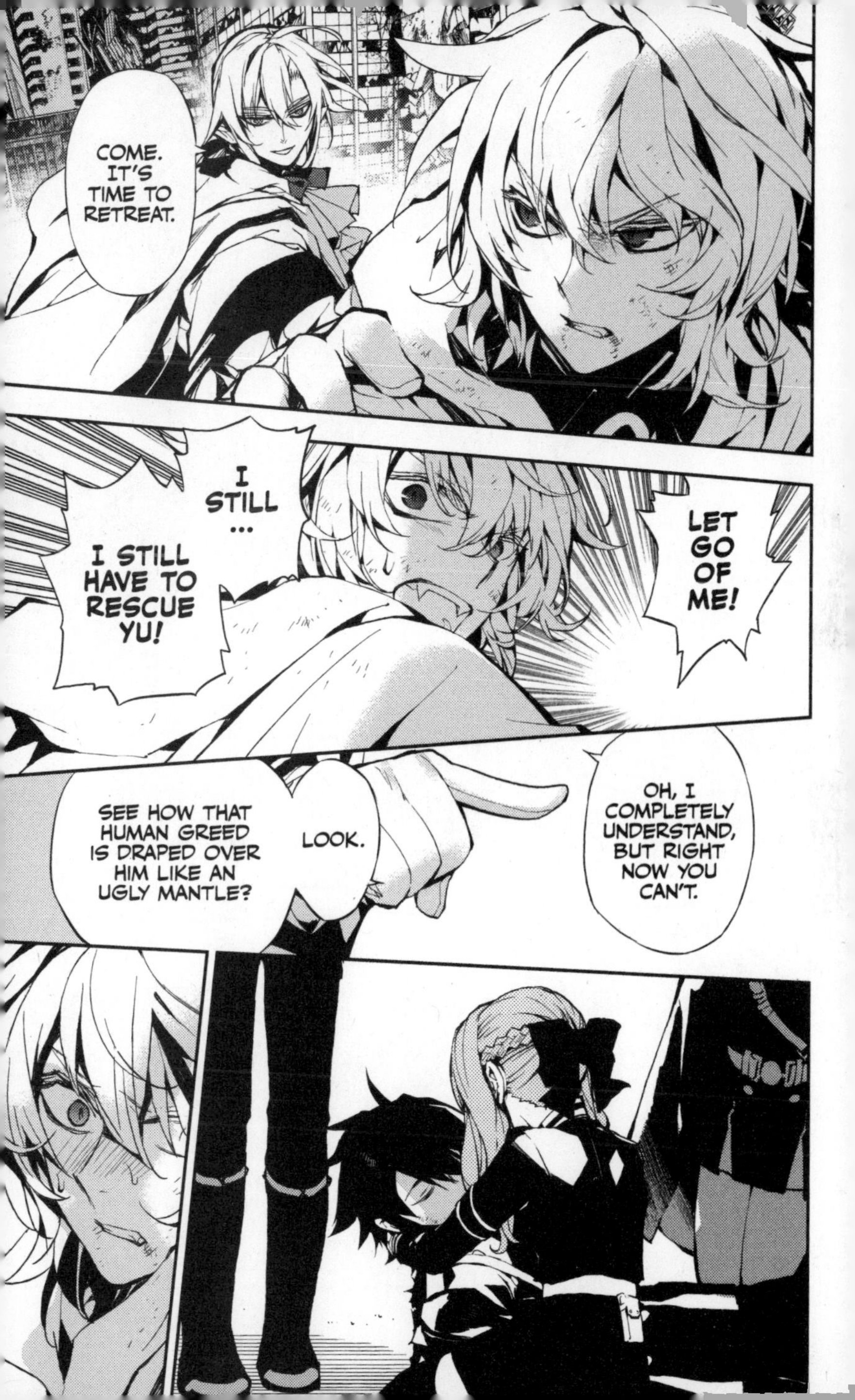
COME. IT'S TIME TO RETREAT.
LET GO OF ME!
I STILL...
I STILL HAVE TO RESCUE YU!
OH, I COMPLETELY UNDERSTAND, BUT RIGHT NOW YOU CAN'T.
LOOK.
SEE HOW THAT HUMAN GREED IS DRAPED OVER HIM LIKE AN UGLY MANTLE?

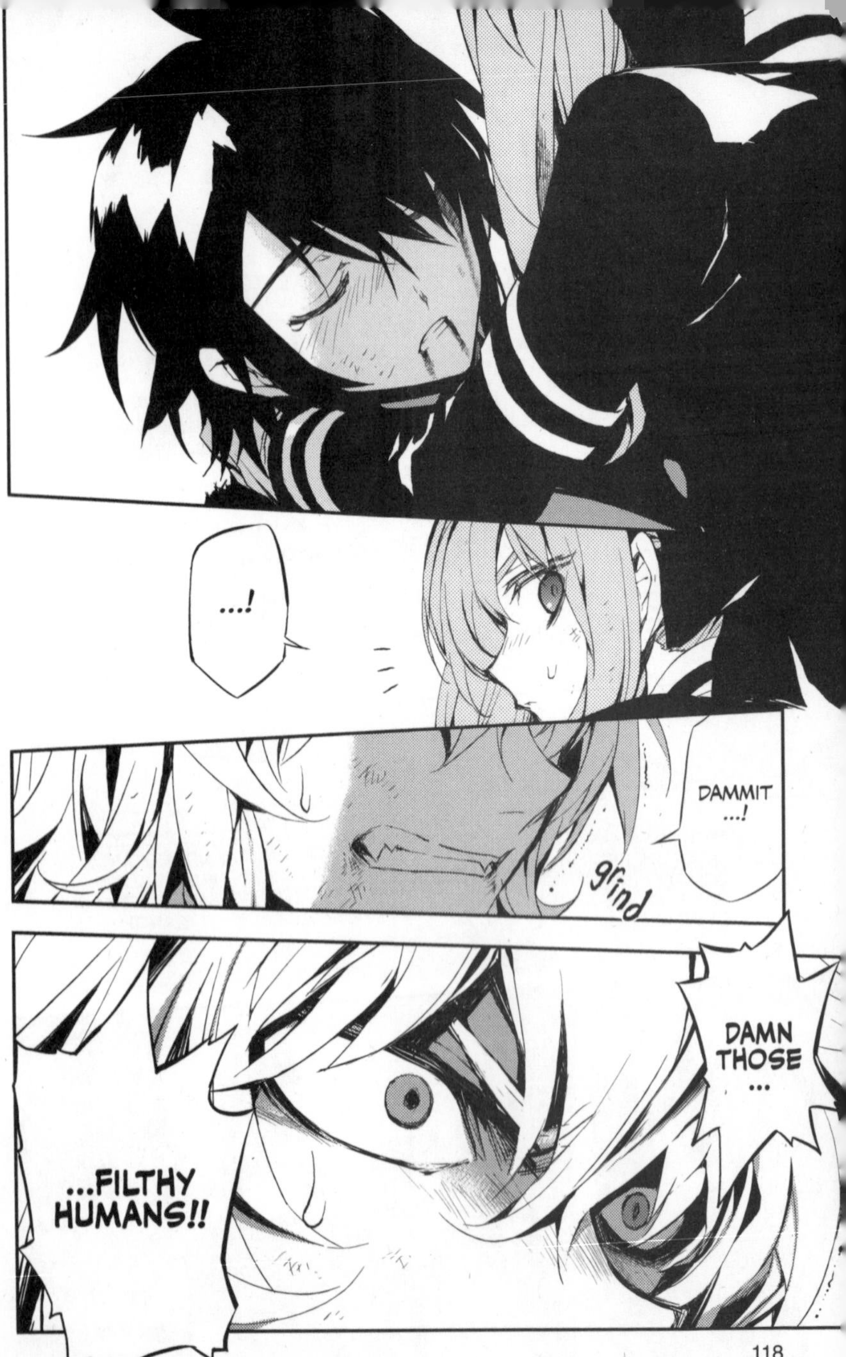
...!
DAMMIT ...!
grind
DAMN THOSE ...
...FILTHY HUMANS!!

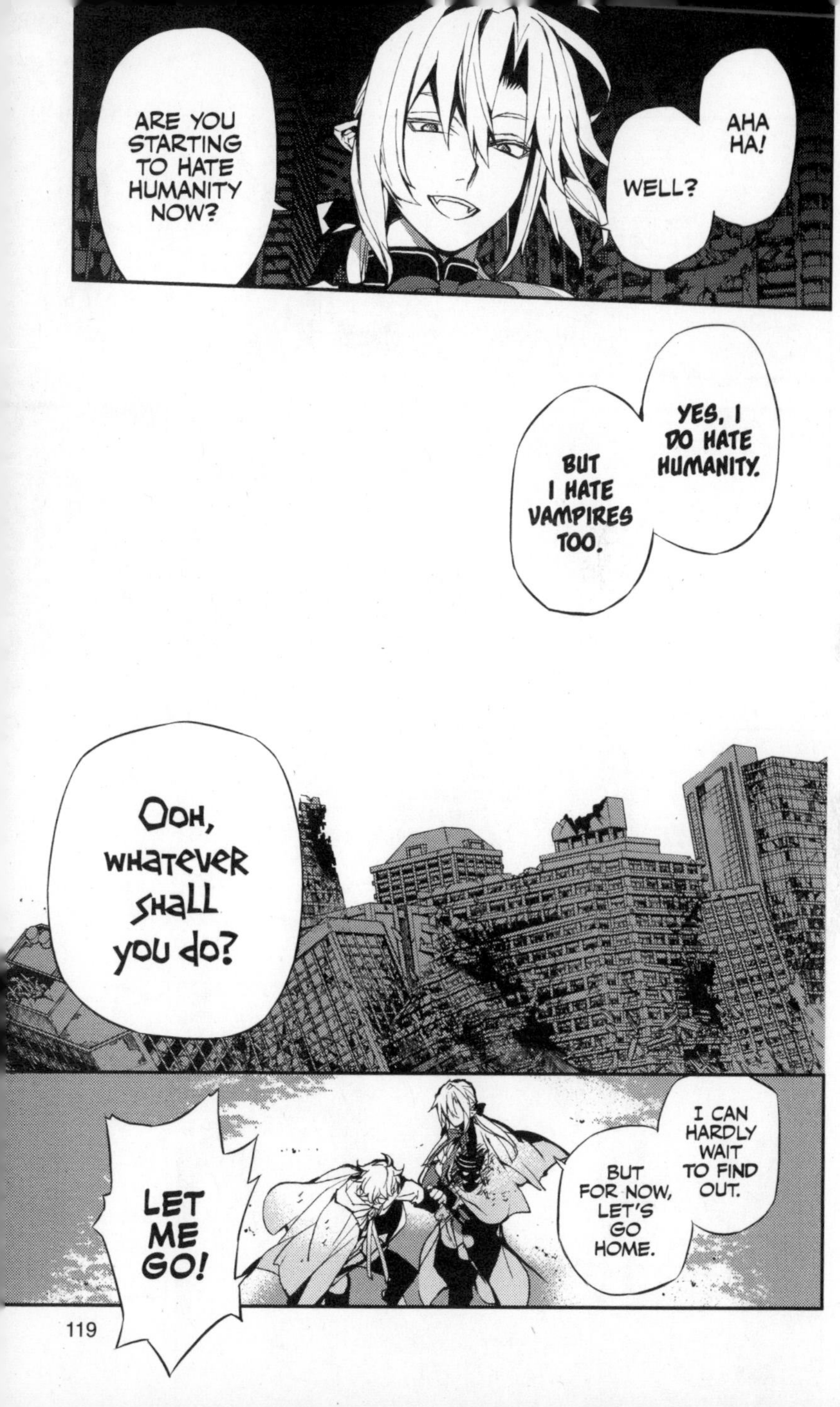
AHA HA!
WELL?
ARE YOU STARTING TO HATE HUMANITY NOW?
YES, I DO HATE HUMANITY.
BUT I HATE VAMPIRES TOO.
Ooh, whatever shall you do?
I CAN HARDLY WAIT TO FIND OUT.
BUT FOR NOW, LET'S GO HOME.
LET ME GO!

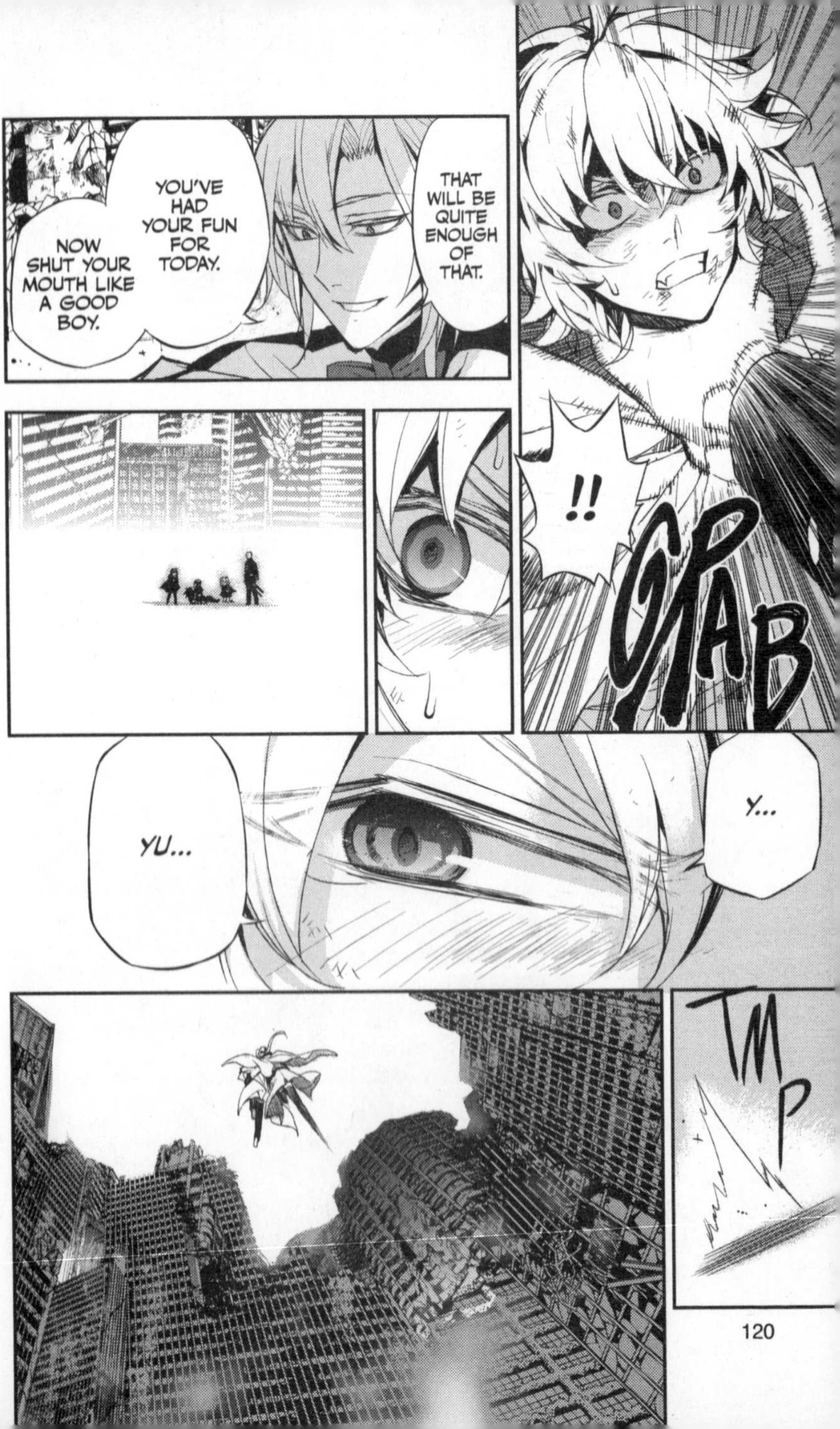
!!
GRAB
THAT WILL BE QUITE ENOUGH OF THAT.
YOU'VE HAD YOUR FUN FOR TODAY.
NOW SHUT YOUR MOUTH LIKE A GOOD BOY.
Y...
YU...
TMP

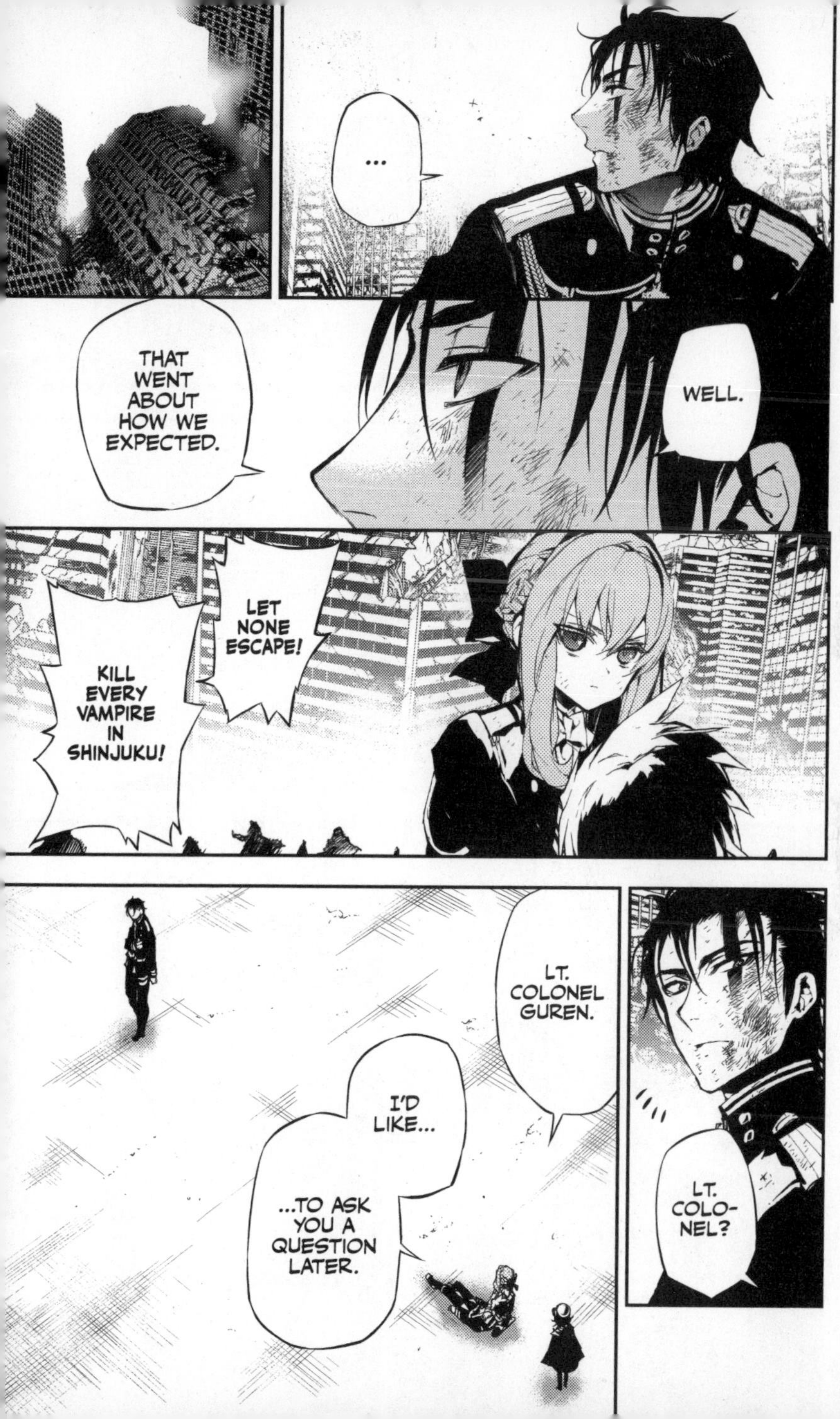
...
WELL.
THAT WENT ABOUT HOW WE EXPECTED.
LET NONE ESCAPE!
KILL EVERY VAMPIRE IN SHINJUKU!
LT. COLO-NEL?
LT. COLONEL GUREN.
I'D LIKE...
...TO ASK YOU A QUESTION LATER.

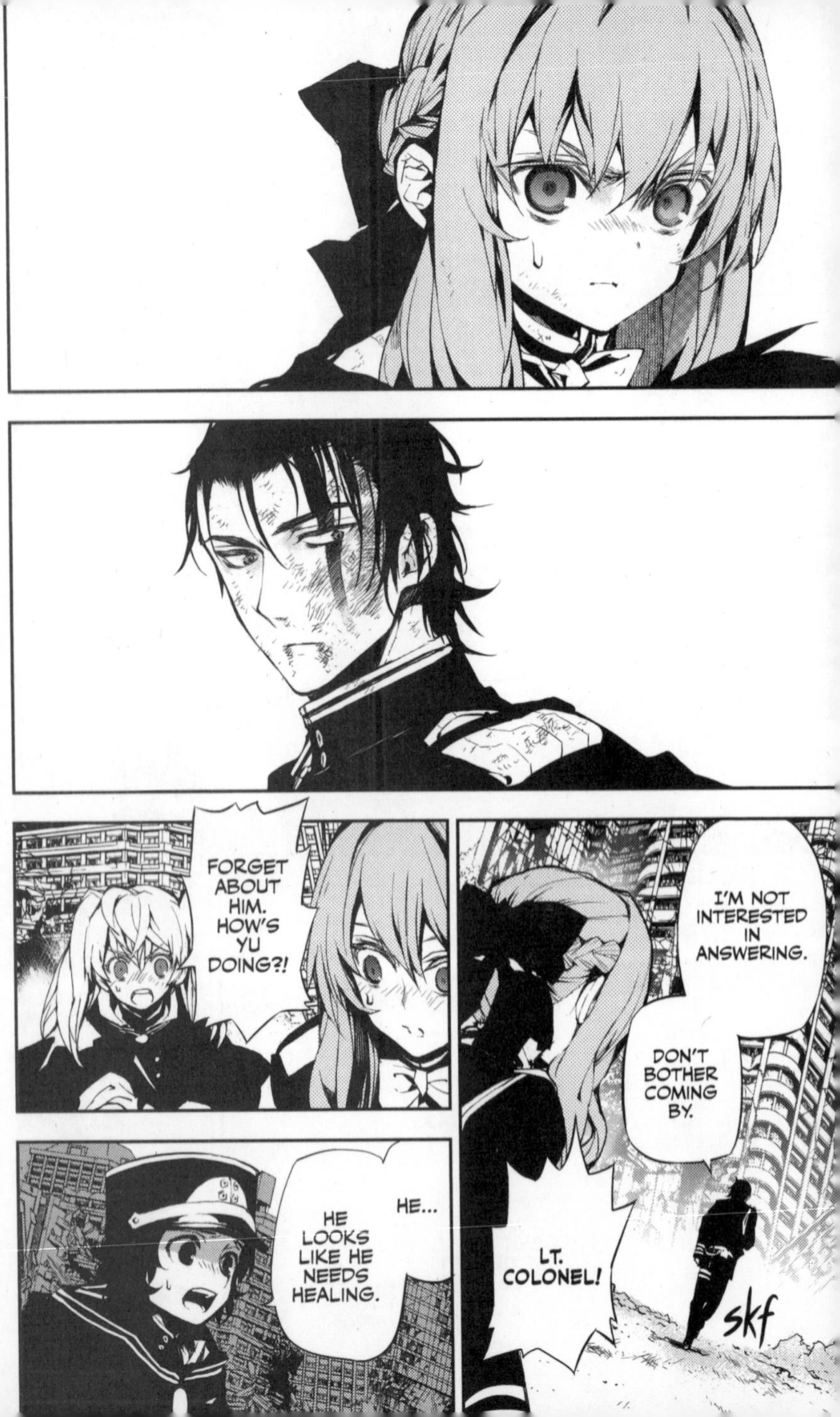
I'M NOT INTERESTED IN ANSWERING.
DON'T BOTHER COMING BY.
LT. COLONEL!
skf
FORGET ABOUT HIM. HOW'S YU DOING?!
HE...
HE LOOKS LIKE HE NEEDS HEALING.

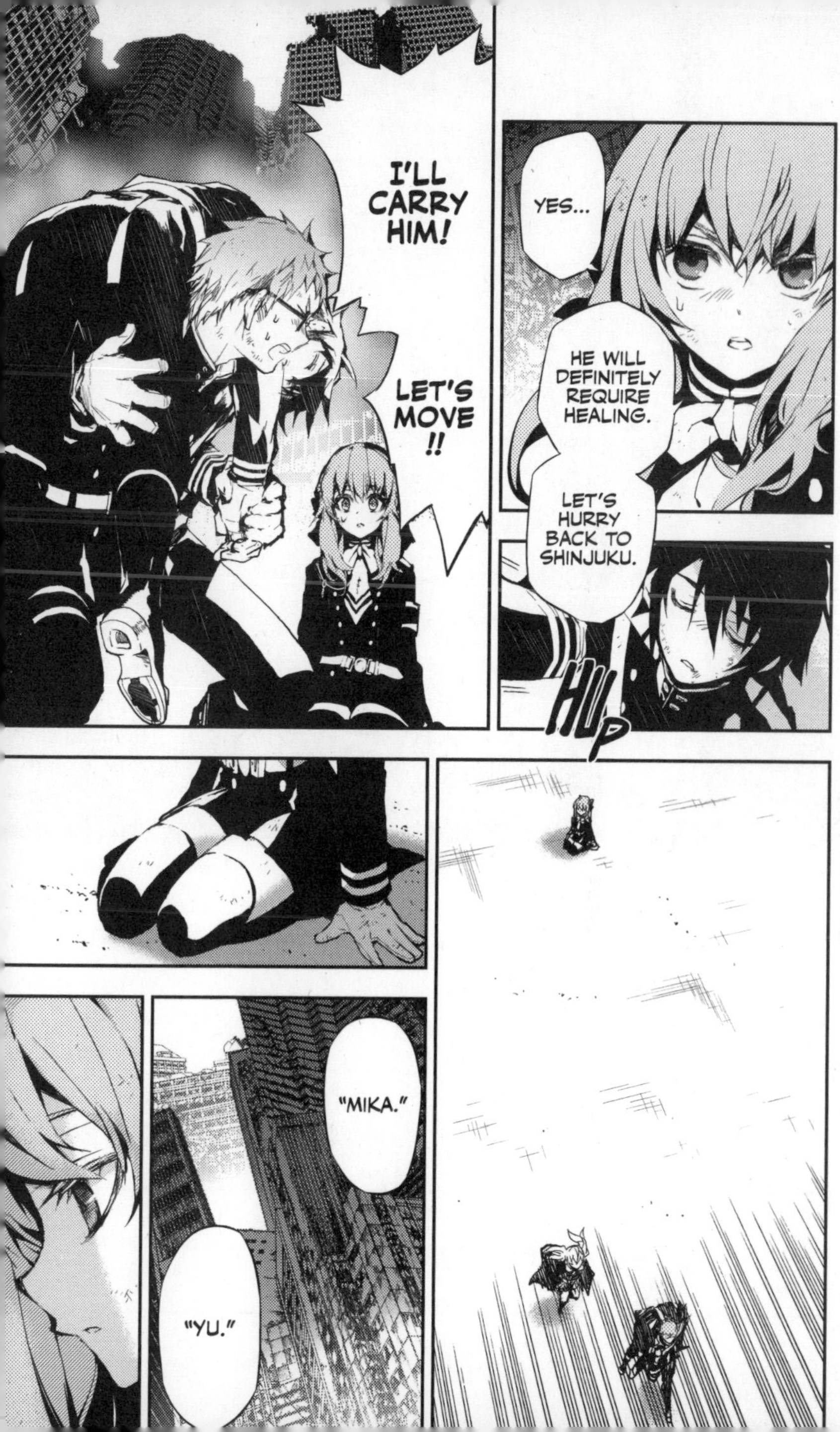
YES...
HE WILL DEFINITELY REQUIRE HEALING.
LET'S HURRY BACK TO SHINJUKU.
HUP
I'LL CARRY HIM!
LET'S MOVE !!
"MIKA."
"YU."

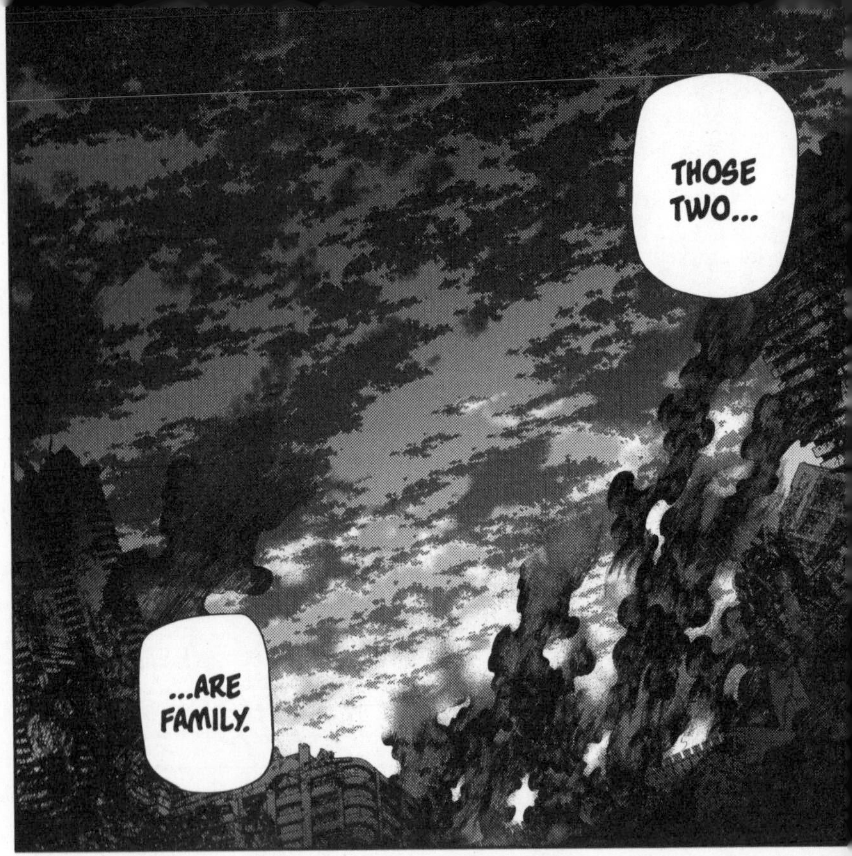
THOSE TWO...
...ARE FAMILY.

Five Days Later

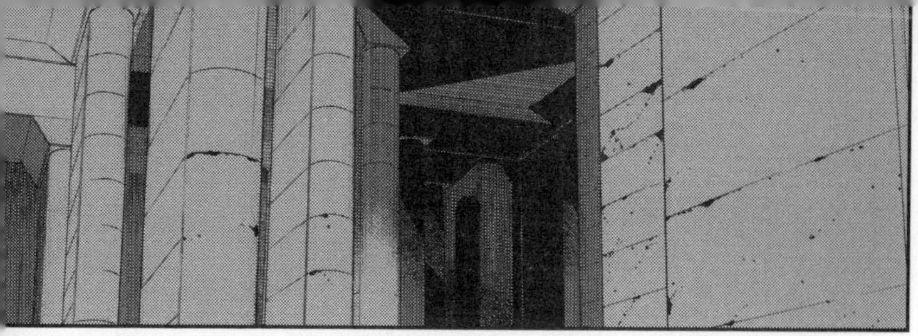

Japanese Imperial Demon Army's Shinjuku Barracks
Underground

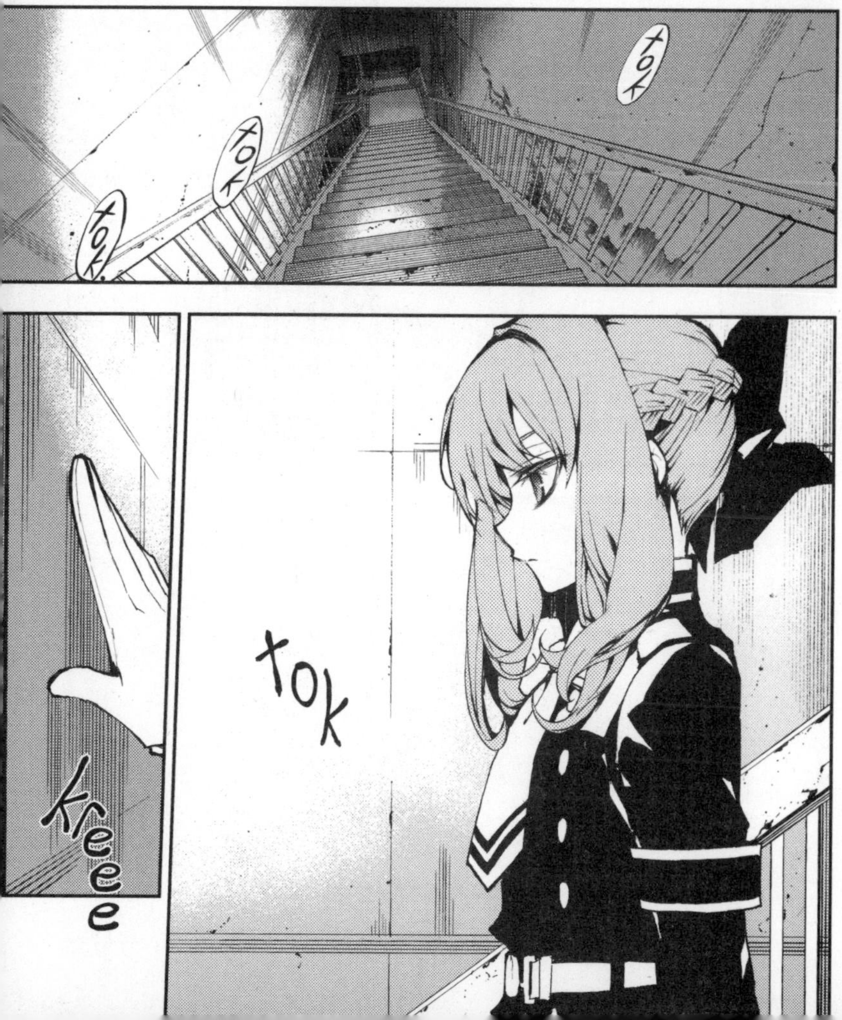
tok
tok
tok
tok
kreeee

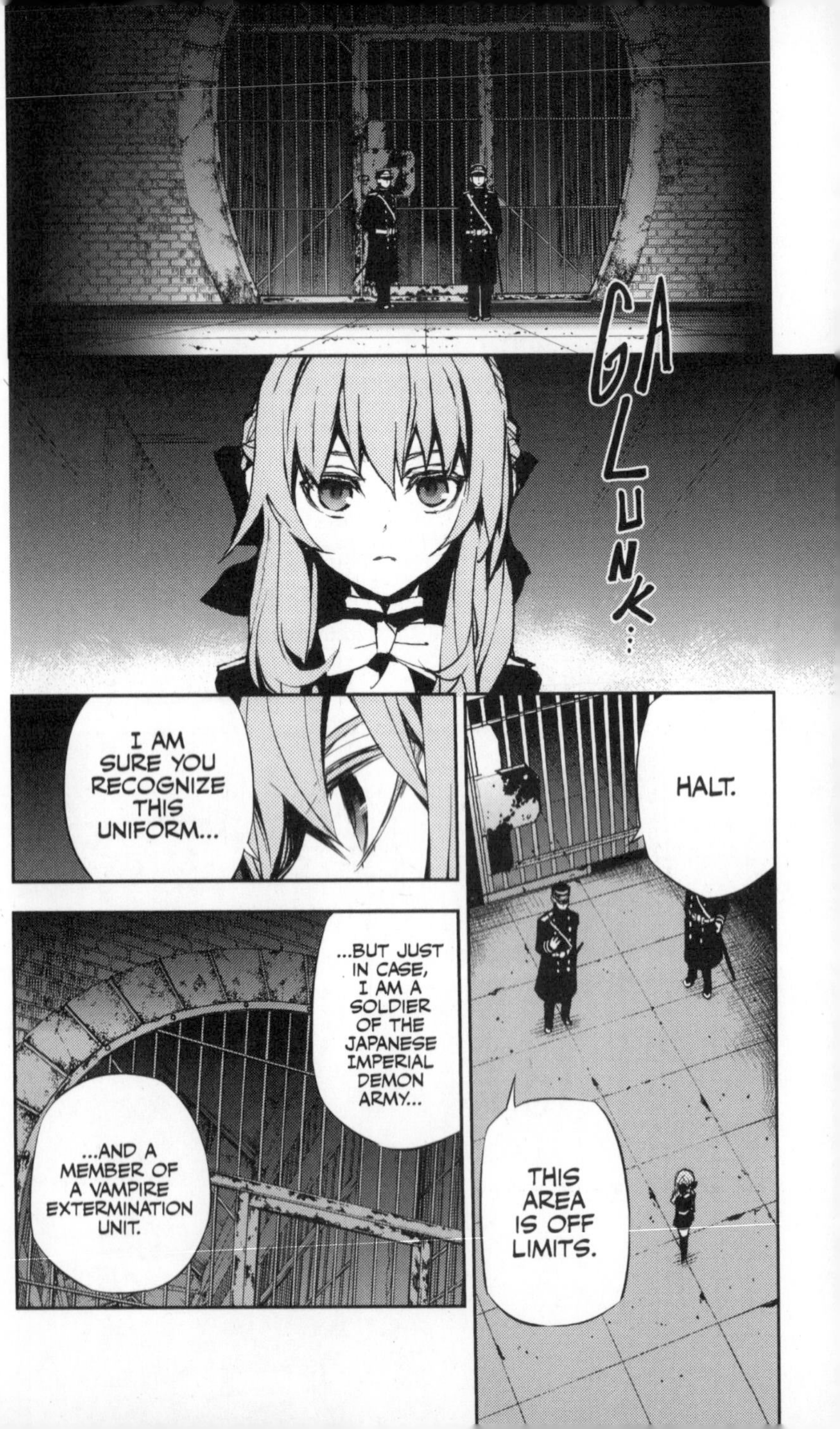
GALUNK...
HALT.
THIS AREA IS OFF LIMITS.
I AM SURE YOU RECOGNIZE THIS UNIFORM...
...BUT JUST IN CASE, I AM A SOLDIER OF THE JAPANESE IMPERIAL DEMON ARMY...
...AND A MEMBER OF A VAMPIRE EXTERMINATION UNIT.

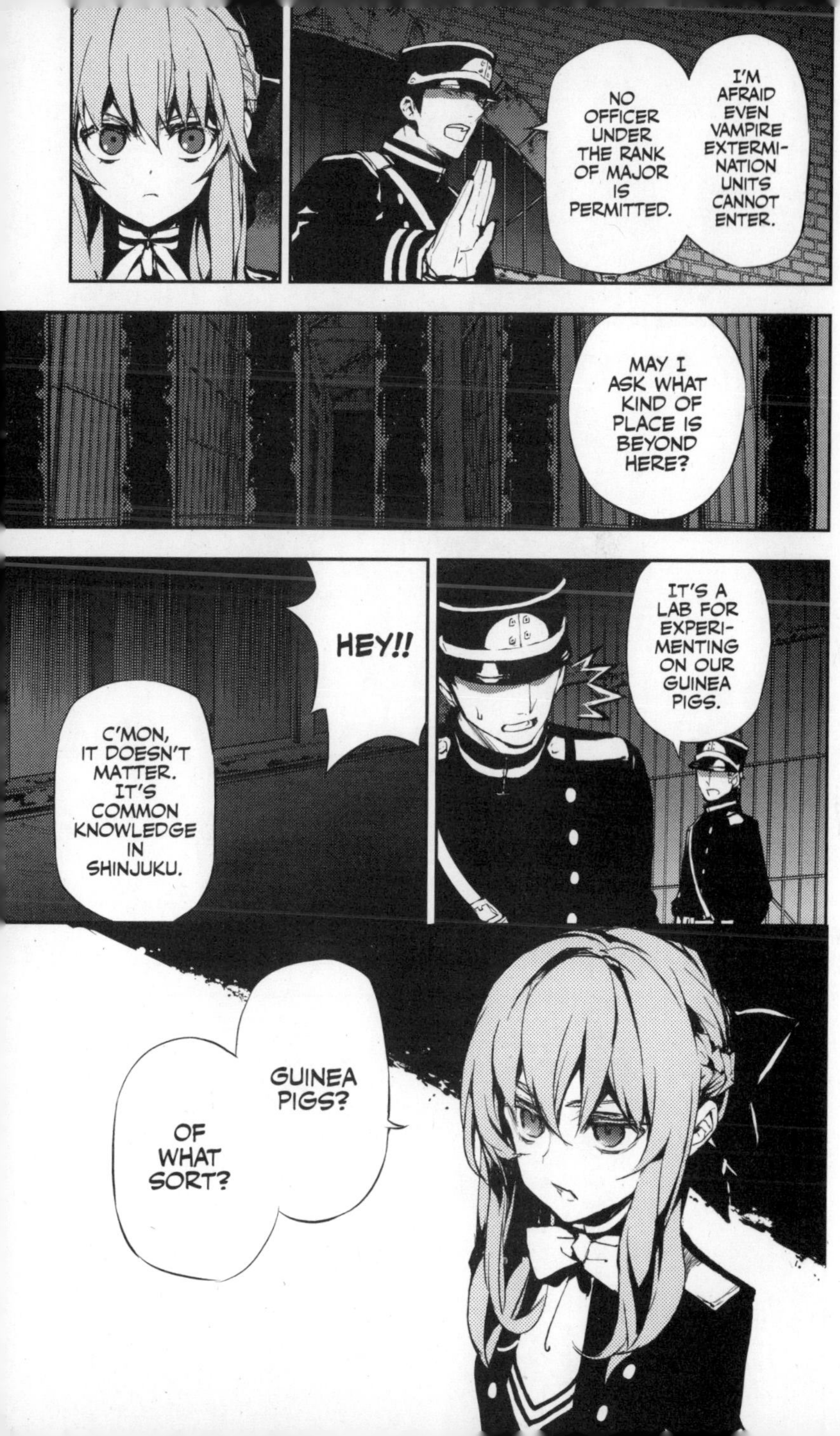
I'M AFRAID EVEN VAMPIRE EXTERMINATION UNITS CANNOT ENTER.
NO OFFICER UNDER THE RANK OF MAJOR IS PERMITTED.
MAY I ASK WHAT KIND OF PLACE IS BEYOND HERE?
IT'S A LAB FOR EXPERIMENTING ON OUR GUINEA PIGS.
HEY!!
C'MON, IT DOESN'T MATTER. IT'S COMMON KNOWLEDGE IN SHINJUKU.
GUINEA PIGS?
OF WHAT SORT?

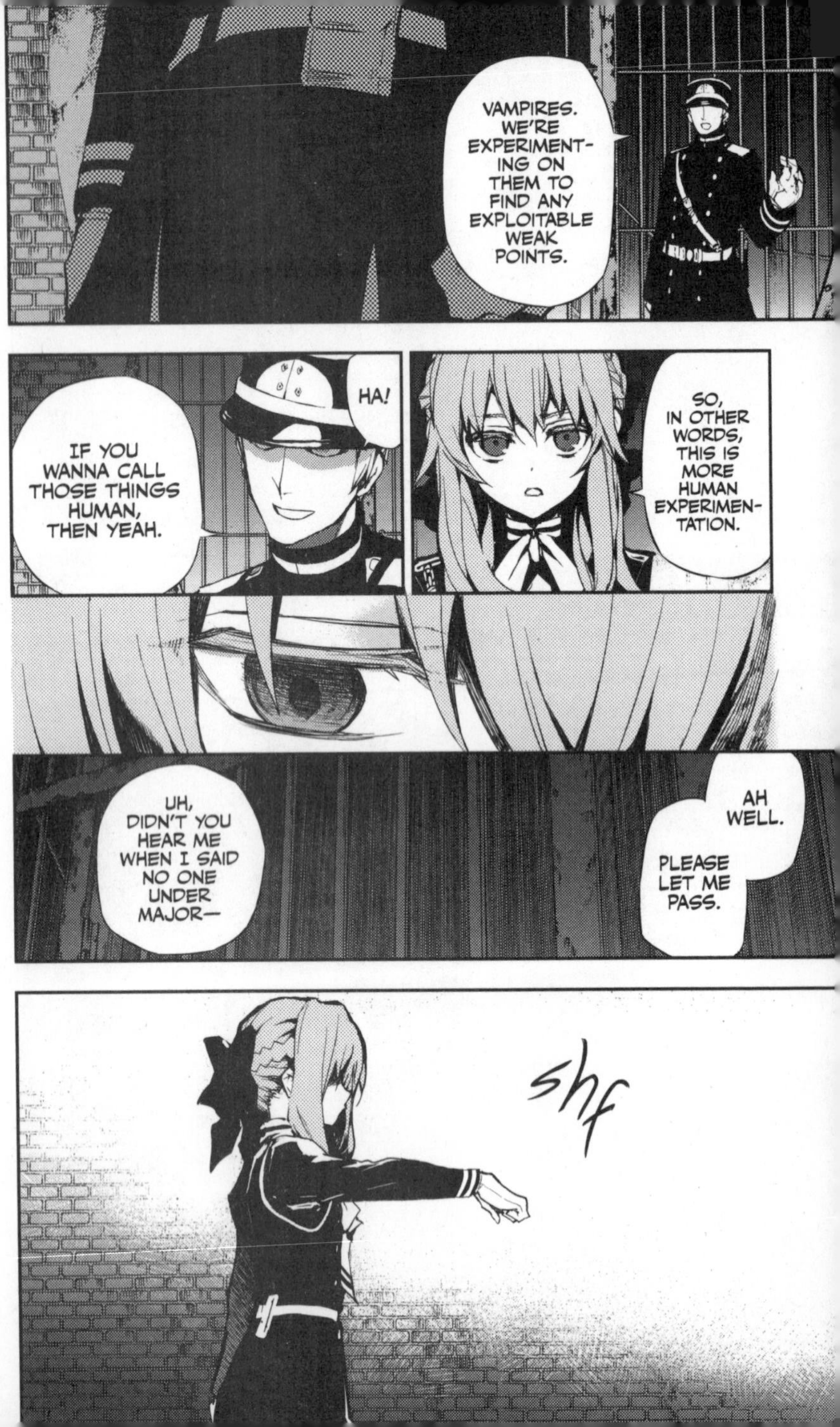
VAMPIRES. WE'RE EXPERIMENTING ON THEM TO FIND ANY EXPLOITABLE WEAK POINTS.
SO, IN OTHER WORDS, THIS IS MORE HUMAN EXPERIMENTATION.
HA!
IF YOU WANNA CALL THOSE THINGS HUMAN, THEN YEAH.
AH WELL.
PLEASE LET ME PASS.
UH, DIDN'T YOU HEAR ME WHEN I SAID NO ONE UNDER MAJOR—
shf

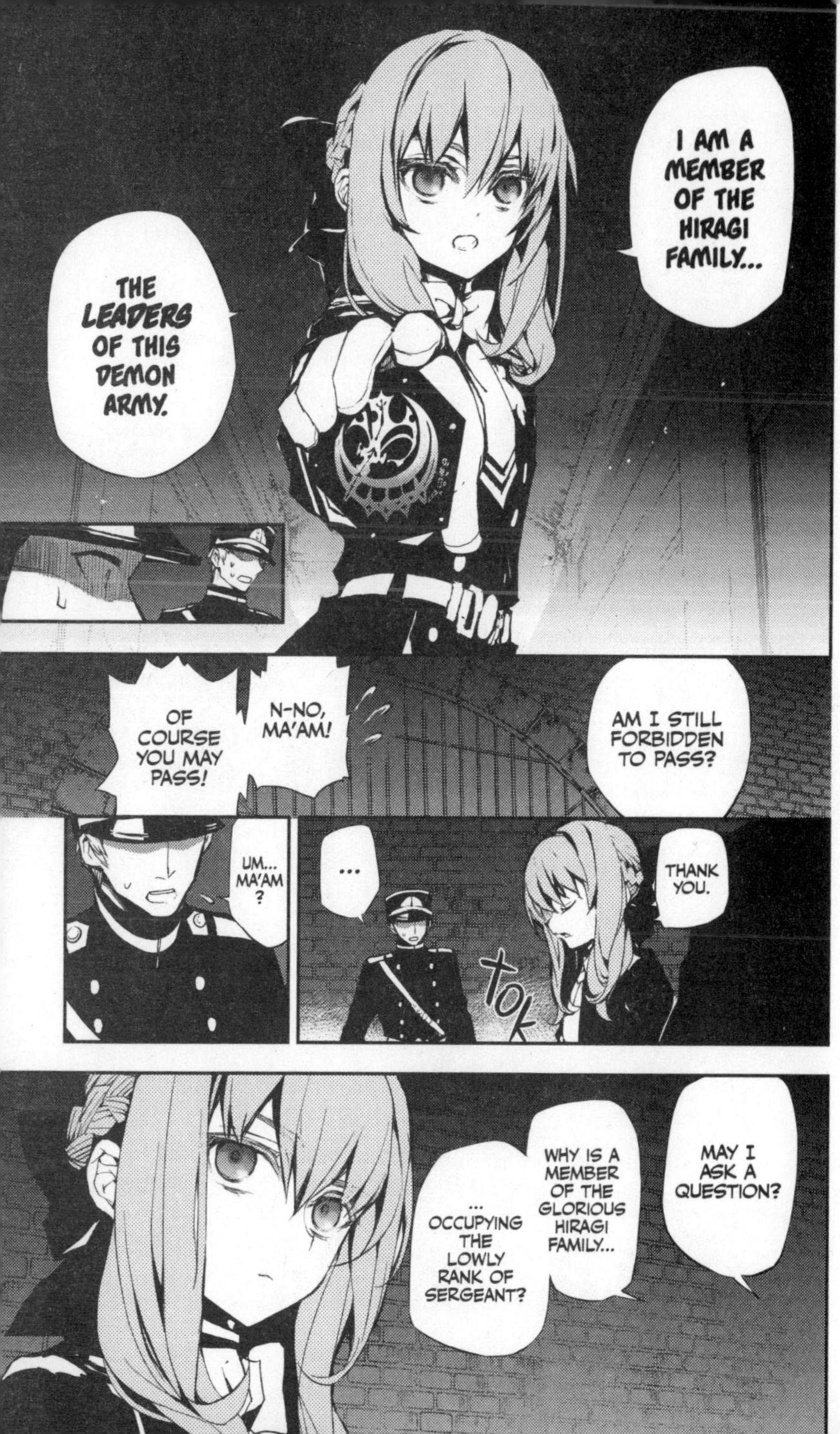
I AM A MEMBER OF THE HIRAGI FAMILY...
THE LEADERS OF THIS DEMON ARMY.
AM I STILL FORBIDDEN TO PASS?
N-NO, MA'AM!
OF COURSE YOU MAY PASS!
THANK YOU.
TOK
...
UM... MA'AM?
MAY I ASK A QUESTION?
WHY IS A MEMBER OF THE GLORIOUS HIRAGI FAMILY...
...OCCUPYING THE LOWLY RANK OF SERGEANT?

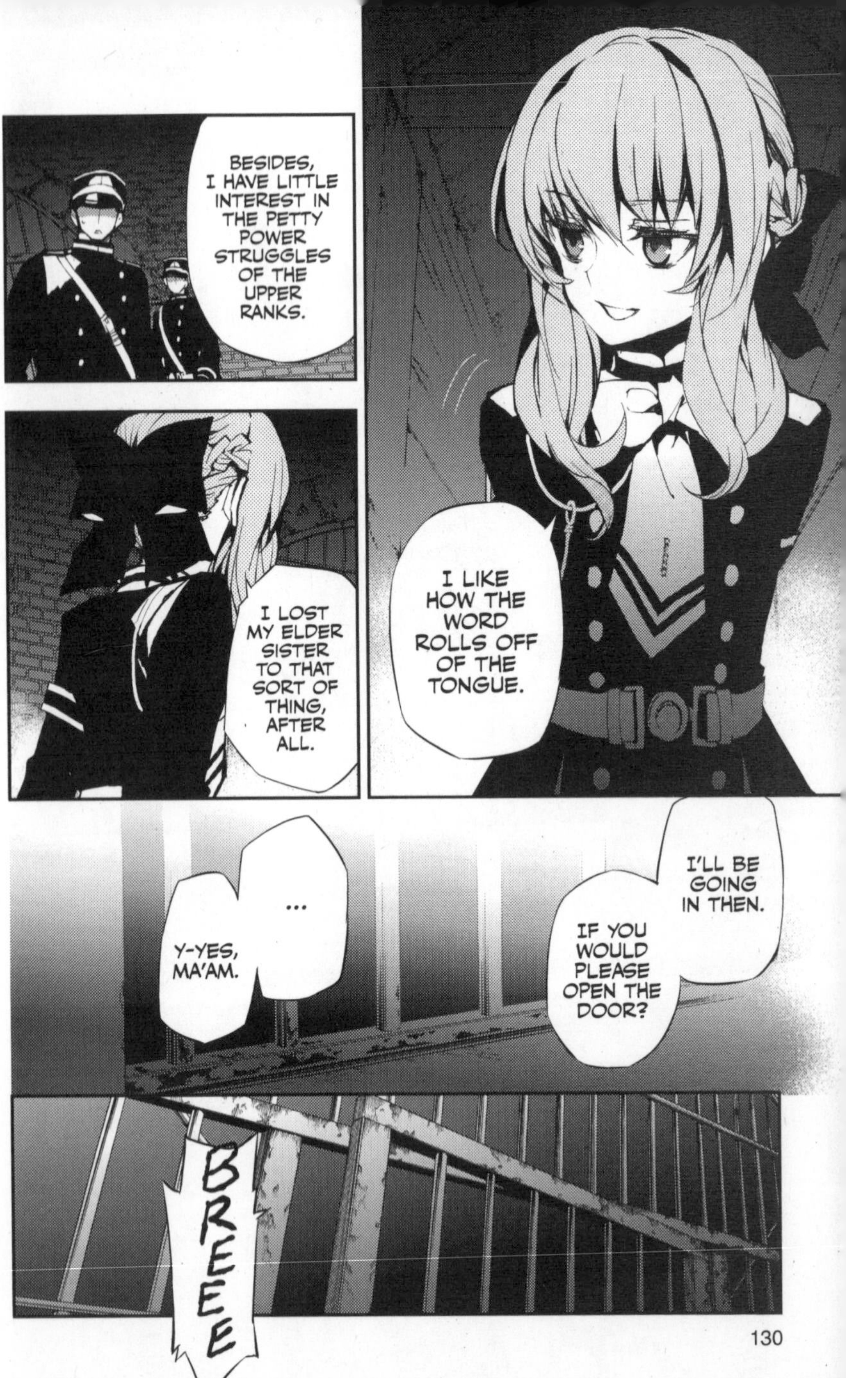
I LIKE HOW THE WORD ROLLS OFF OF THE TONGUE.
BESIDES, I HAVE LITTLE INTEREST IN THE PETTY POWER STRUGGLES OF THE UPPER RANKS.
I LOST MY ELDER SISTER TO THAT SORT OF THING, AFTER ALL.
I'LL BE GOING IN THEN.
IF YOU WOULD PLEASE OPEN THE DOOR?
...
Y-YES, MA'AM.
BREEE

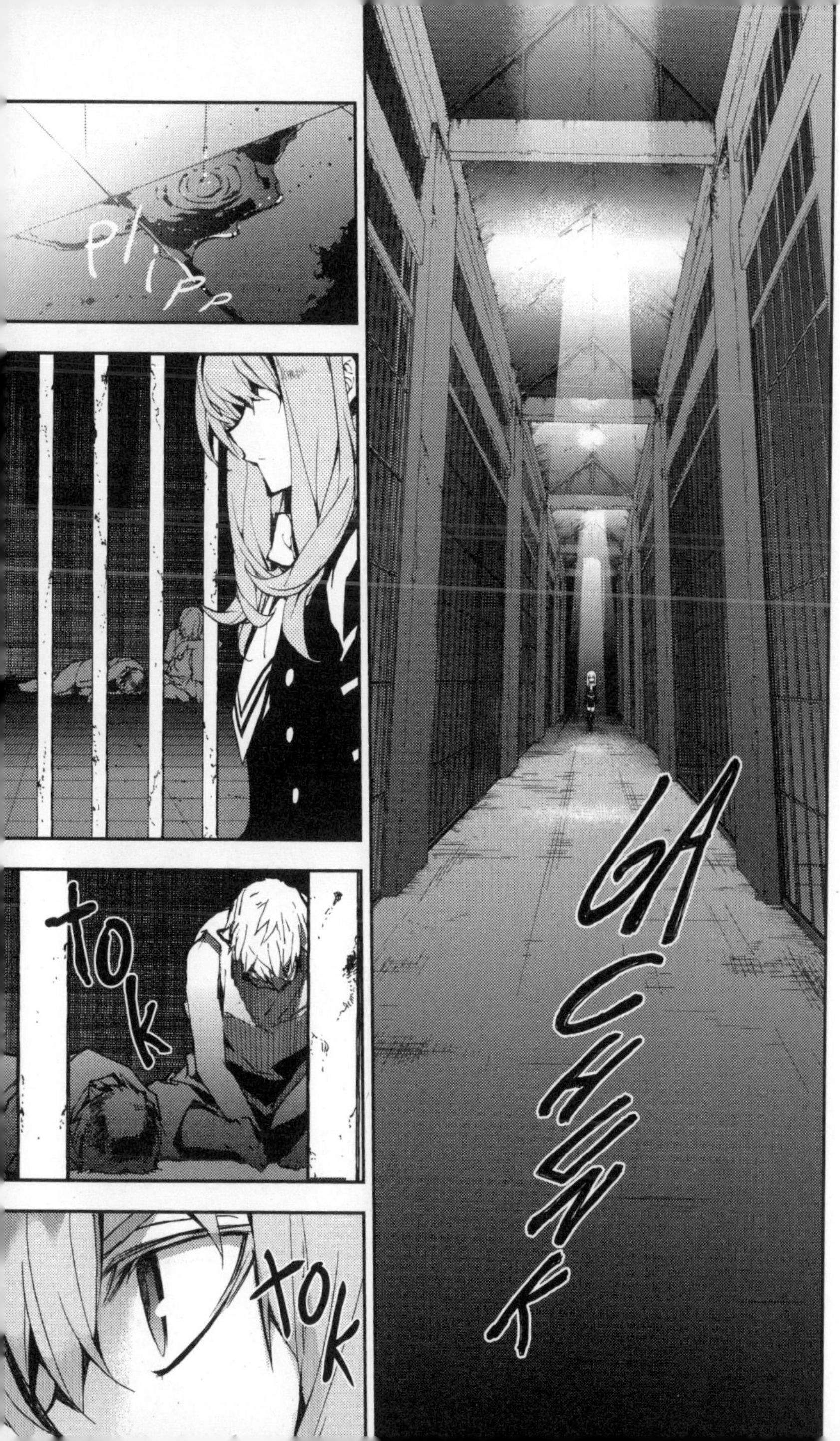
GACHUNK
PLIPP
TOK
TOK

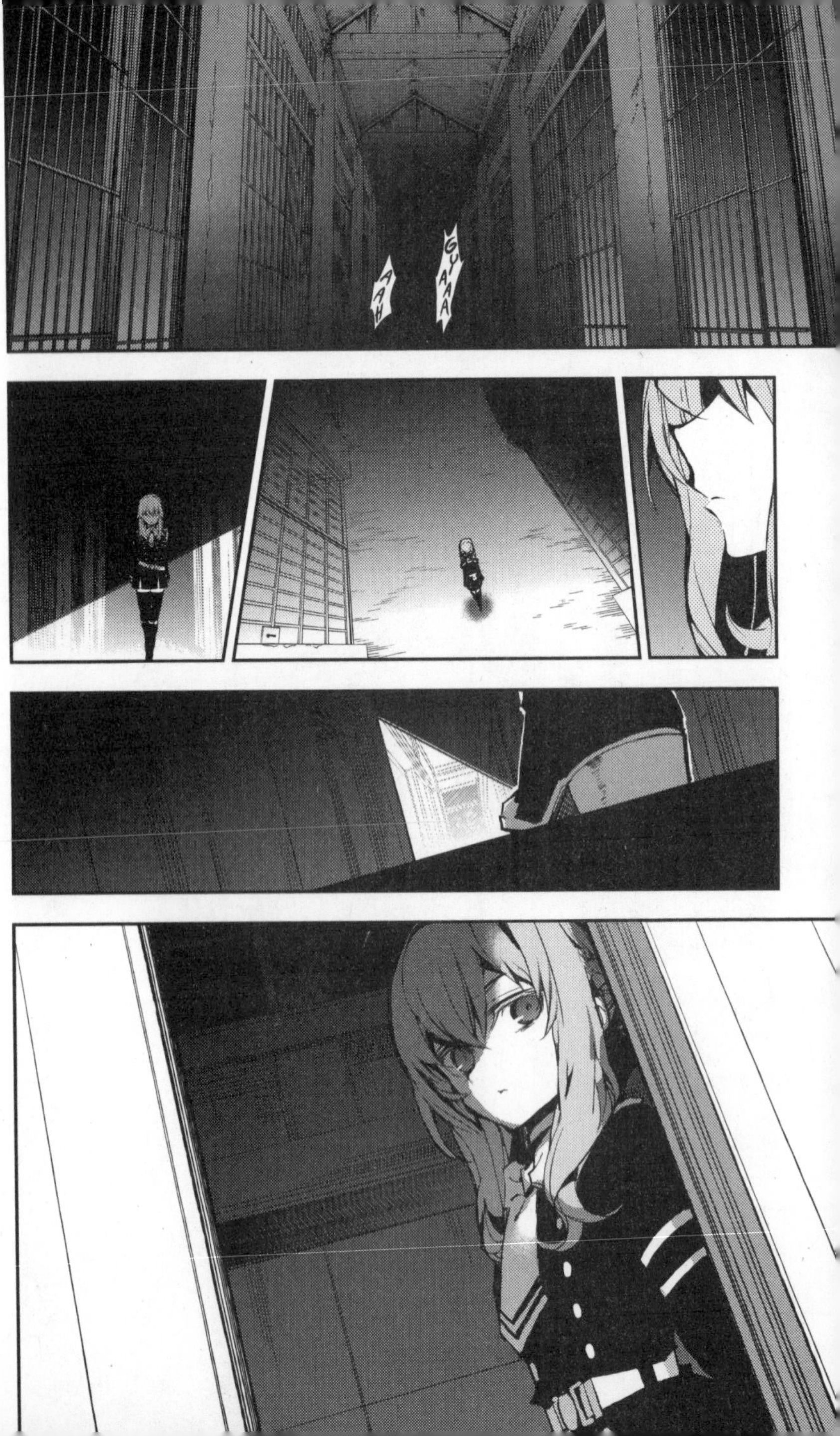
GUAAAA
AAAH

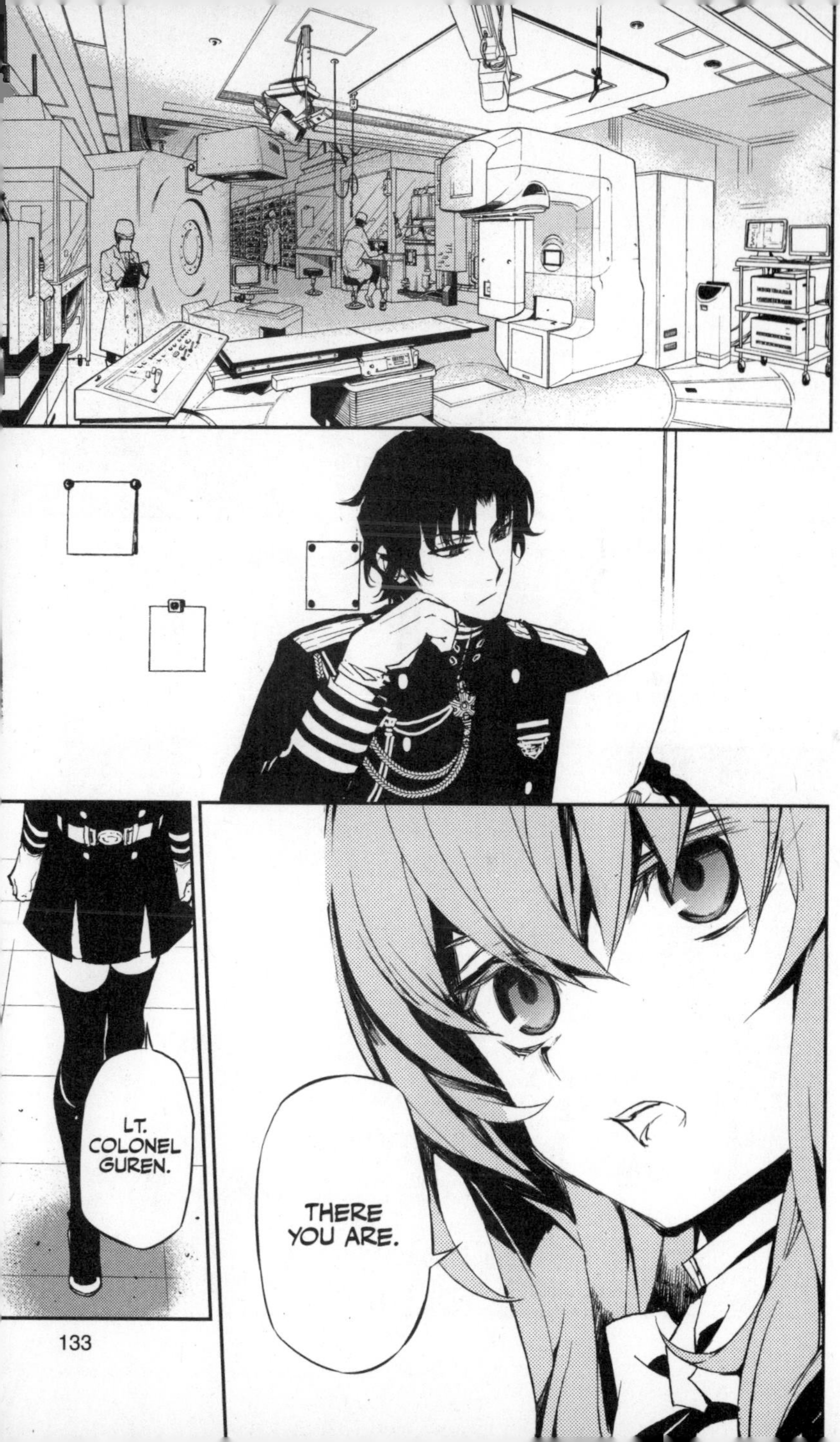
THERE YOU ARE.
LT. COLONEL GUREN.

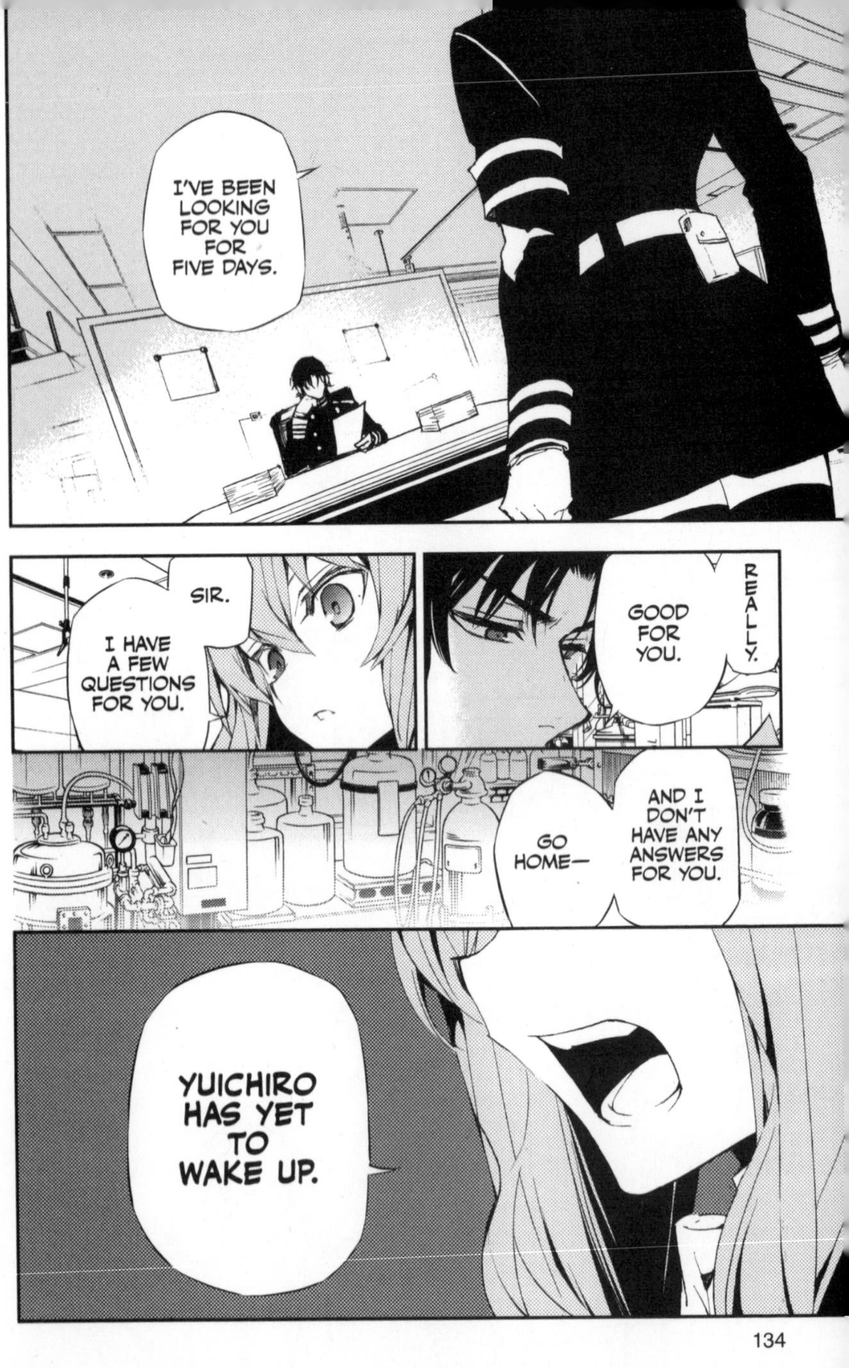
I'VE BEEN LOOKING FOR YOU FOR FIVE DAYS.
REALLY.
GOOD FOR YOU.
SIR.
I HAVE A FEW QUESTIONS FOR YOU.
AND I DON'T HAVE ANY ANSWERS FOR YOU.
GO HOME—
YUICHIRO HAS YET TO WAKE UP.

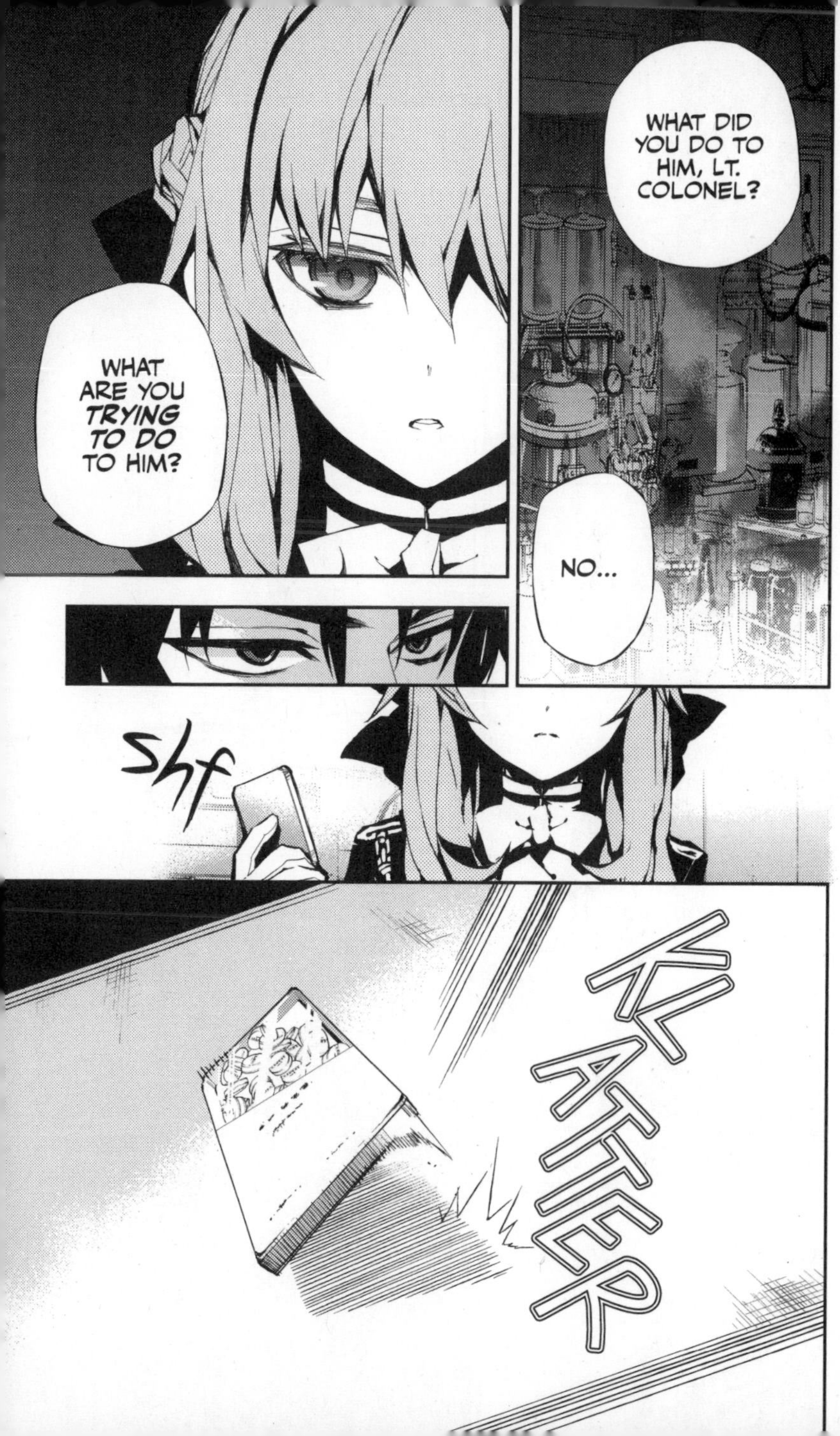
WHAT DID YOU DO TO HIM, LT. COLONEL?
NO...
WHAT ARE YOU *TRYING TO DO* TO HIM?
shf
KLATTER

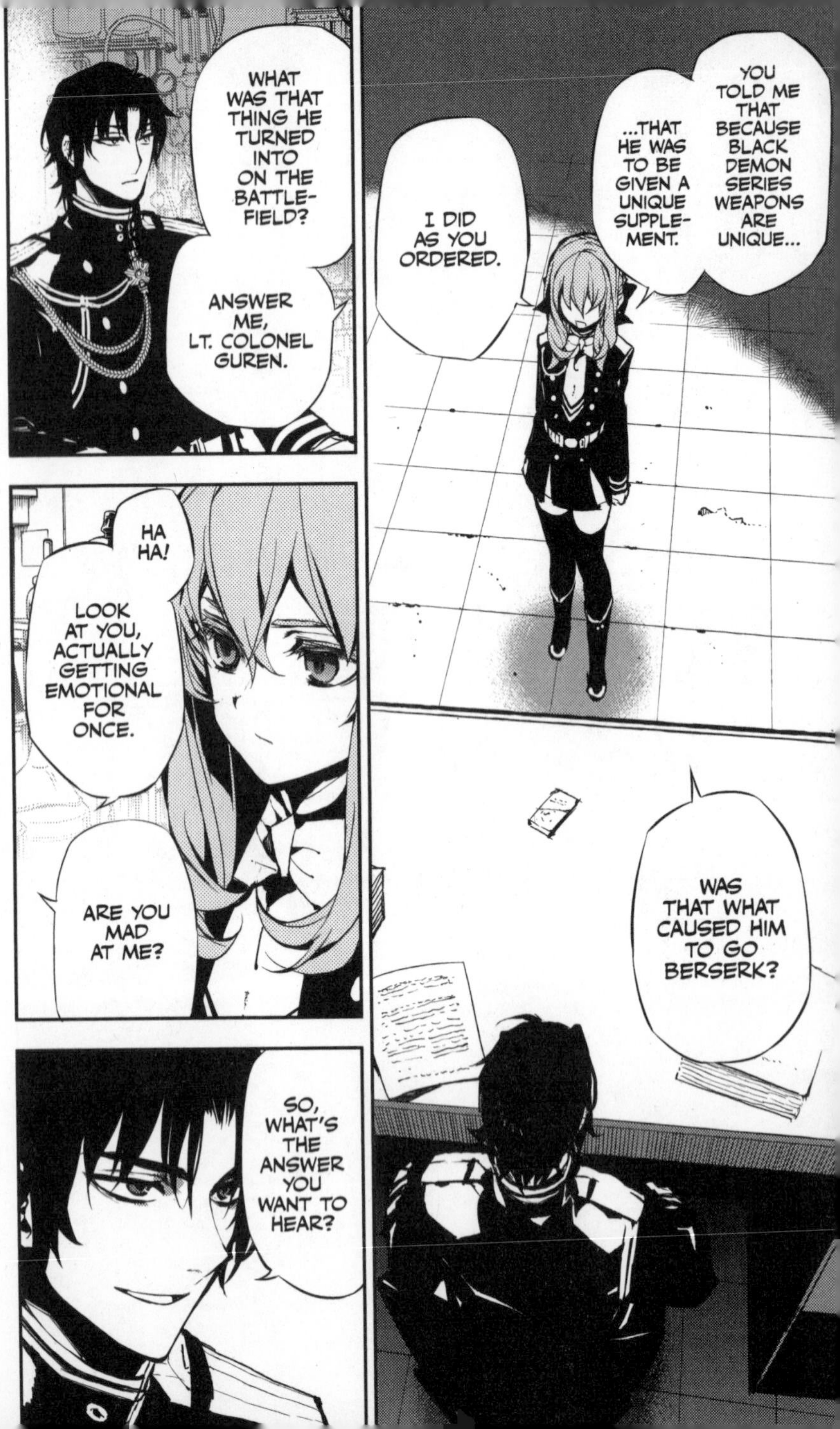
YOU TOLD ME THAT BECAUSE BLACK DEMON SERIES WEAPONS ARE UNIQUE...
...THAT HE WAS TO BE GIVEN A UNIQUE SUPPLE-MENT.
I DID AS YOU ORDERED.
WAS THAT WHAT CAUSED HIM TO GO BERSERK?
WHAT WAS THAT THING HE TURNED INTO ON THE BATTLE-FIELD?
ANSWER ME, LT. COLONEL GUREN.
HA HA!
LOOK AT YOU, ACTUALLY GETTING EMOTIONAL FOR ONCE.
ARE YOU MAD AT ME?
SO, WHAT'S THE ANSWER YOU WANT TO HEAR?

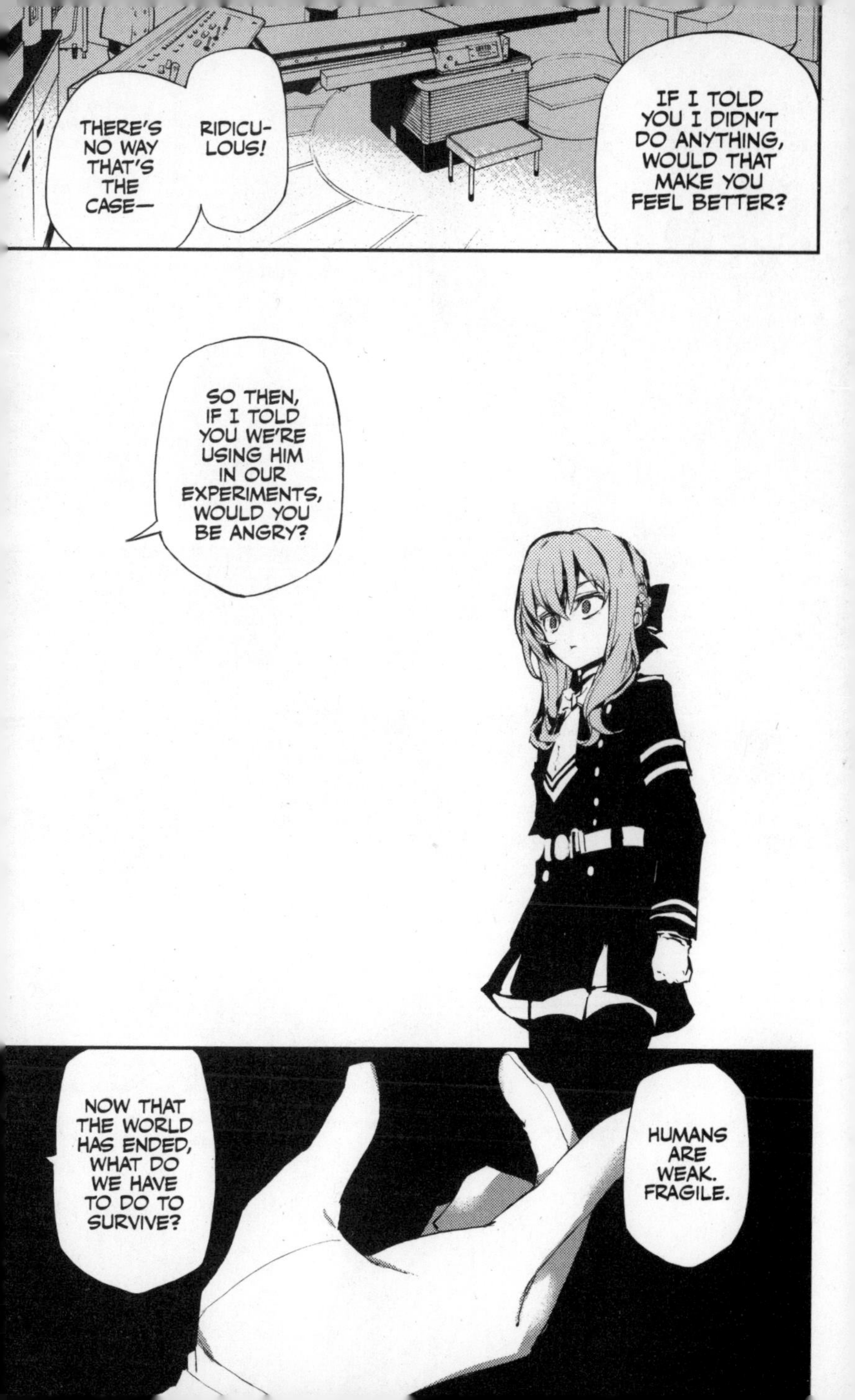
IF I TOLD YOU I DIDN'T DO ANYTHING, WOULD THAT MAKE YOU FEEL BETTER?
RIDICU-LOUS!
THERE'S NO WAY THAT'S THE CASE—
SO THEN, IF I TOLD YOU WE'RE USING HIM IN OUR EXPERIMENTS, WOULD YOU BE ANGRY?
HUMANS ARE WEAK. FRAGILE.
NOW THAT THE WORLD HAS ENDED, WHAT DO WE HAVE TO DO TO SURVIVE?

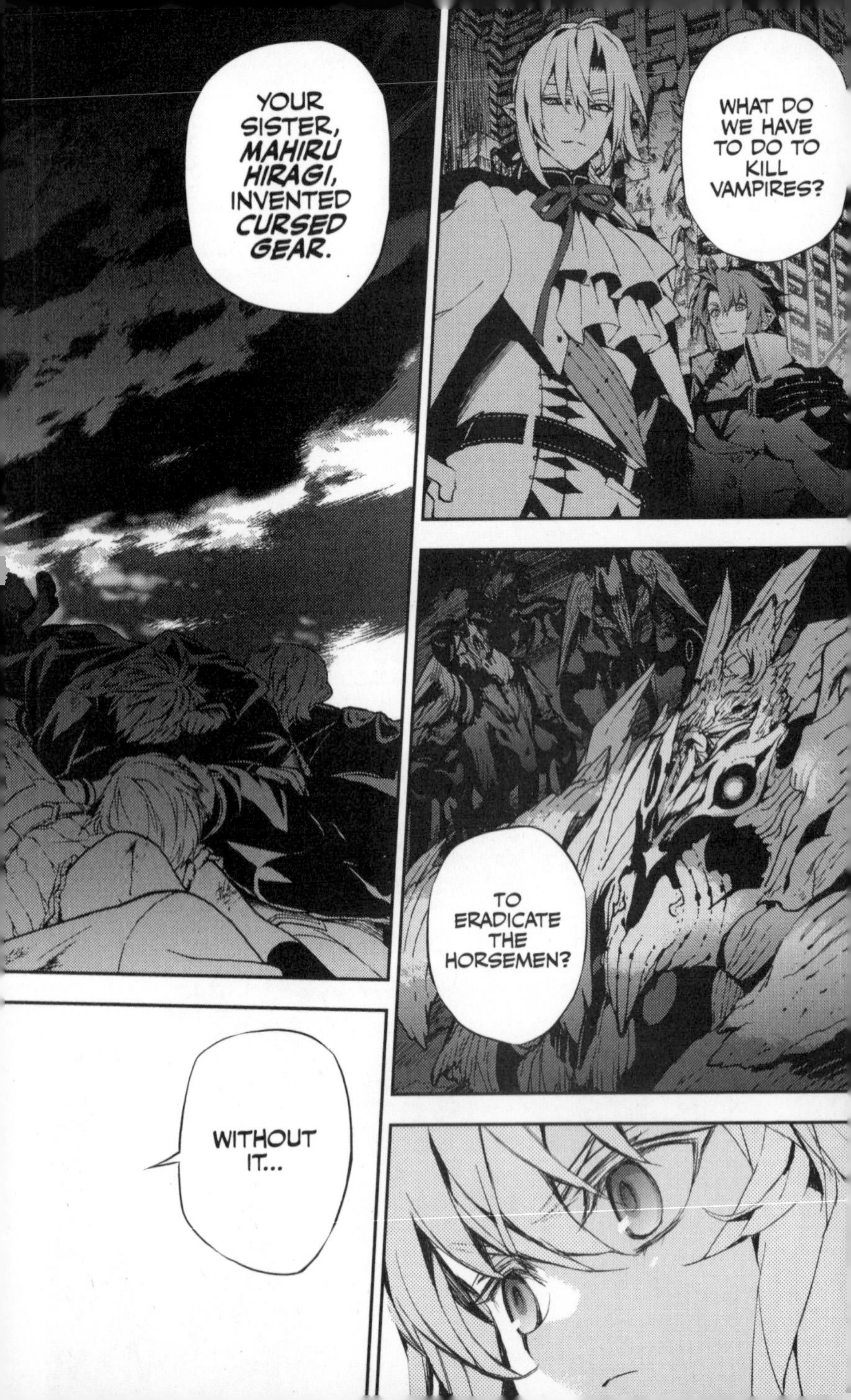
WHAT DO WE HAVE TO DO TO KILL VAMPIRES?
TO ERADICATE THE HORSEMEN?
YOUR SISTER, MAHIRU HIRAGI, INVENTED CURSED GEAR.
WITHOUT IT...

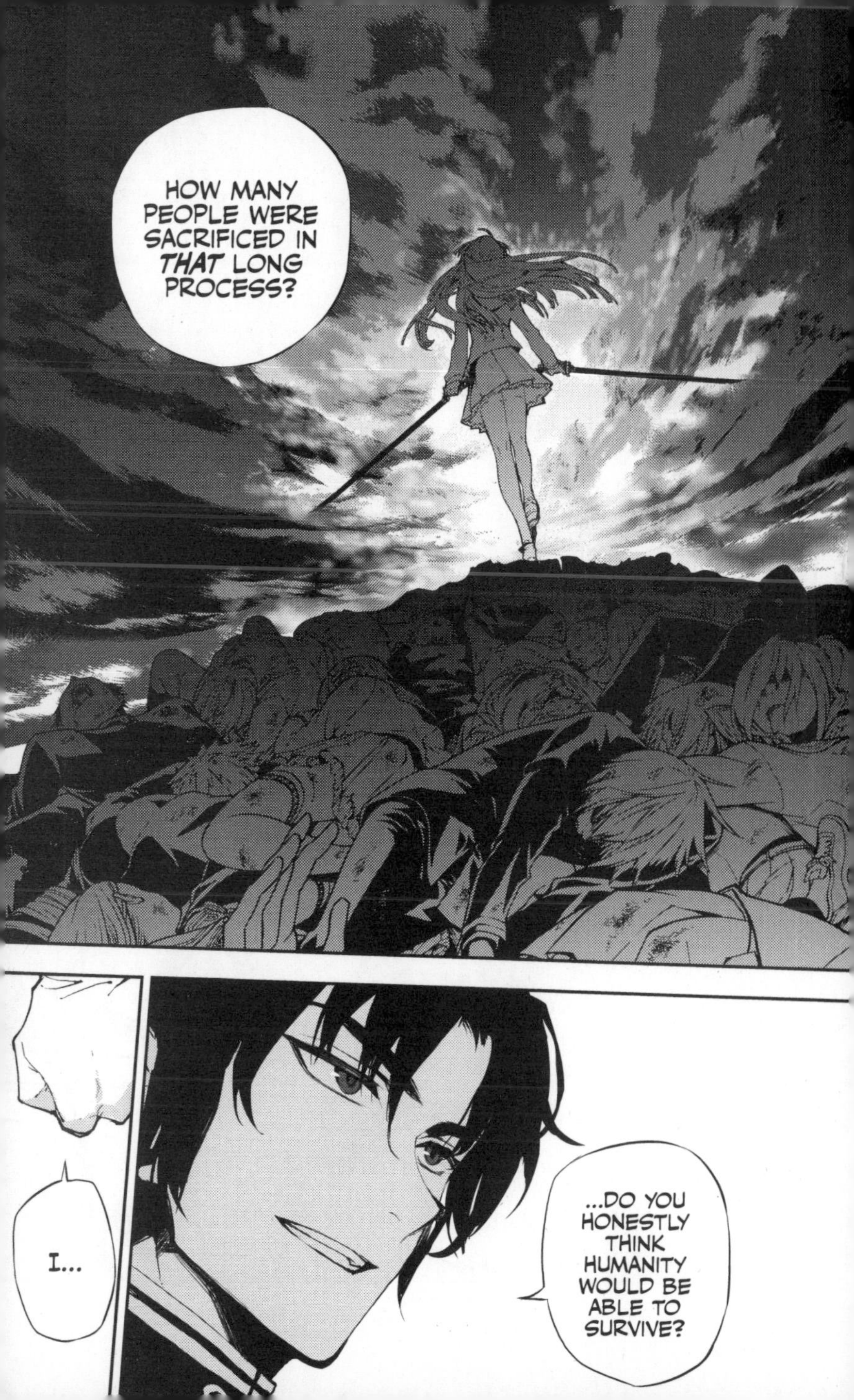
HOW MANY PEOPLE WERE SACRIFICED IN *THAT* LONG PROCESS?
...DO YOU HONESTLY THINK HUMANITY WOULD BE ABLE TO SURVIVE?
I...

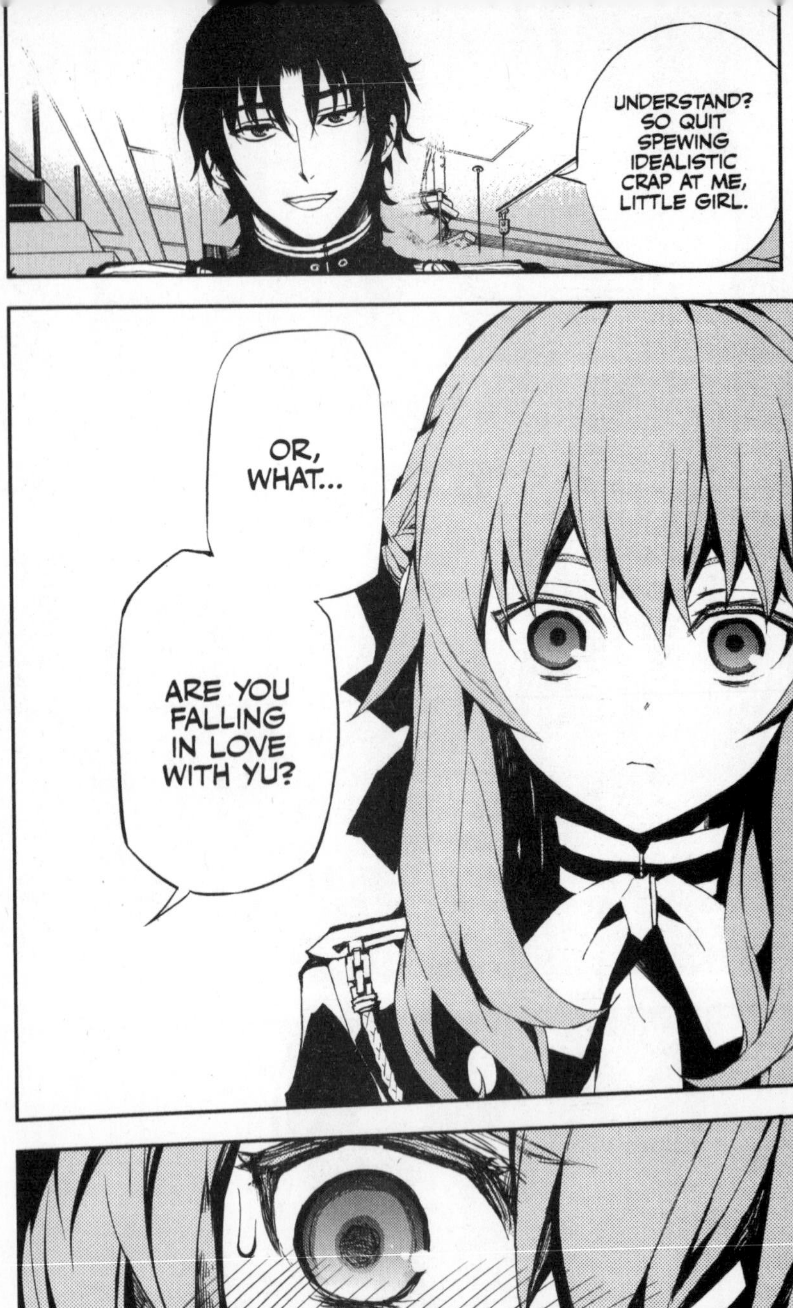
UNDERSTAND? SO QUIT SPEWING IDEALISTIC CRAP AT ME, LITTLE GIRL.
OR, WHAT...
ARE YOU FALLING IN LOVE WITH YU?

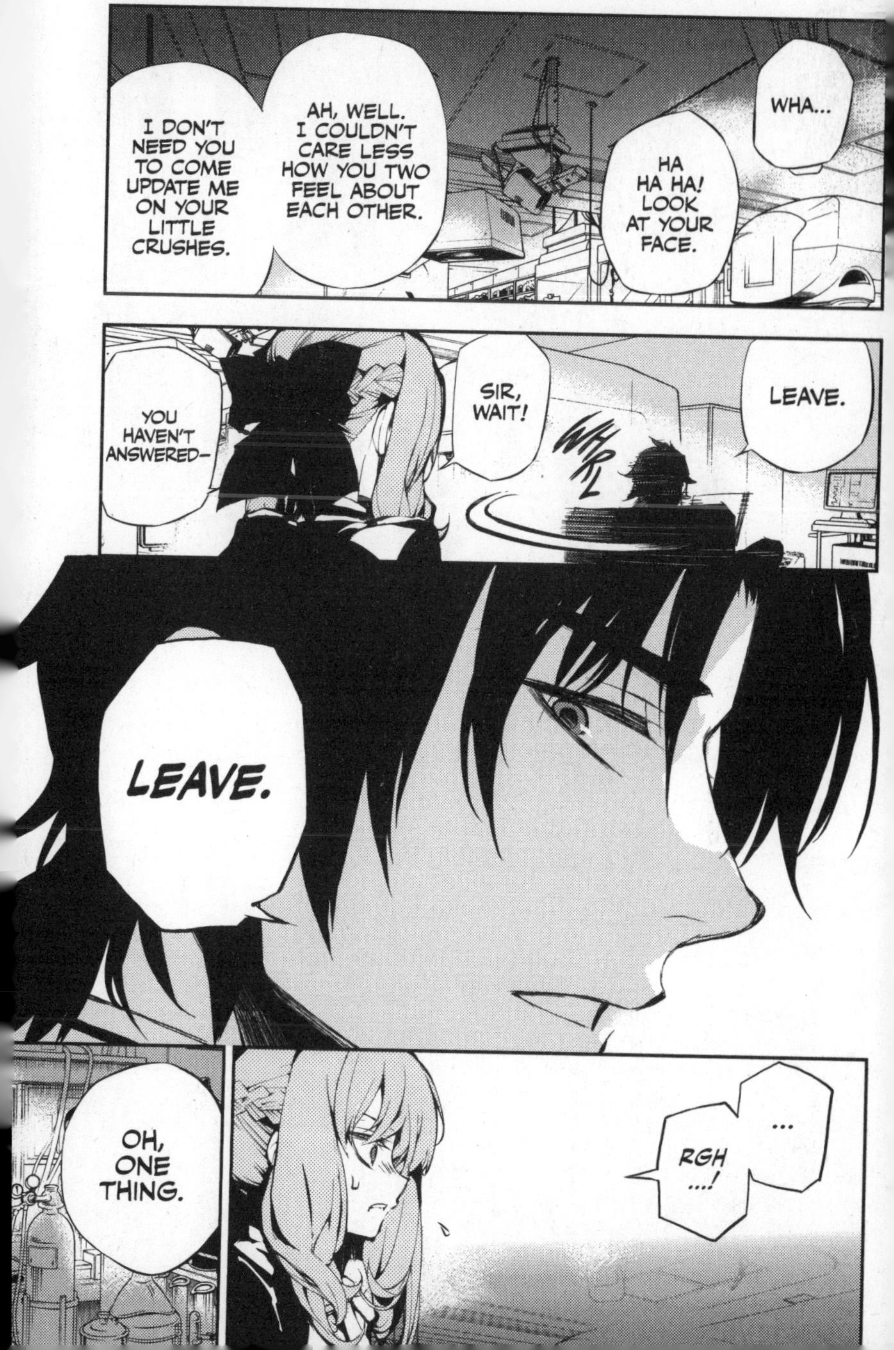
WHA...
HA HA HA! LOOK AT YOUR FACE.
AH, WELL. I COULDN'T CARE LESS HOW YOU TWO FEEL ABOUT EACH OTHER.
I DON'T NEED YOU TO COME UPDATE ME ON YOUR LITTLE CRUSHES.
LEAVE.
WHRL
SIR, WAIT!
YOU HAVEN'T ANSWERED—
LEAVE.
... RGH ...!
OH, ONE THING.

THE DRUGS ARE WEARING OFF.

IT TAKES FIVE DAYS FOR THEM TO WORK OUT OF HIS SYSTEM. HE'LL WAKE UP SOON.

CONSIDER PAYING HIM A VISIT.

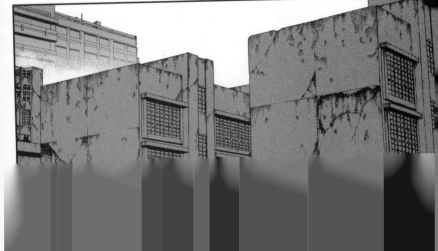

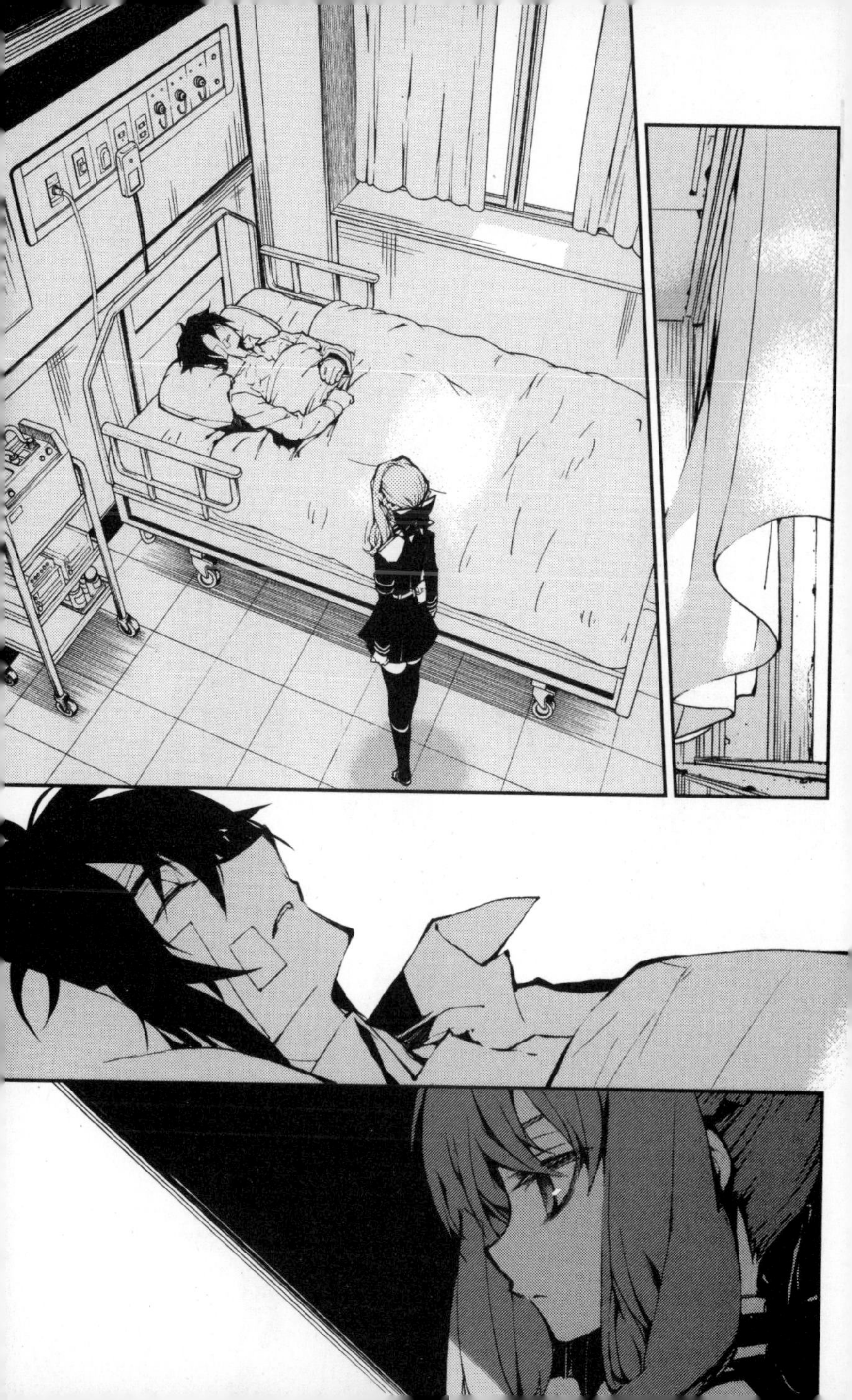

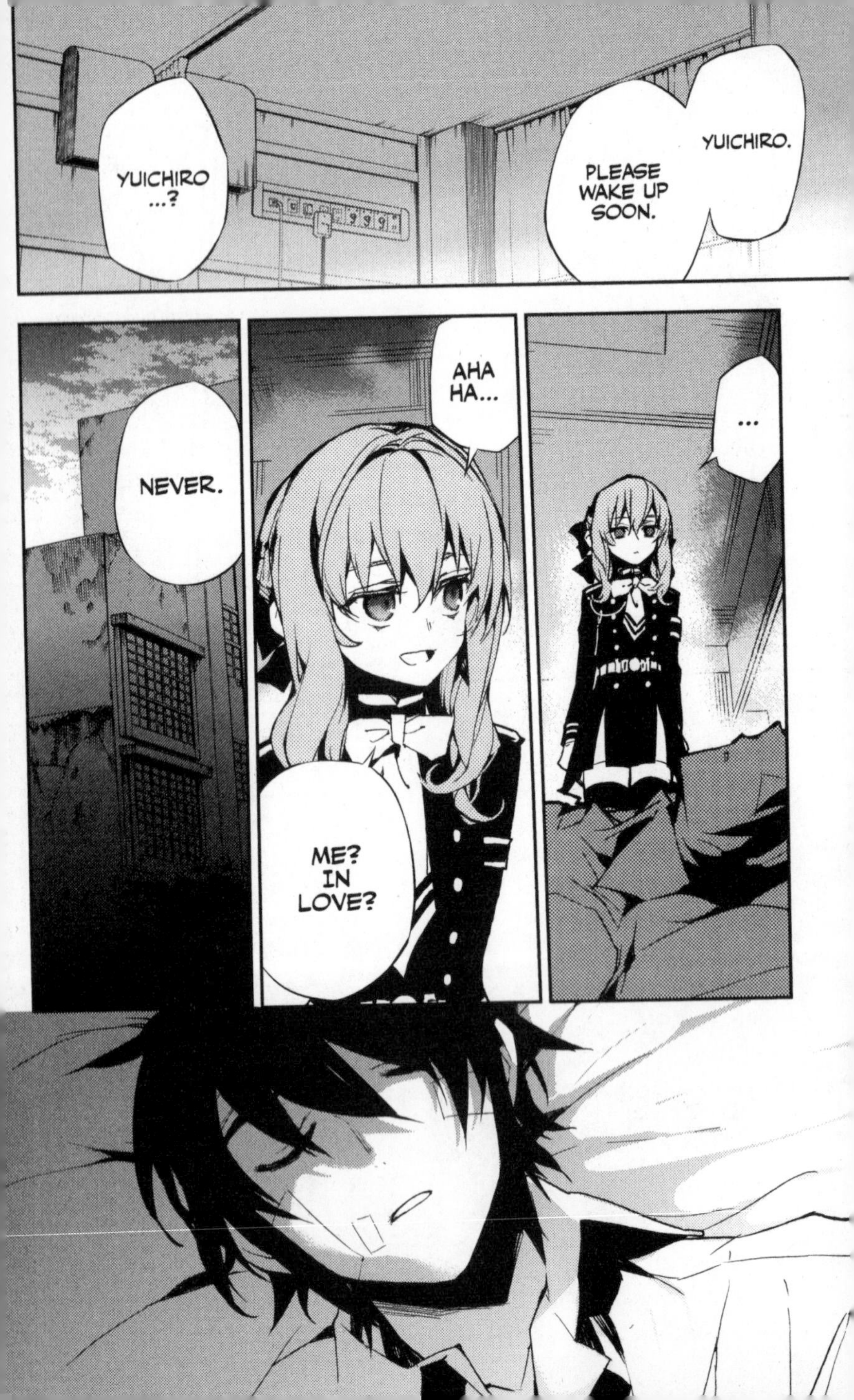
YUICHIRO.
PLEASE WAKE UP SOON.
YUICHIRO ...?
...
AHA HA...
ME? IN LOVE?
NEVER.

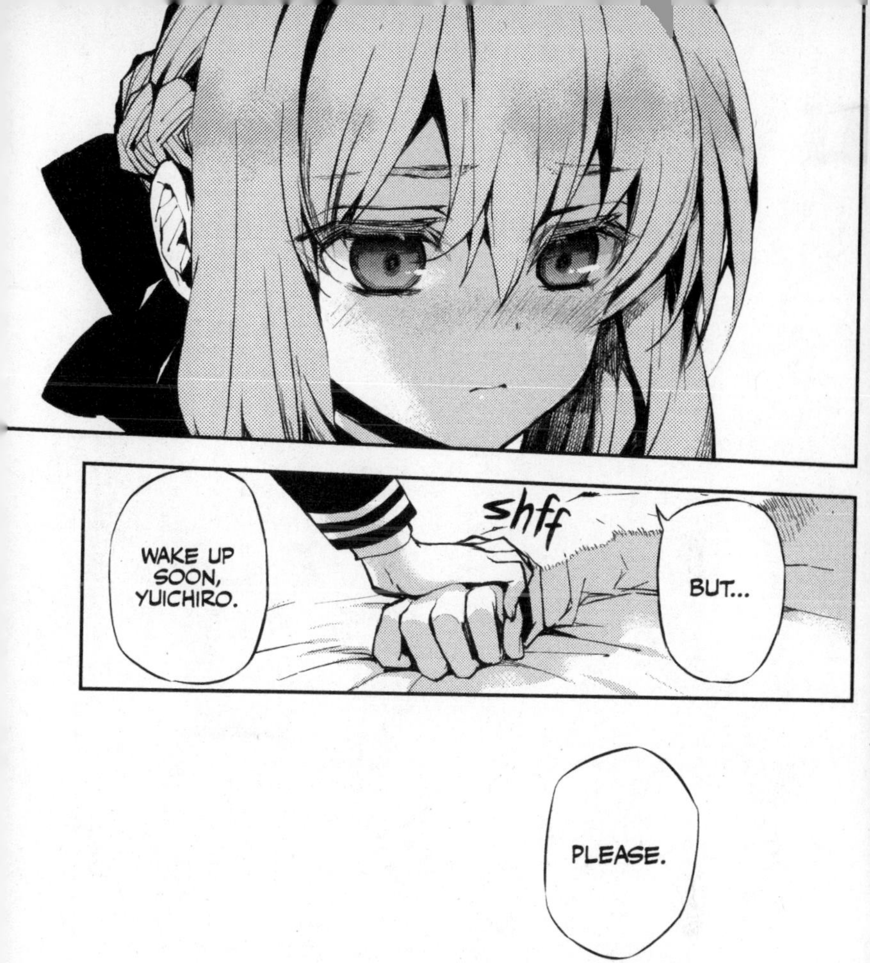
BUT...
shff
WAKE UP SOON, YUICHIRO.
PLEASE.

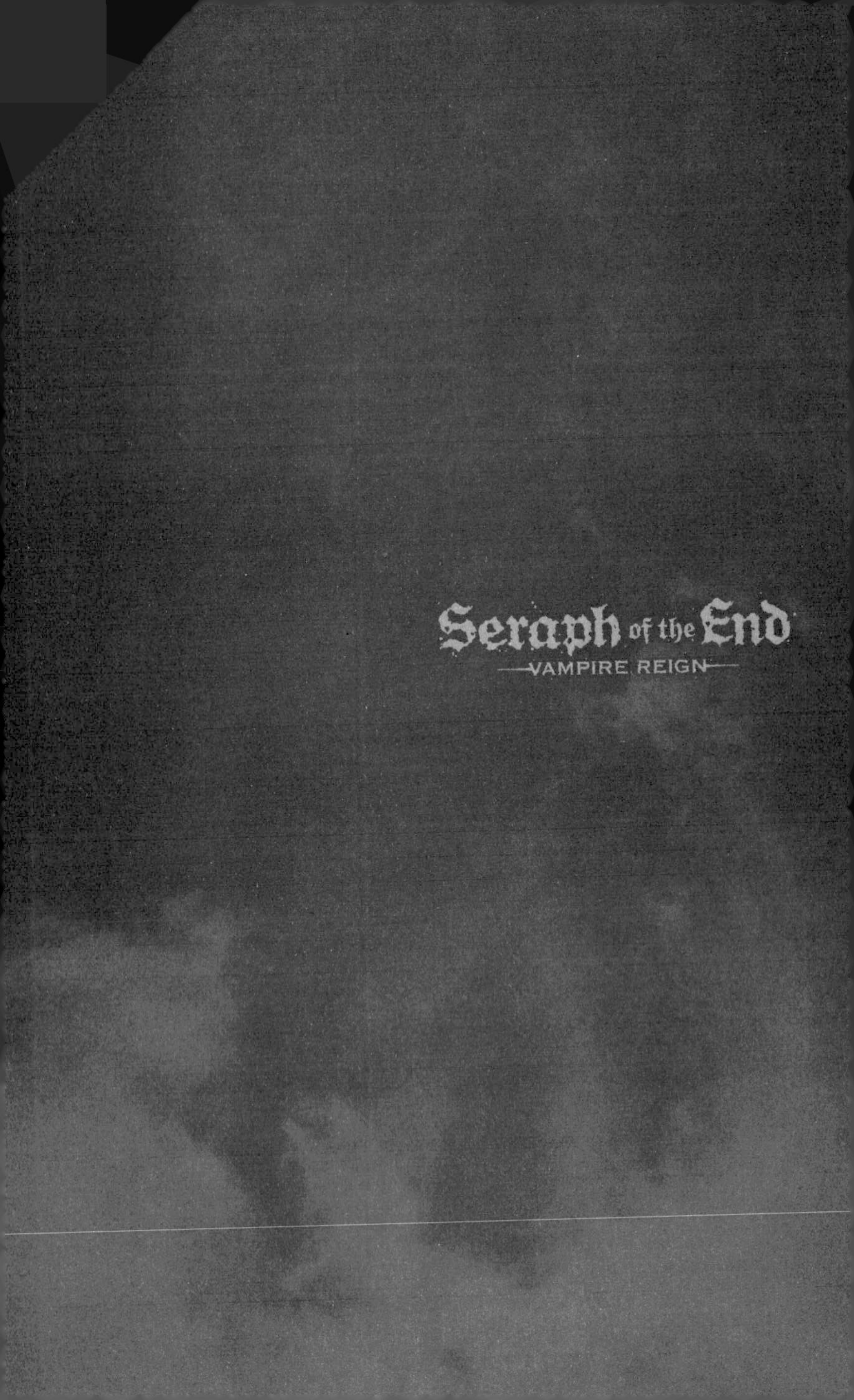
Seraph of the End
VAMPIRE REIGN

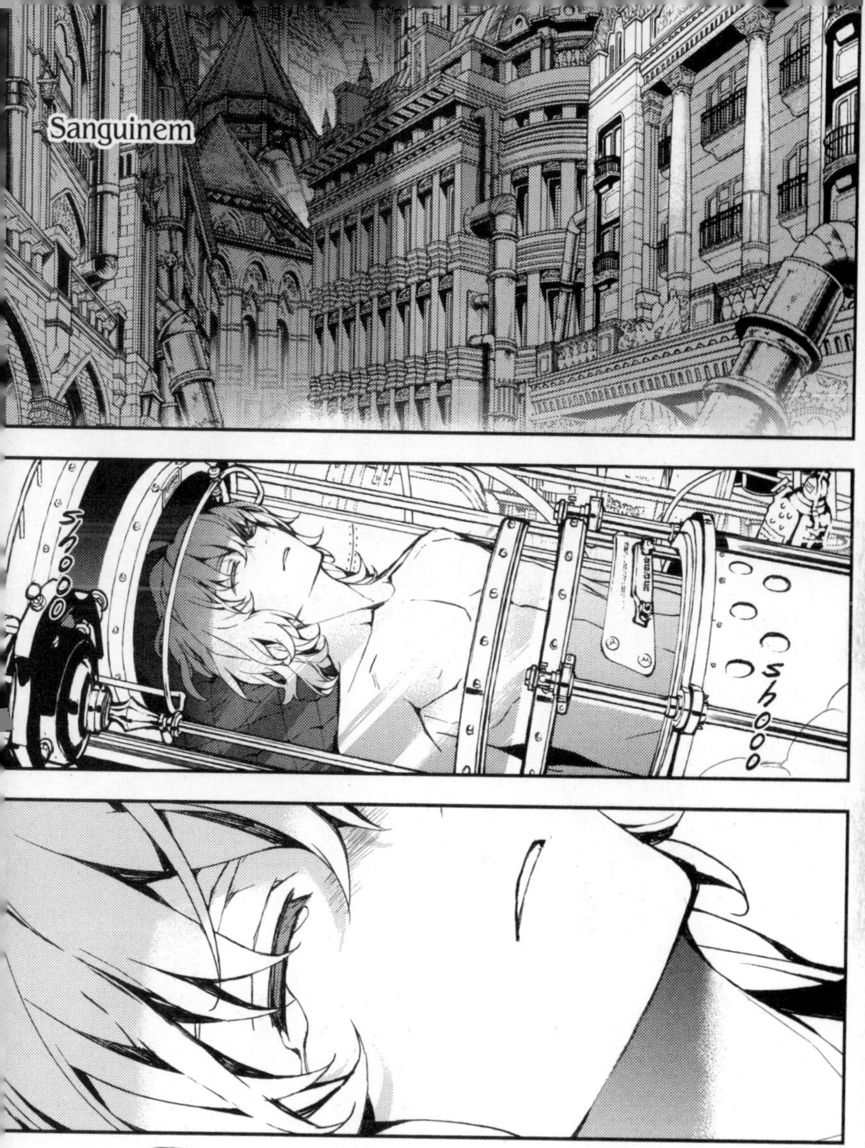
Sanguinem
SHOOOO
SHOOOO

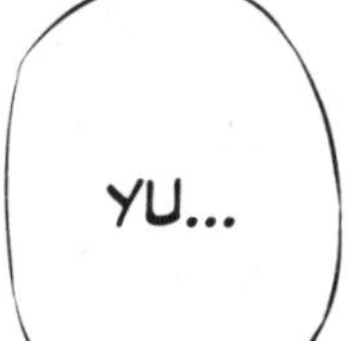
YU...

CHAPTER 15

Complicated Connections

Chapter 15

Complicated Connections

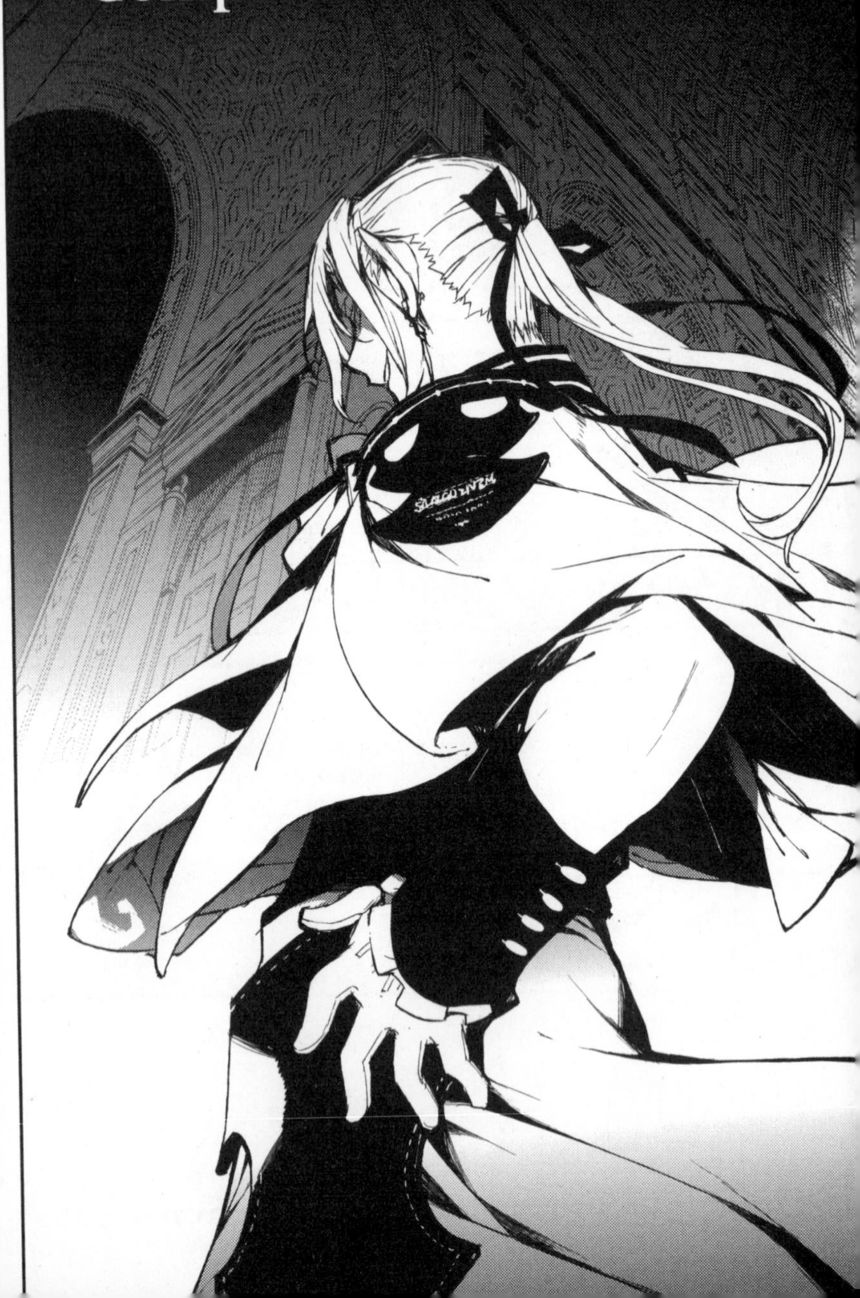

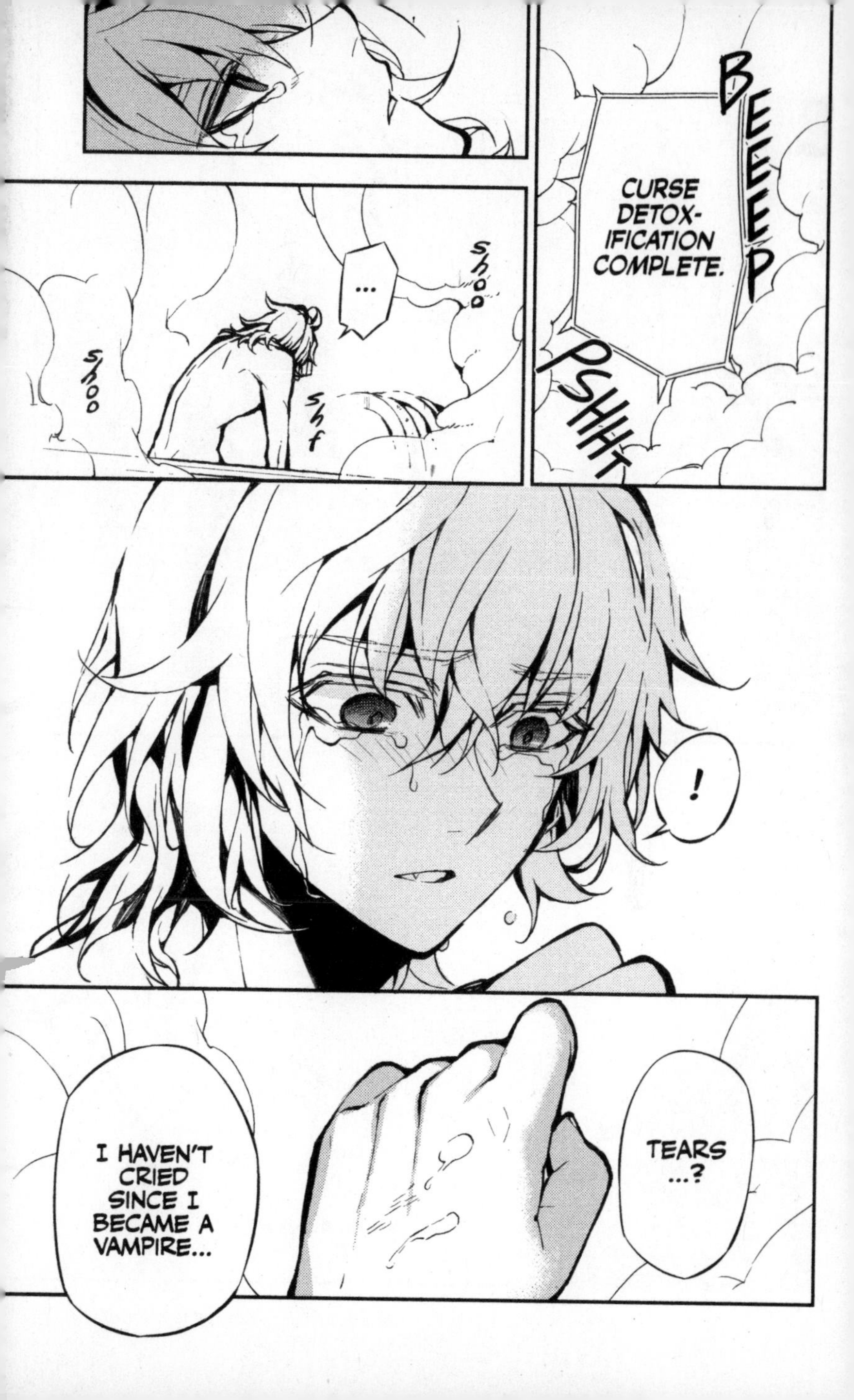
BEEEEP
CURSE DETOX-
IFICATION
COMPLETE.
PSHHHT
shoo
...
shoo
shf
!
TEARS
...?
I HAVEN'T
CRIED
SINCE I
BECAME A
VAMPIRE...

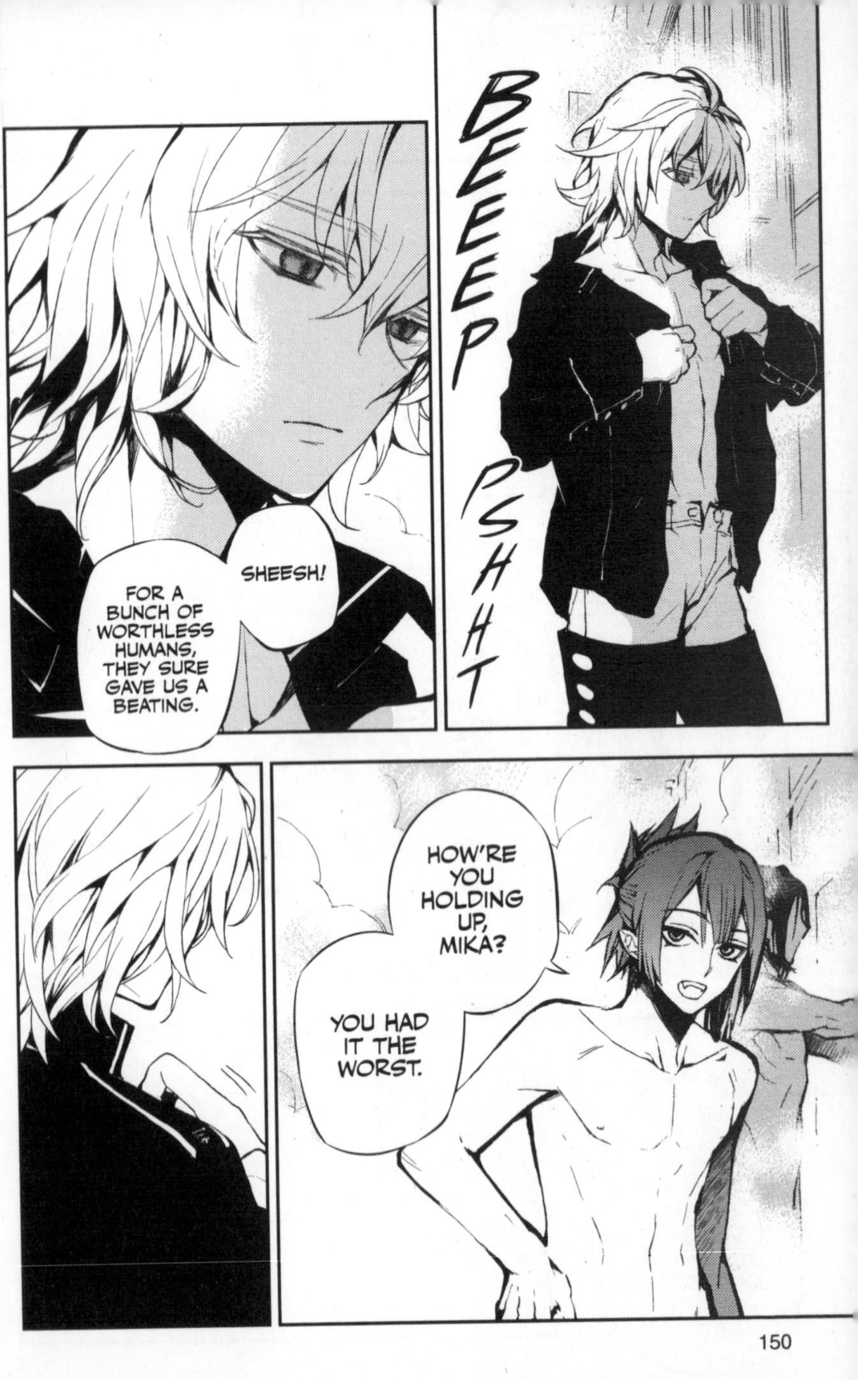
BEEEEP
PSHHT
SHEESH!
FOR A BUNCH OF WORTHLESS HUMANS, THEY SURE GAVE US A BEATING.
HOW'RE YOU HOLDING UP, MIKA?
YOU HAD IT THE WORST.

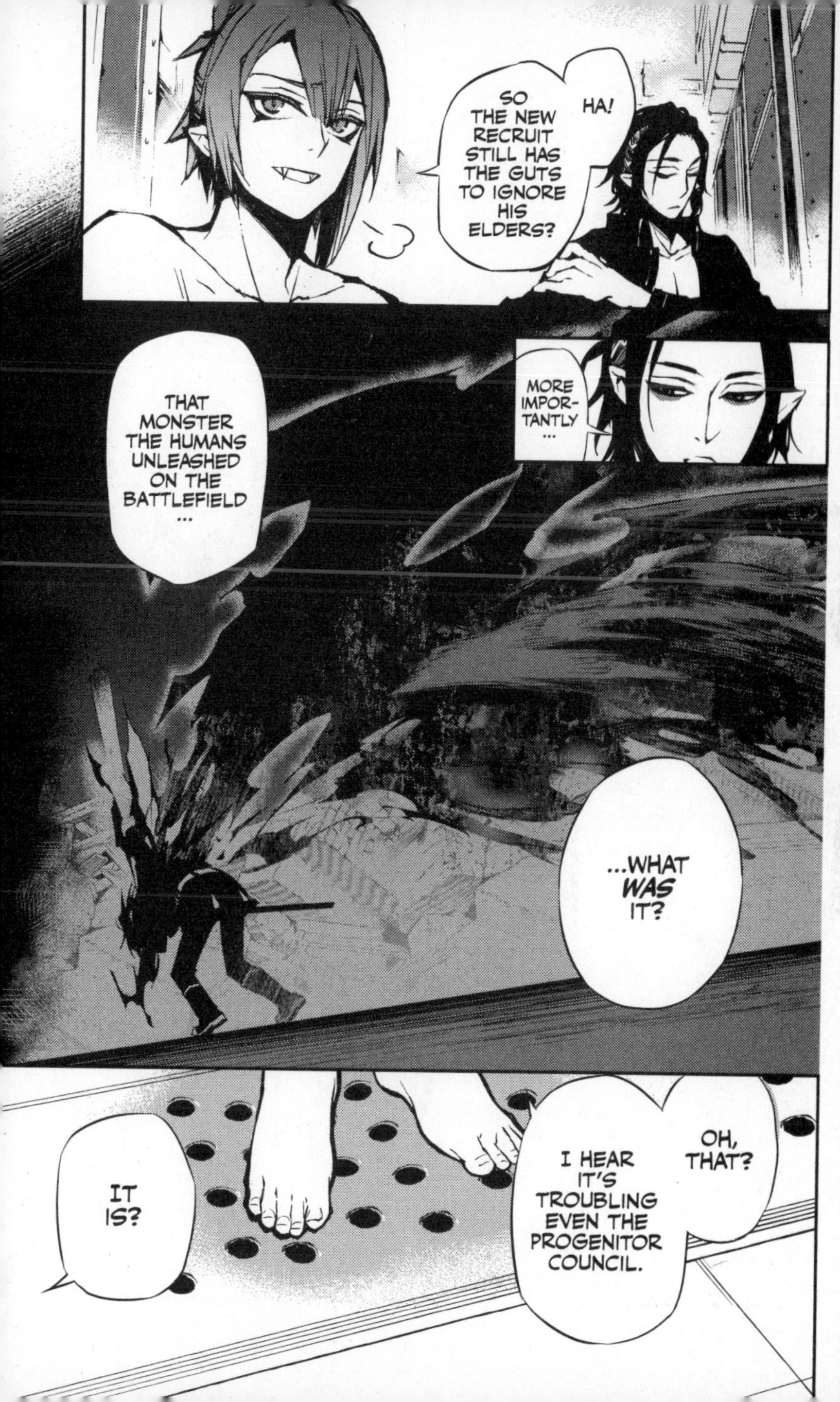
HA!
SO THE NEW RECRUIT STILL HAS THE GUTS TO IGNORE HIS ELDERS?
MORE IMPORTANTLY...
THAT MONSTER THE HUMANS UNLEASHED ON THE BATTLEFIELD...
...WHAT *WAS* IT?
OH, THAT?
I HEAR IT'S TROUBLING EVEN THE PROGENITOR COUNCIL.
IT IS?

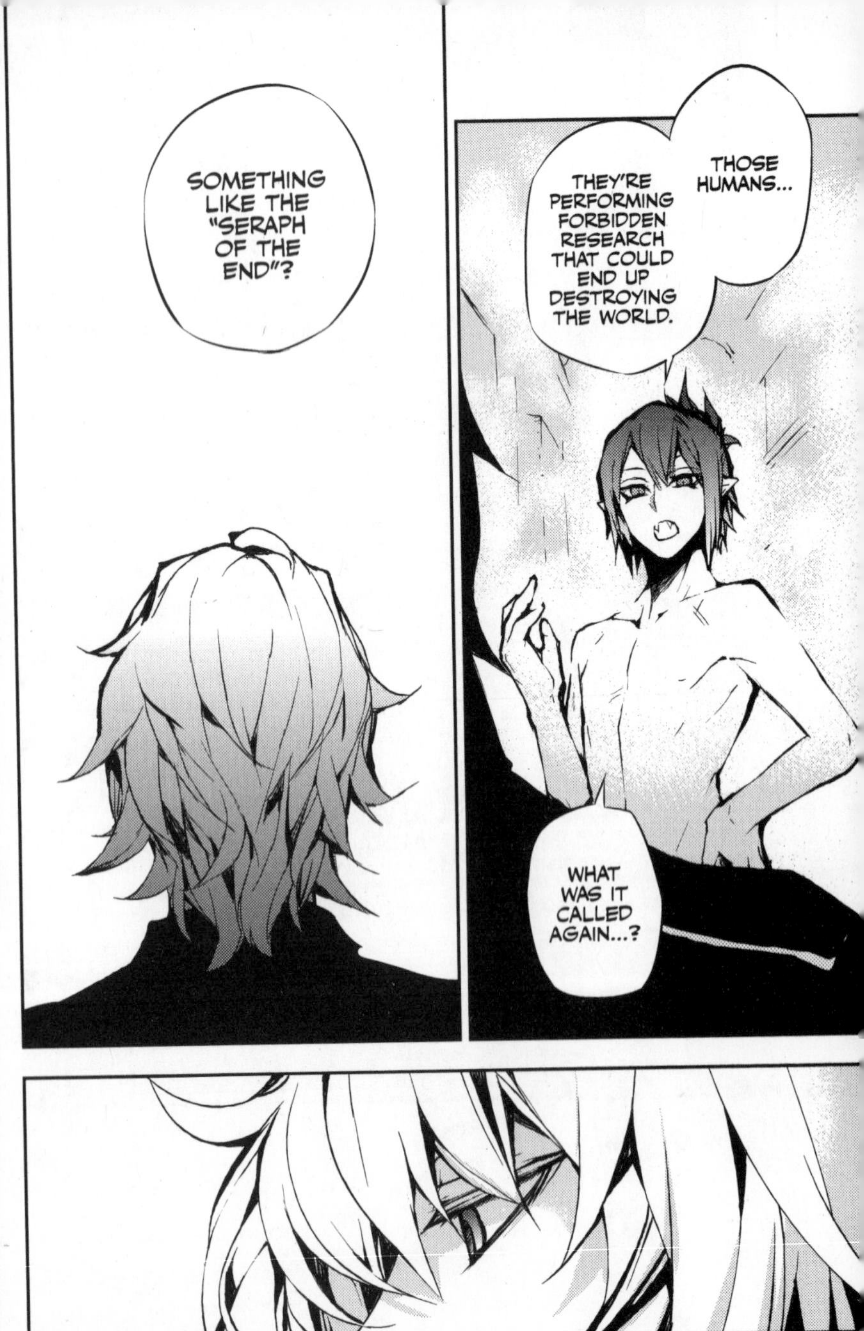
THOSE HUMANS...
THEY'RE PERFORMING FORBIDDEN RESEARCH THAT COULD END UP DESTROYING THE WORLD.
WHAT WAS IT CALLED AGAIN...?
SOMETHING LIKE THE "SERAPH OF THE END"?

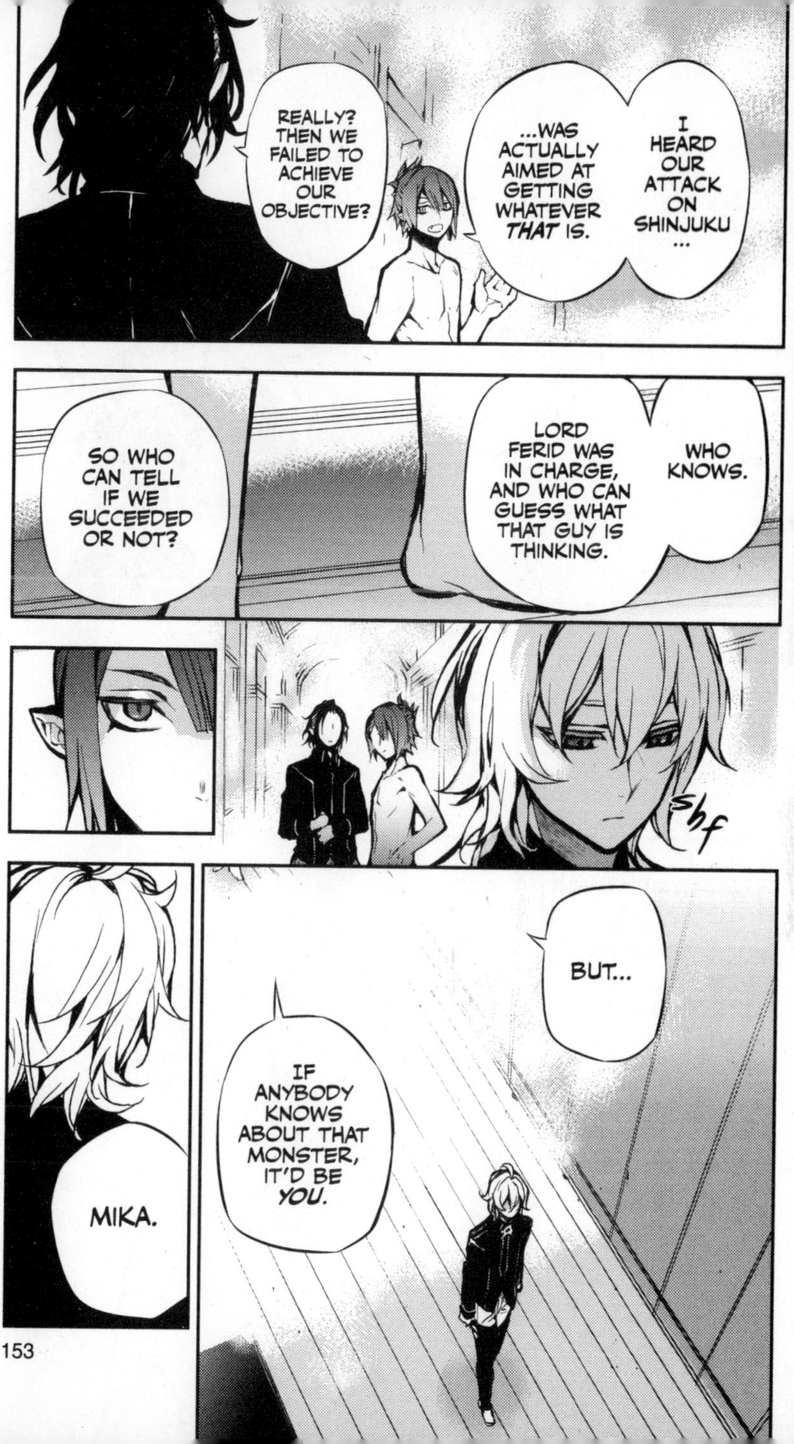
I HEARD OUR ATTACK ON SHINJUKU...
...WAS ACTUALLY AIMED AT GETTING WHATEVER *THAT* IS.
REALLY? THEN WE FAILED TO ACHIEVE OUR OBJECTIVE?
WHO KNOWS.
LORD FERID WAS IN CHARGE, AND WHO CAN GUESS WHAT THAT GUY IS THINKING.
SO WHO CAN TELL IF WE SUCCEEDED OR NOT?
shf
BUT...
IF ANYBODY KNOWS ABOUT THAT MONSTER, IT'D BE *YOU*.
MIKA.

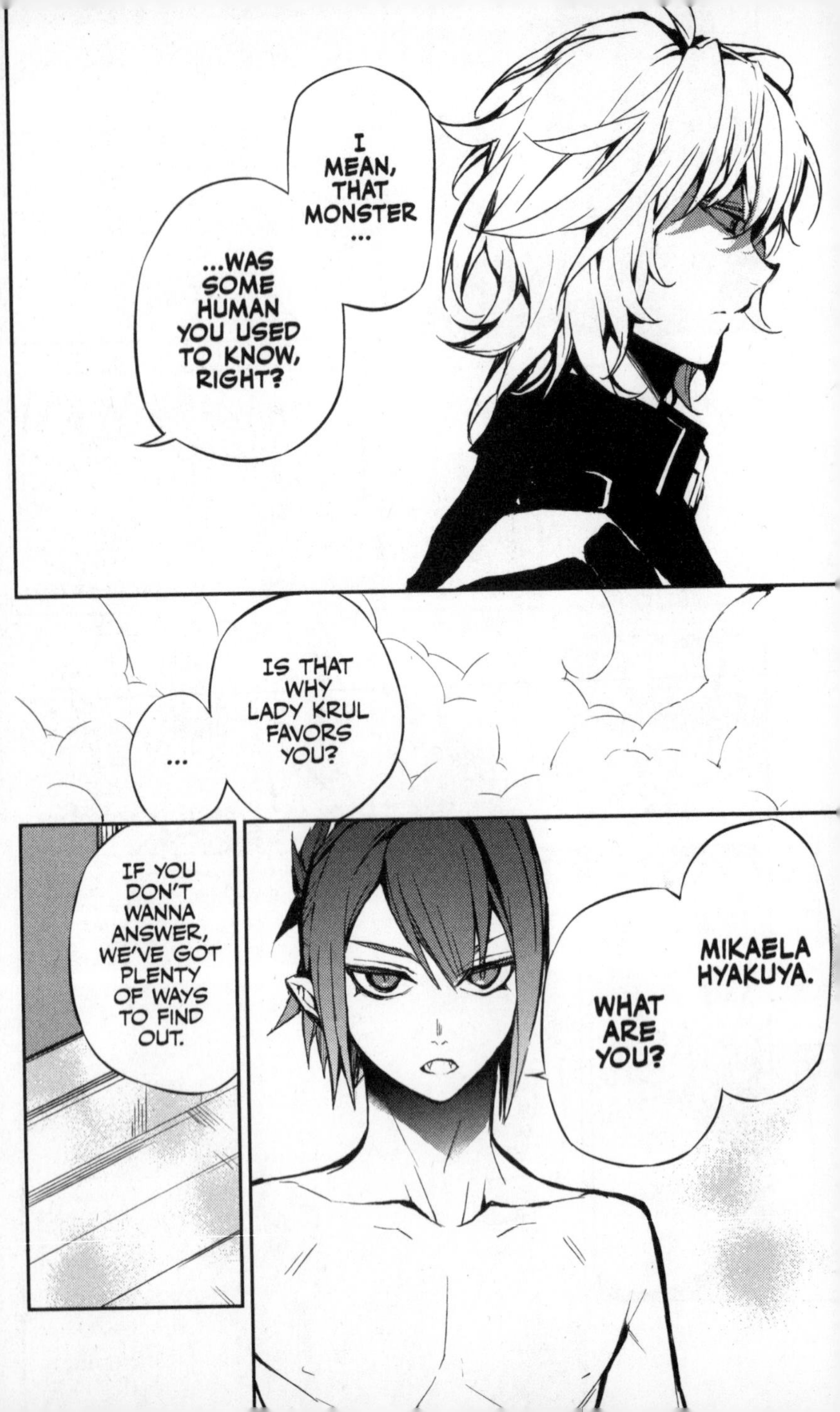
I MEAN, THAT MONSTER...
...WAS SOME HUMAN YOU USED TO KNOW, RIGHT?
IS THAT WHY LADY KRUL FAVORS YOU?
...
MIKAELA HYAKUYA.
WHAT ARE YOU?
IF YOU DON'T WANNA ANSWER, WE'VE GOT PLENTY OF WAYS TO FIND OUT.

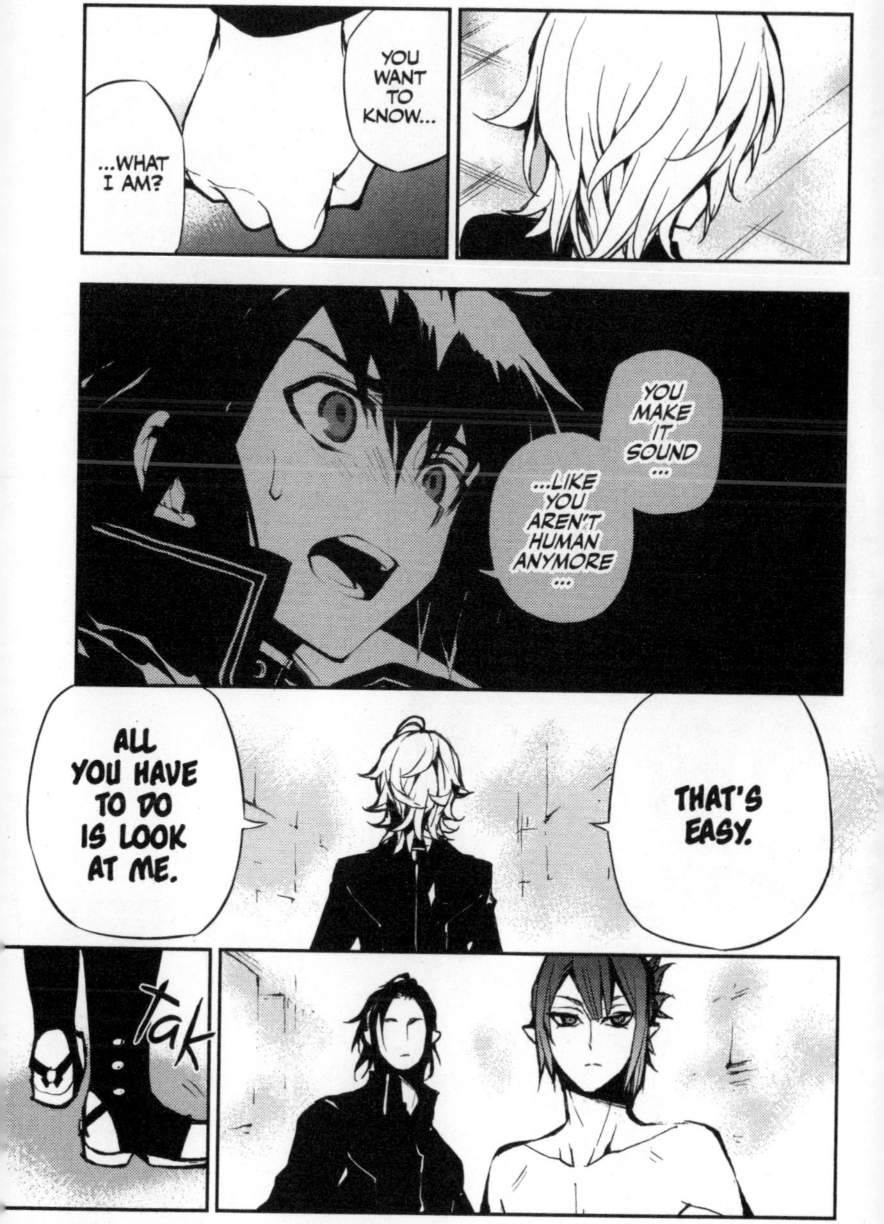

YOU WANT TO KNOW...
...WHAT I AM?
YOU MAKE IT SOUND...
...LIKE YOU AREN'T HUMAN ANYMORE...
THAT'S EASY.
ALL YOU HAVE TO DO IS LOOK AT ME.
tak

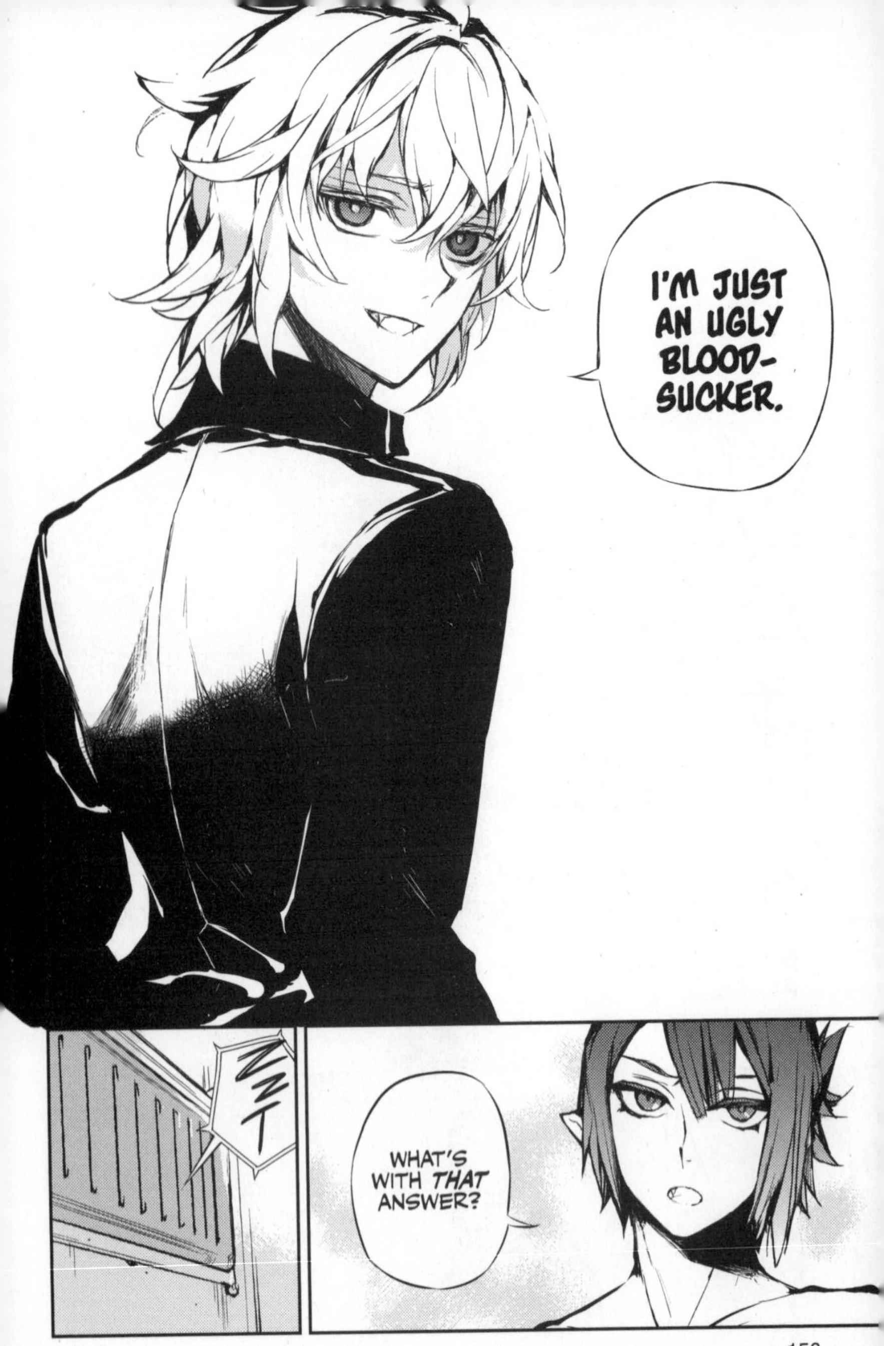
I'M JUST AN UGLY BLOOD-SUCKER.
WHAT'S WITH *THAT* ANSWER?
NNT

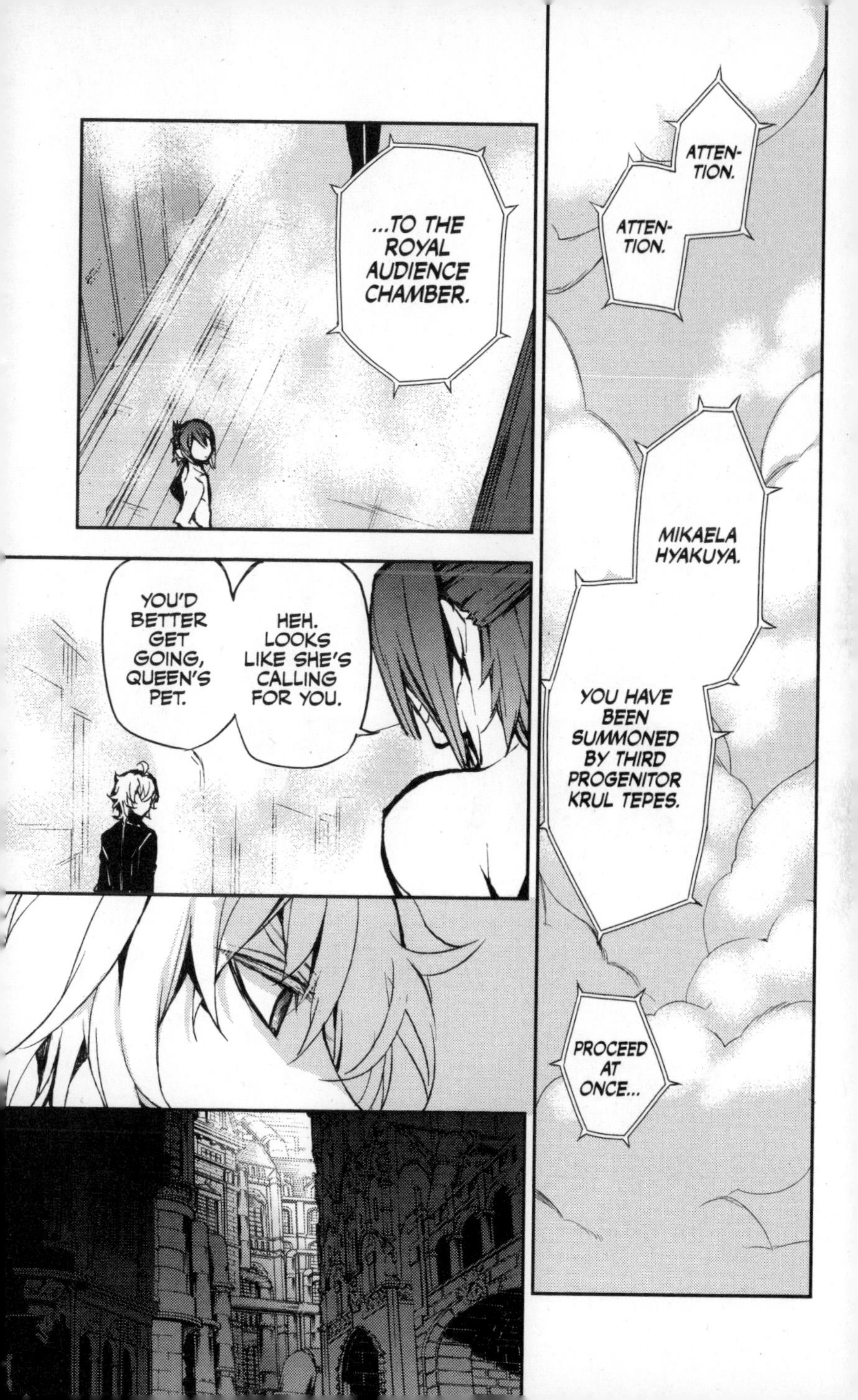
ATTEN-TION.
ATTEN-TION.
MIKAELA HYAKUYA.
YOU HAVE BEEN SUMMONED BY THIRD PROGENITOR KRUL TEPES.
PROCEED AT ONCE...
...TO THE ROYAL AUDIENCE CHAMBER.
HEH. LOOKS LIKE SHE'S CALLING FOR YOU.
YOU'D BETTER GET GOING, QUEEN'S PET.

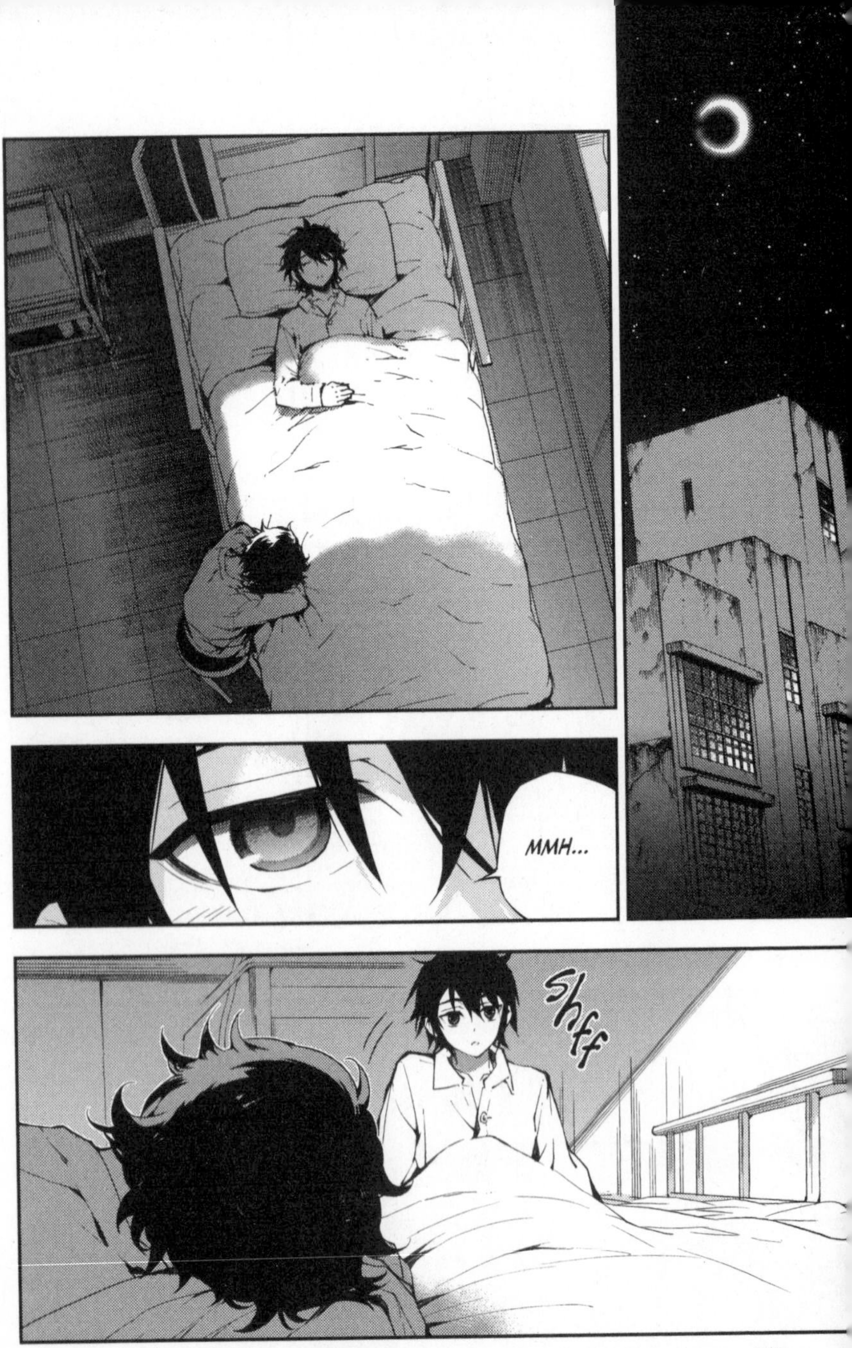
MMH...
Shff

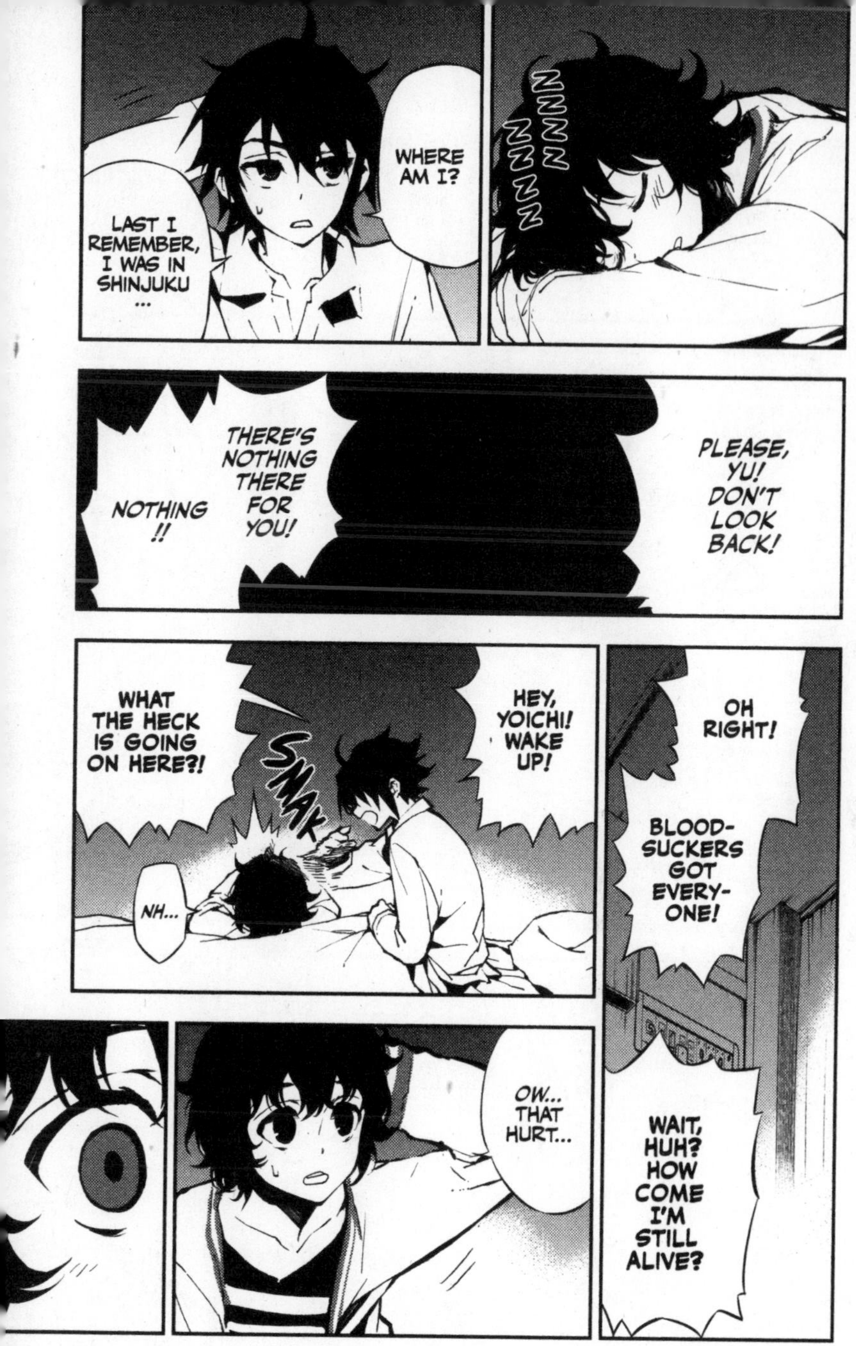
ZZZZ
ZZZZZ
WHERE AM I?
LAST I REMEMBER, I WAS IN SHINJUKU ...
PLEASE, YU! DON'T LOOK BACK!
THERE'S NOTHING THERE FOR YOU!
NOTHING !!
OH RIGHT!
BLOOD-SUCKERS GOT EVERY-ONE!
WAIT, HUH? HOW COME I'M STILL ALIVE?
HEY, YOICHI! WAKE UP!
SMAK
WHAT THE HECK IS GOING ON HERE?!
NH...
OW... THAT HURT...

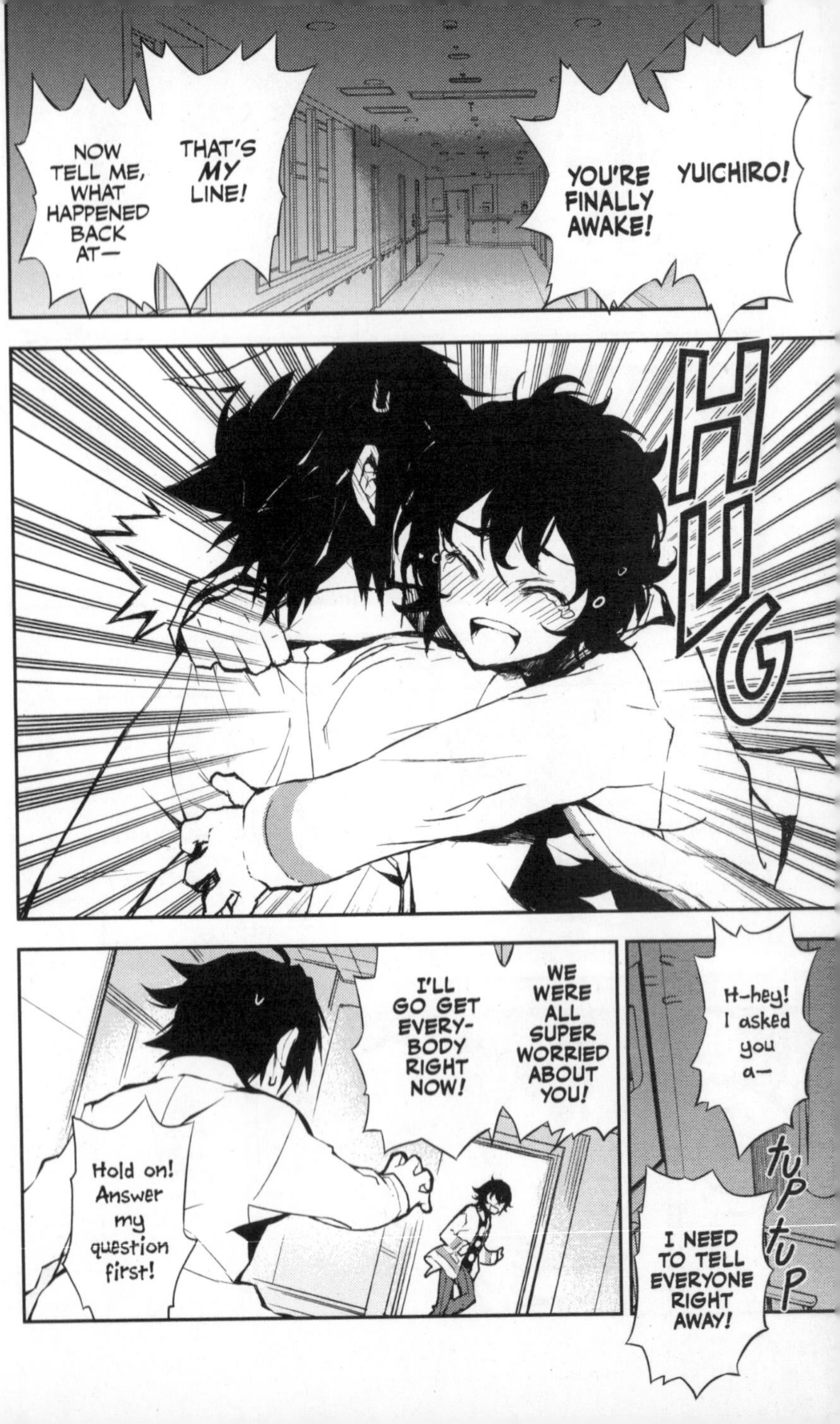
YUICHIRO!
YOU'RE FINALLY AWAKE!
THAT'S MY LINE!
NOW TELL ME, WHAT HAPPENED BACK AT—
HUG
H-hey! I asked you a—
I NEED TO TELL EVERYONE RIGHT AWAY!
TUP TUP
WE WERE ALL SUPER WORRIED ABOUT YOU!
I'LL GO GET EVERYBODY RIGHT NOW!
Hold on! Answer my question first!

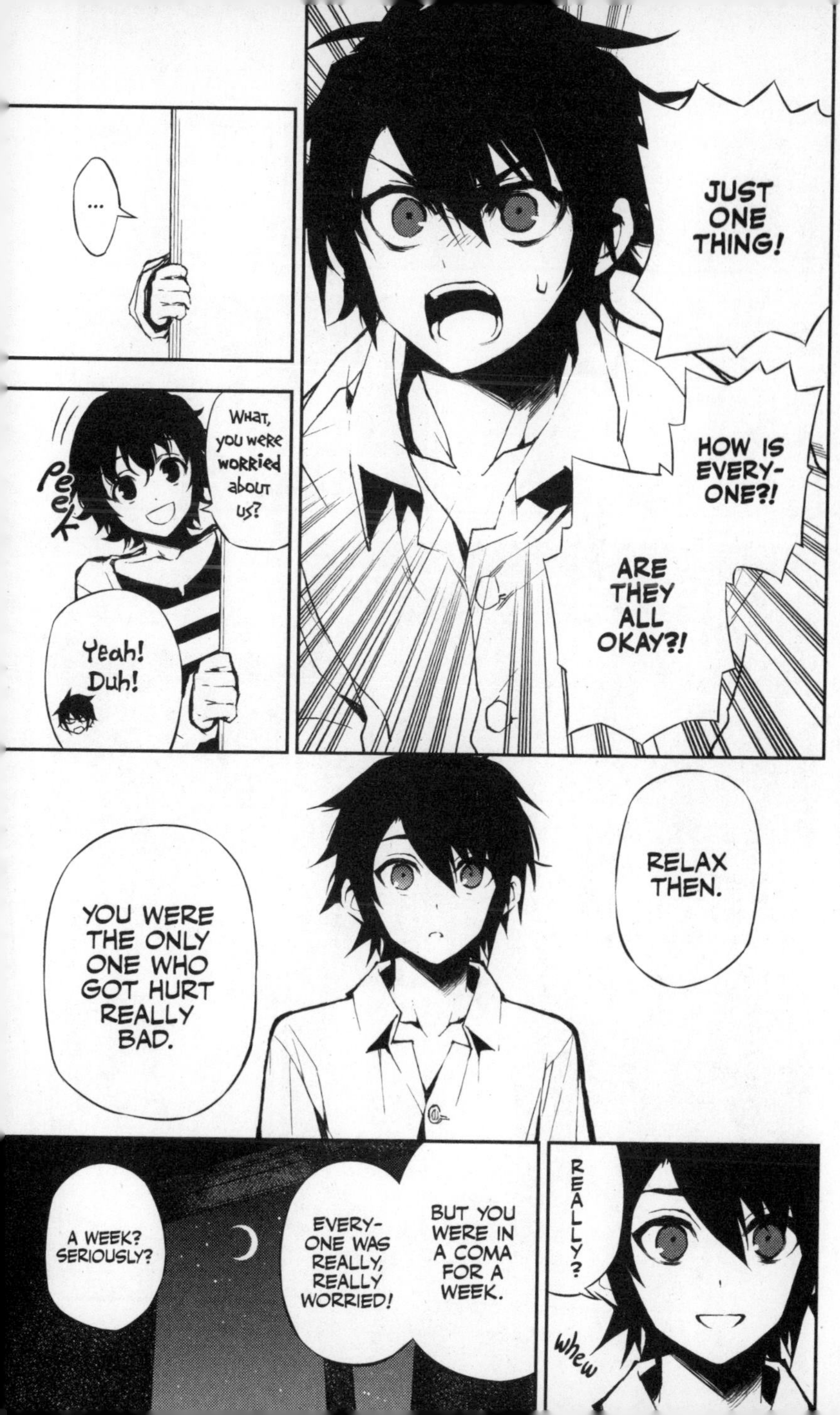
JUST ONE THING!
HOW IS EVERY-ONE?!
ARE THEY ALL OKAY?!
...
WHAT, you were worried about us?
Peek
Yeah! Duh!
RELAX THEN.
YOU WERE THE ONLY ONE WHO GOT HURT REALLY BAD.
REALLY?
whew
BUT YOU WERE IN A COMA FOR A WEEK.
EVERY-ONE WAS REALLY, REALLY WORRIED!
A WEEK? SERIOUSLY?

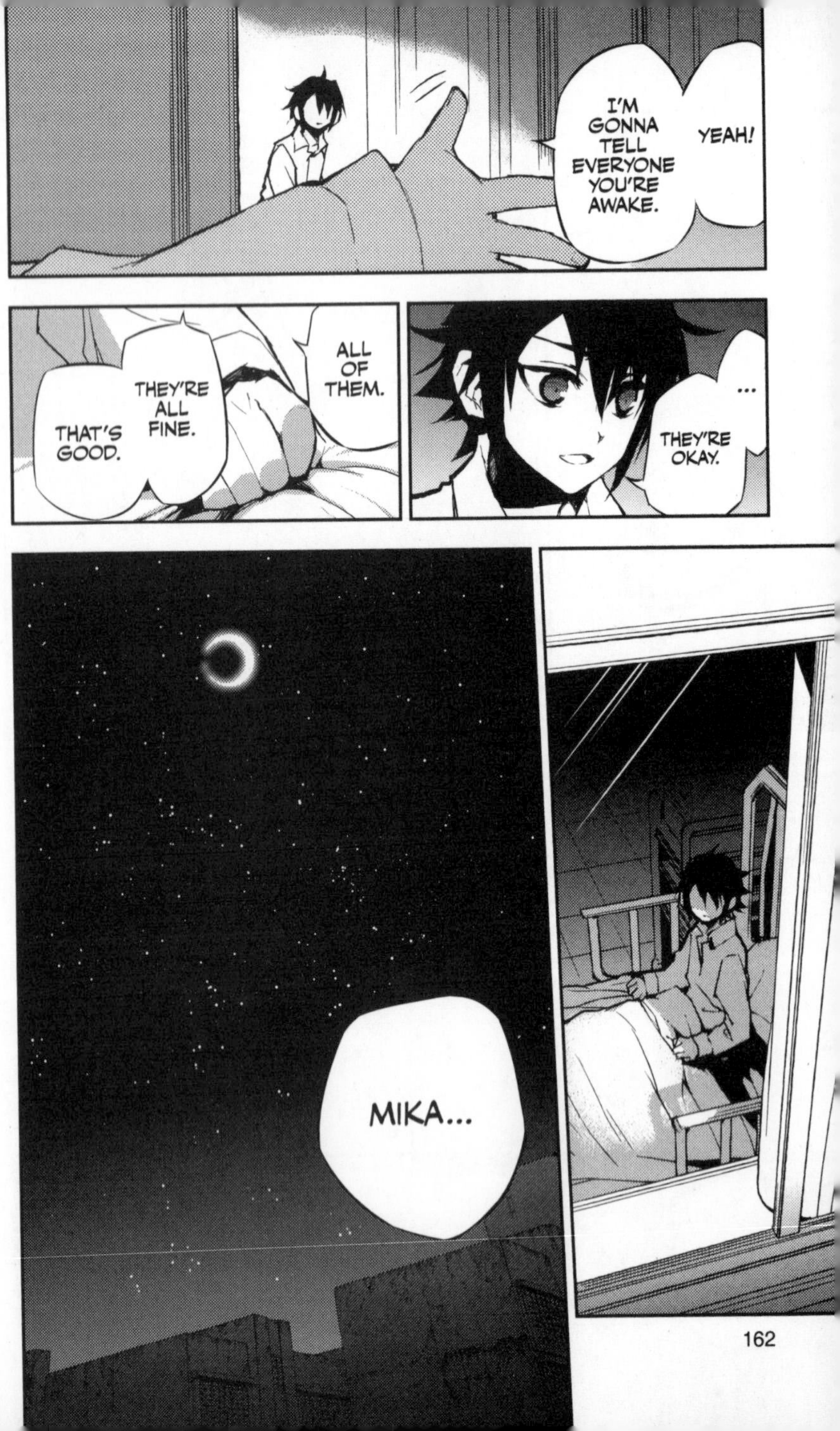
YEAH!
I'M GONNA TELL EVERYONE YOU'RE AWAKE.
...
THEY'RE OKAY.
ALL OF THEM.
THEY'RE ALL FINE.
THAT'S GOOD.
MIKA...

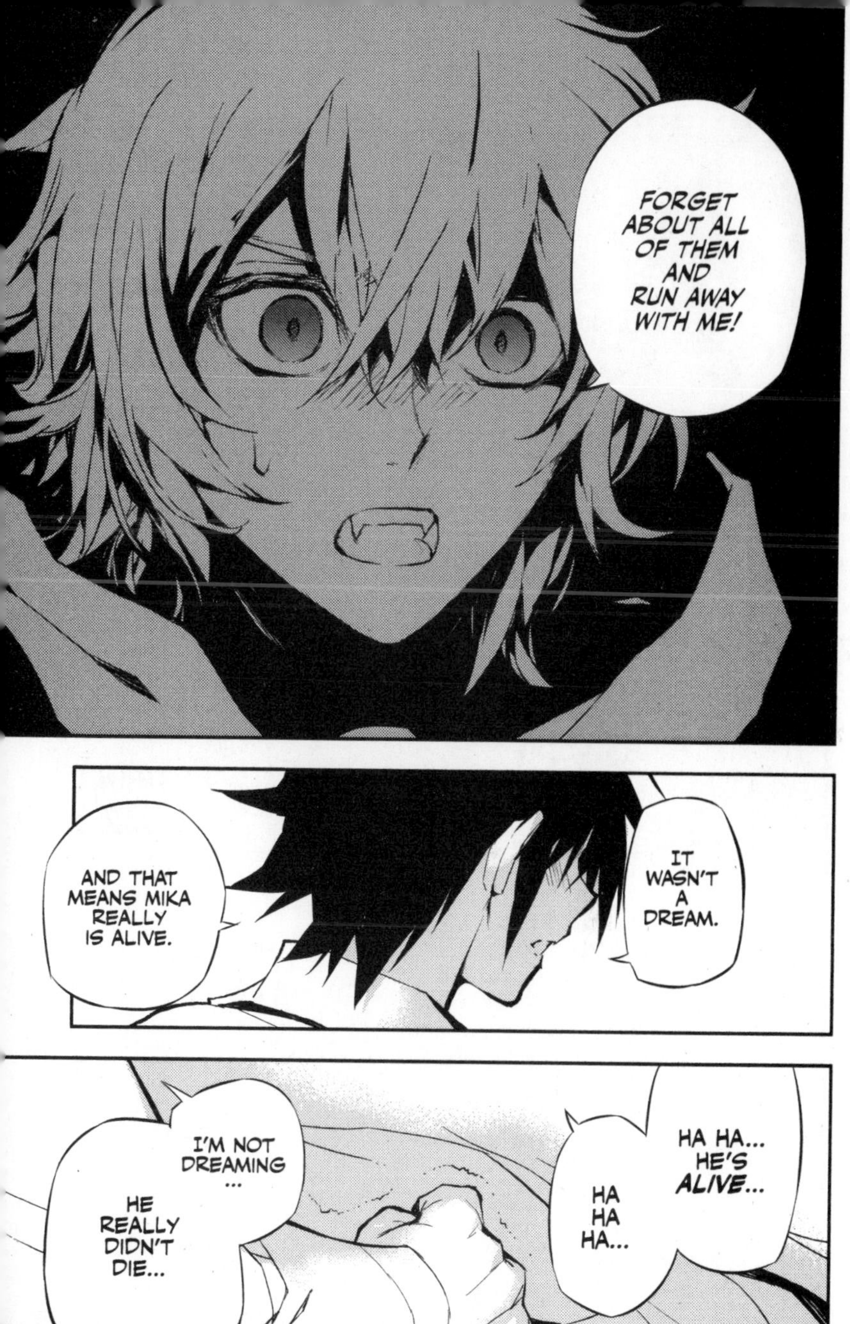
FORGET ABOUT ALL OF THEM AND RUN AWAY WITH ME!
IT WASN'T A DREAM.
AND THAT MEANS MIKA REALLY IS ALIVE.
HA HA... HE'S ALIVE...
HA HA HA...
I'M NOT DREAMING...
HE REALLY DIDN'T DIE...

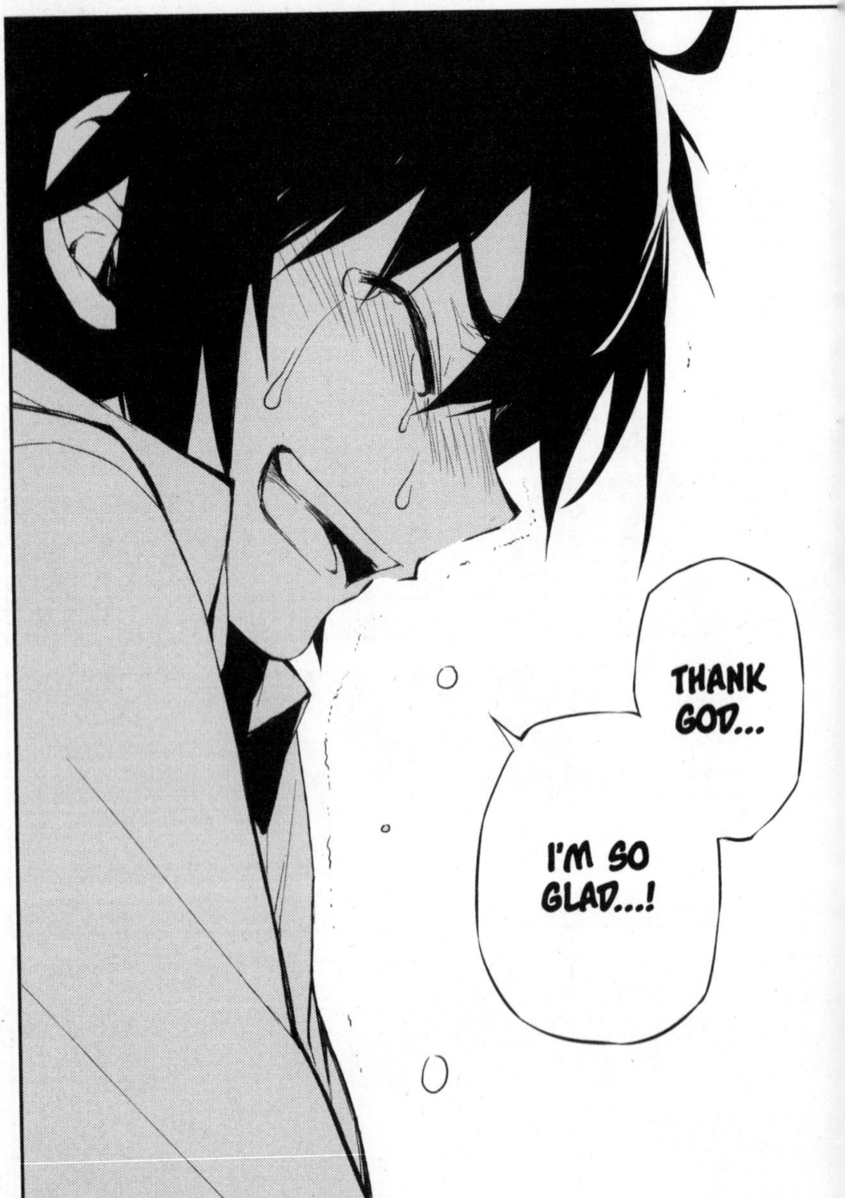
THANK GOD...
I'M SO GLAD...!

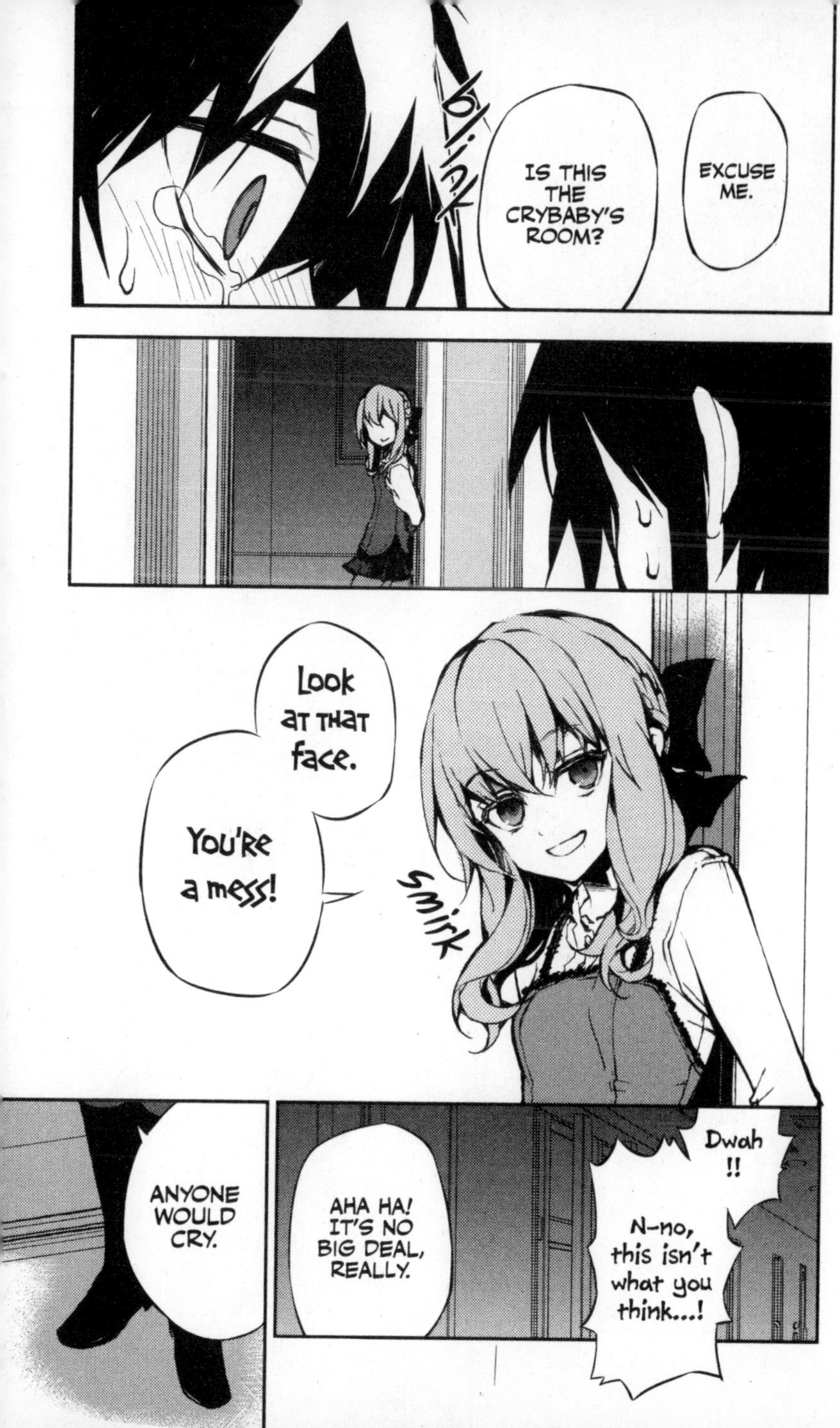
EXCUSE ME.
IS THIS THE CRYBABY'S ROOM?
blink
Look at that face.
You're a mess!
smirk
Dwah !!
N-no, this isn't what you think...!
AHA HA! IT'S NO BIG DEAL, REALLY.
ANYONE WOULD CRY.

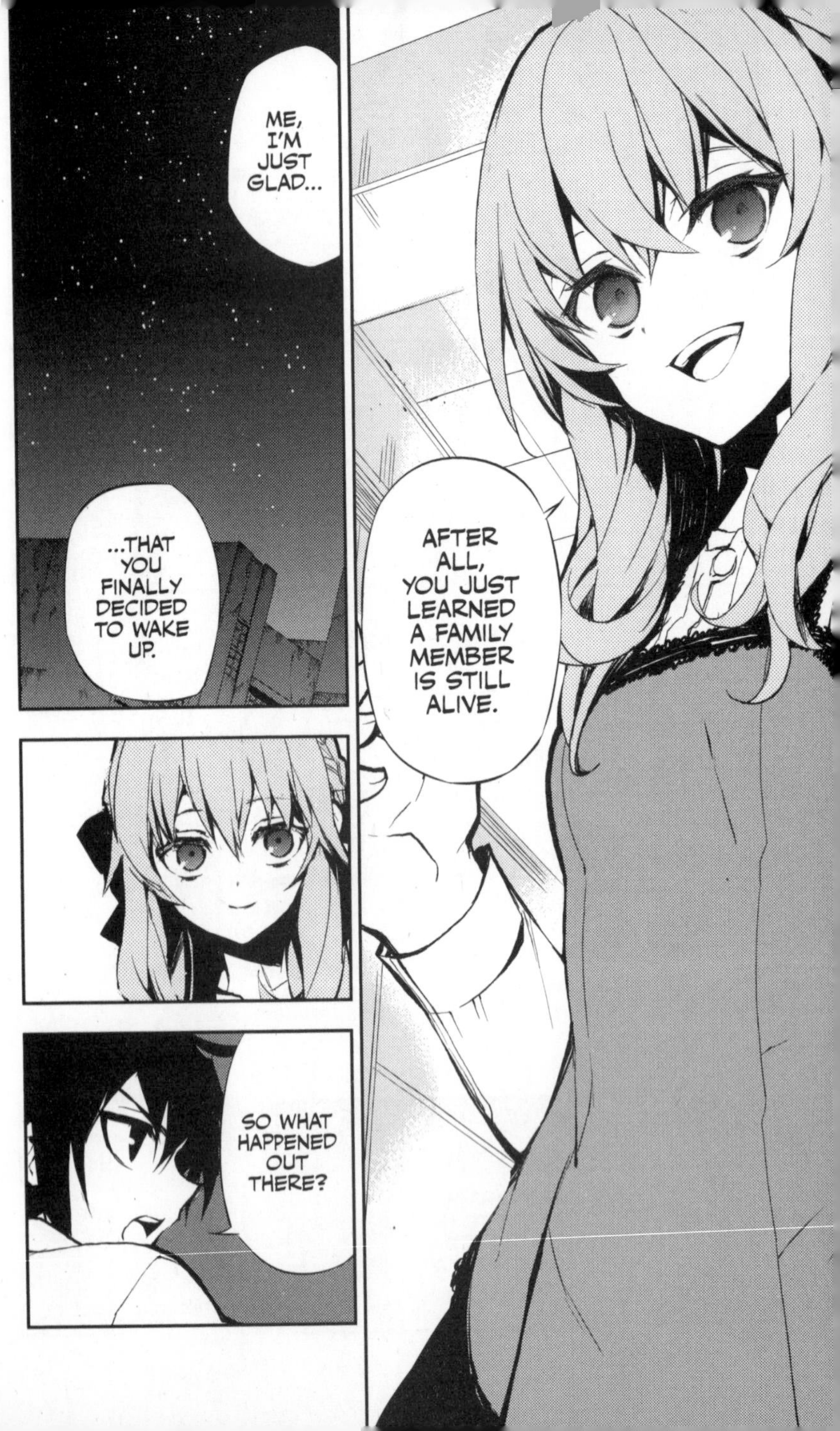
AFTER ALL, YOU JUST LEARNED A FAMILY MEMBER IS STILL ALIVE.
ME, I'M JUST GLAD...
...THAT YOU FINALLY DECIDED TO WAKE UP.
SO WHAT HAPPENED OUT THERE?

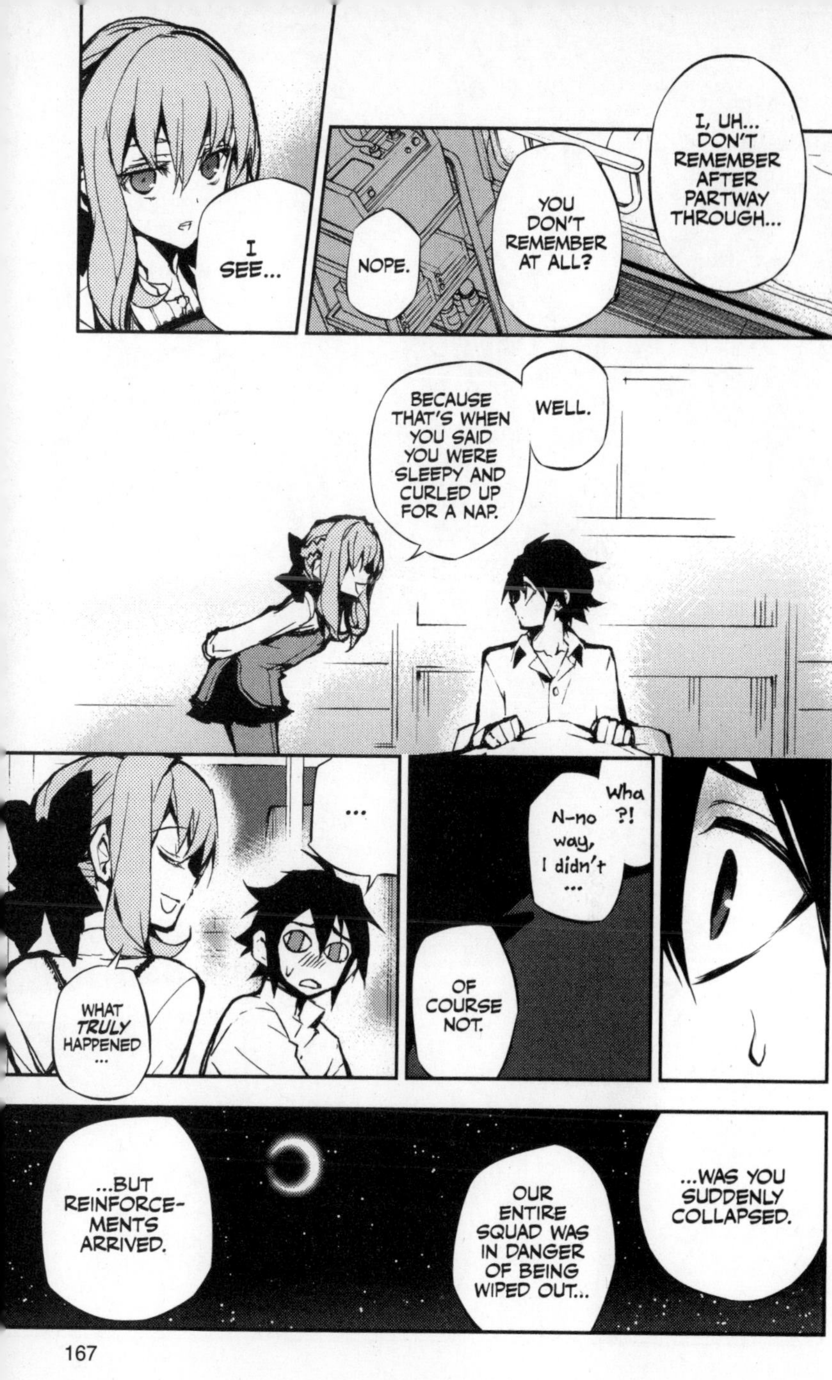
I, UH... DON'T REMEMBER AFTER PARTWAY THROUGH...
YOU DON'T REMEMBER AT ALL?
NOPE.
I SEE...
WELL.
BECAUSE THAT'S WHEN YOU SAID YOU WERE SLEEPY AND CURLED UP FOR A NAP.
Wha ?!
N-no way, I didn't ...
OF COURSE NOT.
...
WHAT *TRULY* HAPPENED ...
...WAS YOU SUDDENLY COLLAPSED.
OUR ENTIRE SQUAD WAS IN DANGER OF BEING WIPED OUT...
...BUT REINFORCE-MENTS ARRIVED.

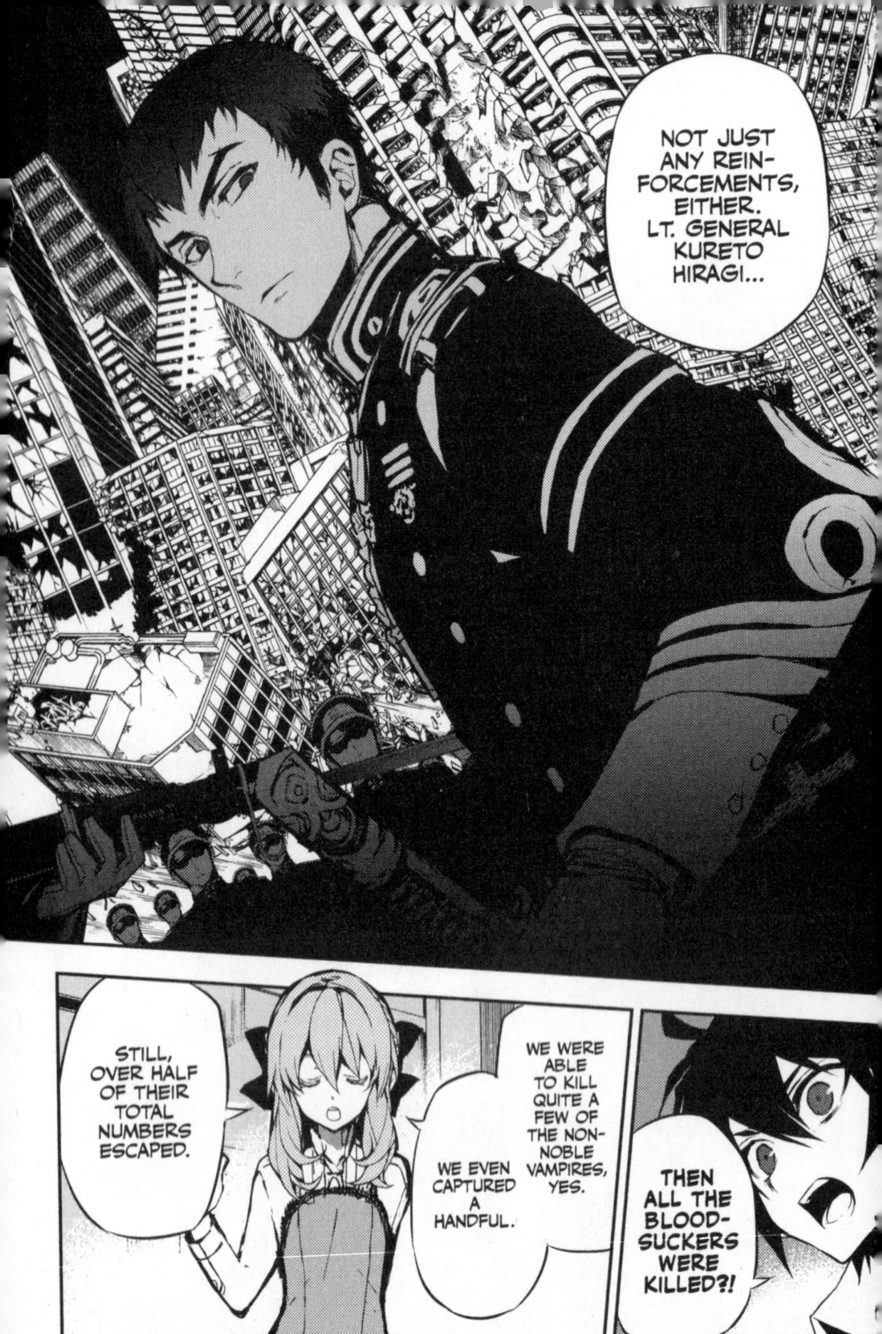
NOT JUST ANY REIN-FORCEMENTS, EITHER. LT. GENERAL KURETO HIRAGI...
THEN ALL THE BLOOD-SUCKERS WERE KILLED?!
WE WERE ABLE TO KILL QUITE A FEW OF THE NON-NOBLE VAMPIRES, YES.
WE EVEN CAPTURED A HANDFUL.
STILL, OVER HALF OF THEIR TOTAL NUMBERS ESCAPED.

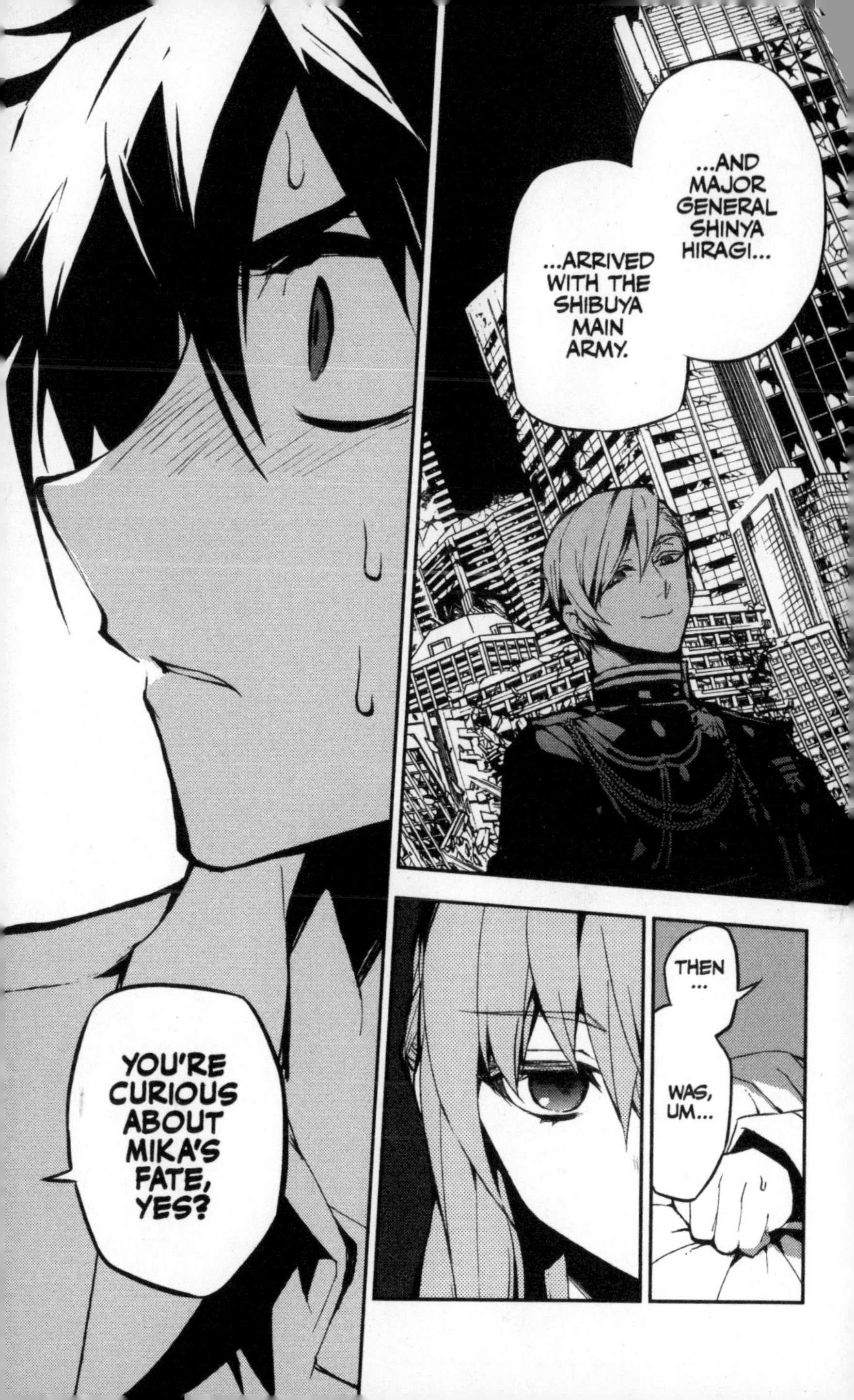
...AND MAJOR GENERAL SHINYA HIRAGI...
...ARRIVED WITH THE SHIBUYA MAIN ARMY.
THEN...
WAS, UM...
YOU'RE CURIOUS ABOUT MIKA'S FATE, YES?

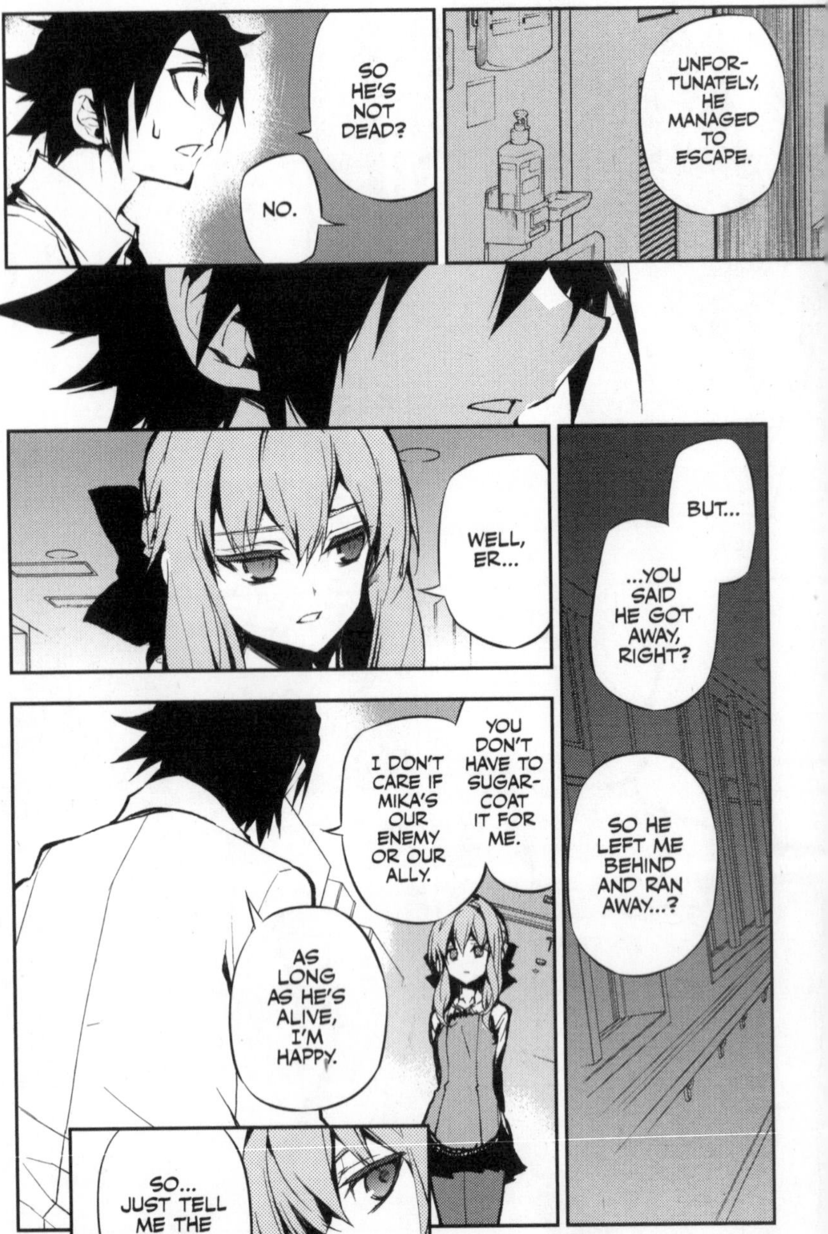
UNFOR-TUNATELY, HE MANAGED TO ESCAPE.
SO HE'S NOT DEAD?
NO.
BUT...
...YOU SAID HE GOT AWAY, RIGHT?
SO HE LEFT ME BEHIND AND RAN AWAY...?
WELL, ER...
YOU DON'T HAVE TO SUGAR-COAT IT FOR ME.
I DON'T CARE IF MIKA'S OUR ENEMY OR OUR ALLY.
AS LONG AS HE'S ALIVE, I'M HAPPY.
SO... JUST TELL ME THE TRUTH.

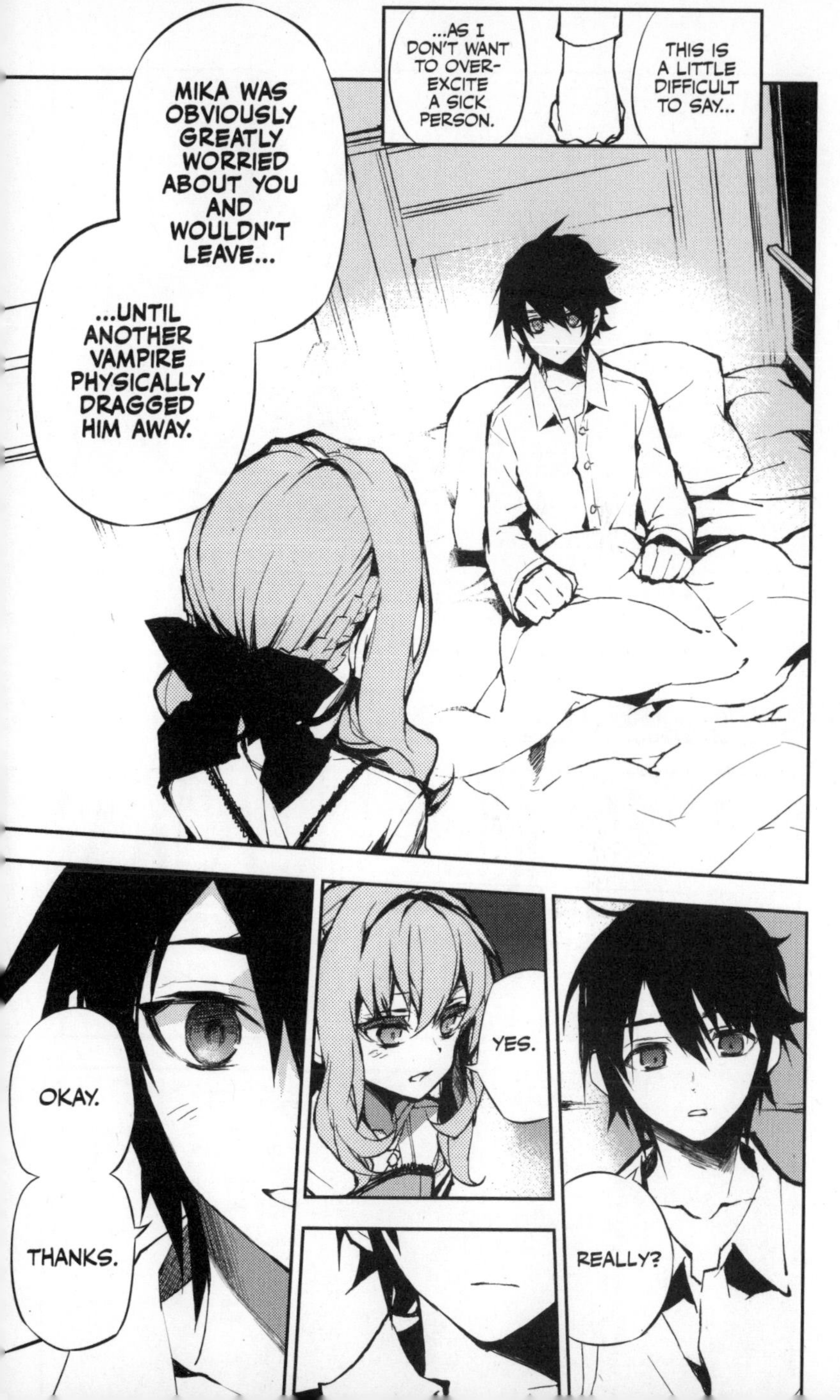
THIS IS A LITTLE DIFFICULT TO SAY...
...AS I DON'T WANT TO OVER-EXCITE A SICK PERSON.
MIKA WAS OBVIOUSLY GREATLY WORRIED ABOUT YOU AND WOULDN'T LEAVE...
...UNTIL ANOTHER VAMPIRE PHYSICALLY DRAGGED HIM AWAY.
REALLY?
YES.
OKAY.
THANKS.

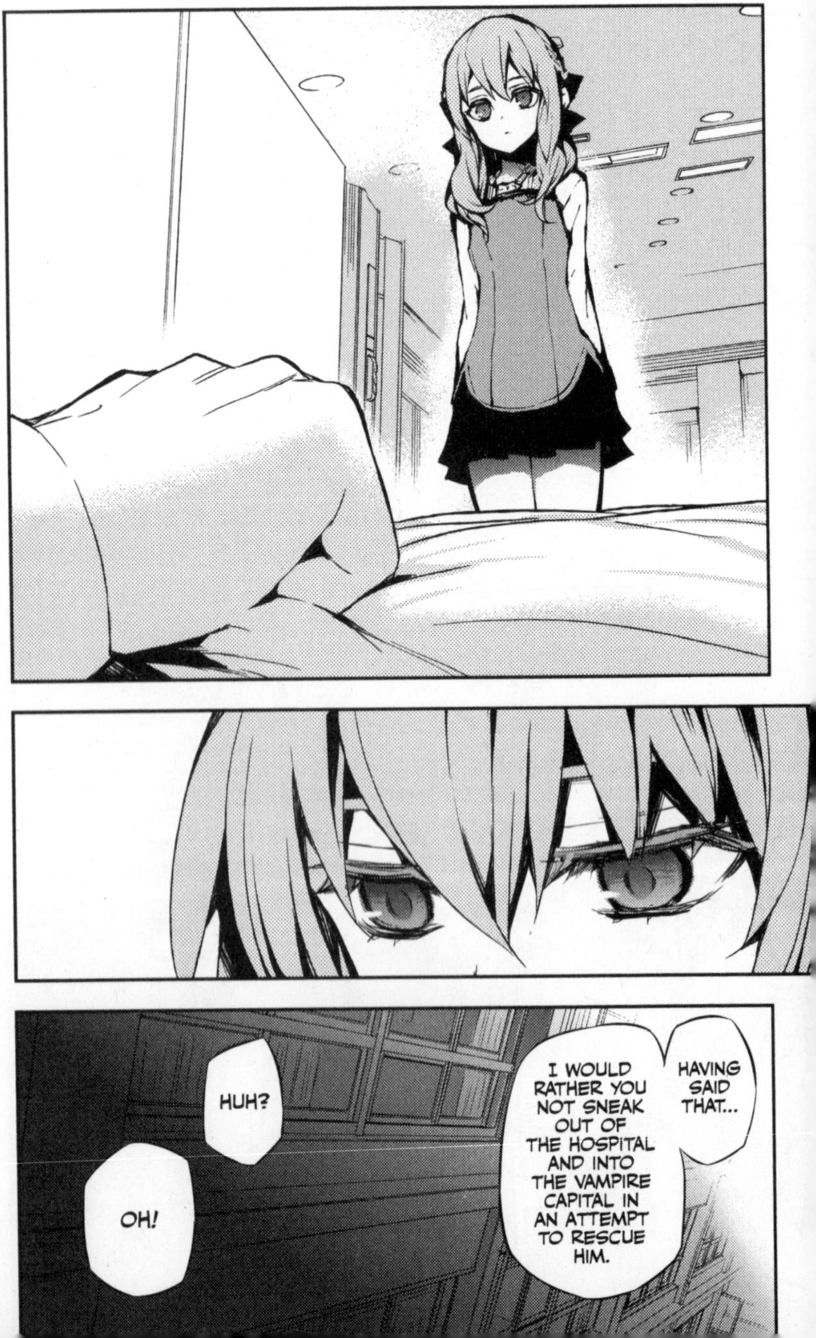
HAVING SAID THAT...
I WOULD RATHER YOU NOT SNEAK OUT OF THE HOSPITAL AND INTO THE VAMPIRE CAPITAL IN AN ATTEMPT TO RESCUE HIM.
HUH?
OH!

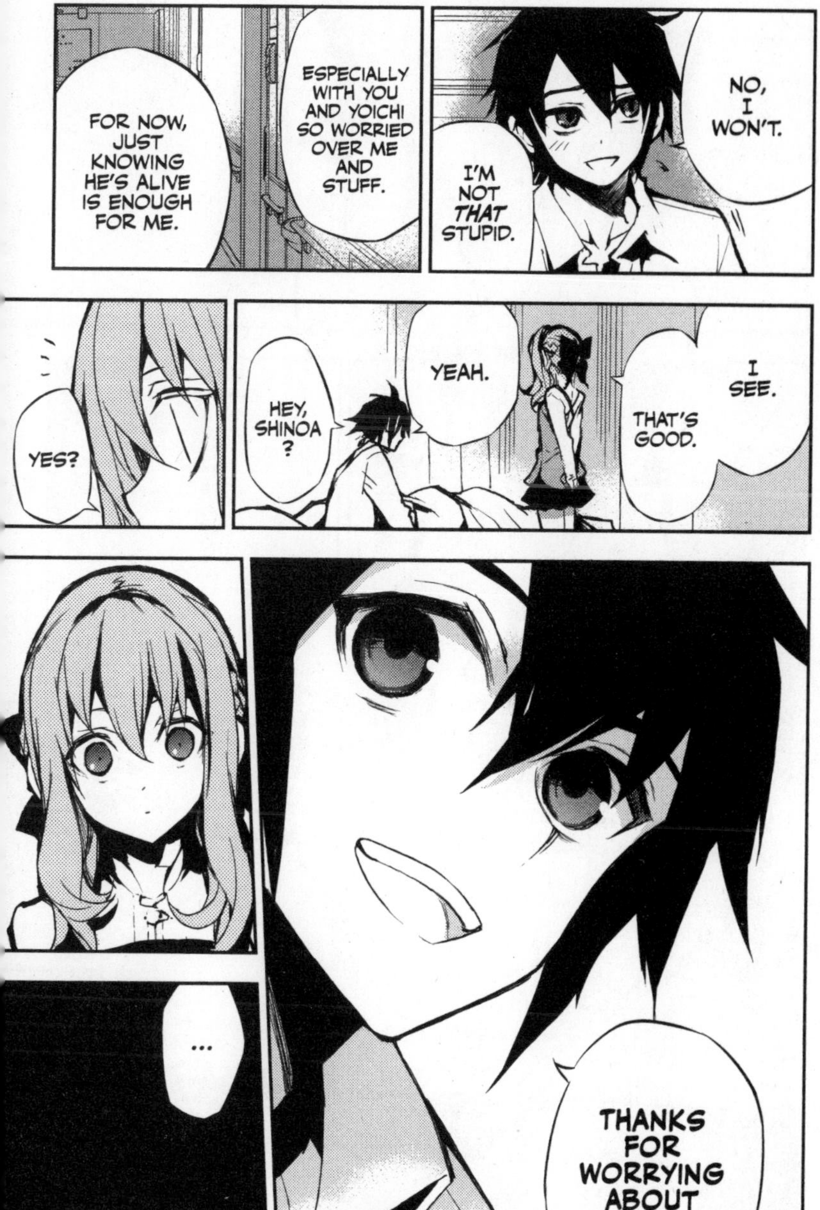
NO, I WON'T.
I'M NOT THAT STUPID.
ESPECIALLY WITH YOU AND YOICHI SO WORRIED OVER ME AND STUFF.
FOR NOW, JUST KNOWING HE'S ALIVE IS ENOUGH FOR ME.
I SEE.
THAT'S GOOD.
YEAH.
HEY, SHINOA?
YES?
THANKS FOR WORRYING ABOUT ME.
...

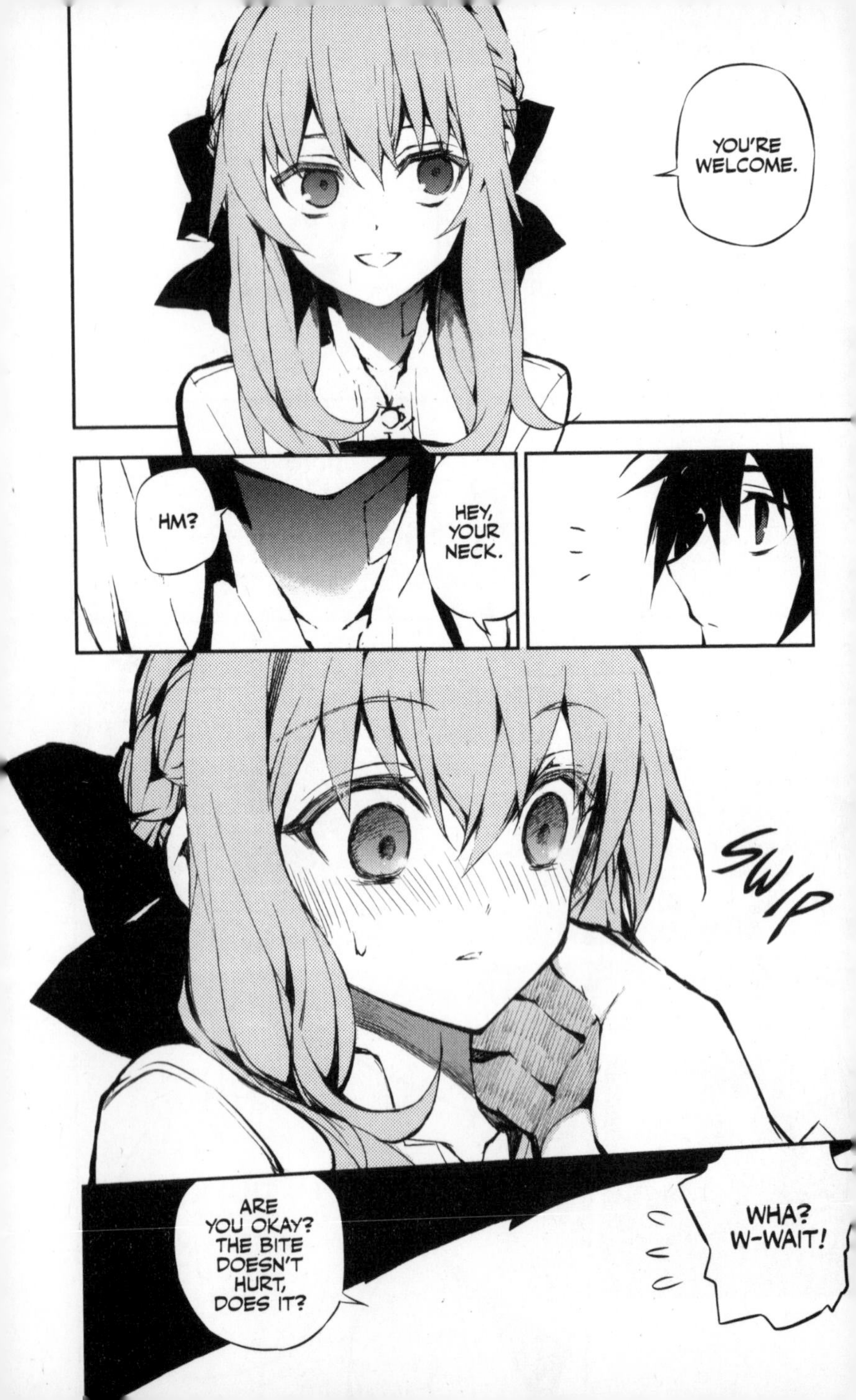
YOU'RE WELCOME.
HEY, YOUR NECK.
HM?
SWIP
WHA? W-WAIT!
ARE YOU OKAY? THE BITE DOESN'T HURT, DOES IT?

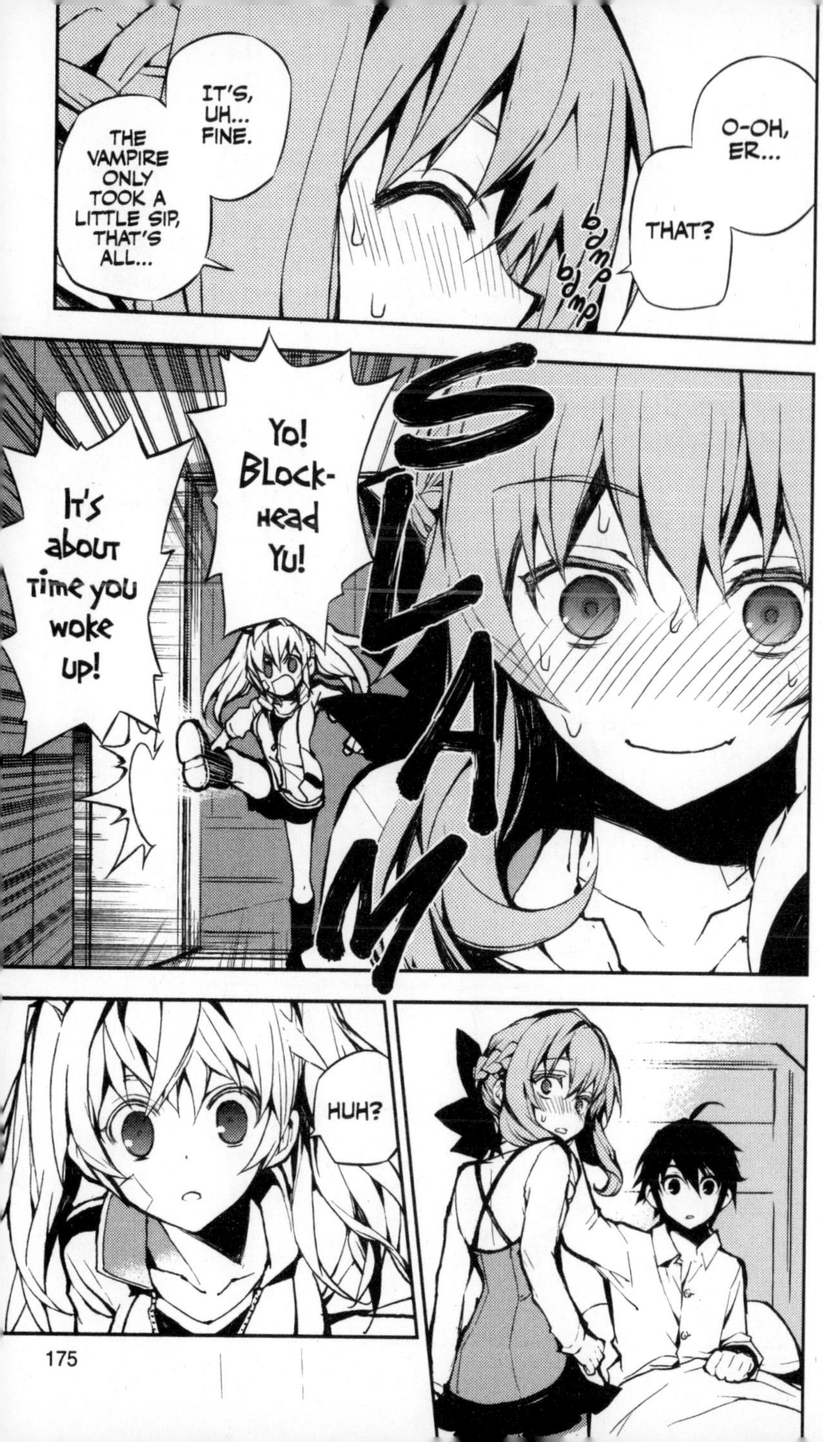
O-OH, ER...
THAT?
b-dmp b-dmp
IT'S, UH... FINE.
THE VAMPIRE ONLY TOOK A LITTLE SIP, THAT'S ALL...
SLAM
Yo! Block-head Yu!
It's about time you woke up!
HUH?

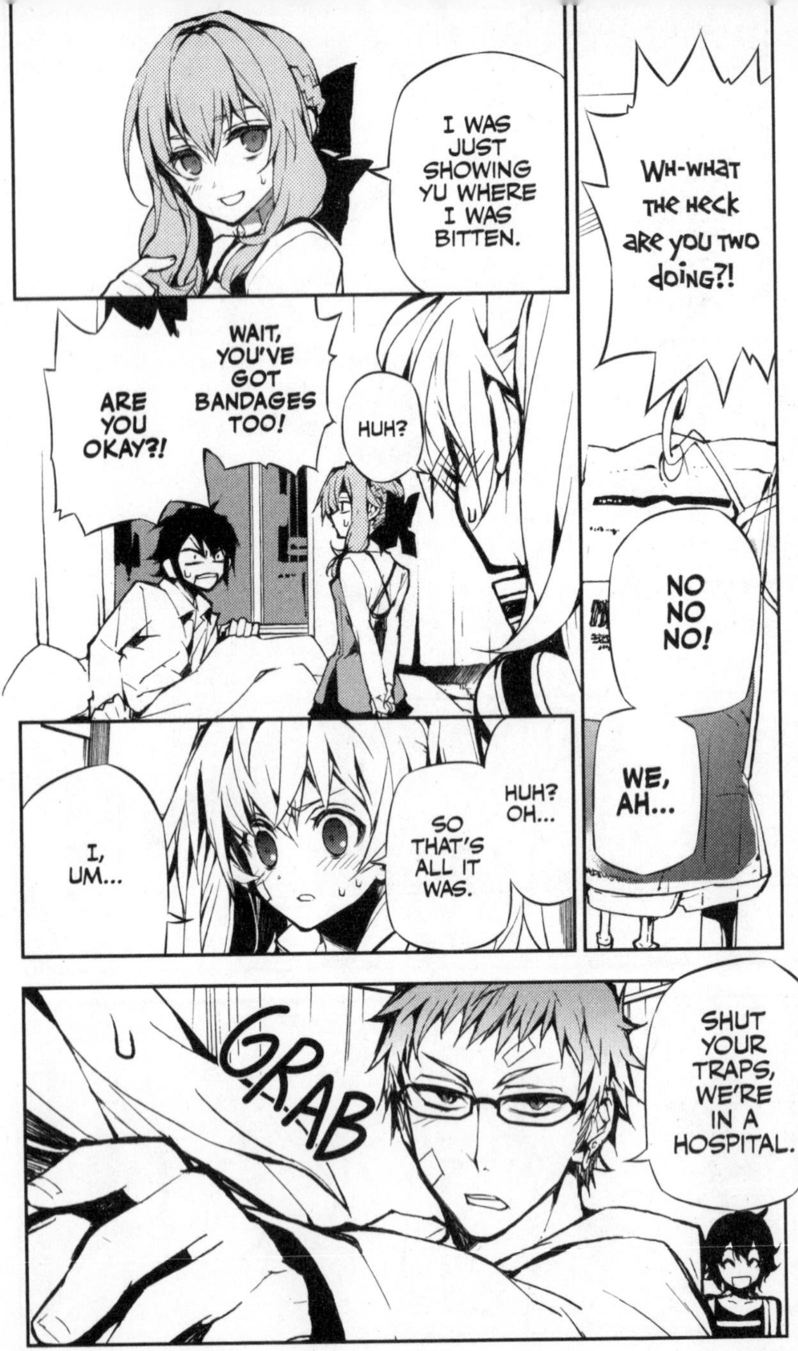
WH-WHAT THE HECK ARE YOU TWO DOING?!
NO NO NO!
WE, AH...
I WAS JUST SHOWING YU WHERE I WAS BITTEN.
WAIT, YOU'VE GOT BANDAGES TOO!
ARE YOU OKAY?!
HUH?
HUH? OH...
SO THAT'S ALL IT WAS.
I, UM...
SHUT YOUR TRAPS, WE'RE IN A HOSPITAL.
GRAB

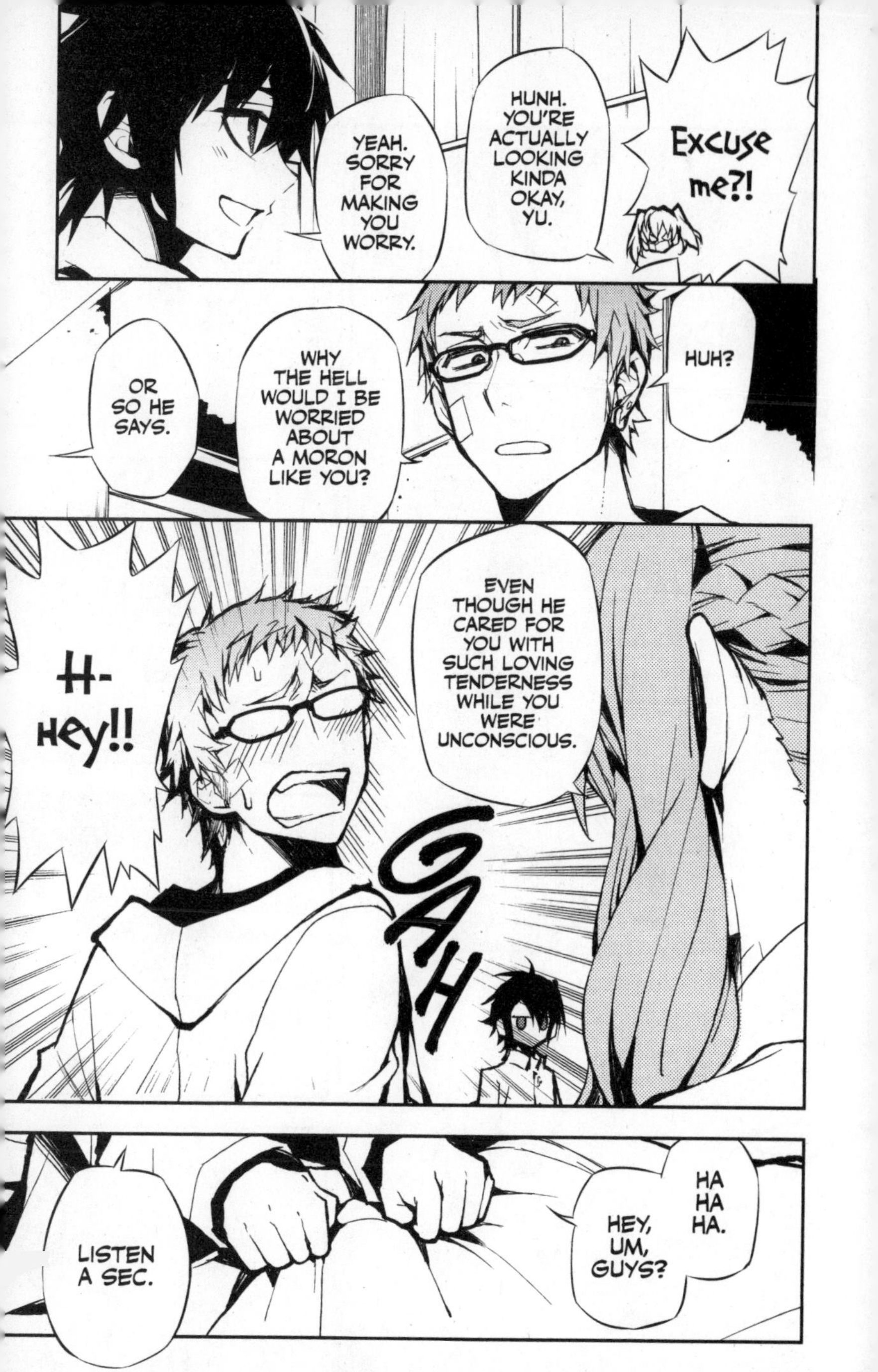
HUNH. YOU'RE ACTUALLY LOOKING KINDA OKAY, YU.
YEAH. SORRY FOR MAKING YOU WORRY.
Excuse me?!
HUH?
WHY THE HELL WOULD I BE WORRIED ABOUT A MORON LIKE YOU?
OR SO HE SAYS.
EVEN THOUGH HE CARED FOR YOU WITH SUCH LOVING TENDERNESS WHILE YOU WERE UNCONSCIOUS.
H-HEY!!
GAH
HA HA HA.
HEY, UM, GUYS?
LISTEN A SEC.

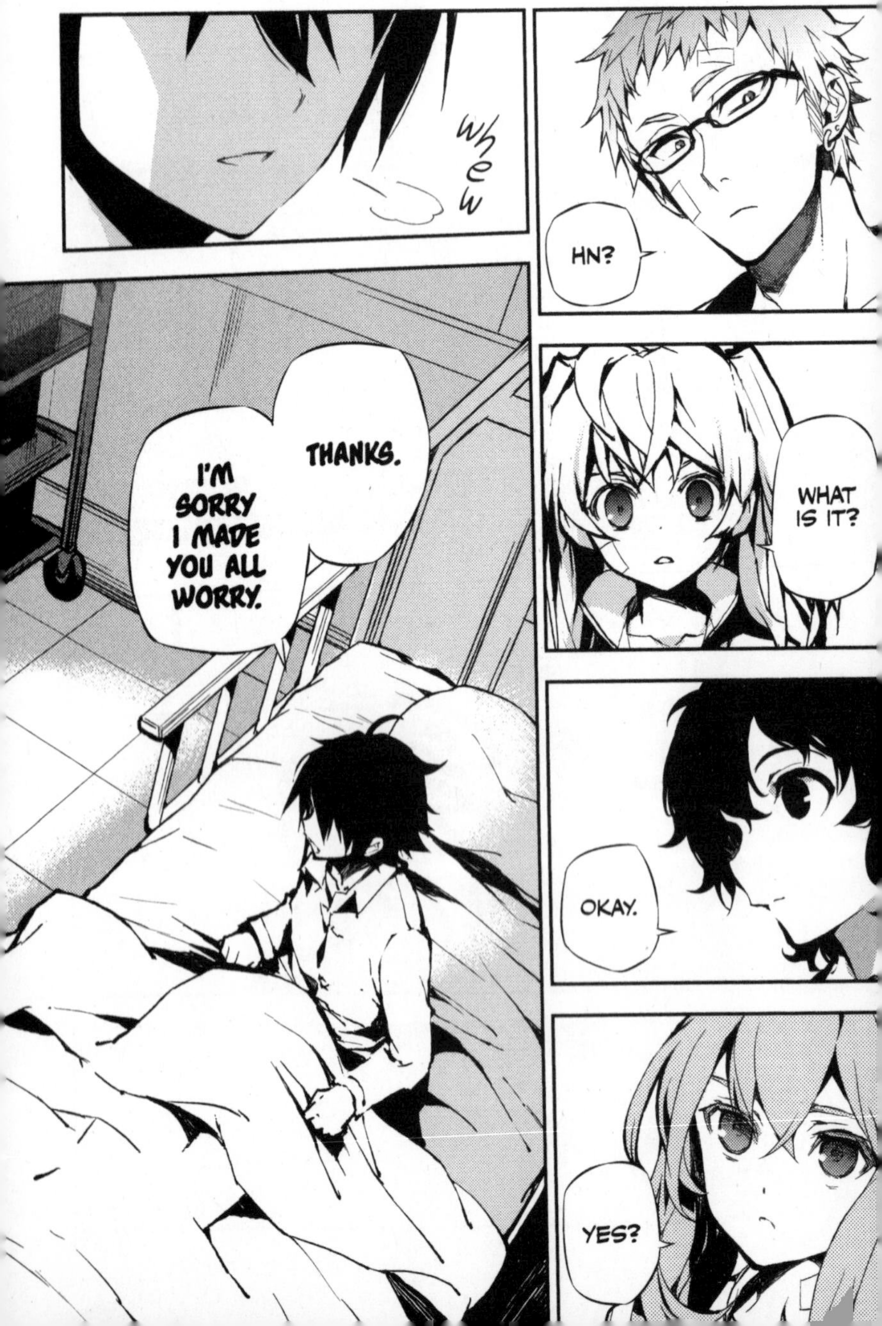
HN?
whew
WHAT IS IT?
OKAY.
YES?
THANKS.
I'M SORRY I MADE YOU ALL WORRY.

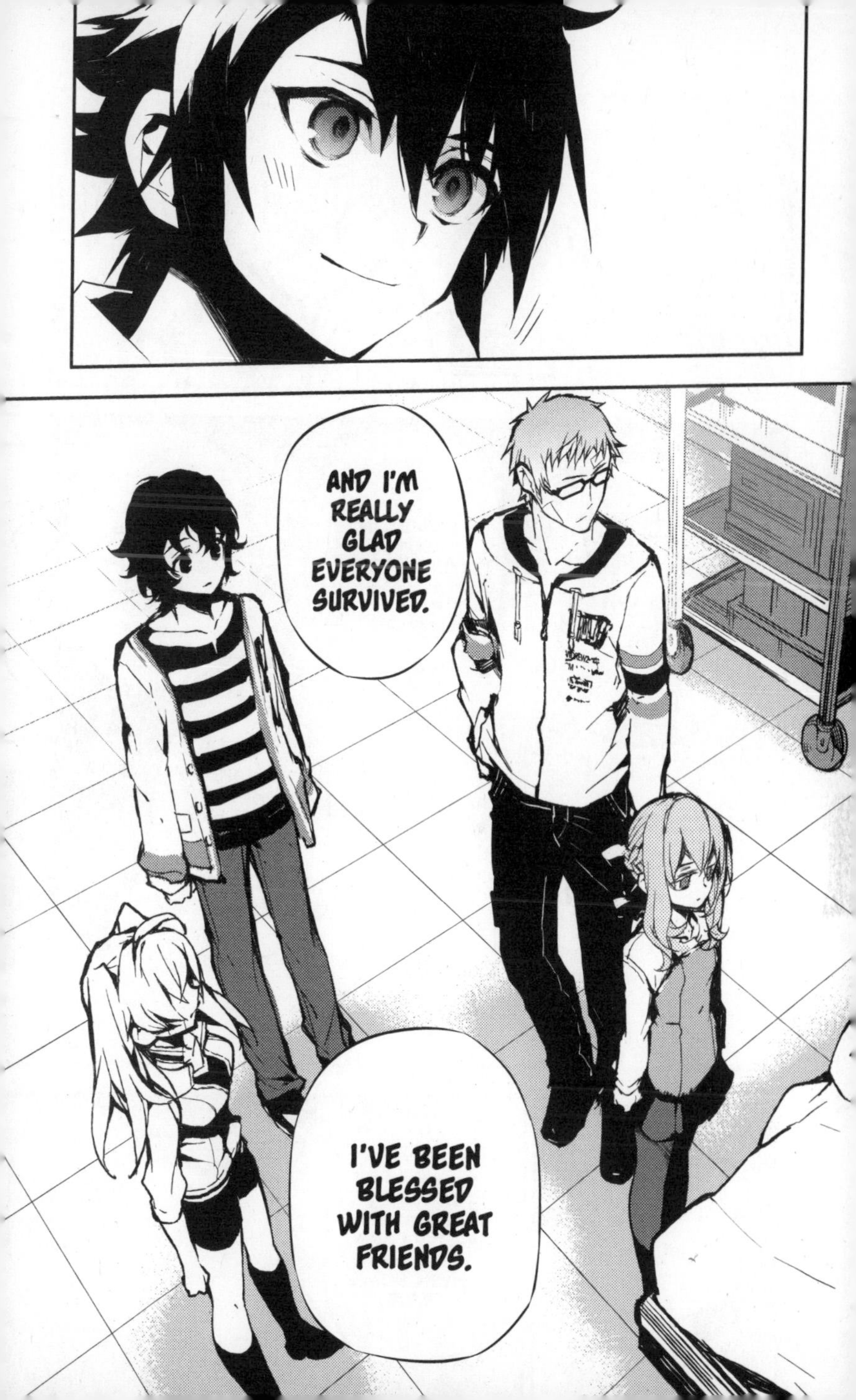
AND I'M REALLY GLAD EVERYONE SURVIVED.
I'VE BEEN BLESSED WITH GREAT FRIENDS.

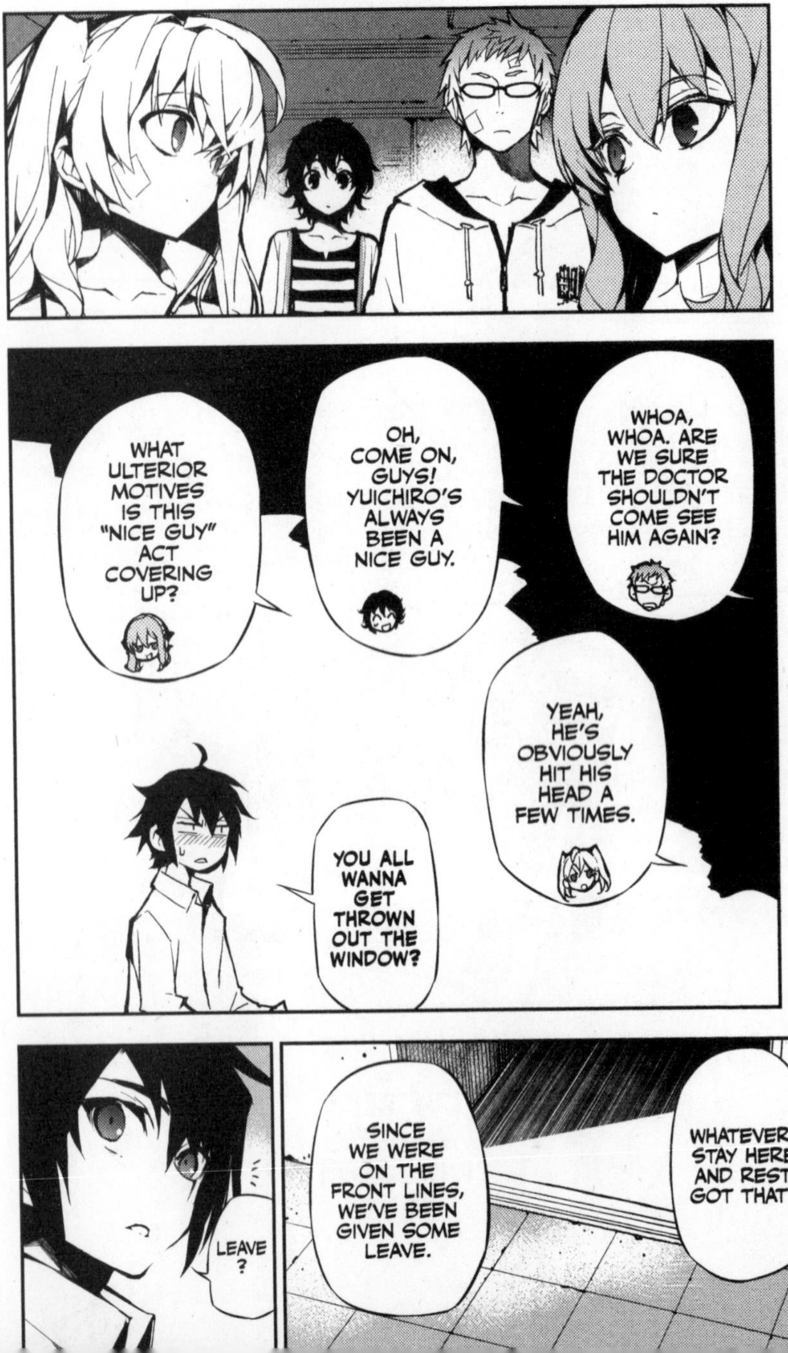
WHOA, WHOA. ARE WE SURE THE DOCTOR SHOULDN'T COME SEE HIM AGAIN?
OH, COME ON, GUYS! YUICHIRO'S ALWAYS BEEN A NICE GUY.
WHAT ULTERIOR MOTIVES IS THIS "NICE GUY" ACT COVERING UP?
YEAH, HE'S OBVIOUSLY HIT HIS HEAD A FEW TIMES.
YOU ALL WANNA GET THROWN OUT THE WINDOW?
WHATEVER. STAY HERE AND REST, GOT THAT?
SINCE WE WERE ON THE FRONT LINES, WE'VE BEEN GIVEN SOME LEAVE.
LEAVE?

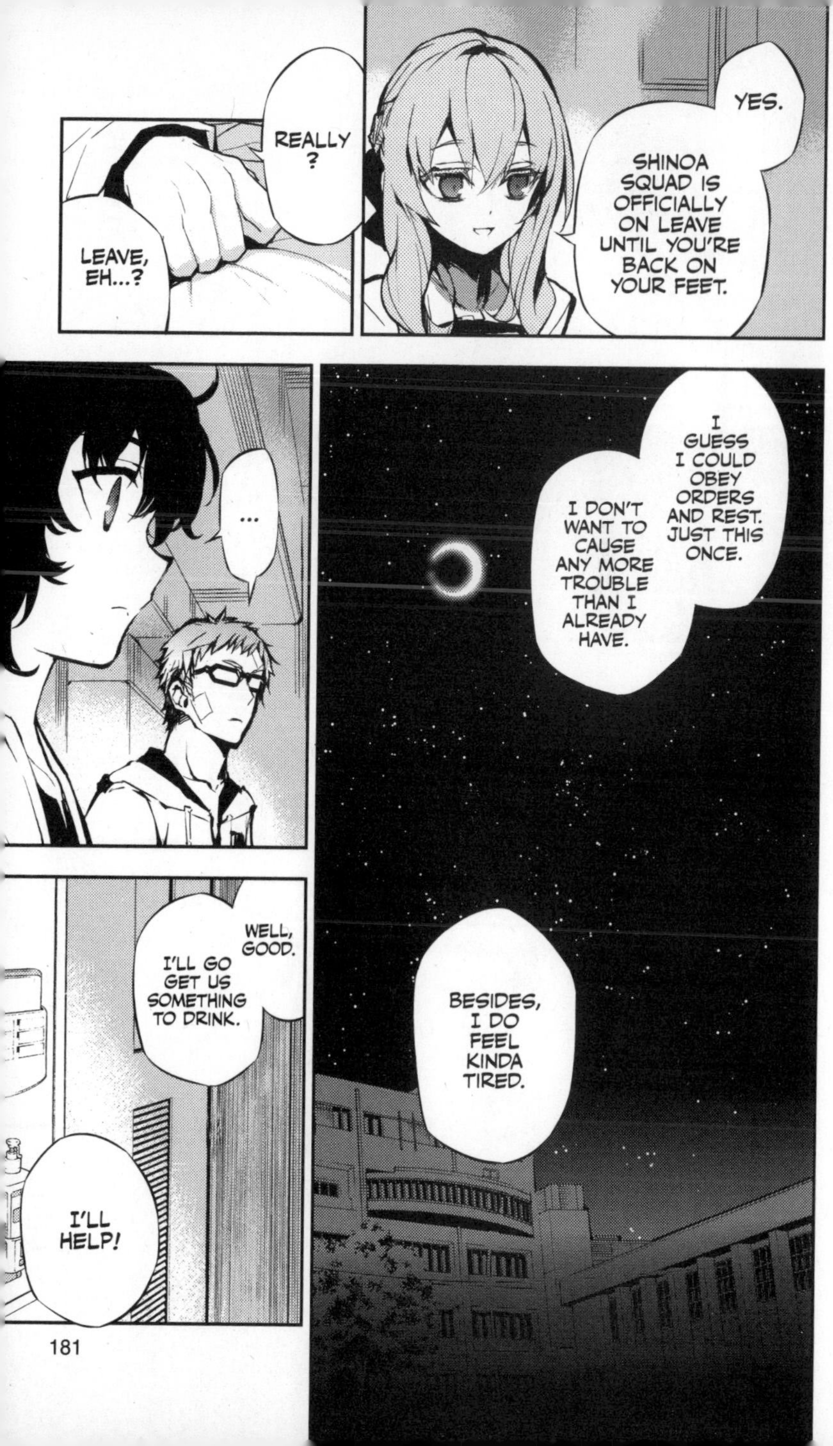
YES.
SHINOA SQUAD IS OFFICIALLY ON LEAVE UNTIL YOU'RE BACK ON YOUR FEET.
REALLY?
LEAVE, EH...?
I GUESS I COULD OBEY ORDERS AND REST. JUST THIS ONCE.
I DON'T WANT TO CAUSE ANY MORE TROUBLE THAN I ALREADY HAVE.
BESIDES, I DO FEEL KINDA TIRED.
...
WELL, GOOD. I'LL GO GET US SOMETHING TO DRINK.
I'LL HELP!

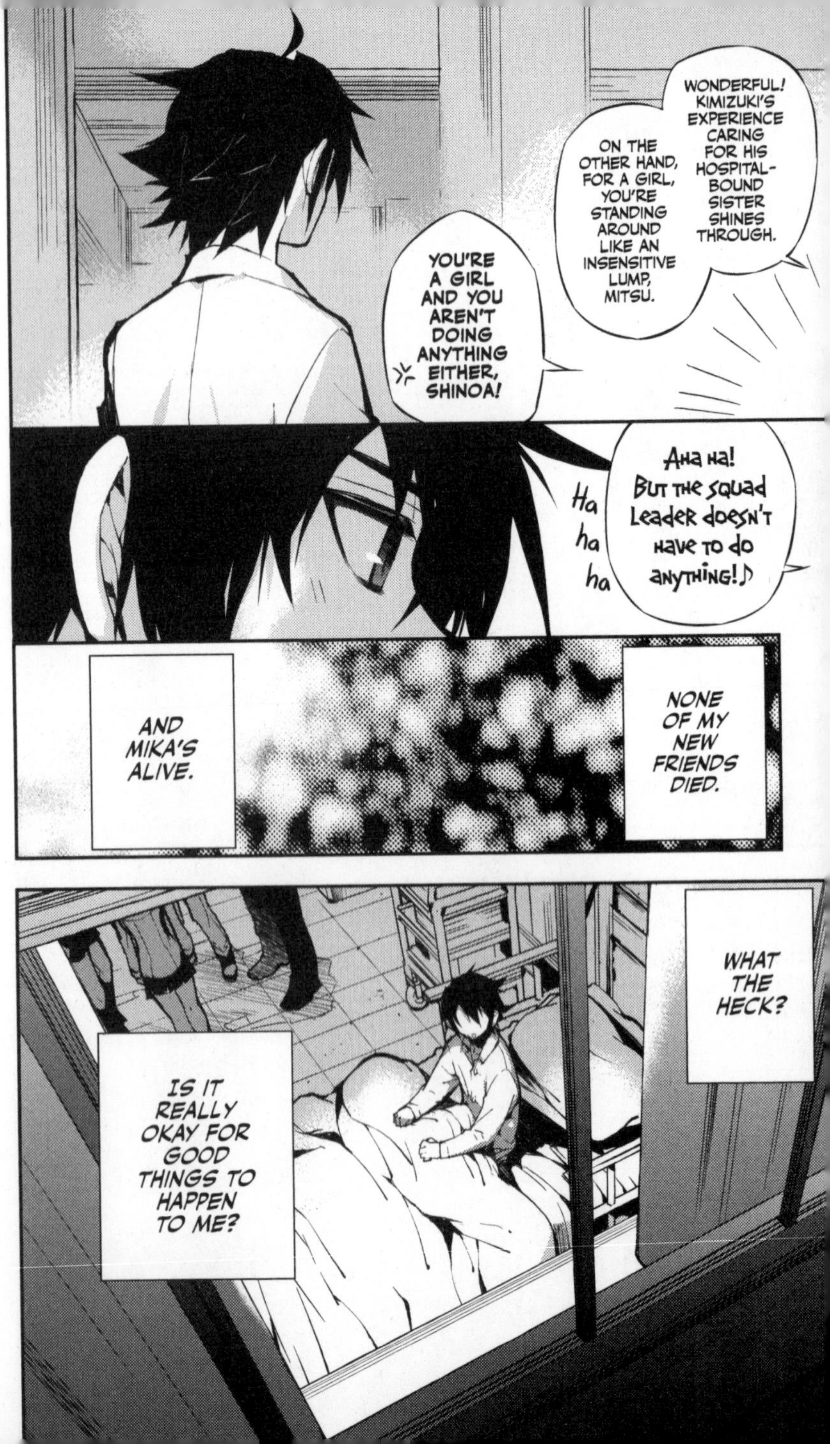
WONDERFUL! KIMIZUKI'S EXPERIENCE CARING FOR HIS HOSPITAL-BOUND SISTER SHINES THROUGH.
ON THE OTHER HAND, FOR A GIRL, YOU'RE STANDING AROUND LIKE AN INSENSITIVE LUMP, MITSU.
YOU'RE A GIRL AND YOU AREN'T DOING ANYTHING EITHER, SHINOA!
AHA HA! BUT THE SQUAD LEADER DOESN'T HAVE TO DO ANYTHING!♪
Ha ha ha
NONE OF MY NEW FRIENDS DIED.
AND MIKA'S ALIVE.
WHAT THE HECK?
IS IT REALLY OKAY FOR GOOD THINGS TO HAPPEN TO ME?

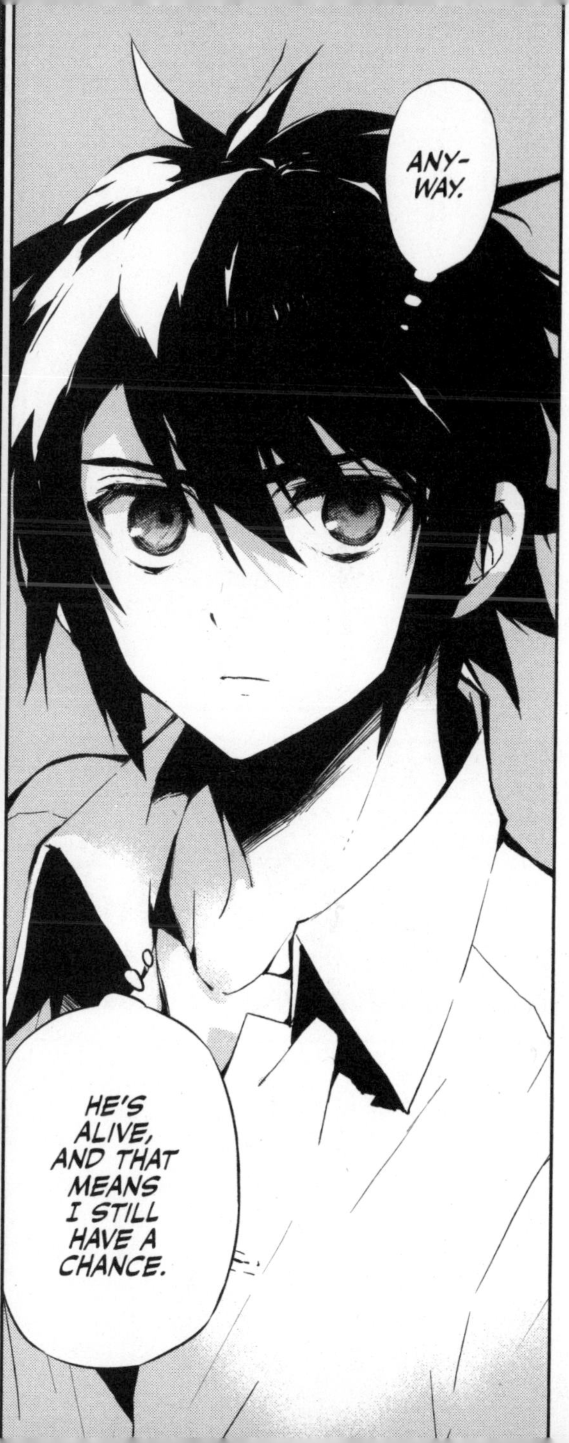
ANY-WAY.
HE'S ALIVE, AND THAT MEANS I STILL HAVE A CHANCE.
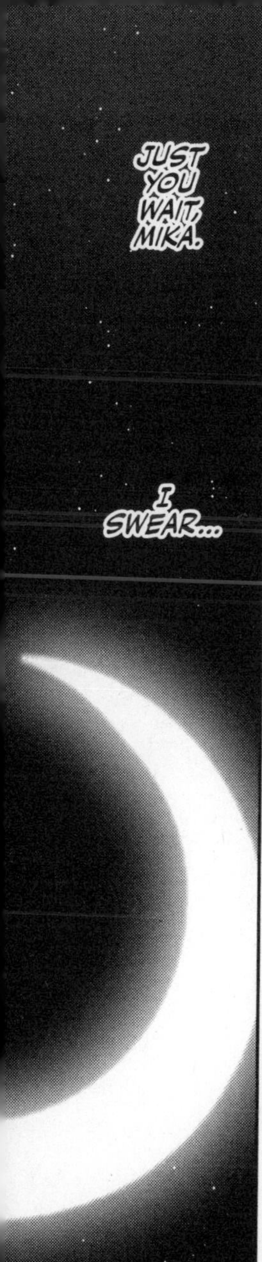
JUST YOU WAIT, MIKA.
I SWEAR...

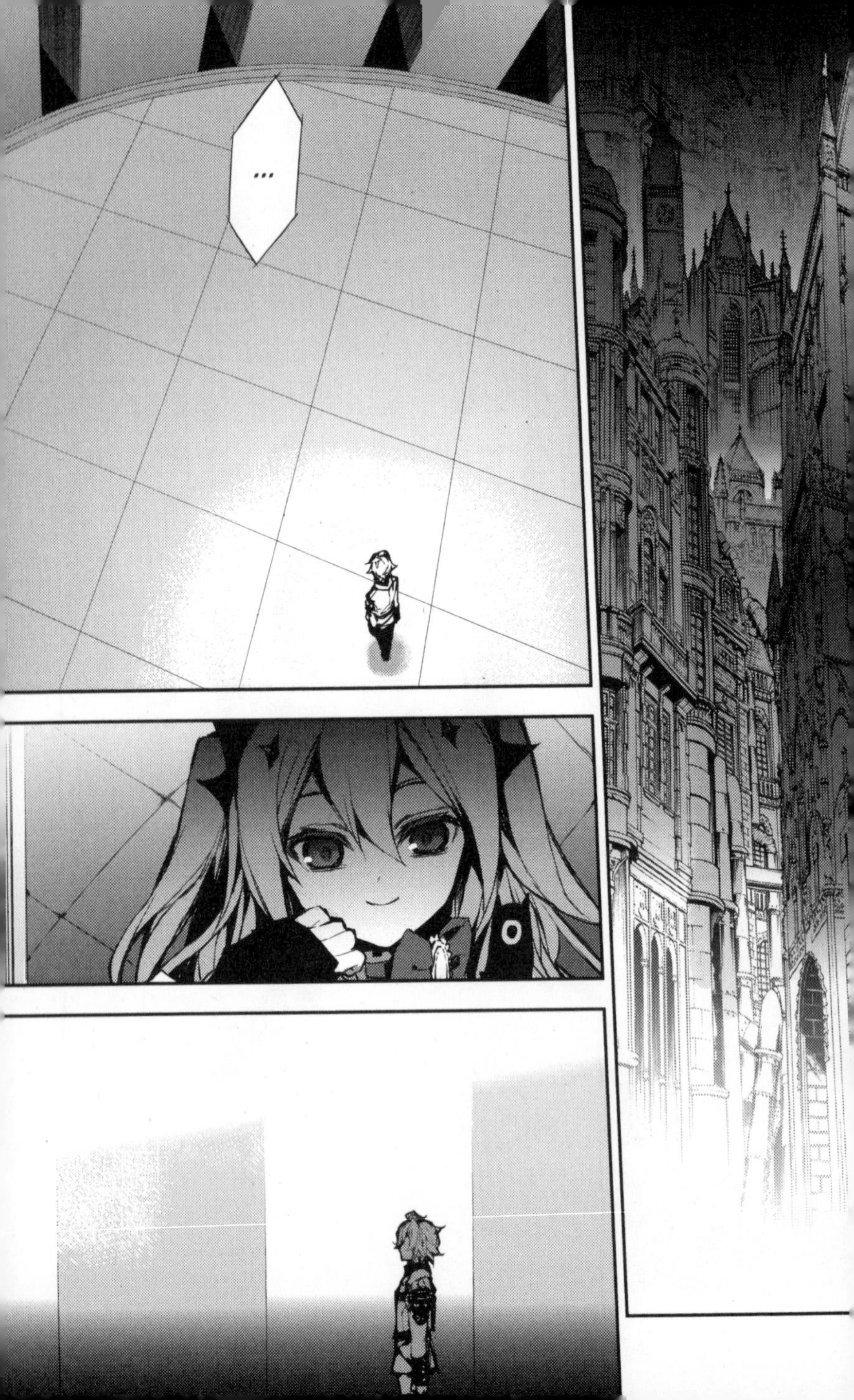
...

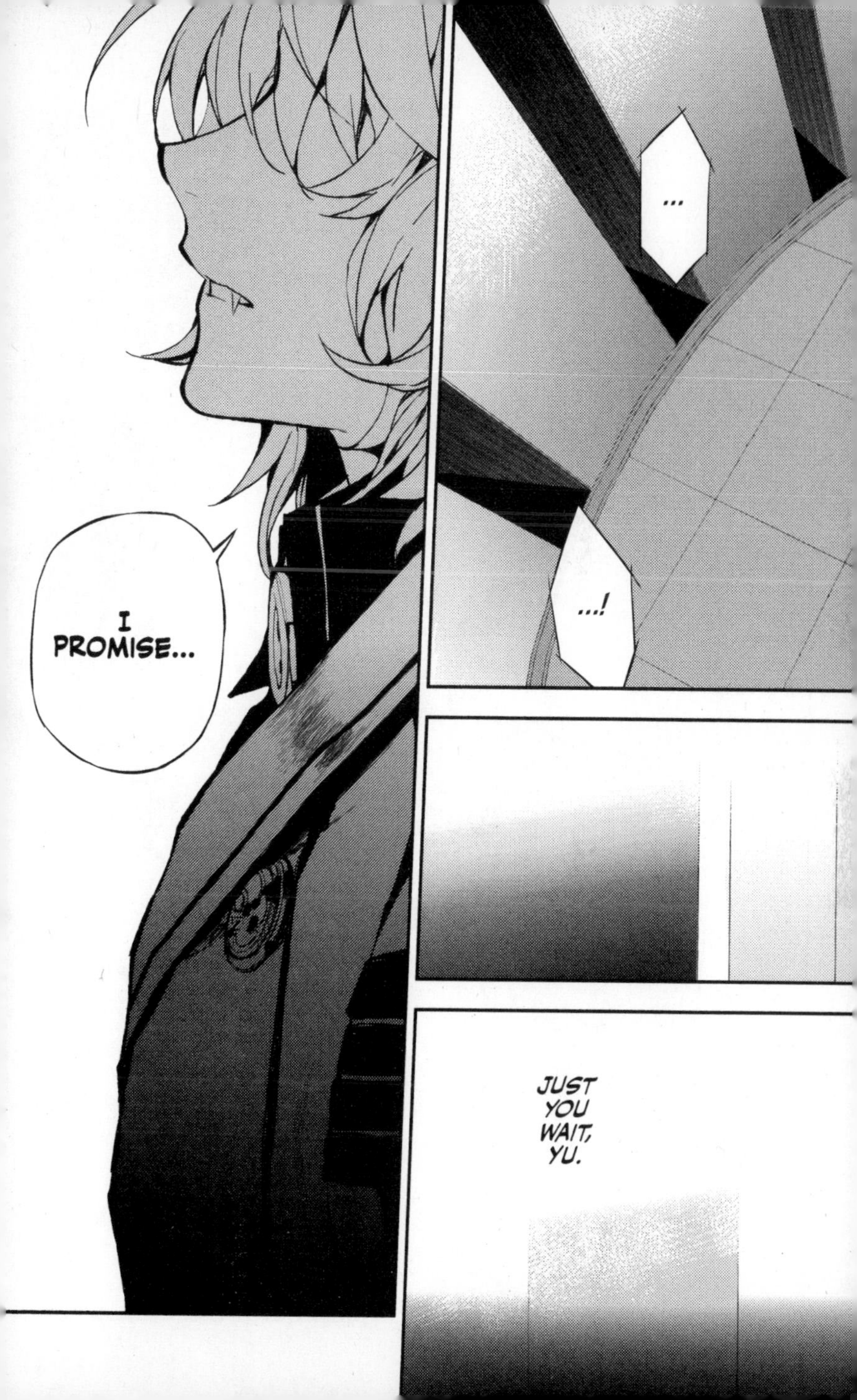
...
...!
JUST YOU WAIT, YU.
I PROMISE...

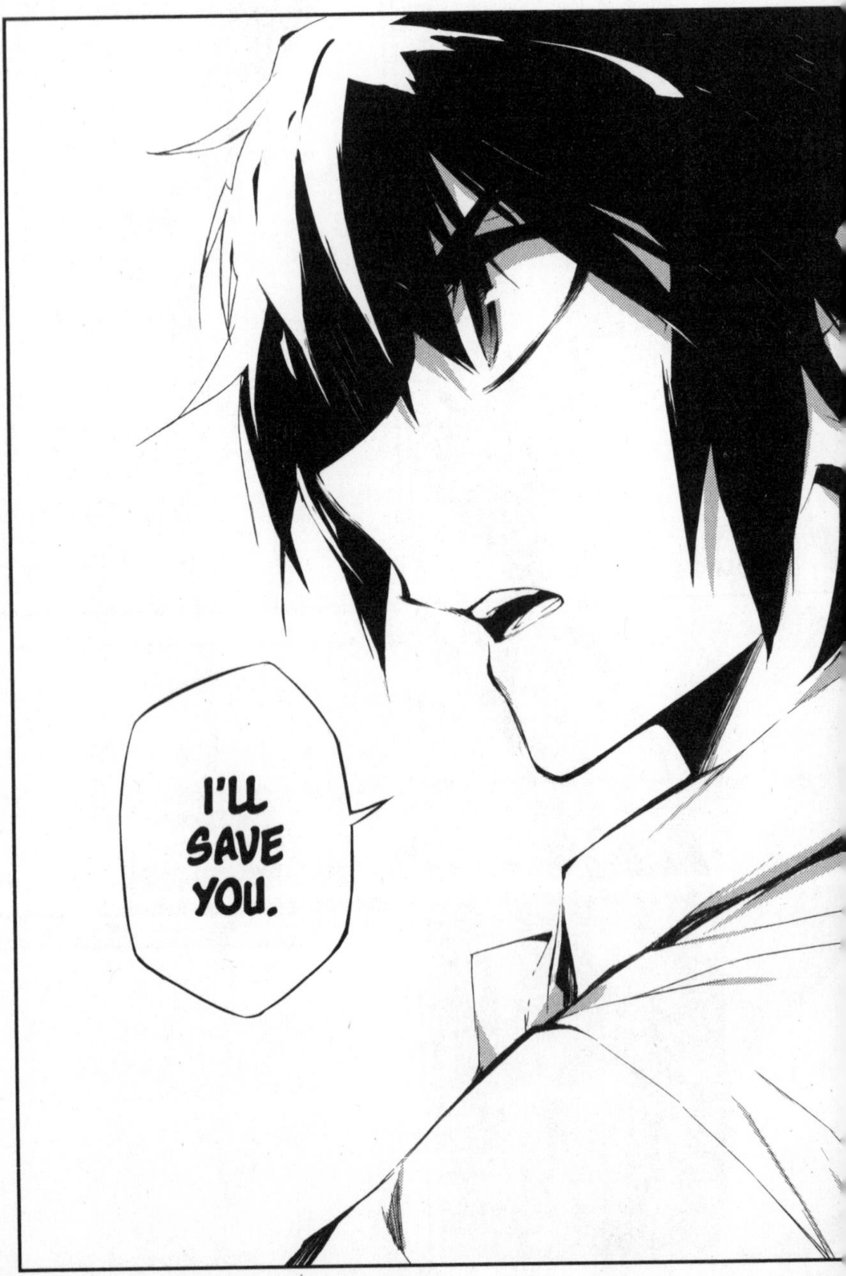
I'LL SAVE YOU.

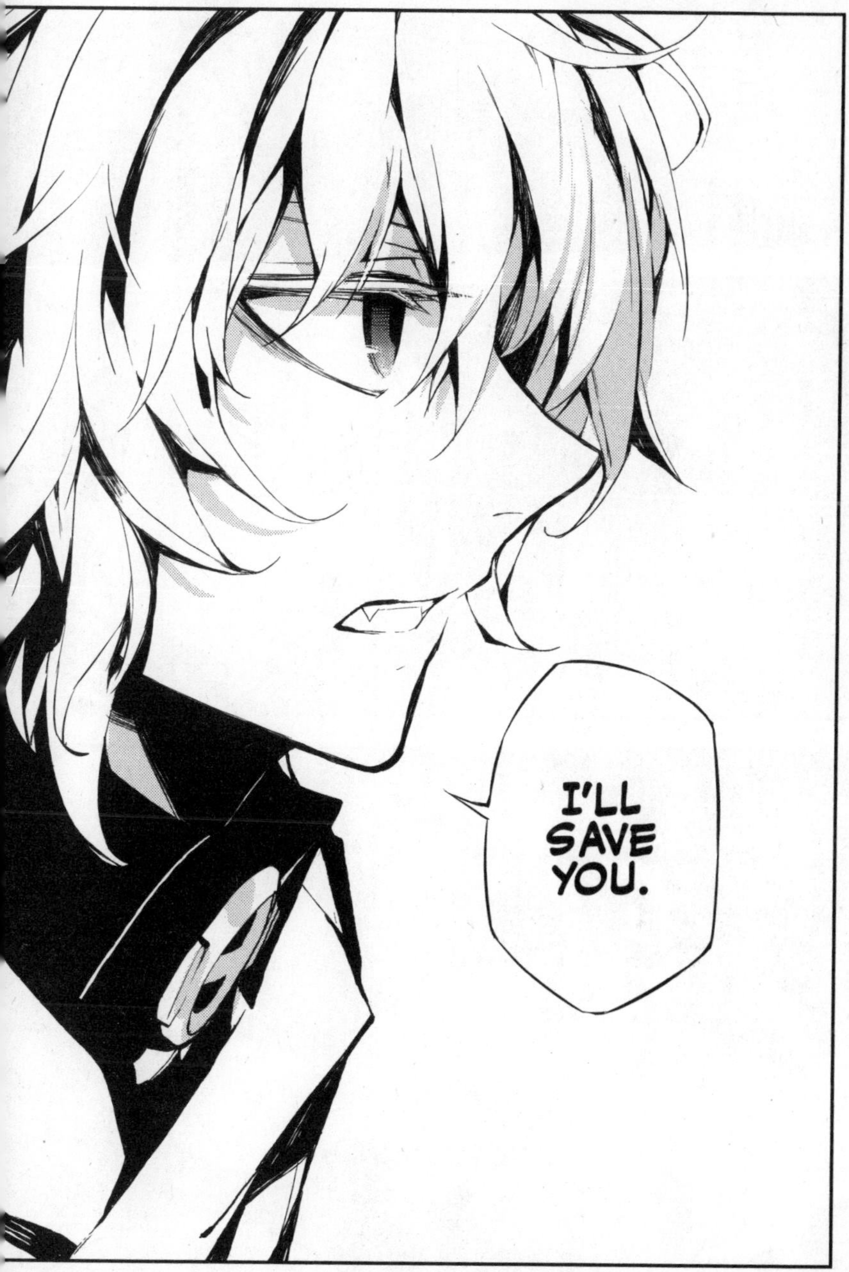
I'LL SAVE YOU.

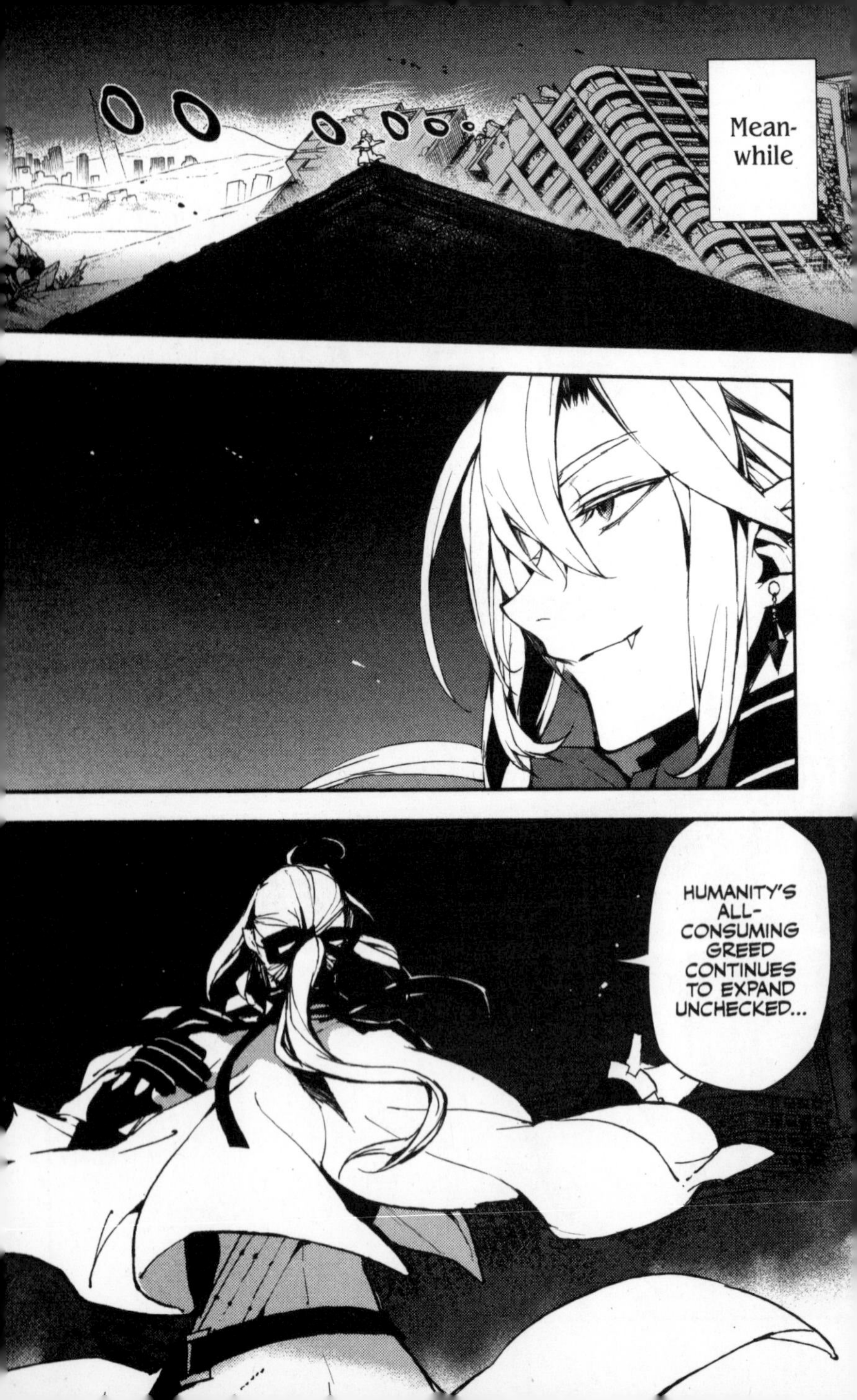
Mean-
while
HUMANITY'S ALL-CONSUMING GREED CONTINUES TO EXPAND UNCHECKED...

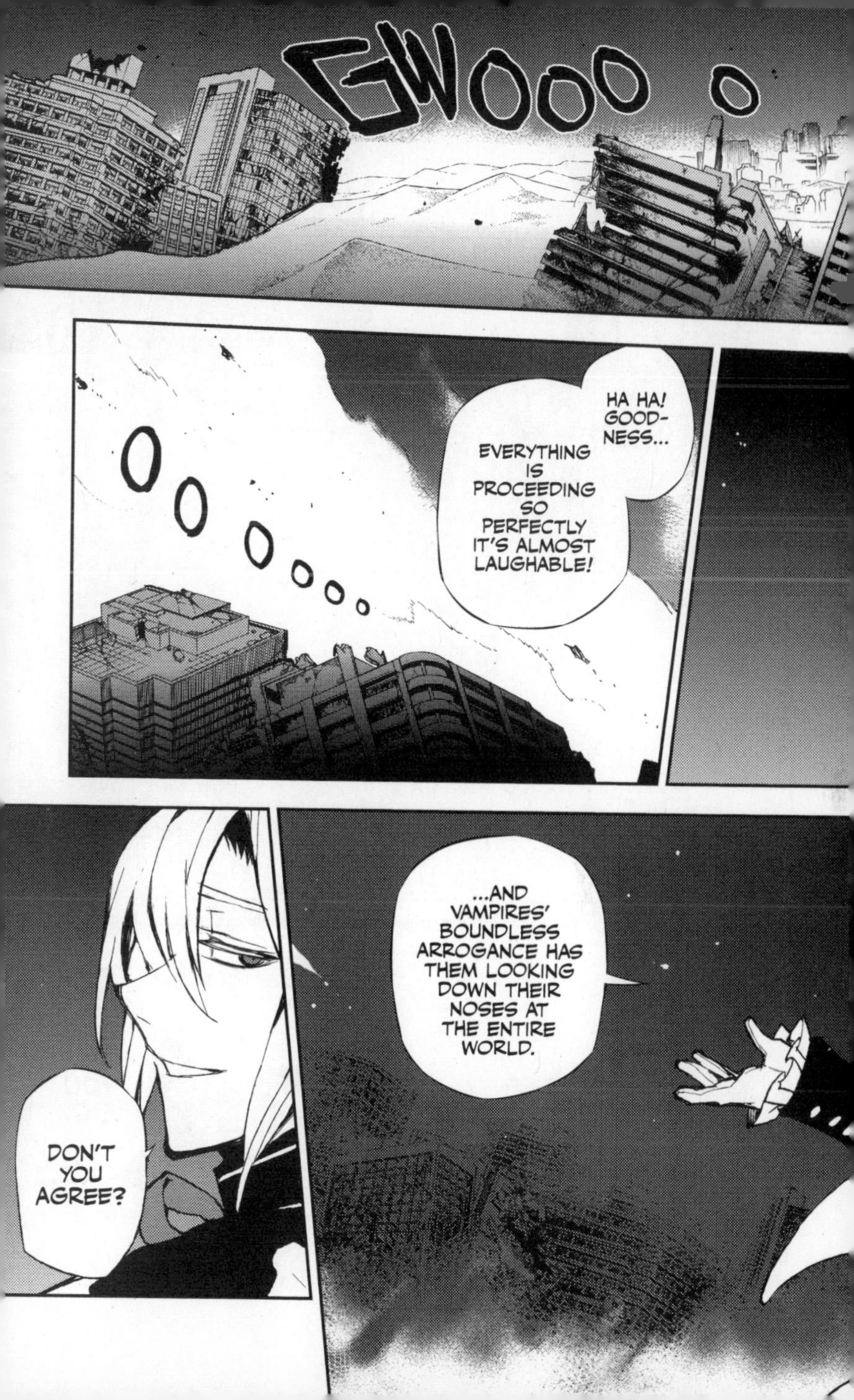
GWOOO O
HA HA! GOOD-NESS... EVERYTHING IS PROCEEDING SO PERFECTLY IT'S ALMOST LAUGHABLE!
OOOOOO
...AND VAMPIRES' BOUNDLESS ARROGANCE HAS THEM LOOKING DOWN THEIR NOSES AT THE ENTIRE WORLD.
DON'T YOU AGREE?

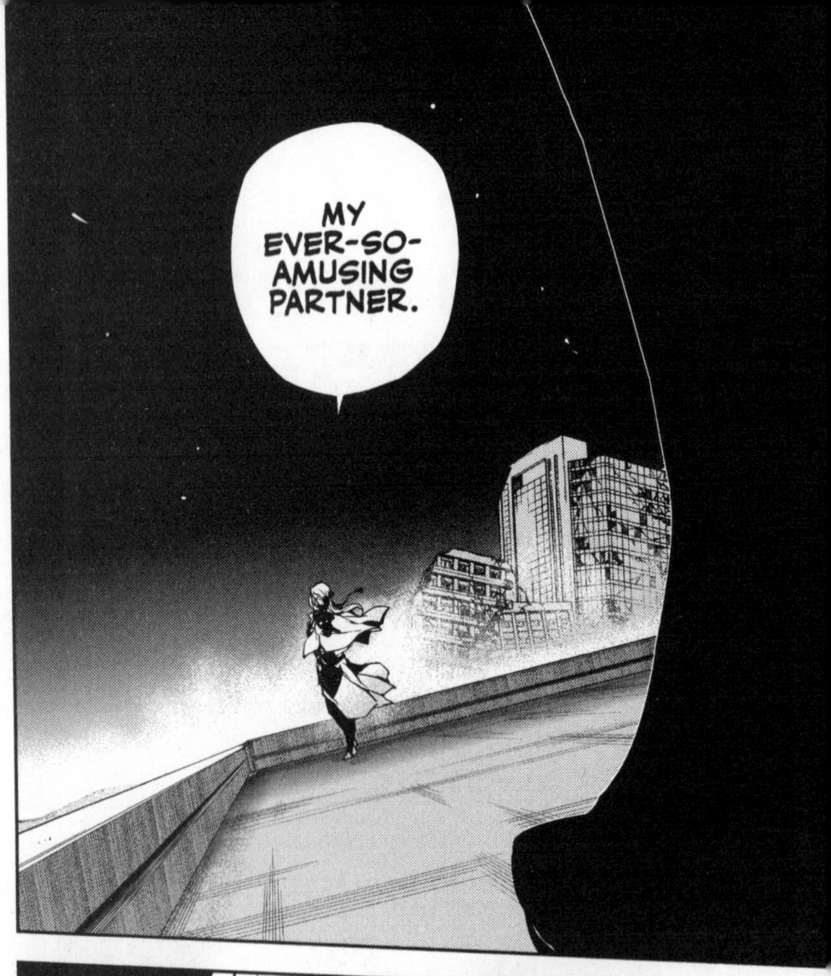
MY EVER-SO-AMUSING PARTNER.

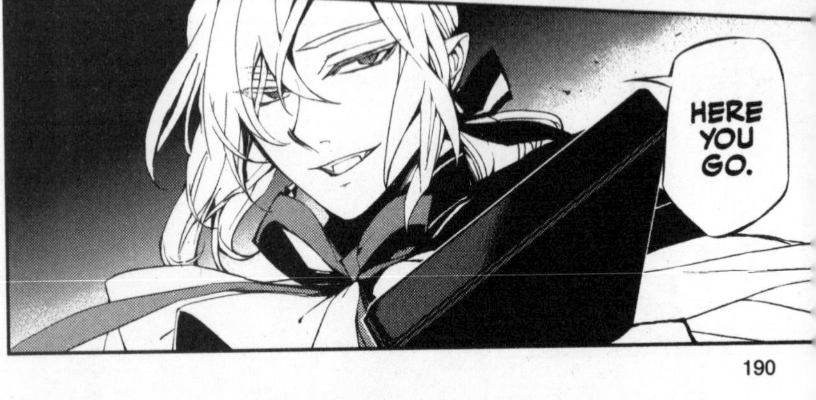
HERE YOU GO.

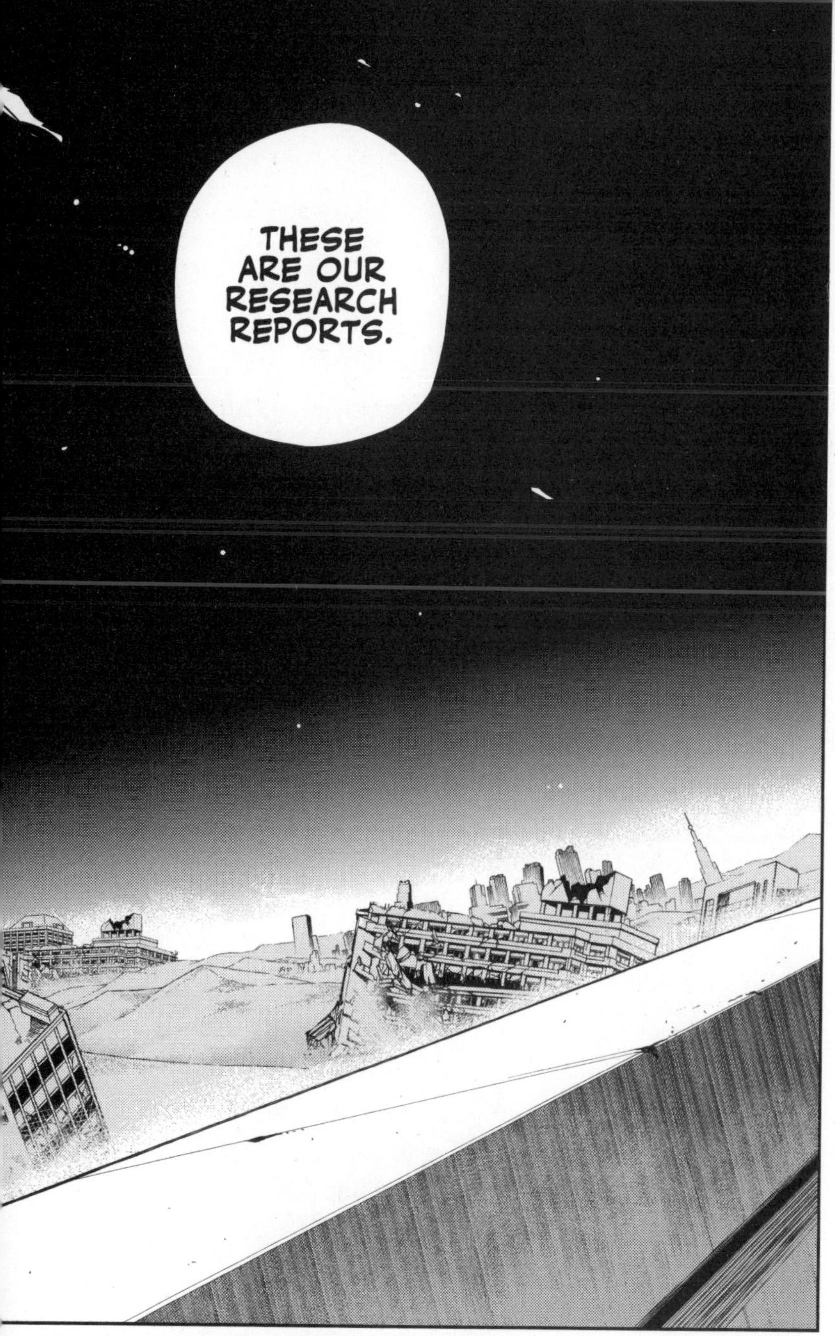
THESE ARE OUR RESEARCH REPORTS.

Seraph of the End: Vampire Reign 4 / END

HELLO, I'M TAKAYA KAGAMI. HERE'S THE FOURTH INSTALLMENT. HOPE YOU LIKE IT!

MITSUBA SANGU

As a daughter of the prestigious Sangu Family, she is an elite warrior. She has an older sister who is the same age as Guren, and was even his classmate in high school. Yes, as you would expect, Mitsuba's sister is a prominent character in the story detailing the world before its end—the light novel *Seraph of the End: Guren Ichinose's Catastrophe at 16*.

Mitsuba is a second daughter, but her name means "three-leaf clover." Her older sister is named "Aoi," which is the name of a two-leafed species of wild ginger. What on earth were their parents thinking when they named them? Who knows. Oh, Aoi will probably appear in the manga starting somewhere in volume 5, so keep an eye out!

SHINOA: "MY, WE BOTH HAVE HIGHLY TALENTED OLDER SISTERS? WE BECOME MORE AND MORE ALIKE EVERY DAY!"

MITSUBA: "YOU'RE THE LAST PERSON I WANT TO BE ANYTHING LIKE!!"

SHINOA: "OH, COME. NO NEED TO BE SHY! AFTER ALL, WE'RE SO CLOSE WE BATHE TOGETHER."

MITSUBA: "WE DO NOT! YOU JUST BUTT INTO MY SHOWERS!!"

Mitsuba's weapon is an enormous axe. Before serialization for this series began, I remember talking with Mr. Yamamoto on the train about how much we loved girls who wield huge axes.

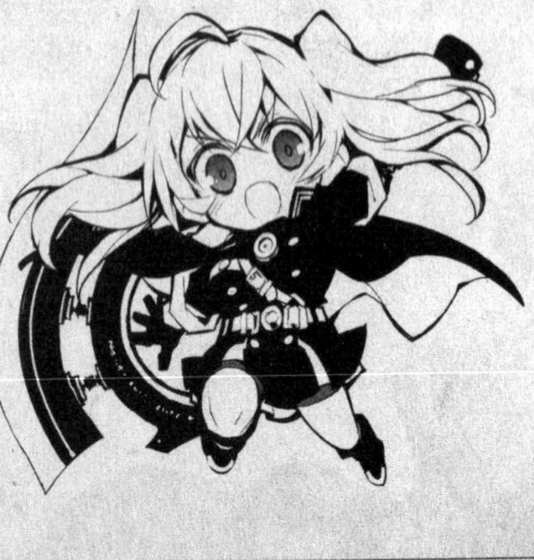

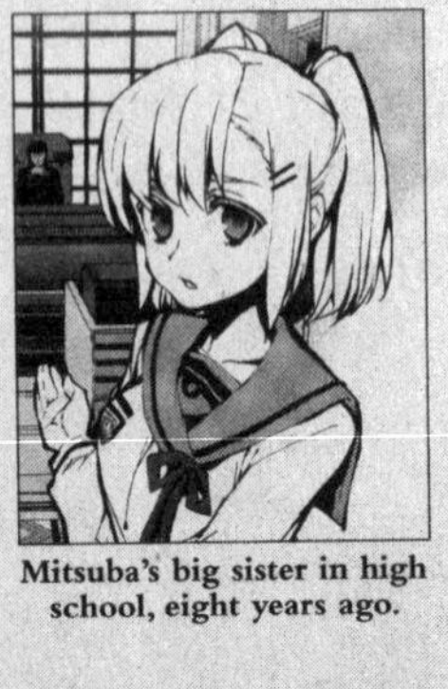

Mitsuba's big sister in high school, eight years ago.

ASURAMARU

This is the demon Yu made his contract with. He lives inside Yu's sword. He's also shrouded in mystery. We have quite a lot set up for his character, but most of it is still secret. Believe it or not, Asuramaru is connected to Guren, and makes a brief cameo in the third volume of the novel. Oh! And eight-year-old Yu also has a cameo. Look for it! How will Yu's and Asuramaru's destinies intertwine? Also...

Demons.
Vampires.
Devils.
Angels.

All of these and the truths behind them will soon begin to pop up in the manga. I hope you're looking forward to it!

ASURAMARU: "YOU DON'T NEED TO BOTHER TELLING ANYTHING ABOUT ME, ACTUALLY. I'M FINE STAYING SECRETIVE. DON'T YOU AGREE, SHI?"

SHIKAMA DOJI: "..."

In case you don't remember, Shikama Doji is the demon who lives inside Shinoa's scythe. Shi first appeared in chapter 3. Both Shi and Asuramaru are still both big unknowns!

Shikama Doji

AFTERWORD

HELLO. I'M TAKAYA KAGAMI. HOW DID YOU LIKE *SERAPH OF THE END: VAMPIRE REIGN* VOLUME 4? I CONSIDER THIS VOLUME THE FIRST MAJOR CLIMAX OF THE SERIES. I MEAN, THERE WAS WHAT HAPPENED BETWEEN YU AND MIKA! ALSO, UNTIL NOW WE KEPT MOST OF THE WORLD-BUILDING LOW-KEY SO THAT READERS COULD GET TO KNOW THE CHARACTERS FIRST. NOW WE WILL START EXPLORING MORE OF THE WORLD ITSELF.

TO BE HONEST, WE HAVE OVER 100 PAGES WRITTEN ON JUST THE SETTING ITSELF (AFTER ALL, WE NEEDED BACKGROUND FOR BOTH THE NOVEL AND THE MANGA). WE'VE BEEN RELEASING TIDBITS SO FAR SO AS NOT TO CONFUSE ANYBODY. BUT NOW THAT EVERYTHING IS IN PLACE, IT'S TIME TO START SHOWING OFF MORE OF THE WORLD!

ON ANOTHER NOTE, I'VE STARTED TO REALLY APPRECIATE HOW WE'VE BEEN DETAILING THE WORLD OF EIGHT YEARS AGO IN THE NOVEL AND LEFT THE WORLD OF TODAY, THE RUINED WORLD, TO THE MANGA. I'VE WORKED ON VARIOUS TYPES OF STORIES, BUT GETTING TO WRITE BOTH A STORY'S PAST AND ITS PRESENT AS THEIR OWN WHOLE WORKS IS REALLY SOMETHING ELSE. NOT ONLY DO YOU GET TO BOIL DOWN THE SETTING TO THE REAL NITTY-GRITTY DETAILS, EACH WORK CAN HAVE SERIOUS INFLUENCE ON THE OTHER.

FOR EXAMPLE, IF SOMETHING MAJOR HAPPENS IN THE NOVEL'S PAST TIMELINE, IT CAN GROW AND EXPAND—IN MY HEAD, AT LEAST—AND MAYBE HAVE SOME BIG REPERCUSSIONS ON THE MANGA'S PRESENT TIMELINE. CONVERSELY, THERE ARE TIMES WHERE I WIND UP THINKING, "AW, MAN! IF I WRITE THAT IN THE NOVEL, I'M GONNA HAVE TO REDO ALL OF THE MANGA SCRIPTS I WORKED ON AHEAD OF TIME!"

HOWEVER, I STILL CONSIDER MYSELF BLESSED WITH AN INTERESTING STORY AND FUN COMRADES (MR. YAMAMOTO, MR. FURUYA, MY EDITORS FROM SHUEISHA AND KODANSHA, AND ALL MY READERS!) IT IS WITH A HAPPY HEART THAT I GO ON...TO DO BATTLE WITH MORE DEADLINES. *UGH.* BUT THANK YOU!

SPEAKING OF THANKING PEOPLE... I SEEM TO REMEMBER GETTING A BIG TWO-PAGE SPREAD AD FOR *SERAPH OF THE END* IN ONE OF THE OTHER STORIES I'M WORKING ON, *THE LEGEND OF THE LEGENDARY HEROES.* NOW MY EDITOR FOR THAT TITLE IS STARTING TO ASK ME WHEN WE'RE GOING TO DO AN AD FOR *LOTLH* HERE, AND I DID PROMISE HIM I WOULD... BUT I DON'T HAVE THE PAGE SPACE THIS TIME EITHER!

SO, RIGHT HERE, RIGHT NOW I'M GOING TO MENTION THAT I'VE STARTED ANOTHER NEW SERIES, *APOCALYPSE ALICE* (PUBLISHED BY FANTASIA BUNKO / FUJIMI SHOBO)! FOR THOSE OF YOU WHO HAVE READ *SERAPH OF THE END* AND CAN'T GET ENOUGH, PLEASE CONSIDER PICKING UP *APOCALYPSE ALICE!* :D

NOW THAT I'VE PLUGGED ANOTHER OF MY SERIES FOR A TOTALLY DIFFERENT PUBLISHER, LET ME REMIND YOU THAT AT THE END OF THE MONTH, VOLUME 3 OF *SERAPH OF THE END: GUREN ICHINOSE'S CATASTROPHE AT 16* COMES OUT. EIGHT-YEAR-OLD YU APPEARS, AND THE WORLD FINALLY BEGINS ITS SLIDE INTO DISASTER. I HOPE YOU LIKE IT!

TAKAYA KAGAMI

A brilliant sketch of Yuichiro by the author!

TAKAYA KAGAMI is a prolific light novelist whose works include the action and fantasy series *The Legend of the Legendary Heroes*, which has been adapted into manga, anime and a video game. His previous series, *A Dark Rabbit Has Seven Lives*, also spawned a manga and anime series.

❝ My desk with the tiltable top finally arrived, and the tendonitis I've been suffering from scribbling too much has suddenly subsided! A new era has begun, everyone! I hope you enjoy *Seraph of the End: Vampire Reign* volume 4 and *Seraph of the End: Guren Ichinose's Catastrophe at 16* volume 3, coming soon! ❞

YAMATO YAMAMOTO, born 1983, is an artist and illustrator whose works include the *Kure-nai* manga and the light novels *Kure-nai*, *9S -Nine S-* and *Denpa Teki na Kanojo*. Both *Denpa Teki na Kanojo* and *Kure-nai* have been adapted into anime.

❝ Yu and Mika finally meet. What trials await the pair now? I hope you enjoy it. ❞

DAISUKE FURUYA previously assisted Yamato Yamamoto with storyboards for *Kure-nai*.

Seraph of the End

—VAMPIRE REIGN—

VOLUME 4

SHONEN JUMP MANGA EDITION

STORY BY **TAKAYA KAGAMI**

ART BY **YAMATO YAMAMOTO**

STORYBOARDS BY **DAISUKE FURUYA**

TRANSLATION **Adrienne Beck**
TOUCH-UP ART & LETTERING **Sabrina Heep**
DESIGN **Shawn Carrico**
EDITOR **Hope Donovan**

OWARI NO SERAPH © 2012 by Takaya Kagami,
Yamato Yamamoto, Daisuke Furuya
All rights reserved. First published in Japan in 2012 by SHUEISHA Inc., Tokyo.
English translation rights arranged by SHUEISHA Inc.

The stories, characters and incidents mentioned in this
publication are entirely fictional.

Printed in Italy

Published by VIZ Media, LLC
P.O. Box 77010
San Francisco, CA 94107

10 9 8 7
First printing, March 2015
Seventh printing, September 2023

viz.com

YOU'RE READING THE **WRONG WAY!**

SERAPH OF THE END reads from right to left, starting in the upper-right corner. Japanese is read from right to left, meaning that action, sound effects, and word-balloon order are completely reversed from English order.

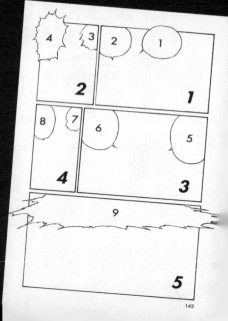